THE SAVAGE PRIDE DUET

SAVAGE PRIDE
SILENT PREJUDICE

JILL RAMSOWER

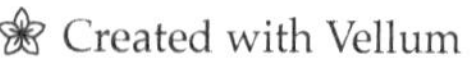 Created with Vellum

PART ONE

This one's to Sarah because Austen will always be better than Brontë.

I am my father's daughter. From his matching set of dimples to his wry sense of humor, I am more like my father than any of my three sisters. Should scientists attempt to genetically engineer a female version of him, I'm not sure they could do a better job than my own DNA, except for my blue eyes and one other critical component—my lack of patience. My father was gifted an eternal wellspring of patience that gives him the ability to shrug off annoying road-blocks to his day and find amusement in otherwise infuri-ating circumstances. Today is not the first day I find myself questioning why I couldn't have acquired a fraction of his even-tempered tolerance.

"I *told* you, I don't know why I'm not on the approved visitor's list. My name is Luisa Banetti. My parents run the Hardwick house and live in a cottage on the property. Just *call* them and ask." I stare expectantly at the new security guard stationed out front of the Tuxedo Park gated entry.

We'd spent the past ten minutes talking in circles about the absence of my name on his guest registry. Tuxedo Park is one of the most exclusive communities in New York. An hour from Manhattan, the priceless estates are nestled in the thickly wooded hillsides around Tuxedo Lake—a serene oasis fervently protected by its wealthy residents. Unlike many security guards, those stationed at Tuxedo Park are paid enough to care who enters and who doesn't. For most of my life, a man by the name of Cleatus welcomed guests during the daytime hours with a smile and a helpful nature. Of course, he'd known me since I was in diapers, so there was never any issue when I came for a visit. However, Cleatus retired six months ago, and now I'm stuck arguing with Sergeant Protocol, who can't seem to grasp concepts outside of a pure black and white palette.

"I called the cottage, ma'am. No one answered." His eyes trail yet again to the black SUV stuck waiting behind my Uber. "I'm going to need you to move so you aren't blocking the entrance while we sort this out."

"This is ridiculous," I grumble under my breath, jabbing my phone to complete the payment for my ride. Using more strength than necessary, I fling open the passenger door and ask my driver to open the trunk.

"What are you doing?" the guard asks warily.

"I'm getting my bag and waiting here with you. If you won't let me in, then you're stuck with me until my family can come pick me up." I haul my scarred black suitcase from the trunk with a grunt when the car door shutting behind us announces that we've drawn yet another party into our little contest of wills. Making a scene wasn't my intent, but it's looking more inevitable by the second.

"Do we have a problem here?" The masculine voice at my back sends a shiver of familiarity down my spine.

Zeno De Rossi.

We don't speak often, but I'd know that commanding tone anywhere.

Of all the possible people who could have pulled up behind me, it had to be Zeno. He'll probably pretend he doesn't know me just to make my life more difficult. My eyes take a long, heavy blink before I turn to face my childhood neighbor.

"Hello, Z," I say with forced calm.

"Luisa," he responds curtly, his deep blue eyes locked on mine.

The guard looks back and forth between us. "Uh, Mr. De Rossi. I'm so sorry for the delay. Miss Banetti here isn't on the registry, and we were trying to get things sorted."

Zeno ignores him, choosing to stare me down instead. "I wasn't informed you were coming."

"I wasn't aware my family had to inform you of my visits." Is he honestly going to keep me from going home? He may have pushed me away through the years, but refusing me entry to the Park would bring him to an all-time low. Incredulity primes my tongue with fighting words.

"Considering the circumstances, the information would have been appreciated." He finally severs our connection with his brusque retort and turns his attention to the Guardian of the Gate. "Luisa is a member of the estate. You can put her on the list of universally approved." He stalks back to his car without another word.

Thanks, Z. It was good to see you, too.

Zeno De Rossi was one of my childhood best friends, but you'd never guess it now. That bridge burned long ago. I suppose he must be visiting his parents as well. Both of us live in the city, but we only see each other a couple of times a year if we happen to be at Hardwick at the same time. Hopefully, that will be the one and only run-in I have with him during my visit. He tends to make me grumpy, and I'd just assume not.

"I appreciate your patience," the guard says, suddenly all smiles. "Let me help you get your bag back in the car."

"Yeah, thanks," I mutter. Opening the passenger door of my Uber, I peer questioningly at my driver. "I'm so sorry about all this. You okay to drive me to my house?"

"Absolutely. After all the fuss, I gotta see what's in here."

I slide into the passenger seat with a weary chuckle. "Happy to oblige."

The gate in front of us coasts open, permitting us entry.

"I had no clue this place existed. If you live here, why on earth don't you have your own driver or like, a car that drives itself?"

I choke on a laugh. "I wish. My parents manage an estate. We're just the help."

"Still, I bet you see some crazy shit in here."

"I guess that depends on what you consider crazy. If you mean obscene displays of wealth, then yeah, all the time." People here may be as varied as those in the city, but they keep it under wraps better. The freak flag isn't so much flown as kept rolled up in the closet only to be displayed at extravagant private functions.

I direct him to my parents' home and give him an extra tip after the long trip from the train station and the delay at the gate. The kid drives off, clearly taking the long way around the lake. I can't blame him—the scenery is gorgeous, and most people will never be granted access or have reason to enter.

My favorite thing about the area is the explosion of color

from the fall leaves. The warm hues are the perfect complement to the chilly, serene landscape. For now, summer is just spreading its wings. Everything is green as far as the eye can see, which isn't all that far since the forest of trees is full of new leaves. The lake isn't even visible from my parents' house, but I know exactly where it is. I know the wooded pathways of the Hardwick estate so well that I could walk them blindfolded. Even now, the shaded trails call to me, urging me to explore. And I will, but first, I need to get my suitcase inside.

After lugging my heavy bag to the front steps, I'm surprised no one has raced out front to greet me. I can only assume they're all out, which is unexpected. At the very least, one of my younger sisters should have been home. They all knew I was coming. Luckily, the front door is unlocked. Mom never sees any point in locking the house when so many other more valuable homes are nearby to lure potential criminals. She isn't totally wrong, but personally, I still believe in the benefit of a good deadbolt.

In this instance, however, I'm glad for her lack of security measures. I let myself inside and take in a deep breath—the smell of aged wood that goes hand in hand with old homes and the cherry tang of my father's cigars. The scent lingers in the upholstery, despite my mother insisting he only smokes on the back porch. Every time I step inside, no matter how many years I've lived away, I regain a sense of my childhood. I cannot exist under this roof without resurrecting dormant emotions and memories. Hugs from my father. Secrets whispered between sisters. School and friends. Arguments with my mother. Her signature brand of chaos can be found in a heap of dishes piled in the sink as well as the living room window framed on either side with two totally different drapes. She'd decided to make new curtains several years ago, then moved on to another project midway through when the winds of her creative mood shifted. She has yet to complete the project, like so many others. No corner of the house remains untouched by her flighty whims.

I love my mother, but she's exhausting—maddening, even—yet visits are worth it to see my dad and sisters. Especially the eldest, Gia. We are only eighteen months apart in age and have always been as close as any two sisters. She's the biggest reason I come back as often as I do. If I could get her to move to the city with me, I would. Her repeated rejection of my offers never keeps me from trying to convince her of the merits of city life. I have no doubt this visit will be no different than the others. I'll urge her to come to the city with me, and she'll find a reason to refuse.

Gia just turned twenty-nine. She's the oldest of us girls, and I can't understand why she won't leave. I get that she's family-oriented, but she has her own life to live. I moved out the second I graduated. Of course, Mom doesn't bother her the way she annoys me. Apparently, Gia got that sneaky strain of patience from my father, along with the uncanny ability to be blind to people's faults—that's her own special gift without a known origin, and it's frustrating as hell. I adore my sister, but she is the worst person in the world to vent to. She'll insist there's been a misunderstanding and assume all parties are acting with the best intentions when I really want someone to empathize about a messy situation. My next-door neighbor did not *accidentally* sleep with my boyfriend, and even if she did, I don't want to hear it.

I digress.

Returning home always involves baggage, and I don't mean of the Samsonite variety.

I shake off the swell of unwanted emotions and take my suitcase to the room Gia and I shared throughout our childhood. We still share the same double bed when I visit, even now as adults, and I wouldn't have it any other way. I slept so many years snuggled up with my big sister that her slumbering form next to me provides instant comfort. A boyfriend or cherished pet could never compare. Gia's love and acceptance are absolute.

Happiness draws my lips back into a broad smile at the same time the front door flings open downstairs.

"Lulu? You here?" Daddy's coarse voice resonates through the house.

My smile stretches farther to a vibrant grin. I abandon my suitcase and zip down the stairs straight into my father's open arms. "Hey, Daddy!" I move from him to my mom, then each sister in turn so as not to elicit any sore feelings by showing favoritism. The entire family has come home to greet me.

Mom begins to chatter before I even finish my hugs. "We heard you'd arrived, but where's all your stuff? I figured you'd come loaded with boxes since your new place isn't ready for another week. You are staying here for the whole week, right?"

"I decided to put my things in a storage unit rather than lug it all here. There's not that much, but it would have been a pain." After living in a tiny studio apartment with another girl for the past four years, I've saved enough to sublet my own room in a two-bedroom place. The new room isn't available yet, but my old lease expired, so I took the opportunity to visit my family … for a whole week. It's longer than my usual stay, which is a mixed blessing. A week is *a lot* of family time.

"Those things are so damn expensive. You shouldn't have wasted your money. We could have had your uncle help you bring it from the city."

"It wasn't too bad. And now, I can sit back and enjoy seeing you all." *Without worrying my stuff will find its way into one of your closets.* Mom has a communal closet philosophy with her daughters. Not a big deal, except that she doesn't take care of other people's belongings any better than she does her own. My budget is tight enough. I don't need her accidentally ruining things that took me weeks to save up for.

"Well," one of my younger sisters Livia starts in, "you couldn't have picked a better time to visit. Although, we won't have as much time for fun stuff, it'll be totally worth it. Mr. De Rossi died, and now *everyone* is coming to town for the funeral. They've already started arriving—so many hot guys —capos and everything. Even Gia could land some deep pockets if she'd do her hair and try a little."

"Liv, have some respect," Gia chides softly. "This is a time of mourning, not a singles mixer."

She rolls her eyes. "Whatever, more for me then."

Marca, the youngest, snickers while I gape in confusion.

"Silvano De Rossi? He died? When? Why didn't you tell me?" My gaze flitters from one person to the next in search of answers. I hadn't been close to the man, but I'd known him all my life. He was a sort of king in my world—both the estate owner and the underboss of the Giordano crime family, of which my father was a member. He'd always been such a guaranteed fixture in my life that it was incomprehensible for him to be gone.

My mother starts to speak, but Dad cuts her off.

"It was sudden. He died not even two days ago. We've been so busy with preparations that we haven't had much time to think of calling." His already sad eyes are rife with loss. I'd been so overwhelmed with my own excitement at seeing him that I'd missed the sorrow so clearly lining his face. A dull ache radiates through my chest.

"I'm so sorry, Daddy." I wrap my arms around him again, this time with the tenderness of sympathy. I may not have been close to Silvano, but he and Dad had known each other for over thirty years. They'd been trusted friends, despite the disparity in their ranks. My father had never been elevated beyond the level of a soldier. Silvano had trusted Dad with the security of his family and the operations of his home—responsibilities that spoke volumes of his respect for my father. A promotion to capo would have been even better, but Dad always seemed satisfied with his station.

"It was unexpected, that's all." The pain lacing his words undermines their brave façade.

"How did it happen? I didn't think he was all that old."

"Just sixty-six. Heart attack."

"It's a shame," Mom adds with exaggerated sincerity. "But it also means a world of work for us. That's why no one was at the house when you got here. Zeno has invited everyone his dad ever knew for the funeral the day after tomorrow. We have to prepare for that and the wake, plus the big house will be totally full for the next few days."

Dad says something about needing to get back over there, but I hardly hear him.

Considering the circumstances. Zeno's words come back to me, and I cringe. Silvano was Zeno's father—a father he idolized. I thought he'd just been rude like so many times before, but now, a sliver of guilt wedges uncomfortably between my shoulder blades that I hadn't been a touch more compassionate.

I'm not even entirely sure why. He is no one to me. Not anymore.

We'd been good friends as children, then … we suddenly weren't. No explanation. No inciting incident. One warm April day, Zeno stopped talking to me. A few years later, he moved to the city while I was finishing high school, and we rarely saw one another since. If our paths did cross, he was curt and aloof, keeping our brief interactions as sterile as possible.

He's grown into an attractive, successful man, quickly making a name for himself in the Giordano family. According to my father, who keeps me somewhat informed on family affairs, Zeno is poised to take over his father's role as underboss. But that isn't what ties my tongue at the prospect of seeing him again this week. More than anything, he stirs up a distressing sense of confusion inside me. For ages, I wondered what I'd done wrong. I'd shed tear after tear with each of his rebuffs in the early days. As I grew to accept the loss of our friendship, my suffering was limited to a melancholy remorse each time our paths crossed. Maturity assured me that his issues had nothing to do with me, but without an explanation, the jagged wound he'd inflicted never seemed to fully heal.

"And to top it off," my mother's voice draws me from my turbulent thoughts, "the girl we'd hired to help Cecelia in the kitchen quit a couple of weeks ago. I was kind of hoping you wouldn't mind giving us a hand, just for these few days."

So that's why I hadn't been informed of Silvano's death. Despite Dad's repeated attempts to keep my mother from gossiping, she always blabs. The death had definitely been major enough for her to at least shoot me a text. She hadn't said anything because she didn't want to scare me off with the imminent possibility of being put to work. She knew this was one of the few breaks I had from work and school, but she didn't care. She would prefer I lighten her load than allow me the chance to change my plans.

I sigh heavily.

Not only had I hoped to relax but working at the house

might mean running into Zeno for a second time. Not that it's my problem—he's the one with issues. I simply prefer to avoid his brooding negativity on my vacation if possible. However, if I don't join my family and help at the main house, I'll hardly see them at all, and that was the whole point of visiting. If alone time had been my goal, I could have crashed at a friend's apartment for the week.

My eyes drift to Gia, who gazes back at me warmly. Any complaints I might have staged melt away at the reminder of her gentle grace and the sight of my father's apologetic smile.

"All right, let's head on over. You can update me on what still needs to be done on the way."

Dad drops a tender kiss on my forehead, chasing away my irritation. "Having you here means the world to me," he whispers.

I am never happier than when I am the center of my father's world, which is often the case as he makes no effort to hide his favoritism. He has my heart, just as I have his, and despite my mother's manipulations and Zeno's looming presence, I will always stand at my father's side if he needs me. After all, it's only a few days. How bad could it be?

CHAPTER 2

My parents use a golf cart to shuttle them back and forth between Hardwick and their cottage. Fitting all six of us is a tight squeeze, so Gia and I offer to walk to the main house. We prefer to catch up privately, anyway. Mom and the younger girls quickly dismiss joining us because of the rising heat. I can't totally fault them. It's not even a quarter of a mile between the main house and our cottage, but it can feel like longer when the sun amplifies the humidity. They slide into their seats and wave as the cart lurches forward.

"This may not be your ideal vacay, but I'm glad you'll be around to keep me company." Gia bumps my shoulder as we walk through the tall grass.

"I'm happy to help. Mom just makes me twitchy."

"Mom? There isn't someone else that made you hesitant to join us at the main house?" Even an older sister as angelic as Gia finds joy in goading a younger sibling.

"You're right. Livia is more obnoxious than ever."

Gia snorts. "You know that's not who I meant."

I shoot her a look from the side of my eye. "If it's Zeno you're referring to, I'd have to care in order for him to rile me up. He hasn't been a part of my world in a very, very long time."

"I suppose. Some people stay with us no matter how long it's been since we were close." Her words resonate with me in a way I don't care to analyze.

"You sound awfully sage for someone who's hardly stepped foot from her Hardwick bubble."

She shrugs. "You don't have to live in the city to learn to read people."

"You're right, of course, except that there are a lot more *learning* opportunities when there are more people. You would have loved my world literature professor last semester. Maybe you two would have hit it off, but I guess we'll never know."

"Is that the same guy you told me had a stain on every shirt he owned?"

A laugh tumbles past my lips from deep in my belly. "Yeah, but that's why he needs someone like you. Someone who loves to take care of people."

Gia shakes her head, but the corners of her lips hook upward. "One more year?"

"Yeah, I've got just enough money saved up for tuition and expenses so that I can limit how many hours I have to work. I'm so ready to get my degree and move on."

"It's been, what? Five years?"

"Almost six," I grumble. "But I've done it all mostly on my own."

"Who cares if you had to spread it out so that you had

time to work—that makes it all the more impressive. You're so determined!"

"I am now, but that wasn't the case early on. If I'd gone straight to college when I graduated high school, I could have been finished by now. Better late than never, right?"

"Absolutely."

Two birds lift off from the grassy covering ahead of us, drawing my eyes skyward. The sun is pushing higher in a clear sky that promises to be a perfect summer day.

"What else has been going on around here that I might have missed?" I talk to my sister regularly on the phone, but she is always more tight-lipped than when we talk in person. She's one of those maddening internal processors who doesn't think to pass on information. It's not that she necessarily makes it a habit not to gossip, but it simply doesn't occur to her. I have to draw the information out if I ever want to learn anything. As I said, it's maddening.

"Nothing, really. Like Mom said, Anna, the kitchen girl, quit. Well, she didn't quit so much as disappear. She was with us for nearly six months when … poof. Gone. She just never showed up for work one day. People do that all the time, but I didn't expect it from her."

"How strange!" I think back to whether I'd met the girl and draw a blank. I rarely see the other staff when I visit and have only been home once during the past six months. I may not have met her, but a sudden departure doesn't necessarily surprise me. Mom supervises the in-house workers, so I could understand if the girl had gotten so fed up that she walked away. If I worked for my mom, I would probably do the same.

I refrain from sharing that thought with Gia. She'd just point out that Mom does the best she can. In my opinion, that's a convenient excuse for bad behavior. It's right up there with "boys will be boys." Bullshit. People will behave as poorly as they are allowed to behave. Mom could stop putting my parents in debt with her ridiculous spending, but she doesn't seem to care. She only thinks of herself. Sometimes, I wonder if living among the rich has given her a false sense of entitlement—as though she has a right to own all the pretty things she sees. I can't explain the source of her issues, but it's been an incessant drain on our family. Even more of a mystery is why my father doesn't stop her. As far as I can tell, he gave up trying with her long ago. Their entire relationship confounds me, though, so I don't try to understand because I'll only end up more confused.

As we near the house, its stone exterior comes into view, surging up over the treetops. A clearing encircles the house with perfectly manicured green grass like a blank wall highlighting the masterpiece of architectural design at its center. I would venture to guess not a penny was spared on its construction. I was told growing up that the home was originally built by a steel magnate akin to Rockefeller or Carnegie. I couldn't even fathom what something like Hardwick would have cost back then.

In my opinion, Silvano De Rossi's dedication to maintaining the integrity of the original design spoke volumes about his person. It would have been cheaper and easier to remodel with modern touches, but he kept the historical accuracy of the home intact. He didn't feel a need to put his own mark on the place. Instead, he chose to honor its original magnificence.

"I wonder what will happen to the house now that Silvano is gone," I muse aloud.

"Zeno already talked with Mom and Dad. He said that he was moving in and would retain their services. I suppose that means not much will change."

Hopefully, that's the case. Zeno is such a mystery that I would never presume to know his intentions. But saying as much serves no purpose, so I merely nod.

The approach of a vehicle into the circle drive snags our attention. When it parks near the front door, I see that Carter Bishop, owner of the neighboring estate, is behind the wheel. He exits the driver's side and immediately turns toward us, meeting us halfway to his car.

"Gia, how are you?" His kind eyes linger on my sister. I don't know him well since he moved in after I left home, but my family is longtime friends with his live-in staff, the Larsons, who worked for the previous owner as well. Our cottages are both near the property line, making them our closest neighbors. Gia has mentioned Carter's name only briefly in passing, but judging by the pink glow of her cheeks, her interest in him is more substantial than I'd been led to believe.

"I'm doing well, thank you," she offers, her gaze flitting to his, then down to her hands. "Carter … Mr. Bishop … this is Luisa, my sister. I can't recall if you two have met."

It's easy to offer him a warm smile as I grasp his outstretched hand. He has an openness to him that is disarming. "I believe we have, but it's been a while."

"Yes," he agrees. "And please call me Carter. It's great to have you here. I mean, not the circumstances, of course, but I'm sure Gia appreciates having you visit." His nervous bumbling is endearing, if not a touch surprising, considering his age and station in life. I've found most middle-aged, affluent men are usually dripping with unearned confidence.

I think I like Carter Bishop.

"The timing was a bit coincidental—I already had my trip planned—but I'm glad I could be here to help. There's a lot to be done."

"I assumed as much." His face sobers. "That's why I wanted to check in with Z and Elena. I want to offer any help I can provide."

I haven't had a chance to think about Elena, Silvano's widow. My heart sinks at how bereft she must be. No matter how poorly my friendship soured with Z, I will always have fond thoughts for his mother. She's a beautiful person, and I hate that she's grieving.

A car door shuts, and I peer over Carter's shoulder to where an elegant woman now stands haughtily next to the car. It's hard to say if she's in her thirties or forties. I've found the wealthy have access to some rather impressive age-defying treatments, so it can be hard to tell, especially at a distance. Her blond hair frames her face in professionally coifed waves that rest a few inches below her shoulders. She's wearing a powder-blue skirt suit perfectly tailored to her thin frame and an expression of unquestionable superiority.

"Carter, dear. I'm sure the staff are busy today, and the De Rossis will need our company far more than these two need our interference with their day." Her voice is more mature than I would have thought, making me lean toward a guess of mid-forties.

He flashes a thin smile. "I'd better get going. I'm sure Z will refuse any help, but please let me know if I can do anything."

"Of course." Gia grins. "I'll make sure to reach out if we need anything."

We both watch silently as Carter joins the woman at the front door. They disappear into the house when greeted by someone inside.

I turn narrowed eyes on my sister once we are alone. "Gia Antonia Banetti, what in the blazes was that?"

Her eyes widen innocently when she looks my way. "What do you mean? That was Carter Bishop, the neighbor."

"I know who he is. Since when does he make you blush like a schoolgirl seeing her favorite boy band?" This is the first time in my adult life that I can recall my sister ever showing genuine romantic interest in anyone. She's not the dating app type and doesn't run into many eligible men at Hardwick, so her options are limited. I'm absolutely ecstatic to discover she has a thing for the handsome man next door.

Her cheeks flush a deeper shade of crimson. "Don't be silly. I was just surprised to see him."

Uh-huh. Right. I slowly shake my head so she knows I'm not buying it, but I don't force her to tell me more. We'll have plenty of time to ease into the subject during the week once she's warmed up to the idea.

"Who was that with him? Did he get remarried?"

"No, that's his sister, Cora. She moved in about a year ago to help with the kids."

Carter was widowed a few months before moving to his Tuxedo Park estate. He's been living there for years now without remarrying, and if memory serves, his two kids are approaching their teens. It makes sense that he might bring in someone, family or otherwise, to help with their undoubtedly busy schedules.

Now that I know his relation to the woman, I note the similarities in their appearance. Carter has the same blond hair with a natural curl that Cora likely hides by straightening and curling to form more controlled, silky waves. They are both relatively petite and not as fair-complexioned as some blonds. As for their natures, I got the sense no two people could be more different. He was attentive and thoughtful while the grass frosted over and died wherever she stepped.

"Poor kids," I murmur. If she's their caregiver, I don't envy them.

"Don't say that." Gia smacks my shoulder. "I'm sure she was just having a rough morning." Her voice lacked the strength of confidence.

"How come you haven't mentioned her before?"

My sweet, considerate, selfless sister raises a brow. "I figure, if I don't have anything nice to say, I shouldn't say anything at all."

I double over in a fit of laughter while Gia fights off a grin. Cora must be a piece of work if she can't even gain favor with Gia. A person has to try hard to fall from her good graces.

"Like I said, poor kids."

Melancholy eclipses her mirth when she nods. "Let's head to the kitchen. I'm sure Mom's wondering where we are."

We bypass the front door and walk around to the servant's entrance at the back of the house. While the building was maintained true to its original character, certain modern amenities such as kitchen appliances and other upgrades were discreetly added to the home in a way that didn't upset the old-world charm. We find the cook, Cecelia, stationed at a twelve-burner Wolfe stovetop overseeing three steaming pots while Mom kneads a massive ball of dough.

"I started to think you two had gotten lost. Your sisters have both been sent out on errands, and I could really use your help upstairs. All twelve bedrooms will be occupied tonight. I've got Laney working on that, but she's been slower than molasses lately. If she's left to do it all on her own, she won't finish until midnight."

Laney is the dedicated housekeeper who lives in a small suite on the third floor and works with Gia. She's in her mid-forties and has worked for the family for more than a decade. It always strikes me as a little odd that she doesn't have her own family and still lives at Hardwick, but Gia is in nearly the same situation, so who am I to judge? Laney seems to like her job and living arrangements, and her opinion is the only one that matters. She reports to my mother, who managed to score a job overseeing the household staff not long after Dad was offered the job as groundskeeper and head of security. Mom's job is a bit ironic since she can't maintain her own home worth a flip, but she somehow manages to perform adequately enough that she has yet to be fired, and by some stroke of luck, her staff turnover rate has been surprisingly low.

Only a few De Rossis live at Hardwick full-time, so a large staff isn't needed. Mom fills in when the family hosts a party or houses guests, but this funeral is an entirely different matter. People will be gathering from all over the country to honor the late Mr. De Rossi, who was intricately involved in politics and who knows what else.

"We'll go ask Laney what rooms still need to be prepared," Gia assures her.

I follow my sister from the kitchen to the walk-in linen closet, where we luck out and find Laney collecting supplies for her next room.

"Hey, Laney." Gia smiles warmly. "Mom sent us to help. Where should we start?"

The thin woman's shoulders slump with relief. "Thank God. I wasn't sure how I was going to get everything done. Most of the bedrooms haven't been used in over a year, so Mrs. De Rossi wants all new sheets put on the beds. I'm also giving the bathrooms a scrub. I'd been working room-by-room doing both, but if you two could get the beds taken care of, I'll finish up the bathrooms."

"Absolutely. What rooms have been done already?"

"It's early, so I've only gotten to the first two on the far east end of the hall. I had enough fresh sheets clean for half the rooms but have stripped the other half already to get those sheets in the wash. Here." She snatches two piles of white linens from the shelf and hands them to Gia, then places a bucket of cleaning supplies in mine. "The next two rooms are queen bedrooms. And do a sweep for any extra touches that may be needed—a quick vacuum of the drapes or the removal of any cobwebs. We don't do a thorough clean of those areas except maybe once a year, so there's no telling what we'll find. But don't tackle too much because we only have so much time." She suddenly stops and takes a shuddering breath. "Heavens, I can't believe this is happening. It was so sudden. He was there one minute and gone the next." When her eyes find us again, they're red and glassy.

Gia places a hand on Laney's shoulder. "It's a hard time for everyone. Try not to overtax yourself, and don't worry about the bedrooms. We have them covered."

Laney nods and picks up her bucket. "Holler if you need me." She gives us a sad smile before disappearing down the hall.

A somberness settles over us that is amplified by the quiet stateliness of the old home. The rich mahogany wood and Persian rugs are a testament to time. Owners will come and go, but Hardwick will long remain. The empty silence in its hallways is a stark reminder of our temporary nature.

"Well"—I shake off the despondency—"let's get started upstairs." *Where the windows will let in some sunlight and cheer.* While I feel bad for the De Rossi family, I prefer not to embrace their sorrow. Maybe it's shallow of me, but I don't like to be sad. For someone like Gia, who is a natural empath, it can be hard to avoid feeling the full extent of another's grief, but I'm not so unfortunate. And as such, it has always been my role to lift her spirits as well.

I flash her an encouraging smile and signal for her to lead the way. We used to play hide-and-seek with Zeno and his brother, Nevio, at Hardwick when we were kids, so I know the house well. Not much has changed within these stately walls, even though it's been years since I've stepped foot inside. Any uncertainty I feel is a matter of me being an outsider rather than an issue of familiarity with the floor plan. If we should run across the new master of the house, he will most certainly deem my presence an intrusion. He made that clear years ago.

As luck would have it, we make it to our destination without encountering a soul. Our first bedroom contains a hand-carved poster bed and other furnishings either original to the house or expert reproductions. There's even an ornate vanity decorated with a set of colored glass perfume bottles. The attached antique mirror is mottled with webbing and flecks of gold—clearly kept for its aesthetic rather than function. The drapes are a heavy tapestry material held back by two giant tassels and match the blue and gold rug beneath the bed. The room is exquisite, if not a tad stuffy from being closed off for so long. If it wasn't for the modern alarm clock on the nightstand, I could swear that I had stumbled onto the set of *Downton Abbey* or some BBC murder mystery show.

"Something is comforting about a house that's been around for so long, as though it's impervious to the changing world around it. Maybe that's why De Rossi moved here from the city—to find a sanctuary for his family," I muse.

"I'm pretty sure it has more to do with the other high-profile residents in the area, but that could have played a part." He had frequently schmoozed with his fellow landowners over the years. I wasn't sure what he did in his role as Giordano underboss, but he was friends with people in high places.

I grab a corner of the comforter and peel it back, mirroring Gia's movements on the opposite side of the bed. "Whatever the reason, I'm glad the family is staying. I'm not sure what would happen to Mom and Dad if they had to leave. I doubt they could afford to be unemployed for long."

Gia is suspiciously quiet after my comment.

I narrow my eyes and study her. "What aren't you saying?"

"Nothing, exactly. I've just had an odd feeling lately. Mom bought several things a while back like a Louis Vuitton bag—things she has no business buying. Then all of a sudden, the items started disappearing. I'm guessing she's selling them, but I'm not sure why, and I'm afraid to ask."

"That sounds about right," I grumble.

We put fresh sheets on the bed, replace the comforter and pillows, then survey the room for any other areas that need attention. Once satisfied with the room, we step across the hall to a more feminine bedroom overlooking the lake behind the house. After briefly losing myself in the view, I join Gia at the bed. We begin our process over again, but this time, when we unfold the new sheet, it's obvious Laney has accidentally given us a king-sized set.

"You run down and grab some queen sheets while I touch up the room," Gia instructed. "The inside of these sconces look like they haven't been dusted in ages." She scowls at the decorative glass fixtures on either side of the arching headboard.

"Okay, I'll be right back." I slip from the room and make my way down the long corridor to the grand stairwell in the center of the house. I take my time now that I'm alone, perusing each piece of artwork and refreshing my memory on the many wonders of the house. I have so many cherished memories of this place from my early years, though each leaves a bittersweet aftertaste when I think of how it all ended. I don't dwell on those memories. In fact, I try not to think of them at all. Some things are better left in the past.

I feel like a ghost passing silently down the halls of Hardwick. I conveniently chose to wear sneakers for my trip out of the city, which is a relief. Anything but rubber soles or the softest of Italian leather would resound throughout the marble entry. I am nearly silent in my descent of the stairs. On the ground level, I curve back behind the stairwell and toward the kitchen on the ground floor. I quickly grab two more stacks of sheets in the linen closet, both set on a shelf labeled queen. When I retrace my route back toward the stairs and the front of the house, the sound of voices carries down the hallway and slows my steps.

Not just any voices. Zeno's baritone rumble.

Soundlessly, I inch forward until I am beneath the stairs, only a dozen feet or so from where Zeno is sending off Carter and Cora at the front door. My heart flutters up into my throat at the knowledge he wouldn't want me here. That I am essentially spying on him.

"Not an intrusion at all. I always appreciate a visit from you both." He speaks with more warmth than I am used to hearing from him, which denotes a genuine affection—something I wasn't sure he was capable of at this stage in his life.

"I hope you know that we're always here for you, Z. Reach out anytime." Cora's saccharine voice claws at my ears until my molars ache. Not an hour before, she had no patience for Gia and me but is now bending over backward for her fellow neighbor.

"I appreciate that, Cora. I'm confident my staff has everything under control."

"Yes," Carter agrees. "I saw Gia on our way in with her

sister who lives in the city. They're a lovely family. Always willing to step up and lend a hand."

Zeno clears his throat, and I strain to catch every word of what he might say about my family. About me. I am shamelessly eavesdropping, but I don't care. Now that they are talking about us, I have to know what he'll say.

"Gia is certainly one of a kind. It's a shame everyone isn't as genuine and honorable."

Carter chuckles awkwardly. "Well, I can't say that I know Luisa well, but in the few minutes we spoke, she seemed genuine enough."

"And that's the problem," Cora interjects. "You're too easily taken in by a pretty face."

Zeno clears his throat to speak, and my heart rate kicks up at the prospect of him defending me. "I will say that she is less abrasive than some of the other members of her family. But they do their jobs well, and that's all that matters."

Less abrasive. That's the best he can say about me? My family has practically been a part of his for decades, yet he talks about us as if we were a necessary evil. His grief doesn't give him the right to be hateful.

Heat scorches up my neck and licks across my cheeks.

My family may not be perfect, but his arrogance knows no bounds. At least my family doesn't treat others like dirt simply because they have more or less money than us.

What an arrogant … self-centered … ugh! Asshole.

My anger and frustration muddle the words in my head. I have to take several deep breaths in order to compose myself.

"Yes, well, perhaps we'll have everyone over for dinner sometime this week." The door creaks open as Carter continues. "I can imagine the circumstances have been difficult for the entire household."

"You're a good man, Bishop," Zeno says warmly.

"Too good, if you ask me," Cora adds wryly. Though it's meant to tease, there is conviction behind the statement. She thinks her brother could use a touch of her callous nature.

Carter clears his throat. "That's a conversation for another day." The sound of hands clasping reaches my ears. "I'll check in with you tomorrow, Z. And don't forget about my offer. I'm happy to help in any way."

"You have my word. You both take care, and I'll see you at the funeral, if not before."

The Bishops say their parting goodbyes, and the door clicks shut.

I should stay hidden. I should allow Zeno to return to whatever cave he's been hiding in and ignore him, but I can't. I'm too riled up to offer him leniency, even when his father has just died. It's his own damn fault. He's the one who packed the heavy baggage I'm lugging around. He's the one who hurt me, and his comments have triggered my anger so thoroughly that it cannot be repressed.

I tug tightly on the reins of my emotions as I stroll forward into the entry. I don't want him to figure out that I was listening, but I need to strike back. I need to hold my ground and take a stand so he won't think he can push me around while I'm here.

For the briefest second, Zeno's back is to me, his hand still clasping the doorknob. My eyes gobble the opportunity to sweep his tall, suited form from top to bottom, only snapping back up to his face when he slowly swivels in my direction.

He is carved stone. Impervious. Untouchable. Breathtaking.

Power wafts off him like mist drifting from the lake. I would be mesmerized by his ominous stature if the air about him wasn't lightly tainted with disdain. Violent blue eyes slice through me with silent accusation.

"What are you doing here?" All traces of the warmth with which he addressed the Bishops have disappeared. His voice is jagged ice scraping against my skin.

"Helping my sister get the house ready." I hold my chin high and hit him with a blast of confidence. I won't let him think he can scare me off.

"You didn't mention you would be at the house."

"Is that a problem?" I challenge.

His eyes flinch the tiniest bit. Almost imperceptibly. "No. There's no problem." As if reconsidering, his jaw clenches. "How long will you be staying with your parents?"

"A week."

He nods as if this news is acceptable, but his nostrils flare and lips thin as though he's conflicted. "Are you helping for the weekend, or will you be at Hardwick the entire week?"

Jesus Christ. He sure does know how to make a girl feel like a pariah.

"I'm not here to harass you, Zeno. I hadn't even heard about your father until I got home. I know my presence bothers you, but my mother asked for my help, and I'm sure you can find a way to ignore me. You've become so good at it through the years. Now, if you'll excuse me. I've got work to do." As soon as I'm done, I turn for the stairs, not giving him time for a response. I'm not interested in whatever demeaning, insensitive garbage he might want to throw at me.

Our exchange goes as poorly as every other encounter we've had in the past ten years. And as always, I deflate upon his departure. My shoulders slump, and my mood darkens. I am equal parts violence and sorrow. If I could hammer him with my fists and force him to remember how we used to be friends, I would. But Zeno De Rossi is not a man to be swayed. He is determined to hate me, and I am not a woman who will beg for acceptance.

CHAPTER 3

Zeno, Age 13

Luisa and Nevio, Age 10

"I THINK WE SHOULD GO TO THE CLIMBING TREE BY THE LAKE. OR *we could play hide-and-seek.*" I look at Zeno and Nevio expectantly, *hoping they'll like one of my suggestions. Summer is drawing to a close, and it's harder to find activities we all agree upon.*

"*You need more people for hide-and-seek. Where's Gia?*" Zeno *asks.*

I pull off a blade of green grass from the lawn beneath me. "She's painting her nails," I grumble. The colors are cool. I like polish as much as the next girl. But I can't stand how long they take to dry. I don't have the patience. Even when I do wait long enough, I inevitably chip them ten minutes later. There's no point. I'd rather skip the wait and play outside.

"*We could go down to the lake,*" *Nevio suggests.*

Z tosses a small rock at the trees. "Nah, let's go for a bike ride."

I jump to my feet. "Okay! You guys wait for me, though." I turn to race back to my house, knowing it will take me longer to get my bike than them. I only take a few strides before Zeno calls out.

"Isa, make sure you wear your helmet."

I screech to a halt and spin around. "What? Why? You never wear one."

"Don't care. You ride with me, you wear a helmet."

"If I have to wear one, Nevio does too." I'm not going down on this ship alone.

"No way!" Nevio groans.

Z smirks. "Fair enough. Now go get your bike. We'll swing by and grab you on our way out."

I leap into action, giggling at the incredulous bellow Nevio releases behind me. Back at the house, I roll my bike out of the shed and clip on my bright red helmet. I check my tires for air, then pedal down our long driveway. The boys are waiting for me beneath a shade tree, Zeno propped against his black mountain bike, and Nevio sitting on his blue BMX style bike wearing a gray helmet and a scowl.

"Let's go up to the clubhouse, then we can coast back downhill on the way home." Zeno throws a long, lean leg over his bike and leads the way. As the eldest, he almost always runs the show when he's around. There are only three years between the two brothers, but it seems like more. Sometimes, Nevio challenges Z, but he rarely wins. Z is way bigger and a little scary sometimes. Nevio is scrappy, but he gets so angry that it hurts his chances. When they fight one another, which happens, Z always comes out on top.

I'm happy to do whatever they decide, so long as I'm not bored and alone.

The clubhouse is about half a mile from Hardwick and is a gathering facility for the community. There is a boat launch for those without water access, picnic tables, and a pier that people use for fishing. Most of the ride there is shaded by a canopy of trees, so even the uphill climb isn't too terrible. When we arrive, we have the place to ourselves. It's probably too hot out for anyone else, but that works for us.

Z hops the curb and leads us over the grass and around the club-house toward the lake on the other side. As we approach the shore-line, the terrain becomes increasingly rocky, especially in the six feet or so of the bank where the water regularly rises and recedes, depending on the weather. I'm not crazy about riding over rocks, but I refuse to show weakness in front of the boys. They already treat me differently because I'm a girl—case in point, my helmet. Whining about the rocks would only make things worse.

I power on along the shore behind the others until my front wheel rolls over an extra-large rock, sliding sideways and toppling me over onto the unforgiving ground. I try to catch myself but am mostly unsuccessful and land on my side with the bike draped over me. I hiss as I scoot away from the offending bike and take in my scraped hands and leg. My hip took the brunt of the fall. Fortunately, my jean shorts kept the skin there safe. The side of my knee wasn't so lucky.

The two brothers throw their bikes down and come running over.

Zeno takes my hand in his and examines my wounds. "Are you okay? Is anything broken?"

"I don't think so." I wince at the stinging now pulsing from multiple places on my body. "It just burns a bit." Tears begin to form in my eyes, but I desperately blink them back. I'm not even sure why I'm crying. I'm not hurt that bad, but the scare has trig-gered my tears.

Nevio stands my bike upright and assesses the front wheel. "I don't think it's bent. Sometimes a fall like that makes the steering all wonky."

Z doesn't acknowledge his brother. Instead, he looks up in search of something, then scoops me into his arms. I cling to his neck, taken by surprise when he lifts me off the ground. I'm a scrawny thing, but carrying me can't be easy. He's stronger than I thought.

Even though I really appreciate him taking care of me, I don't want him to think I'm a baby. "I can walk, Z. You don't have to carry me."

"No, Isa," he murmurs. "I got you."

I believe him. Z would never drop me.

He sets me down on the bench of a nearby picnic table, then squats to look at my knee, slowly lifting my foot to straighten the joint. "How does that feel?"

"Okay."

"How about you try to stand."

I nod and do as he says, putting weight on my hip. "I think it's okay, just a little sore." I sit back down and wipe the moisture from my cheek.

Z reaches up and gently raps his knuckles on my helmet. "Aren't you glad I had you wear that thing now?" he teases.

I chuckle and roll my eyes. "I guess."

He joins me on the bench, and we watch Nevio skip rocks for a few minutes. Once I'm feeling better, I suggest we join his brother, and the rest of our afternoon unfolds as it would any other day. When I go to sleep that night, curled up next to my sister, I recall the feel of Zeno's strong arms supporting me. I'm not sure why it comes to mind, except that it felt so good. I almost wish he were here now so that I could hear the thundering of his reassuring heartbeat.

I fall asleep with that thought in mind, comforted by the fact that I have such an amazing friend.

CHAPTER 4

I TAKE EACH STEP UPSTAIRS WITH CALM CONTROL. ZENO ALREADY stormed away—no one is watching me—but I refuse to look like I'm scurrying away with my tail tucked between my legs. I use the time to recenter myself and remember why I'm here. Zeno may be a dick, but that's irrelevant to me. *He* is irrelevant. I get a week to spend with my favorite people on the planet, and I will not let him ruin that.

When I locate Gia, she's moved to the bedroom next door to where I left her and already has the old sheets piled by the door.

"Housekeeping," I say in a sing-song voice, holding up the fresh sheets.

"I was starting to think you'd gotten lost."

"Nah, only delayed a minute. Come on, let's finish the bed next door." I lead the way back to the unfinished room, and we fall into easy teamwork.

"You know," Gia muses after a bit. "I could get used to working with you. With Anna gone, we'll need to take on someone new. You and I could get an apartment together nearby."

"As tempting as it is to be closer to you, school and Mom make that impossible."

"I figured, but I had to mention it. We could even hold off until after you graduate. I could do the extra work until then."

"Oh, no." I grin. "If one of us is making a move, it's *you*. I'm going to have my own bedroom now. We could share, like the old days."

Gia won't meet my gaze. "I know how excited you are to have your own space. And besides, I hate to leave when Marca is still here," she says softly. "Liv and Marca need me now more than ever. They need a good influence in their lives." She's not wrong, but I hate that the burden falls on her. I'm not bothered enough to volunteer myself, but I understand.

"Livy may be a lost cause, as much as I hate to say it. I couldn't believe how insensitive she was about Mr. De Rossi's death right in front of Dad. All she's interested in is getting her hooks in a man with money."

"Trust me, I know," Gia grumbled.

"As much as we want to help guide Marca, she's an adult now, too. She may not even stay with Mom and Dad much longer. You sure the girls are the only reason you want to stick around?" I watch my sister closely.

A delicate flush creeps up her neck.

"Tell me something is going on between you and Carter," I urge.

"There isn't, I promise."

"But you'd like there to be?"

"Isa, he's a wealthy widower, twelve years older than me, with two kids and a real estate empire. And I'm … *me*."

"And?" I gape.

Her answering smile is so sorrowful that my chest clenches. "It's just not meant to be."

She continues with her task, effectively ending the conversation, but my thoughts continue down a dark path. I hate that she doesn't see her own value. Aside from her loving temperament, she looks like an angel on earth. While my hair is a sandy color, she's the only one of us girls who managed to snag Dad's blond hair. Gia's long waves are spun silk, and her warm brown eyes shine with love and acceptance. She's a few woodland creatures shy of being a living, breathing Disney princess. It baffles me that she doesn't see the immense worth of all her amazing qualities. I would find a way to show her how the world truly sees her if I could, but my attempts would be meaningless unless she's willing to believe in herself.

What irony. The humility that makes her so loved by everyone she meets is the very reason she can't comprehend their adoration. Then again, maybe it's best to leave things alone. I love her exactly the way she is, and if Carter or any other man isn't willing to swoop in and claim her, she's better off without them. The only person worthy of Gia's perfection is a man who appreciates his good fortune in earning her affection.

We spend the rest of the day in lighter spirits, finishing our work minutes before guests begin to arrive for dinner. Gia stays with Mom to help Cecelia with the meal while I walk back home with Livia and Marca. Dad is already at the cottage enjoying a cigar on the back porch when we arrive. I pause to say hello while my two sisters bolt inside and up to their room.

"I'm going to get stuck making dinner, aren't I?" I ask Dad wryly with my eyes trailing after the girls.

"That's the first time Livia's put in a full day's work in ages. You'd have a better chance conjuring dinner from thin air than getting her to help." His rounded lips draw deeply on his cigar, making the embers on the end spark with life.

"She's twenty-three! What's her problem?"

"I prefer not to ask that question. It only brings on a headache."

I roll my eyes and head into the house. Dad hasn't forced Livia or Marca to do much of anything—ever—so I don't know why I expect him to now. I guess I'm no better because I can't summon the energy for an argument about his need to be firm with them. Instead, I check the fridge and find enough ingredients to throw together a simple meal.

The girls come down to eat, and as usual, Livia does most of the talking. Marca's eyes light up when she watches her older sister, and it worries me. Marca is intelligent. She's quiet and more rational than Livia, but her desire to gain her big sister's approval has more sway over her than it should. Especially when Livy is such a hot mess. Throughout dinner, I try to engage with Marca but find Livia often interjects her opinions. Separating the two would be a difficult feat—more of a challenge than I am up for at present. With food in my belly and a long day on my feet, exhaustion fills my limbs with lead. I pile the dishes in the sink to be dealt with later and join my dad in the living room.

He pats the sofa next to him. "Come sit with me, Lulu."

My chest warms in anticipation of snuggling with my dad. I miss having quiet time with him, just the two of us. Sinking into the old sofa, I sit with my knees up and lean into his side with his arm curled around me.

"Tell me about school. You've been able to keep your grades up while you work?"

"It's a lot of reading and essays, but I manage."

"You love to read, so hopefully, it's not too much of a burden."

I laugh. "Yeah. It would be more enjoyable if I wasn't graded on that reading, but overall, I like my classes."

Daddy grins down at me with adoration in his sad eyes. His eyelids sag above his eyes in a way that makes him look weary, regardless of whatever he's actually feeling.

"I love hearing that. I only wish I could have helped you more so you didn't have to juggle work and school."

His words remind me of Gia's concerns about Mom and possible financial troubles. It's not a subject I normally discuss with my dad, but G has me a little worried.

"Daddy? Is there anything going on with Mom that we should know about?"

His brows furrow. "What do you mean?"

I shrug. "Gia mentioned she thought Mom might be selling stuff—that maybe finances were tight. I thought I'd check and make sure everything was okay."

"There is absolutely nothing for you to worry about. And besides, you should know by now that your mother's life choices are not your problem." His words are reassuring, but the remorse in his coffee-colored eyes breaks my heart. It's not the first time the emotion has aged his features.

I try to smile, but the result is brittle and frail.

"Hey," he says with renewed energy. "I forgot to mention earlier than Z asked about you today."

Dad's attempt at a subject change successfully wipes my mind of all previous conversations. Shock and curiosity are now my only companions.

"When?"

"This afternoon. He asked how school was going and what your plans were after you graduate."

He what? After we'd already talked and he'd acted like he couldn't wait to get rid of me, he'd gone out of his way to ask my father about school and my plans? I can't make a lick of sense out of it.

"I'm sure he was only being polite. He couldn't care less about my plans, trust me."

"Don't go judging him right now. He's been devastated at losing his father—you know how much he adored Silvano. And besides, just because he's not charismatic like his brother doesn't mean he doesn't care. Sometimes that's easy to misinterpret."

Dad always assumed Z stopped hanging out with me because he was older than me, and that was the nature of maturing. I know there was more to it, but it's not worth arguing over. "Where is Nevio, anyway? I figured he'd have come home as soon as he got the news of his father's passing."

"I think he's supposed to get in tomorrow for the wake. There's no telling with him."

That's something to look forward to. I haven't seen Nevio in ages, and he is always loads of fun. Maybe not so much now, considering the circumstances, but it will still be good to catch up.

Dad tilts his head closer. "You three used to be thick as thieves."

"That was a lifetime ago."

"True." He sighs. "There was a time when Silvano and I used to wonder if something might develop between you and Zeno, considering the way you looked up to him."

The laugh that slips past my lips is tinged with bitterness. "Z doesn't want anything to do with me."

Dad frowns, but his eyes spark like the ends of his cigars. "I'd say that's his loss, then. But I'm not sure anyone is truly deserving of you."

I'm about to brush off his compliment when I realize he's having the same conversation with me that I had with Gia earlier today. And he's right.

"Thanks, Daddy." I rest my head on his chest and try to sear the moment into my memory banks. Mr. De Rossi's passing was an unfortunate reminder that loss is often unexpected, and every hug from my dad is worth cherishing.

CHAPTER 5

THE NEXT MORNING, I SLIP FROM THE HOUSE EARLY TO CATCH UP with my childhood friend, Grace Larson. Knowing I'll have to help my family all day, I made sure to set up a visit with her before going to bed. Aside from Gia, Grace is my closest friend back home. She and G are in similar situations in that they both still live with their parents, but Grace is not so content with the arrangement. Gia stays because she feels compelled to, while Grace stays because she believes she has no other options.

Back in her teens, Grace was diagnosed with polycystic ovary syndrome or PCOS. It wreaked havoc on her hormones and caused her to struggle with her weight. She's worked hard to balance her hormones and do what she can, but it hasn't been easy. Grace is funny, clever, genuine, and one of the best people I know, but her size and health have affected her confidence. Plus, her family has even less money than mine. Dad may be a glorified grounds keeper, but he's also technically a member of the Mafia, which brings in extra funds. Mr. Larson is a modest man with no criminal ties. Curvy and penniless, Grace has convinced herself that no man could possibly want her. It's heartbreaking.

On the bright side, she's improved her mindset over the years, focusing on finding happiness rather than obsessing over what she lacks. The last time we spoke, she told me about her aspiration to move to the city. Living among a variety of people from all walks of life would help her immensely. I hope she'll make the move. Plus, that would be one more friend close by.

When I approach her house, she's waiting for me on their porch swing.

"Oh, Isa, I've missed you!" She jumps up and meets me in a tight embrace.

"I've missed you, too, Gracie. FaceTime just isn't the same as a real visit." The radiant grin on her face warms my heart.

"No, it's not. You look as fabulous as ever, of course! How have you been?"

"I've been really great! Finally moving to a better apartment and almost done with school. This was supposed to be a happy visit until I got here and found out about Silvano. I feel terrible for Elena and everyone."

"Oh, I know! Such a shame. Hey, you want to walk a bit while it's not too hot yet?"

"Absolutely. We could head down to the water. I haven't had a chance to make it down there yet." I hook my arm in hers, and we move in step toward the trees separating the lake and the house.

"Sorry to hear you ended up getting put to work."

"Gia and I got to spend the day together yesterday, I had

dinner with my dad last night, and now I'm getting to spend time with you—I'd say that's not so bad!"

She squeezes my arm in hers, and we grin at one another as though we're still teenagers. I've made some good friends in the city, but something is special about a childhood friend who's been there through braces and breakups from day one.

"Mr. Bishop told us to make sure we helped you all out if you need anything. Not that he has to tell us to do that, but he wanted to make sure we knew he wouldn't need us at the house if something came up over at Hardwick."

"I got to talk with him briefly yesterday. He seems very thoughtful." I pay extra attention to how Grace responds. I'm curious about her opinion now that I'm seeing our neighbor in a new light.

"He's exceptionally kind. His sister can be nasty, and I'm not sure why he tolerates her, but he's great in every other way." It seems Cora Bishop is universally disliked.

"Does Gia ever go over to the house?" I ask nonchalantly.

Grace slows and studies me from the corner of her eye. "I'm not sure what you mean. She sometimes drops cookies by for the kids. But I don't see her over often."

"I was just curious."

"Well, I'll say this. I *have* noticed when she and Mr. Bishop are together, they gravitate toward one another. His kids absolutely adore her. Do you think something is going on with them?" Her eyes brighten with romantic hopefulness.

"There's nothing official between them, but I think Gia wishes there were."

"Why doesn't she make a move? She's absolutely stunning, and he definitely likes her."

I breathe deeply through my nose and resume our walk. "She's convinced he's out of her league."

Grace snorts, and we both start giggling.

"I'm sorry, but that's the most absurd thing I've ever heard. She's so gorgeous with her golden hair and warm brown eyes. Her figure is to die for, and she's so incredibly sweet. Why on *earth* wouldn't he want her?"

"I agree. But *some* people don't see themselves clearly." I peer at her meaningfully. "*Some* people think that simply because they don't have a lot of money or fit into a certain size of jeans that they aren't good enough." A single brow arches high on my forehead.

Grace shoots me a dry stare. "I get where you're going with that, but *I* am no *Gia*."

"You two aren't the same person, but that doesn't mean you don't have just as many admirable qualities." I raise my hands in surrender before I ruffle her feathers beyond repair. "I'll stop there. Just food for thought."

"I'll keep that in mind," she says with a smirk.

We walk for several seconds in silence before I launch us into a new topic of conversation. One I'm hesitant to share but know of no one else who would fully comprehend my jumbled feelings on the matter.

"I ran into Z yesterday."

All of us kids used to play together when we were young, though I was closer to the boys than Gia or Grace. She wasn't as affected by Zeno's transformation, but she consoled me through bouts of tears and knows what I went through. She knows about our years of awkward encounters and my endless frustrations, and unlike Gia, Grace will offer to help me spike his coffee with a laxative rather than lecture me about being understanding.

"And?" she prods.

"He would have incinerated me from existence if he could have. I just don't get it. He looks at me like I killed his dog and hung its severed head on my wall, and every time we're together, he finds a way to point out my family is nothing but staff. At this point, it's hard for me to deny his arrogance. All I can figure is that he's worried someone might think he has a relationship with *the help*."

"What an ass."

"No kidding. If he's worried about me crushing on him, he's got another thing coming. I wouldn't date him if he was the last man on earth. Not after the way he's behaved over the years."

We emerge at the waterfront and slow our pace to admire the sweeping view.

"Fortunately, you don't have to put up with him for long. Once you're back in the city, you can do whatever you want." Her voice was edged with nervous excitement.

"Are you still considering moving?"

She bites her full bottom lip and nods. "I've crunched all the numbers, and it may take me a bit longer to finish saving the money, but I think I can do it. The biggest hurdle is the initial cost of getting over there and finding a job, but I'm almost ready. If I'd been better about saving over the years, I would already be hunting for apartments. Oh, well."

I clap my hands and jump with excitement surging up inside me like little champagne bubbles. "Oh, Gracie. I'm so excited for you! Anything you need, just let me know. I'll help you move or whatever you need."

"Don't get too excited yet. It'll still be a while, but it's in the works." The tightness in her smile and the glimmer of nerves in her eyes speak to how desperately she wants this new adventure and how anxious she is about making it happen. Grace and I are both twenty-seven years old. If I were her, I'd be itching to get out of my parents' house as well.

I take her hand in mine and squeeze. "You'll make it happen, Grace. I know you will."

"Thanks, honey. Your support means the world to me."

"Of course, I support you! Now, we better head back to the house. I'll need to head to Hardwick soon." I roll my eyes and sigh dramatically.

Grace giggles. "You better keep me posted on how that goes. I want to hear *all* about it."

When we get back to her parents' house, the sun has risen up over the trees, and her dad is standing out front talking with Carter and Zeno beside a fancy four-wheel-drive golf cart. All three men are casually dressed, which would otherwise be unremarkable had I seen Zeno in anything other than a suit since we were children. He looks like a corporate Grecian god when suited in sleek Armani, but formfitting jeans sculpted to his corded thighs are equally as mesmerizing, maybe even more so because of the rarity of its occurrence. A good three-piece suit may be the equivalent of sexy lingerie for men, but the gentle drape of a soft cotton shirt molded over muscle should never be discounted. The sight of a casual Zeno De Rossi threatens to scramble my brain.

It's fortunate I have absolutely no interest in him because the sight of so much masculine perfection might stir up a girl's hormones. Not me. Only righteous indignation here. Woman scorned and something about wrath. Yeah. That's it.

"What did your dad just say?" I whisper to Grace.

She eyes me curiously as we approach the men. "He said he wondered where we'd gotten off to. You okay?"

"Yeah. Shh." I grin and swath myself in feminine grace. "Hello, gentlemen. Is there something we can help you with?"

Mr. Larson waves his hand. "Not at all. Mr. De Rossi here was going to borrow some chairs and tables for the wake tonight, but they're in storage. I'm about to have a look at what condition they're in."

"It appears the rental company we contacted double-booked," Zeno explains. "Now, we're shy some seating."

"It won't be a problem, Z," Carter assures him. "We'll get the chairs all cleaned up and brought over. You don't need to worry about a thing."

"Absolutely," Mr. Larson agrees. "I've got it covered. You can head on back. I'm sure you have plenty of other arrangements to be made." Then the older man turns back to me. "I hear you're helping out as well, Luisa. I'll bet that's a big relief for your mom."

"It is, and she's probably wondering where I'm at, so I better get to the house." I give a parting smile and start to turn.

"No reason to walk. Mr. De Rossi is headed that way. Surely, he wouldn't mind giving you a ride."

Zeno's gaze collides with mine.

My heart stumbles, skipping over beats and rushing blood to my face. It takes every ounce of my composure to formulate a coherent response. "Thank you, but the walk will do me good." My eyes stay locked with Zeno's, neither of us willing to withdraw.

"The temperature is already rising," Z points out in a low rumble. "If you're out for long, you'll burn."

"I appreciate your concern, but I'd say the heat is far *less abrasive* than a jostling ride in a cart. But thank you for the offer." With my parting jab at his own heartless words, I sever our connection and turn to Grace. "I'll see you later."

His hostile stare burns at my back as I walk into the knee-high grass.

I can't believe what I've done—thrown his words back at him like an armed grenade. He'll know now that I overheard him, assuming he cares enough to remember what he said. Would that bother him? I haven't the slightest clue where Zeno is concerned. All I know is that I stood up for myself, and the resulting high has me convinced I could conquer the world.

CHAPTER 6

WHILE OUR PARENTS ARE AT THE VIEWING, US GIRLS GO HOME TO quickly clean up and change. There's not time for much, but I'm able to rinse off, fix my hair in some semblance of an updo, and add a thick layer of smoky eye shadow to make my blue eyes pop. After I dab on an extra coat of mascara, I slip on one of Gia's dresses and a pair of heels since I didn't bring anything appropriate to wear. We're close enough in size that it works.

Several guests are milling about when we return to the De Rossi house. Gia and I go directly to the kitchen to check on Cecelia and the food preparation, not that there is any concern. Mrs. De Rossi wanted us to participate as guests and not employees, so everything was kept simple—finger foods and self-service for the most part. We'll keep an eye on the food and bring out more when needed while still getting to visit with other guests. My parents, in particular, will appreciate the chance to catch up with people they haven't seen in years. According to my mother, Mrs. De Rossi had initially suggested bringing in caterers, but Gia and Cecelia jumped in and refused before Mom could get out her acceptance. Hosting Silvano's closest friends and family was their way of paying respects, as they explained it, which sounds just like Gia. I have no complaints. I'd prefer to have responsibilities because they give me an excuse to escape any small talk.

Once everything is set out and ready on the plaza outside, I wander back inside as Nevio De Rossi slips through the front door. While Zeno is rigid strength with sandy hair and shards of blue ice for eyes, Nevio is relaxed charisma shining from beneath espresso eyes and a single perfect dimple. He's rarely at his parents' house, so I've only run into him a couple of times through the years. He hasn't changed much from his youth, as far as I can tell. Nevio was the idea man. He came up with games for us to play and told stories better than anyone I've ever met. Even after Z stopped hanging out with us, Nevio and I were close. At least, as close as we could be, considering we went to different schools even before he left for boarding school our junior year. He and I are the same age while Zeno is three years older, but personality played a key role in our continued friendship rather than age. Being friends with Nevio was as easy as breathing.

The second our eyes meet, he flashes that trademark dimpled grin. "Look who's here." He holds out his arms to draw me in for a hug, which I readily accept.

"I'm so sorry about the circumstances, but it's lovely to see you."

He pulls back and studies my face as though I'm a ghost come back to life. "I can't believe it's you. And you're every bit as beautiful as the last time I saw you, which was entirely too long ago."

The girlish giggle that tumbles from my lips is foreign to me, but that's what Nevio does to people. Women, especially. They flock to him by the dozens, or at least, they did in high school. I never could keep up with his latest interest. Knowing that side of him as well as I did kept me from developing any foolhardy attachments to him.

I wonder if he's settled down now that we're older. He's not wearing a ring. Not that I'm interested—just … curious.

"Did you make it to the viewing?" I ask.

"No, I came straight here. I'm not sure why people want to look at the dead body of a loved one. Seems morose to me. I choose to remember Dad without the smell of embalming fluids."

"Ah, well, I guess I can understand that. Your family is all still over at the funeral home, though."

"Perfect, I can get settled without any hassles. Zeno would prefer I wasn't here at all, so it'll be easier this way."

"I thought I was the only one." The snarky comment rolls off my tongue, but once it's out, I realize what Nevio has implied and am curious what he means.

Nevio grins devilishly. "Oh, no. He outright asked me not to come last night. Trust me, you're not alone."

I'm a little shocked. I knew the two weren't super close, but I didn't realize it was so bad that Zeno would keep Nevio from his own father's funeral. "That's awful. You have every right to be here." Not just the right, he should be welcomed home by his family. Is Zeno that jealous of his brother's easy nature that he can't stand to be civil even at their father's funeral? The absurdity of it balls my hand into a fist tight enough to risk leaving crescent-shaped marks in my palm.

Nevio takes my hand in his and coaxes my fingers to open. "I don't let him get to me, and you shouldn't either. Let me run up and put my bag in my room, then we can visit."

He brings my hand to his lips, placing a tender kiss on my knuckles.

Butterflies tickle the inside of my chest, causing my breathing to stutter. "Yeah, you get comfortable. Then you can tell me what you've been up to lately."

"Be right back." He winks, then strides swiftly up the stairs.

He's only out of sight for a matter of seconds before the front door opens, and Elena De Rossi enters with Zeno towering behind her. Her eyes are glassy and tired, and her poor nose is red. I can't imagine how hard it would be to lose a husband so suddenly. How heartbroken she must be.

"Elena, I'm so incredibly sorry." I greet her with a hug, hoping she feels the sincerity in my condolences.

"Thank you, Luisa. It's been quite the shock, but it's lovely to see you." She pulls back and smiles, sorrow staining her features.

"You just missed Nevio. He ran upstairs to get settled." My eyes flick to Zeno, curious for his response, but his face is inscrutable. Not a lick of emotion. I'm not sure what I expected—maybe a hint of strain from mourning his father. Perhaps irritation that his brother has come despite his wishes. *Something.* They say everyone grieves differently, but I'm not sure Zeno De Rossi has sufficient human emotions to grieve. I always thought he looked up to his father, which would make this all that much more painful, but on the surface, Zeno is all business.

"Oh, that's great news." Elena gently touches my arm. "Everything here going okay?"

"Perfectly smooth. A few guests have already begun to gather out back. I was going to help receive people while Gia kept an eye on the refreshments."

"You don't need to do that," Zeno announces. "I'll stay up here and greet people. You two head outside and mingle."

"Are you sure, dear?" his mother asks.

Z places a kiss on her cheek and offers her an uncharacteristically gentle smile. "Yes, I'm fine. You two go on." No matter how detached he may appear, he has a soft spot for his mother.

Seeing the briefest glimpse of his armor slip tugs at my conscience. He may have hurt me in the past, but his father just died. I would never be so uncaring toward anyone else in such circumstances. No matter how thoroughly he attempts to suppress his emotions, I know he has them. I know who he used to be underneath the stoic mask. He used to be my friend, and while I can't write off his mistreatment toward his brother and me, I also don't want to believe he's totally heartless. Maybe it's naïve of me, but my common sense of decency demands I show some compassion.

"You want me to bring you a drink and maybe a plate of food?" The offer tumbles from my lips without thought. It's the least I would have offered to anyone else who lost their father, and Zeno should be no different.

"Some water would be appreciated … thank you." He seems almost as surprised by my offer as I am.

I nod and flee toward the kitchen to escape his penetrating gaze. Bottles of water sit on the counter, but they're warm. After a little digging, I'm able to find a chilled bottle in the back of the fridge. I wrap a paper napkin around the cold plastic to help with the condensation and head back to the front of the house. Zeno is greeting two couples, both in their mid-sixties by the looks of it. I pause, tucking myself away where I can watch them without interrupting.

Z shakes hands with the men and smiles appreciatively at their wives, accepting their condolences graciously. One of the gentlemen pats him heartily on the back while saying something they all nod to in response. Zeno motions toward the back of the house, and they wander off to join the gathering. When they are out of sight, his head falls back, and his chest heaves on a tormented breath.

His unguarded display of weariness draws out my own breath until my chest feels hollow and cold. My inner skeptic whispers that Zeno is simply annoyed at the imposition of hosting, but my gut is convinced that's a lie. Zeno isn't as immune as he'd like everyone to believe.

I step forward, drawing his gaze. Blue eyes, infinite as a clear summer sky.

"Here's your water. Are you sure you don't want anything else?" I extend the bottle, and our fingers brush in the exchange. Ribbons of electric current unravel up my arm and bury themselves deep in my belly, where a pool of warmth gathers. I do my best to ignore the sensation.

"No, nothing else." His voice is the gentle rumble of distant thunder, sending a chill down my spine.

I offer a thin smile and turn to leave.

"Luisa," he calls, hailing my attention.

I pause and peer at him over my shoulder.

"Thank you … for being here."

I don't know what to say. Shock ties my tongue. Instead, I nod and flee from the confusion that threatens to overthrow my system. I don't know what's going on. Why did he thank me if he doesn't want me here? Is he merely out of sorts, or maybe he's playing games with me? No, that doesn't seem right. I saw him moments ago when he thought no one was watching. He wasn't in a place to be playing games.

Even if it isn't a game, that doesn't mean he won't go back to being his aloof self as soon as his grief passes. He's shown me over and over who he is through the years; I won't let a couple of days of civility dupe me into believing he's something he's not.

I shake my head, trying to clear my jumbled thoughts. Stepping onto the flagstone patio, I spot Grace talking with Gia and make my way over. Respectful of the somber mood, we greet each other quietly and fall into light conversation. In half an hour's time, the patio is teeming with people, all talking amongst themselves in a mostly reserved fashion. I spot a number of familiar faces—the governor and his wife, a woman I believe to be one of our senators and a handful of B actors and singers. I'm sure other famous people are present, but I'm not the best at names and faces. Regardless of who they are, there is one commonality among them all. Everyone around us reeks of money. Having grown up around the wealthy, it normally doesn't bother me, but even I feel out of place in this setting.

"Can you guys believe this turnout?" Livia hisses when she joins our circle.

I cringe. "Liv, it's a *wake*, not the red carpet."

"I *know*." She rolls her eyes and crosses her arms over her chest. "That doesn't mean it's not a great place to meet people." Her irritation suddenly fades, and her eyes brighten. "Look over there, by the pool. See that gorgeous guy with the tattoo on his neck? That's Renzo Donati, underboss of the Moretti family and *totally* available."

"How do you even know that?"

Liv shrugs. "I asked Daddy."

"Asked me what?" Dad appears unexpectedly behind us with Mom at his side.

"The names of the available deep pockets here tonight. I've got my sights set on Renzo. Think I'll go introduce myself." Her eyes are glued to her target, and I'm already feverish with embarrassment.

"Livia Banetti, don't you dare!" I hiss, then look at my dad for reinforcement.

Dad purses his lips and rolls back on his heels. "Livy, this really isn't the place."

Not exactly the admonishment I was hoping for.

"Come on, Tony," Mom cuts in. "If not here, then where? It can hardly hurt for her to say *hello*. Here, Liv, take my drink. It's always easier to flirt with a drink in your hand."

Jesus Christ. How do I share DNA with these people?

Dad says nothing as Livia strolls coyly in the direction of her target. I'm contemplating crawling under a table when a microphone clicks on, and tapping resonates across the crowd. We all turn toward the house, including Mr. Donati's group, effectively cutting off Livia's access to him. I breathe an enormous sigh of relief. Her efforts won't be thwarted so easily, but for the time being, it's safe.

"If I could have your attention, please." Zeno's commanding voice lassos the crowd, and I am no different.

My eyes are drawn to him and greedily consume his suited form. My ears strain in curious anticipation of what he might say. My heart falls to my feet when his searching gaze locks on mine.

One second.

Two seconds.

Three seconds.

The evening breeze tugs at strands of my hair, but Zeno's gaze is unnervingly steady. Only after the crowd has quieted does he clear his throat and release me from his hold. I take a shaky breath to center myself as he begins his address.

"On behalf of my family and me, I want to thank you all for coming here tonight to celebrate the life of my father, Silvano De Rossi." He pauses, his throat bobbing as if he's struggling with his words. "I didn't always agree with my father, but my respect for him was immeasurable. He was insightful, clever, passionate, and his loyalty was beyond reproach." Zeno's gaze drifts back to mine, his features hardening before he looks away. "He has touched all of our lives in ways we will never forget. But if he were here with us tonight, I'm confident he wouldn't want us to mourn. 'Life is about finding the silver lining,' he'd say. So please, raise your glasses with me in honor of a man who lived life with abandon and who will never be forgotten." He lifts a crystal champagne flute in his hand, the crowd mirroring his movement in a choreographed wave. "To Silvano." His voice thunders overhead.

"To Silvano!" A chorus of voices cheers to the memory of a cherished family member, friend, and associate. The voices are mostly buoyant, but sniffles can be heard all around. Nothing blurs together gratitude with sorrow the way death does. Even for those not particularly close to the deceased, the mix of emotions is unavoidable. I grieve for the family who is clearly hurting, but I am so grateful it's not my father dressed in his best suit, laying stiff in a silk-lined casket. The emotions are so intense that I even take a long look at my mother and say a silent word of thanks that my time with her is not yet over. These not so gentle reminders of our own mortality are a blessing in that way.

I wonder if Zeno feels the same. If this display of the fragility of life will spur him to embrace his brother and heal old wounds. I could only imagine that would be the ultimate silver lining for Silvano. For his death to unite his children. What father wouldn't want his sons to be close?

Judging by the way Zeno purposely ignores Nevio's presence as the family accepts condolences, not even death will bridge these troubled waters.

# CHAPTER 7

"Gia!" The excited cry draws my attention behind me to where two kids have ambushed my sister in a double hug, a girl clinging to her middle and a boy giving her a shy one-armed side hug. The joy on Gia's face warms me from the inside out.

"*Boston, Emily,*" Cora Bishop hisses. "What did I say about behaving yourselves?" She yanks at their arms, tugging them away from Gia.

G tries to discreetly assure the kids that she appreciates their affection without further upsetting Cora.

"They're only children, Cora," Carter says in a soothing tone. "No one will begrudge them a little happiness at seeing a friend."

"They need to learn to be respectful at times like these. They can't grow up laughing and giggling at funerals and such."

Carter's eyes darken unexpectedly. "They know all too well about loss and funerals, in case you've forgotten. Let them be." His clipped warning is the first backbone he's shown in my presence and helps raise him, in my estimation. His children lost their mother, so it's imperative that he protect and nurture them. The hole in their hearts will never fully heal from that loss, but the wound may be less destructive with the right influence.

I peer at my sister and the adoring way she gazes at the Bishop kids. Her forgiving, loving nature would be the perfect balm for their souls … if fate would give them that chance.

"Gia, I think I need an introduction." I raise my brows at the two blond children.

"Of course! This young man is Boston, and he turned twelve last month."

I extend my hand with a broad smile. "Hello, Boston. It's lovely to meet you."

He grins bashfully, eyes flicking up at his father's approving smile.

"And this," continues Gia, "is Miss Emily. She is ten and going into the fifth grade in the fall." She says the last part with emphasis to impart the impressive nature of such an accomplishment.

Again, I extend my hand. "How exciting! Will that be your last year of elementary school?"

Emily shakes her head. "No, at my school, sixth grade is the last year of elementary."

"Ah, very good. You'll just get more homework once you move to middle school, so no rush," I assure her.

"That's what I keep telling her," Boston pipes in with the puffed-out chest of authority.

All of us adults, except Cora, of course, smile at the innocence of youth.

"Have you two had a chance to get some food?" Gia asks. When the two shake their heads, she scoops their hands in hers. "Come on, I'll take you over to the food table."

The three disappear into the crowd, giving room for Zeno to slip into our circle. I'd been too distracted to notice his proximity and wonder how long he's been standing there.

"Zeno!" The scowl falls instantly from Cora's face, which is now alight with devoted concern. "How are you holding up?"

"I'm fine, thank you." His response is respectful, but I get the sense he's growing tired of issuing the same assurances. "I hope everyone is enjoying themselves as much as can be expected. Did you try any of the champagnes?"

"Yes, and your toast was so touching." Cora's hand comes to rest over her heart.

Her antics make my skin crawl. I itch to scream at her to have some self-respect and stop throwing herself at the man. Instead, I down the remainder of my drink and let the bubbles burn all the way down.

"I see you were able to get a glass," Zeno directs at me.

Cora scoffs. "Not everyone knows how to appreciate a good vintage."

If it wasn't for your ridiculous simpering, I could have sipped the champagne as it's intended. "Who says I didn't appreciate it?" I shouldn't make a big deal about her rudeness, not here in the middle of a wake, but I never could keep my mouth shut when it came to standing up for myself. Cora may have learned she can push my sister around, but I am not my sister.

"It's not your fault." There's condescension in her tone, and I can't wait to hear what she says next. "How often could you possibly have had an opportunity to drink a good Dom Perignon?"

I flash my teeth in a caustic grin. "Fortunately, I don't have to have it often to appreciate it. In fact, I'd say the opposite is true. Being accustomed to luxury would likely make a person more apt to overlook it, whereas someone who has little access would cherish the tiniest taste of opulence."

"Don't look now, Z, but I believe Miss Luisa is calling us spoiled." She cups her hand around his bicep and leans against him to emphasize their mutual station in life. And the manner in which she used my name is not lost on me either—patronizing, as though she's referring to a child. She believes herself so far above me that I'm surprised she can see me at all.

Zeno chimes in before I can shoot back a reply. "I'm not so sure that she did, but either way, she's free to think of us as she will. People have always assumed a great many things about me. That doesn't make them true." He makes his statement without looking at either of us. His comment was technically directed at Cora, but I take it upon myself to respond.

"People have to formulate their own opinions when questions go unanswered."

Zeno's arctic eyes collide with mine. "And that is an unfortunate consequence over which I have no control."

"It's not in your control to correct them?" I should stop and leave him alone. His father died, for Christ's sake, but words leap from my mouth without my consent.

"No," he bites. "It's not."

A sweltering tension descends between us, making my skin too tight for my body. Only Cora is left standing with us, and she fidgets as though our exchange has made even her uncomfortable. Seconds tick by in silence until someone swoops in and saves us.

Nevio, the antithesis of awkward discomfort, uses his superpower of congeniality to lift the oppressive tension from around us. "I saw you three from across the way and thought I'd join your little conversation, but now, I'm not so sure."

I flash him a relieved grin. "Oh no, now that you're here, you're stuck." His levity is exactly what we need.

Nevio drapes his arm around my shoulders and tucks me into his side. "I can't think of anyone I'd be more delighted to be stuck with. Right, Z?" He's being sweet, yet I get the sense he's also goading his brother.

My smile falters a touch.

Zeno's lips never even twitch. "I'm sure you'd love to catch up, but I believe Luisa has responsibilities to tend to." His dismissal stuns me. I'm not even a paid employee, and we were encouraged to mingle tonight, but he's sending me to work? Is this some kind of reminder that I'm beneath him after I challenged him before?

"Well, then"—Nevio's tone is laden with defiance—"I'll just have to help her with whatever she needs to do."

"I'm afraid that won't work. Too many important people are here who we need to talk to."

Nevio chuckles darkly. "You're the one poised to fill Dad's shoes, brother. I'm nothing but a mere soldier in this organization. You've seen to that. Nothing I say to anyone here will be of consequence."

"We are not discussing family matters here." Zeno's words bite like the end of a whip. He's growing noticeably more agitated, and I am increasingly more uncomfortable being used to come between the two men. This is not the time or the place.

I pull out from beneath Nevio's arm and rest my hand on his chest. "There's no reason to argue. I'll be here for the rest of the week, and these people are only here tonight. I wouldn't be comfortable keeping you from them. Do what you need to do, and we'll catch up later."

His eyes are as dark as the starry sky overhead and equally as fathomless. Nev may be more charismatic than his brother, but both are endlessly complicated. I can't tell if he'll push the issue further, and my nerves fray with the uncertainty.

Eventually, he offers a regal bow. "As you wish." His nod to my absolute favorite childhood movie, *The Princess Bride*, earns him a beaming smile. I can't even believe he remembered. Nevio winks, allowing me to relax, then follows his brother's lead into the crowd.

As soon as they go, I escape toward the kitchen, breathing a deep gulp of cleansing air. The tension from multiple awkward conversations has seeped into every part of my body, including my lungs. I've been taking shallow, measured breaths like a rabbit caught between two wolves. The replenishment of oxygen makes me slightly dizzy. I smile at the feeling. Maybe it's the champagne. Or a little of both. Either way, I'm free for a moment, and that's a relief.

I coast slowly past the refreshments table on the way inside to assess what needs to be restocked. When I enter the kitchen, Cecelia has retired for the night, and the place is empty. I load up a tray with provisions and make my way back to refill the food table. Once I've returned to the kitchen and rinsed the tray, I drift to the window where I can watch the party rather than rejoining the guests. It's peaceful in the kitchen. I can only hear a faint murmur of voices over the hum of the refrigerator. The lights strategically placed throughout the landscaping make a stunning nighttime scene. There aren't any houses right on the waterfront, so the lake disappears in the dark, especially when the moon is new as it is tonight. It's a perfect evening for a gathering. The stars are extra vibrant in the black velvet sky, and the evening air is a comfortable reprieve from the heat of the day.

At least one-hundred and fifty people are scattered about the flagstone plaza. I'm pleased that so many of Silvano's friends and family could come together. A man who impacted so many people should be honored properly. I recall a time when I was maybe six years old and had wandered over to the De Rossi house in search of the boys after Gia and I had gotten into a fight. Nevio and Z weren't home at the time, but instead of returning to my own house, I wandered onto the Hardwick plaza to entertain myself. I wasn't ready to go back and face my sister, so I used water from the stone fountain to finger paint fading designs on the flagstone. Silvano must have noticed me playing alone, which was unusual when so many kids lived nearby, and joined me by the fountain.

"I believe there's chalk in the garage somewhere—that way, your drawing doesn't disappear quite so quickly."

I've heard Mr. De Rossi yell at his boys, so I know he can be scary, but right now, his voice is calm and soothing, so I'm not worried. If anything, I'm surprised he's come out since he's usually busy with work.

"I like the way it fades. That's the cool part," I tell him.

He nods as though he understands now. "What are you drawing?"

"A house for myself without my sister where I'm the only one who gets to play with the toys. She says I mess up her doll's hair and won't let me play with it, but I don't. I always brush her hair *carefully."*

"Ah … now I understand."

"Gia's just being mean cause she's older than me."

"Well, I suppose you could move into my house. It would mean never seeing your sister again—no birthdays or Christmas morn-

ings with her. No riding bicycles or painting with her. And you two share a room, right? You'd have to sleep all by yourself."

I look up at his huge house behind us. It's fun to play hide-and-seek in, but I'm not sure I want to be there all alone. No more Gia? No cuddles at bedtime. No singing while we clean up our room together. No sharing treats or laughing at cartoons together. No more Gia hugs.

When I look back at Mr. De Rossi, I can barely see him through the tears.

He squats until his eyes are right in front of mine. "Sometimes we get angry, but we forgive our family. Always. They are the best part of our lives."

I nod. "I'm gonna go home, now."

He smiles, and I take that as my cue to leave. I run all the way back home. When I step through the doorway to the room I share with my sister, she's on the bed, crying.

"What's wrong?" I ask, confused why she'd be upset.

Gia sits up, eyes round. "I'm sorry I got mad. You can play with my dolls."

Dolls forgotten, I run to the bed and climb on, wrapping my arms around my big sister.

Mom found us an hour later, asleep on the bed in each other's arms. It wasn't the only fight we ever had, but it was the last time I wished away my sister. Silvano had a way with people, even children. He was good at hearing people, which is a rare quality to possess.

Lost in the memory, I don't notice someone entering the room until a throat clears behind me. I startle, hand on my chest, when I whip around to find Zeno leaning in the kitchen doorway.

"I'm sorry to frighten you. I just wanted to see if you needed any help."

"I thought you and your brother had to mingle with your

guests." *Away from the help.* My sympathy for his loss shrivels as I recall his arrogant refusal to allow Nevio time with me.

"Whoever thought it was a good idea for a grieving family to host a party was a masochist." His lips thin with the attempt at a smile. "It's fine if I'm gone for a few minutes." He's allowing me to witness how drained he's become over the past few days, a glimpse into his struggles. It's been unquestionably challenging, and I realize I haven't given him much grace. Someone in the midst of a crisis should not be judged according to their behavior during that time.

Yes, but why would you cast me away to the kitchens in front of my friend, then sneak away to help me?

Confusion puts me off balance, so I say the only thing that comes to mind. "I don't think I told you yet, but I'm sorry about your dad."

Pain, unfettered and raw, lances through him. "I've heard that so many times tonight, and every time I express my appreciation, put on a brave face, and assure people we're managing well … that everything is fine. But it's not. There's nothing fine or fair about this." His agonized words hang in the quiet between us, filling the gaping distance. Neither of us moves to step closer to one another, though we are at opposite ends of the room. There's a safety to our distance as if a protective bubble exists around us and neither of us wants to risk upsetting the balance.

I can't tell what's unfolding between us, but I'm entranced and don't want it to end. No matter how angry he makes me, there will always be an even larger part of me that desperately wants to call him a friend again. I can't fathom why after so many years, but it's the truth. The hint of an olive branch from him assuages years of hurt and confusion.

"You're right. It's not fair at all," I say softly. "Life is utterly unpredictable—that's why we have to make the most of each moment we have." To forgive and forget. To embrace our families and hold them close even when we're angry. His father was the one to teach me that.

"And what would you have me do to make the most of this moment?"

My eyes glance out the window to the gathering of people. "You could take advantage of the opportunity to see family."

"And if I don't want to go out there?"

I peer at the pile of bowls and flatware in the sink, then bite my lip with a smirk. "There's plenty of dishes to be washed."

Zeno huffs an almost laugh, then slips his suit jacket off his shoulders. He deposits the jacket over the back of a chair and rolls up his white shirtsleeves to his elbows before ambling toward me.

I can't believe this is happening.

Have I stumbled into some alternate universe where my life is unrecognizable? A week before, if I'd been told I'd be back home doing the dishes with Zeno De Rossi, I would have fallen over laughing at the absurdity. Yet here I am, sliding on an apron before handing Z one of his own.

"Can't have you getting all dirty."

"A little dirt never hurt anyone," he murmurs. "Now, where do we start?"

We work in companionable silence for a half hour. Even if I knew what to say, I wouldn't want to interrupt the moment. I'd planned to leave the mess for Cecelia to clean in the morning, but there'd been something compelling in Zeno's manner that overrode my petty grievances. He'd offered up a rare showing of vulnerability. I hadn't stolen this knowledge by watching him covertly. He'd come to me with his shields lowered, something he hadn't done for years.

We get most of the dishes either loaded in one of the two dish washers or cleaned and set on towels to dry. No one interrupts, and for once, our history is forgotten. We are simply two people helping each other complete a necessary task.

Once I've hung up my apron, I wander back to the window. "People will start leaving soon. You should be there to say goodbye."

He's quiet, so I turn back to see what he's doing and find him staring at me. The intensity radiating off him sends a zing of adrenaline through my veins.

"You have your father's smile," he rasps softly. "You don't much resemble him otherwise, but when you smile, it's impossible to miss."

It's such a random comment, I'm not sure how to respond. Since I adore my daddy, I choose to take it as a compliment, which draws out the very smile he mentioned … that is, until Zeno winces in response.

"I need to go." He slips his jacket back on without looking at me. "Thank you for the distraction." His eyes flit to mine just briefly before he flees the room.

I'm left in utter dismay, totally at a loss.

My eyes feel glued shut, heavy with sleep. If light weren't pouring in through the windows, I could swear I'd laid my head on the pillow only minutes before.

Gia is sitting on the edge of the bed wrapped in a towel with wet hair hanging limp on either side of her face. "It's time to get ready, sleepyhead."

"Ugh," I groan. The funeral. "I hope you have something for me to wear because I got nothin'."

"We can scrape something together. Now get up before one of the others beats you to the shower." Her reminder of our limited bathing resources spurs me into action. Two bathrooms for a single family may sound reasonable, but when four sisters are trying to get ready at once, it's a nightmare.

I manage to snag the bathroom, still steamy from Gia's shower. The scalding water brings me back to life, especially when I run through all that happened the night before. I told Gia the basics of what had happened after we'd curled up in bed last night, but talking it through with her hadn't provided any further insight into the situation. Zeno's contradictory behavior has left me even more confused than ever. I don't know what to think, but I decide that maybe there is no conclusion to draw. Maybe this is a time of grief, and there is no logic or reason to anyone's actions. I'd like to believe his attitude toward me is changing, but that may not be the case.

No matter the source of his behavior, my visit home has become more than I bargained for—confrontations with the man who broke my heart as a child, and now, a funeral. Will the good times ever end?

We load into Mom's 4Runner, and everyone's remarkably quiet. I give thanks for small miracles because I'm not up for drama. After Livia threw a fit about having to change when Dad rejected the short skirt she'd picked out, we are all running a bit late and low on patience.

The church parking lot is already packed when we arrive. Cars will be parked down the street for blocks once the service begins. That's the way it is for someone of such importance as a Mafia underboss. Silvano's death will draw in family, both blood and otherwise, from all over the country.

We make our way into the sanctuary and select one of the few remaining pews with open seats. Mom is seated next to me, and I notice she keeps scanning the crowd, craning her neck to look at new arrivals every few minutes. Her odd behavior sets me on edge. I find myself peering over my shoulder without any idea why.

"Who are you looking for?" I ask in a whisper, growing irritated.

"Huh? No one. Just curious who came." She sits back casually, but I don't buy it. With Mom, there's no telling.

I glance around one more time and note many of the faces from last night, but the service today includes even more people, most of whom are unfamiliar to me. The procession to the gravesite will require a large police presence to navigate traffic, which is always odd because families like ours don't mesh well with cops. Sending Silvano off with a police escort seems wrong, but our funeral train will be far too long to execute without assistance.

Within minutes, it's standing room only in the church. The mood is somber with a respectful undercurrent of reunion as many people greet old friends for the first time in months or even years. Sorrow and gratitude, hand in hand, make yet another appearance.

The ceremony lasts almost an hour. Zeno speaks briefly, along with his mother. Yet again, Nevio does not say a word, and I wonder if that is his choice or if Z refused him the opportunity.

A priest conducts a short Mass, and Christiano De Bellis, the boss of the Giordano family, gives a respectful speech about his former second in command. He's somber, but I don't get the sense he caters much to emotion. He rose to become boss for a good reason—ruthless power resounds in every word he utters.

Eventually, we all filter back into our cars and take the slow, winding drive out to the cemetery. Marca and Livia chatter in the car, but I hardly pay any attention. I'm lost in a sea of my own thoughts.

As we exit the vehicle at the graveside, I swear I see my mom take a swig from a flask. If she were truly struggling with grief over Silvano's death, I could understand, but I've watched her over the past couple of days and know she isn't overly affected.

"Mom, are you drinking?" I ask once I've got her out of earshot of the others.

She shoots a glare at me. "That's not any of your business." With her attention fixed on me, she stumbles in the grass, catching her footing before she falls.

I help steady her, recalling when she slipped away during the funeral service to go to the bathroom. She'd also been surprisingly quiet on both car rides. "Exactly how much have you had?"

She yanks her arm from my grasp. "I'm allowed to be upset. It's a funeral."

"Everything all right over here?" Zeno appears from thin air, his voice a quiet warning. "Of course, Z," Mom gushes, suddenly all sunshine and rainbows. "We were just talking about finding the Larsons. Luisa here has always been such good friends with Grace, the poor girl." She leans in as if imparting a great secret. "She would be such a cutie if she wasn't so chunky."

"*Mom*, that's enough." Mortification isn't sufficient enough to describe how I feel. If I could, I'd jump into Silvano's casket and let them bury me with him. Judging from the heat blazing across my cheeks, they have to be bright red.

Swallowing back any semblance of pride I may have had, I turn to Zeno and attempt a smile. "Everything is fine. I'm sorry if we were drawing attention." I tug my mother toward the crowd and pray he doesn't realize she's tipsy at his father's funeral. I don't know what's gotten into her, and I'm afraid to find out.

We manage to locate the Larson family among the crowd and stand with them beneath two majestic oak trees. The graveside portion of the service is short, with only a few words spoken by the priest, yet somehow, it makes me even more heavyhearted than I was at the church. So few can witness a casket perched above a deep hole in the ground while grief-stricken families struggle to breathe without sharing in the pain of the experience.

Once the elegant silver box is lowered beyond our view, Elena steps forward and tosses a single red rose to be buried with her husband. The act reduces her to sobs, her face crumpling with heartache. Zeno places a hand on her shoulder, a surprisingly cold gesture considering their relationship and the circumstances. Nevio, with tears in his own eyes, pulls Elena against his chest, wrapping her securely in his arms.

Was Z trying not to look soft in front of his fellow made men? I can't imagine why he would be almost robotic with his mother when she was so distraught. Last night, he'd been almost tender with her, but now there's no sign of that Zeno.

The crowd slowly dissipates over the course of a half hour. Some people feel the need to pay their respects to the family, while others simply drift back to their cars to leave the family in peace. Daddy makes no move from our spot beneath the trees, so neither do we. I've peered at him countless times throughout the morning and can't fathom what he must be going through. He looks ten years older than usual today, but there is no other trace of emotion. It's almost as though the loss has overwhelmed him to the point of emptiness. The sight makes my heavy heart break wide open.

I go to his side and take his warm, calloused hand in mine without saying a word. His fingers squeeze mine in return, assuring me that he's in there … somewhere.

The Larsons stay with us, along with Carter and Cora Bishop. They all talk quietly, but I stand silent in solidarity with my father.

Nevio is the first of the family to free up and come our way. His bloodshot eyes draw me toward him for a hug. I don't want to sever my connection with my dad, but Nevio is just as troubled. He was there for his mother, and I want to be there for him because Lord knows his brother won't be.

"I'm so sorry," I whisper.

He nods and pulls back, taking my hands in each of his. "I just wish we'd been closer while he was alive." His soft words are directed at the ground, only loud enough for the two of us. "Zeno found ways to make sure that never happened. He was even the reason I was sent to boarding school. Did I ever tell you that?" When he peers up at me, there's turmoil in his mocha irises.

I'm stunned—at a loss for words for several seconds. "No, I had no idea. I thought it was all about grades." How could this be the first time I'm hearing about this? Why hadn't he said something long ago?

Because he was gone before you knew what happened, then your paths rarely crossed.

I suddenly feel like a wretched friend.

He smiles, but there's no humor in it. "Grades were the story they told everyone. It's only ever been about Zeno. That's why I'm rarely ever here anymore; no point in coming home when I'm unwelcome here."

I have so many questions, but this isn't the time or place to pick at old wounds. He's suffered enough today. All of them have.

I squeeze Nevio's hand and look back toward my family to discover Zeno has joined them, and to my horror, Livia is chattering his ear off.

"I told Mom last night that it was so great having such a large gathering at Hardwick that you should have them more often. Maybe a Fourth of July barbecue or something."

Holy shit. Did my little sister just tell Zeno she had fun at his father's wake?

I cannot even begin to understand how her mind works. All she thinks about is what Livia wants and what's best for Livia. She doesn't care that others are grieving, and her petty machinations are beyond embarrassing. Her words are out faster than I can apologize on her behalf. And if that isn't bad enough, my mother voices her hearty agreement.

I glance at Gia in a silent plea for help. Her eyes slowly drift shut with embarrassment.

Zeno may have no tolerance for his brother, but he manages to remain polite, if not a touch austere, with my family, though heaven knows they don't deserve it.

"The house hasn't seen company like that in a while. Next time, hopefully, we'll be celebrating something much more uplifting." His eyes drift to mine, an inscrutable energy passing between us before his gaze drops to where my hand still clasps his brother's. When his stare reconnects with mine, the link is no longer present, and I'm met with cold indifference.

I feel cut off and dejected in a way I can't explain. A part of me wants to yell at him and demand an explanation. Why should it bother him if I hold hands with his brother? He couldn't possibly be jealous. He's never shown the slightest sign of interest in me. How can you be jealous over something you don't want?

"Zeno, Nevio, Antonio." Christiano De Bellis joins our circle and nods at each man in greeting. "And this is Gemma if I recall correctly." He extends a hand toward my mother, who tosses her red curls and grins.

"Yes, it's lovely to see you."

"And these are your girls, Antonio?" Christiano peers at all of us.

"The four here, yes. Gia, Luisa, Livia, and Marca. And these are our neighbors, the Bishops and the Larsons."

We all smile and wave.

"Lovely young ladies, wouldn't you say, Savio?" He draws a finely dressed young man into the group, who smiles graciously and nods his greeting. "This is Savio, my nephew. Antonio, you haven't been to the city in a while, but Savio is one of the young men looking to take over the most recent organizational vacancy." He's being vague because outsiders are present, but the rest of us are all aware he means Silvano's role as underboss. Someone will need to take over soon.

"That would be quite the honor," Livia says with a coy smile, seemingly oblivious that Zeno is the other capo vying for his father's old job. For those of us who know, the situation is endlessly awkward. Why bring up something like that at a funeral? Either Christiano was insensitive or he'd done it on purpose to goad Z. Either way, it makes him look like a jerk.

Savio nods and smiles but doesn't say anything further about his ambitions. Instead, he offers Zeno a private word and a handshake of condolence. He appears to recognize how uncouth his uncle's statement was and doesn't wish to dig the hole any deeper. My first impression is that I'd like him if we ever had the chance to talk. Some of the Mafia sort can be self-important, but I don't get that sense with him. I'm not sure how that would bode for a future as boss. A certain degree of arrogant ruthlessness is central to the role.

"The whole family appreciates you both coming out," Zeno interjects. "I hope you'll be staying for lunch at the house."

"We have to get back to the city, I'm afraid," Christiano says. "I've got a meeting with some important people, and I'd like Savio to join me." He looks smug, and it makes me want to knock him on his ass.

Zeno's eyes blaze with intensity, but I'm not sure if it's anger, jealousy, or grief stoking that fire. When he speaks, his words give no hint at emotion. "I'm sure he'll be an asset at any negotiation."

"Yes, and it's important I give thorough consideration to all my options before I make a decision."

"I know you'll do what's best for the organization. Now, if you'll excuse me. I need to get back to the house and check on our guests." Zeno's words are clipped, as though he's reached his capacity for tolerance. Without waiting for an answer, he turns to collect his mother, who had migrated to the grave for a final private moment with her husband.

The rest of us offer our goodbyes to Christiano and Savio before returning to our cars. I am bone-weary as I plop into the back seat, but our day isn't even half over.

"You okay, Daddy?" I had thought I'd run upstairs and freshen up after we made a brief stop at home before going over to Hardwick, but when I spot my dad standing on our porch, staring into the trees, I have to check on him. He hasn't been himself all day, even taking into account his grief.

He's quiet, and we both listen as a breeze rustles the leaves on the trees around us.

"These past couple of days, I've been thinking a lot about how I've led my life and the things I could have done differently." He gives me a sad smile and wraps an arm around my shoulders. "I ever tell you how we ended up here at the cottage?"

I rack my brain and realize he hasn't. "I guess I assumed Silvano needed someone, and you offered to take the job."

"Not exactly. We were young when we got married—your mom especially. I was twenty-three, and she was only eighteen. Nowadays, having a baby before you're married isn't uncommon, but back then, it was still frowned upon. Your mom got pregnant after we'd been dating for only a couple of months."

My jaw grows slack as my father proceeds to rewrite the history of their relationship, erasing the doctored story I'd been told while growing up and had believed wholeheartedly.

"I had no money and was new to the family, but Silvano took me under his wing. He'd moved up the chain of command quickly and had become a top-ranking capo in his mid-thirties. He'd gotten married two years earlier, in part to position himself to be underboss. He bought Hardwick to solidify his roots and give his new family a place to grow up alongside the other powerful residents at Tuxedo Park. Zeno was born close to the time they moved in, and Silvano recognized his need for help at the house. He wanted someone who was connected and knew I was in a situation. He approached me one day and said that if I planned to marry your mom, we could move to the cottage rent-free and work for him. I love the city, but I couldn't pass up the opportunity for my kids to grow up in a place like Hardwick." Dad pauses, turning his sad eyes to meet mine. "Who knows what would have happened without Silvano's intervention. He changed our lives, and … I … I'm not sure I showed him the gratitude he was owed. Now he's gone, and I can't do anything to right the matter."

I'd been told from the time I was little that my parents were madly in love, so much so that they'd eloped only months after meeting. Gia was born within a year, but it had never occurred to me to question the timeline. To question whether they'd ever loved each other in the first place.

I feel like time and space are colliding to warp the world

around me until things I've known all my life suddenly look unfamiliar.

"Did you want to marry Mom?"

Dad's face softens. "Your mom has a vivacious spirit that's infectious, even more so when she was younger. I knew she'd always keep things interesting, and I got you out of the bargain, so I have no regrets."

That wasn't exactly a yes. My parents' relationship was never one I would strive to replicate. They lead mostly separate lives, and Dad usually can't be bothered to deal with Mom's antics. They aren't partners so much as roommates, but that didn't seem so problematic when I thought the relationship had originated out of love. Now, I wonder if my dad has lived his entire adult life in misery.

"I just want you to be happy, Daddy."

"I am, Lulu. Especially when you're here." He squeezes me affectionately as Mom steps out the front door in leggings and a T-shirt.

"Are you not coming to the lunch?" I ask with surprise.

"I'm not feeling so great, so I'm gonna stay home and rest. Elena won't miss me with so many others there, but you can call if you need me." She crinkles her chin in a show of remorse, eyes dancing between the two of us before she slips back inside.

I look at Dad, my brows tightly knitted. "What's going on with her?"

Dad sighs. "No idea. Come on, let's get the other girls and go."

ELENA HAD INSISTED on a catered lunch so everyone could attend the funeral without worry. Gia can't help but check on things as soon as we enter the house, but otherwise, we are off duty. The luncheon is elegant yet casual. White linens hang from round tables set up all over the plaza. Each table is adorned with an artfully designed floral centerpiece and eight flatware settings. A buffet table sits at the far end of the plaza along with a drink station and a small table filled with desserts. Some people eat while others mingle, and a few children play in the grass off to the side.

Carter and Cora are already seated at a table and wave us over when we step onto the plaza. More precisely, Carter waves us over while Cora sips on her water and pretends not to notice us.

"Have you already had a chance to eat?" Gia asks, accepting the seat Carter pulls out for her next to him.

"No, we wanted to wait for you all."

"I'm so sorry you had to wait, but that's very thoughtful of you. We ran home to freshen up. Mom wasn't feeling well, so she stayed at the house."

Carter's brows furrow. "I hope she's not sick."

I'm pleased to detect genuine concern. He isn't simply saying the polite thing or feeding Gia what she wants to hear. He really cares about people, which is an unusual quality in my experience.

"I think the past few days have overwhelmed her. Nothing to worry about." Gia smiles. "Let's get some food. You've waited long enough!"

He helps her again with her chair, and I exchange a glance with my dad. He shrugs, and I stifle a laugh. We each fill our plates, then return to the table and eat. Conversation is easy, which is a relief. With Mom absent, both Livia and Marca manage to be on their best behavior. That or Liv is simply preoccupied scoping out the guests for potential dates. Either way, lunch is a pleasant change of pace, and I'm thoroughly grateful.

Livia is the first to finish and excuses herself from the table. I'm not sure where she's hurrying off to, but I'm afraid to ask, so I don't question it. Marca stays seated with a frown. I get the sense she wanted to follow her sister but was refused. I have no doubt Marca is much better off right where she is.

Minutes after Liv disappears, Zeno wanders over to our table.

"Z, we have a seat open here. Why don't you join us?" Carter stands and motions to the unused place setting Mom would have occupied had she been with us. The seat next to me.

His eyes shift from my father to me before he stiffly lowers himself into the white folding chair. My teeth grind together at his palpable discomfort. After witnessing his ability to be civil, his irritability toward me feels like an even greater affront.

Maybe you should sit next to Cora, who is equally as disappointed with her present company.

"I can't stay long. I'll need to check in with my mother. Today has been exceptionally hard on her."

I could tell you were worried by the way you didn't comfort her at the funeral. I have to bite my tongue to keep my thoughts to myself. I'm tired of the whiplash I get trying to keep up with his moods. One minute, he's opening up and helping me, and the next, he can hardly stand to occupy the same breathing air as me. My patience is wearing thin far faster than it should, considering he just buried his father.

"Surely, you have enough time to get a plate of food," Carter says.

"No, I'm not hungry. I hope you've enjoyed everything, though."

"Of course," Cora coos from across the table. "Everything has been lovely today."

"Excellent," Z murmurs. His eyes lift to mine but slice away as if I've somehow sent him a telepathic electric shock. "I have to get going, actually. Make sure you get some dessert before you go, and if I don't see you before then, thank you all for coming."

"You're leaving?" I blurt, my control finally shattering.

I'm sick of feeling like a leper in his company, especially when we're around anyone else. He can't get away from me fast enough. And if that isn't bad enough, he forces his brother away as well, like he doesn't want my taint to spread to anyone in his family.

"I have over a hundred people at my house right now. I have obligations," he says tersely.

I lean in and whisper, "I don't believe it has anything to do with that."

Zeno turns to the others with a tight smile. "If you'll excuse us, please." He stands and wraps his long fingers around my upper arm, carefully tugging me along with him as he leaves the table. He doesn't stop until he's dragged me through the French doors of his office and tucked us away from prying eyes. We stand inches away from each other, his towering form caging me with my back to the drapes.

The waters in his oceanic eyes are raging when he blasts me with his stare. "Do you have something you'd like to say to me?"

My chest rises and falls as I struggle to catch my breath—not from the walk but from the adrenaline surging in my veins. A cataclysmic storm has been brewing between us since the moment I came home.

Maybe even for years.

I've tried to be tolerant and understanding, considering he lost his father this week, but my own hurt has grated away at my patience. "Your need to escape our company ... *my* company ... has nothing to do with checking on your mother or any other responsibilities." The bottled-up emotions I've been carrying spew out with my words.

"Then what exactly are you implying?" He's so close. Close enough for me to smell the spice of his cologne and feel the fiery heat radiating off him. He's nearly as furious as I am, but he's doing his absolute best to rein in his temper.

Good. Let him be angry.

Let him show me proof that the friend I grew up with is still in there somewhere behind the heartless machine he claims to be.

"I think you're arrogant—too proud to be seen with the help. *That's* your problem—your damn pride. You want to become king of the Giordano family and can't possibly associate with a lowly soldier and his family. You're hardly near us for two minutes before you can't wait to get away. *That's* what I think."

I expect my attack to instigate an all-out war, but it has the opposite effect.

A veil of placid indifference falls in place over Zeno's features. The tendons no longer strain in his neck, and the fine lines of fury gathered at the corners of his eyes simply vanish.

The change is instant and absolute.

When he finally responds, his words are a jagged cliffside, coarse and brutally sharp. "I don't want to be your family. You're absolutely right. But if I'm to blame for the situation, then it is my *loyalty* rather than arrogance at fault. Loyalty drives me to forgive when I cannot forget because family is everything. If you think me weak because of it, that is *your* problem. Do not pretend you are without flaws of your own. Your intentional ignorance keeps you from seeing life's truths. If our mutual shortcomings combine and lead you to conclude that I am something I'm not, then little can be done to correct the matter."

Zeno takes a slow step back before turning and stalking out of sight into the hallway.

I feel as though his departure has stranded me alone on a small island. I am bereft, and I don't know why. My hands tremble as I look around with unseeing eyes and attempt to sort through what happened.

He mentioned forgiveness, but what had been done to him to require his forgiveness? Who had hurt him? Surely, he couldn't mean me. I'd done nothing but act as a punching bag for his bad temper.

I think back to that painful week when our friendship ended, but just as I have tried countless times before, I can't identify the reason for his rejection of me. He insinuated I was failing to recognize something obvious, but how could I possibly change that if he didn't give me a hint? If arrogance wasn't behind his behavior, what was?

I slump helplessly onto the worn leather sofa in his father's office. It may be Zeno's office now, but the room hasn't been touched. It holds tight to his father's memory. Mementos sit on shelves along with books and framed photos of a happy family. The essence of him is so strong in this room that I almost feel like he's still here. Still alive.

"What am I missing, Silvano?" I whisper, only to be met with silence.

CHAPTER 10

Zeno, Age 14

Luisa and Nevio, Age 11

"Why do you guys always have to play Halo?" I groan, flopping onto the sofa in the game room at Hardwick. The boys got a new Xbox 360 for Christmas and have been glued to it ever since. Some of the games advertised on TV look fun, but I don't like any of the games the boys have—mostly shooter games and race cars. Blech.

"Because it's awesome," Nevio says without taking his eyes from the screen. "Why don't you go play with Grace if you don't like Halo?"

"She went to Connecticut for Easter to visit her aunt. The whole family went."

"And Gia?"

"She asked Mom to show her how to use the sewing machine."

No idea why. I'd rather do a million other things before I'd ask to learn how to sew. So dumb.

"Hey!" Nevio cries. "Why'd you pause it?"

We both look at Zeno, who stands and tosses his controller on the couch.

"How about I go find the old Game Boy for you, Isa? I think we still have the Mario Cart game with it. Would that work?"

I grin so wide my cheeks ache. "Yeah, that works." Z is the best. If I had a brother, I'd want him to be exactly like Zeno.

He gives me a knowing smirk and jogs out of the room. For the next several minutes, I deal with Nevio moaning about his game being interrupted. I throw a pillow at him, which instigates a pillow fight. We shriek and chase each other around the room with sofa pillows clasped in our hands. I get a particularly savage strike in and laugh hysterically as Zeno returns in the corner of my vision. When I look at where he stands frozen in the doorway, my grin melts from my face.

"What's wrong?" I ask, ignoring Nevio's return strike to my gut.

"You need to go home." Zeno's body is rigid, and his angry glare makes me feel six inches tall.

"But the Game Boy? I thought we were all hanging out." My voice is barely a whisper because I don't understand what I've done to be sent home.

"Now, Luisa!" he yells, pointing at the door beside him.

Zeno is scaring me. I glance beside me at Nevio, who looks confused as well. There's an apology in his eyes, but he doesn't argue with his brother. All I can do is tuck my chin and slink from the room, hoping his bad mood passes quickly.

I want to cry as I walk through the spring grass on the way home, but I don't. Instead, I veer from the worn path and walk down to the lake. I need to be alone. I spend at least an hour skipping rocks along the smooth surface of the water, wondering what I did to upset Zeno. Whenever I think of how he glared at me, my chest feels hollow, and I want to curl into a ball.

Midmorning the next day, I walk to Hardwick and slip in through the kitchen door like I always do, making sure to tell Cecelia good morning. I'm equal parts nervous and hopeful about seeing Zeno. Even when Nevio makes Z really mad, it only ever lasts a day. I have convinced myself that whatever got into him will have passed, and we'll all hang out today like usual.

I find the boys together in the main family room, watching TV. "Hey, guys. Can I watch with you?" My gaze darts warily back and forth between them.

Nevio turns to smile at me briefly. "Sure. The Scorpion King is on."

Zeno doesn't tell me to leave or acknowledge my presence at all, for that matter, so I find a spot on the large sectional away from him and turn to the screen. Not even five minutes later, Z pushes off the sofa and storms from the room.

"He still upset?" I ask Nevio.

"Yeah, he's been extra quiet. No idea why, but I wouldn't worry about it. He can be moody like that."

I wish it were that easy. I can tell in my gut that Z is upset with me, and I want to fix it. Zeno's anger feels so much worse than when Gia or Grace get mad at me. Maybe because he's older and cooler. I don't know. I just want to make it better.

We continue watching the movie for almost an hour before I can't stand it any longer. I have to go find Z and apologize. Nevio doesn't take his eyes from the movie as I slip from the room. The house is quiet, especially once I'm upstairs away from the sounds of the TV. The silent hallways at Hardwick are always a little creepy, but I'm more scared of Zeno staying mad at me than anything.

When I get to his room, the door is shut. I knock softly, not wanting to bother him but knowing I have to do something so that we can be friends again.

"What?" Z barks from inside.

"It's Isa. Can I come in?"

I stand in the huge hallway while a nearby grandfather clock ticks away the seconds. Could Z be so mad that he'd never talk to me again? I wait long enough until I begin to give up and am about to leave when the door creaks open.

Zeno stands tall above me. Taller than I remember him being, though I see him all the time. His anger makes him look enormous and a little scary. "This isn't going to work anymore, Luisa. I'm not interested in hanging out with the housekeeper's *daughter. Plus, you're a kid, and I'm a teenager. That's the way it is, so you need to get over it." His voice reminds me of a dog's warning growl. There's no hint of teasing on his face or in his words.*

Zeno is telling me he's done being my friend.

I blink back tears and push past the ache in my chest. "But ... what about this summer—bike rides, and hide-and-seek, and climbing trees, and..."

"That's not my problem. Maybe Nevio will play with you." Zero emotion. In fact, the more upset I become, the angrier he gets. Too angry for me to argue with him.

He's cutting me from his life the way Daddy trims weeds from our garden, and I can't do anything about it.

I turn and walk toward the stairs, speeding my stride with each step I take. By the time I make it outside, sadness leaks from my eyes in heavy droplets. I walk home, each step heavier than the last. It takes me a full half hour to make the short walk. By the time I reach our front door, I want to crawl under my bed and cry for days.

Z NEVER FORGETS HIS ANGER, *no matter how many times I try to reach out.*

One week later.

One month.

One year.

I've lost my friend forever, and though I don't cry about it anymore, the loss of his friendship is like a broken bone that won't heal. Reminders of him are everywhere, stirring up a dull ache when I let myself remember how much fun we used to have. Sometimes, I wonder what would have happened if I'd simply played Halo *with them instead of fussing. But it's pointless to think about because I did fuss, and nothing has been the same since.*

"Mind if I join you?" Gia pokes her head out the door to where I'm sitting on the back porch.

"Not at all. In fact, there's something I wanted to tell you about."

"How intriguing. I'm all ears." She sits on the bench next to me with her knees angled toward me.

"I was talking with Nevio after the funeral today, and he implied that somehow Zeno was responsible for him being sent to boarding school. Do you know anything about that?" I'd been thinking about what he'd said all afternoon and about Zeno's comments as well.

"No, but I wasn't ever as close to them as you were. Zeno had already graduated and moved out when Nevio went away. How could he have been responsible?"

"I'm not sure. I could have sworn I was told he left because of grades, but he said it had nothing to do with that.

He didn't say anything more, and I wasn't going to push him while we were standing at his father's graveside."

"Of course, not. I'm surprised he even mentioned it."

"He was upset about not being closer with his father. Says he blames Zeno."

Gia sighs into the night air. "Those guys were always competitive, and Z was Silvano's mini-me. I could imagine that was hard on Nevio. He and his dad butted heads all the time—Silvano never could understand Nevio's laid-back temperament. Look at their positions in the family. Z has advanced faster, and Nevio probably feels like he lives in his brother's shadow. I can't imagine my father being my boss and knowing he refused to promote me above an entry-level position while my brother was poised to take over."

"Very true. Though, that doesn't exactly explain how Zeno could be responsible for Nevio being sent to boarding school. I don't know what happened, but I hate that something obviously came between them." *Between all of us.*

"Maybe when the time is right, you can ask one of them."

"We'll see. It's a conversation that needs to take place in person, and I'm not here very often. Who knows what kind of mood they'll be in over the next couple of days."

"Speaking of moods, you never did tell me what you and Z talked about after lunch. He sure seemed upset."

My shoulders sag. "I lost my temper and made some accusations. He said words of his own. It wasn't particularly pretty."

"Oh, Isa. I'm sorry." Her delicate hand comes to rest on my forearm, and I appreciate her understanding.

Unfortunately, her empathy connects with the emotions I've been battling to keep suppressed and enables them to push to the surface. My chin quivers, and tears pool in my eyes.

"It's just been a crazy couple of days, and I wasn't prepared." The words are spoken on a breath because my voice has abandoned me.

Spending time with Zeno after only the briefest of encounters for years is an emotional landmine. To learn he's pushed Nevio away as well makes me want to rage at him even more. Then there's my family. The issues beneath my parents' roof are so vast I want to run back to the city to hide from the oppressive weight of it all. Gia and her hopeless longing. Livia's inability to consider anyone but herself. And now, my parents' marriage was little more than a sham.

Coming home has been so disheartening that I'm already dreading future visits. I'll still come back, but the thought is daunting, and I hate that. I want to look forward to spending time with my family.

Gia scoots closer and pulls me into a hug. "Don't cry, Isa. Everything will work out, I promise." She's using her most comforting mom voice, and it's almost enough for me to believe her. I desperately want to believe her.

"I'm okay, just tired." I squeeze the last of the tears from my eyes before pulling away and wiping the moisture from my cheeks. "Thanks, G. You always find a way to make me feel better."

"I'm glad because I can't stand to see you cry."

I smile reassuringly. "Such a softy."

"Guilty. Now, if you're okay, I'm going to head to bed. You coming?"

"Let me text Grace, and I'll be up." She'd reached out hours ago, but I'd been too distracted to reply.

"Sounds good." Gia kisses my forehead and disappears inside.

The woods are dark, but the kitchen light casts a soft glow on the patchy grass beyond the back porch. Most of the other lights in the house are off. Mom and Dad went to bed an hour ago, and Livia has yet to come home from wherever she disappeared to.

After checking my phone, I respond to Grace's message asking about the day without going into detail about Nevio's comments or my encounter with Z or my father's revelations. Those are conversations better had in person, but I'm not sure I even want to do that. Partly because I fear giving voice to my worries will make them all more real. Other parts simply feel too personal. Maybe once I sort things out in my head and figure out how I feel about it all, I can share, but until then, the things I learned today will stay with me.

I stand and stretch, my body tight from sitting on the hard bench for so long, then quietly make my way inside. As soon as I shut the back door, I hear whispered voices coming from the living room. I strain my ears and realize there's only one voice—my mother—and she's talking frantically to someone on the phone. Unable to help myself, I silently move closer until I can make out her end of the conversation.

"I told you, I'll get the rest … No, you don't need to do that … but … I'm not being difficult, I swear … Okay … A week? … There's no way … Please, Aldo … Aldo?" She's quiet for several counts before her fist pounds the sofa, and she hisses a string of curses.

I peer around the corner at where she sits perched on the edge of a sofa cushion, her small body forlornly curved in on itself with her head dropped back, eyes cast skyward. She looks despondent, but it only makes me angry. I hate that she's the reason Gia can't move on with her life. If my mother could get her shit together, maybe she could have been a real mom and not leave that for her eldest daughter to take on. The daughter she'd never meant to have.

"What was that all about?" My voice is a deadly blade slicing through her moment of self-pity.

Mom shoots upright, her face sculpted in innocence. "Hey, Lulu. I didn't realize you were down here."

Obviously. "What was the call about, Mom? It have anything to do with why you've been selling things?" I'm not letting her leave this living room until she tells me the truth.

She stands and waves a hand at me as though I'm being silly for asking questions. "It's nothing. I borrowed a little money from a friend, and she needs it back sooner than I expected."

"How much?"

"How much what?"

"*Jesus*, Mom! Don't be difficult. How much damn money do you owe?" I want to smack the wide-eyed look right off her face. It's an act, and it's wasted on me.

Like any animal being forced into a cage, she lashes out. "Don't act all high and mighty around me. Just because you're getting some fancy degree doesn't make you better than us."

"And you're not going to redirect this conversation. Tell. Me. What. You. Owe."

Her lips purse and eyes narrow as she studies me, weighing her next move. My inflexibility on the matter must register because her chin lifts defiantly in preparation for her surrender.

"Originally, it was fifteen, but I paid off five, so now it's down to ten." She straightens a stack of magazines nonchalantly on the coffee table as if she's just told me about tomorrow's breakfast options rather than unloaded a financial bomb in our living room.

"Are you talking … thousands?" My mind is utterly blown. "You owe ten *thousand* dollars to someone?" How does that even happen? They don't pay a mortgage or rent. Three of their daughters are grown and should be independent. They have one car between them and never travel. Had Mom racked up ten grand in debt from merely buying shit?

My legs want to give out, but I have the upper hand and refuse to hand it over to her by looking weak.

"You never worried about my finances before, so there's no reason to start now. You'll go back to the city and your fancy life in a few days, so it's not your problem anyway. Forget about it."

I want to listen to her. I don't want to make this my problem, but I have to. Something about the way she panicked worries me. Mom gets herself into all kinds of predicaments and always brushes them off. This is different. Something about this debt has Mom worried.

"Who lent you the money?" This time my words are eerily soft.

I know I've hit the crux of the problem when her lip trembles. She slowly sits down on the sofa, her eyes intently studying her fingers as they fiddle with a hole in her leggings. There is a sincerity to her actions, but it won't gain my sympathy. Whatever mess she's in, she got herself there. I may assure her and even help her, but I won't feel sorry for her.

"His name is Aldo Consoli. He's … he's a bookie. I make a bet here and there, nothing major. I gave it a try one time because there was this Fendi purse I *really* wanted, but I knew we could never afford it. I figured, what does it hurt to chance a couple of hundred on a bet? Instead of buying a crap purse I didn't want with the money, I'd use it to at least try to get the bag I wanted. And I did it—I made five grand from nothing. It's the most incredible feeling, Isa, like winning the lottery. I got the purse then made a couple more bets with the rest of the money. I won three more grand and felt like I was on top of the world, but then I had a bit of a dry spell. Things didn't go so well for my next few bets, but a race was coming up that I felt great about. I *knew* that would get me back in the money. I felt so good about it … I still don't know what went wrong. One minute, I was swimming in cash, and the next, I was fifteen k in the hole."

A bookie. There never was a friend. She owes money to a *bookie*.

Fuck.

Fuckfuckfuckfuckfuck.

This is so much worse than I assumed. Ten grand is a lot, but ten grand to a bookie is serious trouble. My stomach churned into an angry knot as her explanation unfolded, and now, there's a real chance I might vomit.

"This … Aldo—he's associated with *the family*, isn't he?"

She nods, and I have to keep myself from lunging at her and wrapping my straining fingers around her throat.

When someone on the street doesn't pay their bookie, they can end up dead, but Mom is technically a part of the family —she's protected as Dad's wife—but that means Dad assumes her debt. They won't kill a member of the family over a debt, but they could easily rough him up. And maybe even worse, he'd be disgraced forever. As if not advancing past soldier at his age wasn't bad enough, my dad would be labeled a deadbeat.

"Does Dad know?"

"No, and he doesn't have to." She jumps up and rushes over to me. "I'll find a way to pay it off. I'll … I don't know, but I'll find a way."

"*How*, Mom? How the hell are you going to come up with ten grand in a week without Dad knowing?"

Her brows knit together as she chews on her bottom lip. "I

don't know, Lulu." Her helpless whisper claws at my skin. I'm so angry I could scream.

"Don't call me that. Don't you ever call me that again." Lulu has always been my father's nickname for me. That's how Gia pronounced my name when I was born, but it became my dad's term of endearment for me. I don't want her tainting something so special. "This conversation isn't over, but I'm going to bed. I can't deal with this right now."

I've had more than I can take for one day.

I leave the room without waiting for a reply. There's nothing for her to say. When I finally make it upstairs, Gia is already in bed, sleeping peacefully.

I envy her. Sleep won't come easily for me tonight.

Needing to at least try to relax the tension now coiled in my muscles, I take a hot shower. The heat soothes my body, but it does little to wash away my fears. I can't bear to let my dad suffer such a disgrace. The thought alone sends a bolt of searing pain through my chest. He's only ever done what he thought was best for his family; he doesn't deserve to be humiliated, no matter what the family code of honor says. It's not his fault my mother is irresponsible and selfish.

Once I'm dried off and in an oversized pajama shirt, I crawl into bed with my worries. They haven't subsided, but at least I'm more disheartened than angry. Unfettered rage makes for a poor bedtime companion.

I close my eyes and try to drown out my thoughts when I hear a sound in the hallway. The only people upstairs should be us girls, so I immediately assume Livia has finally come home. She's old enough not to have a curfew, but I wasn't crazy about her disappearing without a word. I tell myself that arguing with her now is beyond my capacity, and it's best if I let it go. Then I lay, straining to hear more sound, wondering if it was her at all. Maybe it wasn't, and she's still out. Maybe she's been hurt.

I sigh deeply and slip from the bed. At some point, I'd think my brain would be exhausted with itself and quit, but no such luck.

The bathroom door is shut with the light on. I test the knob and find it's unlocked. When I open the door, Liv is sitting on the side of the tub, half-naked with her red curls plopped in a messy pile on her head. She looks so much like Mom and is equally as bad at making decisions for herself. It hurts my heart to witness.

"Lu-*ees*-a," she hiccups with a blinding grin. "What are you doing up?" Her words are slurred but not enough for me to worry about alcohol poisoning. Some of the scathing comments I'd considered die a quick death when I realize she's drunk. No point in arguing with a drunk Livia.

"Hey, little sister," I whisper. "You been having fun?"

She puts her finger to her lips as if telling me to be quiet when she's the one with the volume problem. "I've had such a lovely night." Her eyes drift shut as she smiles again.

"I'm glad to hear it, but you never told anyone where you were going. That's not safe, you know."

"Don't be such a Worry McWorry Face. Everything is going to be fine. You … you take my word." She struggles to take off her bra and put on a sleep shirt as she talks. Watching her is rather entertaining, but I give in and help.

"Some of us have to worry because *others* of us don't worry enough."

"There's no need, silly. I'm going to marry someone rich, rich, rich! So why worry?"

"Orrr," I draw out. "You could make your own money and not rely on someone else to take care of you."

Livia collapses into a fit of giggles, snorting, then snickering some more. "You're so funny, Lulu."

Apparently, everyone was going to resurrect that nickname tonight.

"All right, Livy. Let's get you to bed."

I help her up and get her tucked in before returning to the bathroom to tidy up. When I crawl back into my own bed next to Gia, I am well and truly exhausted. My worries finally coalesce into a fat, gelatinous blob in the back of my brain, enabling me to hide from them for the moment. I focus on Gia's slow, even breaths, and before I know it, I'm drifting into a deep, dreamless sleep.

I HAVEN'T FELT *this well rested in ages.* It's the first thing I think as I stretch in bed. I must have slipped into a coma because I feel like I've slept for a week. When I open my eyes, I confirm that the sun is well into the sky. I've slept much later than I intended. Now that the funeral is over, I don't need to help my family with work, but I still hadn't meant to sleep half the day away.

After I roll myself out of bed, I pull on a pair of booty shorts and give my teeth a quick brush before confirming I'm alone in the house.

Thank God. I need a few minutes of peace and quiet. No drama. No more surprises.

I slip a pod in the Keurig and open my phone to start scrolling on social media when a knock sounds at the front door. My parents don't get many visitors, especially unexpected visitors, since guests have to be approved at the gate. Assuming it's probably Mrs. Larson stopping by to see my mom, I open the door wide. Only, it's not Mrs. Larson. It's not anyone I know.

"Can I help you?" I ask warily, crossing my arms over my chest when I remember I don't have a bra on.

The man on our front porch grins the most seedy, serpentine grin I've ever seen. His black hair hangs down over his forehead, and his eyes are a smidge too close together. He's not big, but somehow, he's not any less intimidating for it. If he were walking toward me on a sidewalk, I'd find a reason to cross the street.

"That depends. I'm looking for Gemma, but judging by those eyes, you must be one of her girls."

Most people don't think I look a ton like my mother because I don't have her billowing red curls, but my eyes and nose are just like hers. That never bothered me before as much as it does right this second. I don't want this man to find me familiar, and I especially don't want to bear any resemblance to the woman I call a mother.

"They're at work right now." I study the man to sort out who he is, but in my gut, I know. This is the bookie my mom owes money to. The reason she was scared out of her mind. "Are you Aldo?"

He rocks back on his heels with a grin that makes me want to pumice my eyeballs. "Hey, look at that. It's like I'm famous. Your ma tell you about me?"

"Not exactly. How did you get past the gate?"

His tongue plunders his teeth like he's got the holy grail stuck back there. "You got a lot of questions for a girl. You wanna go on a date, we can *talk* all night long. Right now? I got some business to handle."

I say nothing. I certainly don't want to go on a date with this creep, nor do I want to piss him off. He accepts my silence for the rejection it is, shrugs, and continues.

"I've been in the area for three days for this damn funeral, and I wanted to get this shit with your mother finished by the time I went home, only she's managed to avoid me at every opportunity. I'm gettin' real fuckin' sick of chasing after her."

So that was why Mom was so out of sorts the past few days. That was why she was drinking and why she bailed from going to the luncheon. She was hiding.

"I heard her talking to you last night on the phone. I thought she had another week to pay you."

The corner of his mouth fish-hooks up in a smirk that bleeds into a snarl. "No, sweet thing. She was asking me for another week. I told her she better get my money by to-fuck-ing-day."

"And if she doesn't pay you?" I can't totally irradicate the fear from my voice.

"I suppose that's between your pops and me."

"Look, he doesn't know anything about this, and I don't want him hurt because of it. What if … what if I helped my mom pay her debt? If I promise I'll get you paid by the end of this week, would you give me that time?" I'm not sure what I'm doing, but I have to at least try to buy more time.

Aldo's lecherous gaze drifts down my body, my skin itching with the invisible stain of his touch.

"I'd give you all sorts of things if you asked nice enough."

I desperately want to slam the door in his face, but I know I can't. "Time. All I need is a little time, and you'll get your money."

"Suit yourself. End of the week, no more extensions." He winks and turns away, calling over his shoulder. "I'll be in touch." He doesn't have a car in the driveway, but he could have parked it down the street to catch Mom off guard. Or maybe he jumped the wall around Tuxedo Park, and that was how he got in. All I know is I'm glad he's gone.

I shut the door and bolt it, leaning back against the aged wood and sliding down to my bottom. My knees bend up toward my chest, and I hug my legs as though I'm a little girl again. I feel like I could be. These mounting problems weigh too much for my shoulders—as though I need an adult to come rescue me. But it's an adult who got me into this mess. My own mother. Now, I have to find a way out for all of us.

CHAPTER 12

I NEED TO FIND GIA AND TELL HER WHAT'S GOING ON.

Forgetting all about my coffee, I throw on some clothes and start toward the back door. It feels safer, like Aldo might still be waiting for me out front. And with that thought, I detour to my parents' bedroom and grab one of my dad's pocketknives. I can't be too cautious where Aldo is concerned.

Fucking creep.

I open the back door and almost pass out when there's someone on the other side. Nevio's fist is raised as though he were about to knock, but my already frayed nerves elicit a momentary panic that I'm about to be attacked. I shriek and flinch, slamming the door shut in his face. Recognition registers seconds too late, and when I open the door to apologize, poor Nevio is still wearing a look of shocked confusion.

"Oh my God, I'm so sorry!" I start to laugh at the absurdity of my morning.

"You okay? I didn't mean to startle you." He flashes that signature smile, brows drawn up good-naturedly.

"Yeah, I'm totally fine—just didn't expect someone to be standing there." And now that my brain has caught up with real time, I process that Nevio has come by the house. Not only has he stopped over for an unannounced visit after years of not seeing each other, but he's come to the back door, which all strikes me as a tad unusual, but not totally out of the question. When we were kids, we always let ourselves in and out of the back of our houses because it was easier than walking around to the front, and as children, we weren't encumbered with a need for formality. But we're adults now, and as far as I know, Nevio hasn't been to our house in ten years.

"I thought I'd stop over to visit. I would have called, but I don't have your number."

"You're right. I don't think we've ever exchanged numbers." I pull out my phone. "What's yours? I'll shoot you a text."

He reads off the digits, and I'm hopeful we'll stay in better contact.

"I was about to walk over to your house in search of Gia. You can keep me company on the walk."

"Absolutely."

I make sure to lock the door behind me before following Nevio into the grass. "I didn't get a chance to ask before. How long will you be staying at Hardwick?"

"I suppose that depends on a couple of things," he muses.

"Like what?"

"Like how long you'll be here." The honesty of his answer

startles me, and I'm not certain if he's sincere or merely being his flattering self.

"Oh, yeah?" I glance over to find his warm brown eyes already watching me, and I can't help the smile that creeps across my face. "Surely, I'm not the only factor in that decision."

"You play a bigger role than you might think. I spent a lot of years trying to get you out of my head, but after seeing you again, I'm not sure what I was thinking."

My stomach bottoms out with his words.

Am I reading into his meaning? Did he mean to imply he had a thing for me back then? That he *has* a thing for me now?

I'm stunned speechless for a solid minute. "Nev, what are you saying?"

We slow to a stop, my eyes searching his face for a semblance of understanding. Growing up, we'd been close, but it never went beyond anything but friendship. When he left for boarding school, I didn't have a cell phone of my own yet, so we couldn't text, and we didn't call or write very often. I missed him, but my life was full with friends and school such that I moved on quickly. It never occurred to me he harbored deeper feelings for me.

I don't know what to say. Ten years is a long time. I'm not as idealistic as I was as a girl, but he still seems to be the same carefree playboy he's always been. That's not exactly the type of man I go for at this stage in my life. Maybe back then, if I'd known how he felt, but now … I'm not so sure.

Nevio raises his hand and gently guides a lock of hair behind my ear after it escaped from my hastily plopped bun. "I'm saying I've missed you and would love to spend a little more time with you. I normally don't like coming home, but with you here, I don't want to leave."

I smile and look anywhere but at him as I'm engulfed in

an ocean of awkwardness. "I'll only be here for a couple more days."

"It's a chance to reacquaint ourselves. That's all I'm asking." He eases us back into our walk, which is not overly hot now that a line of clouds has overtaken the sun. "I'd love to hear more about your life in the city. Where did you end up settling down?"

"Over in Brooklyn. I'm finishing my degree in English lit at St. Joseph's. I'm a little older than the average student, but I've been paying my own way, so it's taken me some extra time. Not to mention, I got a late start."

"Hell, I'm impressed you went after what you wanted and are achieving it. Not everyone can say they've done that." He smiles warmly at me. "I remember how much you loved reading. English lit sounds perfect for you. Are you wanting to teach one day?"

"That's the part I haven't totally figured out. I've been so concentrated on getting through school that I haven't had a chance to fully consider what I'll do once I'm done." That's not totally true. I know what I want to do, but I'm just not sure how to make it happen. I want to write my own stories—create my own characters and watch them evolve into multi-dimensional people—but the process is daunting, and I'm not sure I want to tell anyone until that first book is complete. The pressure I put on my own shoulders is more than enough. I'd rather not have to bear the expectations of others as well.

"That sounds perfectly reasonable. I don't believe anyone can truly know what they want from their lives until they've lived a little. If I'd gone to college, I wouldn't have had any idea what degree program to pick. That was one of the perks of having my life already decided for me."

Both De Rossi boys had followed in their father's Mafia

footsteps, but I'd always assumed that was because they wanted to and not for any other reason. The suggestion that my assumption could be wrong shocked me.

"Were you forced to join the family?"

"No, not exactly. It was more like an expectation, and I wasn't a fan of school, so going to college was never an option. I could have lived off my father's money easily enough, but then I'd have felt like even more of a failure than he and Zeno already thought I was."

"Why would they think that?" I balk.

"Why were both of them always hard on me? My father didn't think I was tough enough, but Z just had a stick up his ass. He wanted to be the favorite and saw me as nothing but competition." His words are spoken with a cool impassiveness that reminds me of the hard layer of ice coating a frozen pond, hiding the treacherous water below. Nevio was concealing a world of raw emotion centered primarily around his brother.

"Yesterday, you mentioned something about Zeno being the reason you were sent away in high school." I'm feeling a little awkward about pushing for an explanation on such a delicate subject, so I technically don't ask a question. I figure he can take the hint and offer an explanation or sideswipe the issue entirely if he chooses. He was the one who brought it up in the first place, but still, I don't want to intrude on a private matter.

Nevio shows no signs of being uncomfortable, launching into his account of what happened so many years ago. "Z started acting funny his senior year of high school. He was distant and more uptight, but he also began to work for the family, so I assumed he was acting tough to fit in. He wasn't around much, and while I missed the friendship I'd had with my brother, there was little I could do to change matters. You and I were only around fourteen at the time and starting our sophomore year. After Christmas, everything got so much worse."

"I remember that Christmas. Mom let us have Bailey's in our hot chocolate—it was the first time I got a little drunk. Or at least, what I thought was drunk. Now, I'd say I was barely tipsy. I remember laughing our asses off." The memory brings a broad smile to my face.

Nevio smiles as well, but his eyes bear a sadness to them at the same time. "That's one of my absolute favorite memories. Unfortunately, it's followed by one of my worst. Two months after that, I overheard Z talking to Mom and Dad about me. He insisted that I needed more discipline and that the only way I'd stay out of trouble was to be sent away to school. He argued specifically for a military school on the West Coast. I couldn't believe what I was hearing. My own brother was trying to exile me from the family for no good reason. I wasn't getting in trouble at school or making bad grades; *he* was the sole instigator. It's the same reason he didn't want me here for the funeral and asked only this morning when I'd be leaving." Nevio looks at me, pleading in his eyes. "Can I be totally honest with you, Luisa?"

"Of course, you can."

He glances up at the house looming before us. "He's never said anything directly, but in my gut, I'm certain it's always been about you."

"Me?" I blurt, totally caught off guard.

"I don't want to put you in an awkward position, but I want you to know the truth. To understand. I think you and I were getting close, and he saw that, so he found a way to keep me away from you. It didn't click with me until years later. I had a lot of time to think while I was away at school, and it's the one thing that made sense. He wanted a clear line drawn between our family and anyone he deemed *lesser* than. I told him once that I wanted to ask you out, and he told me I was a fool. That I'd end up like your dad, stuck at the bottom of the organization with no hope of success. I told him he was being absurd. I think he was stepping in to make sure nothing developed between us. He probably thought he was protecting me, but it wasn't his call to make."

I'm dumbfounded. It makes sense in a way, but it's still hard to imagine someone could be so shallow. "Why would he be so narrow-minded? Our parents are friends. We grew up together."

Nevio shrugs. "Dad groomed him from the day he was born to lead the Giordano family. There's no telling what he said to Zeno to warp his thinking. Being friendly with a soldier's family is one thing but marrying into it is another."

I shake my head in wonder that anyone could cling to such archaic principles. I wonder if that's what happened that day so many years ago. Had he run into his father and been given a reprimand about hanging out with me? It's all so odd. People marry whoever they want—Mafia jobs aren't some makeshift caste system. At least, I'd never gotten that impression. But once I start thinking about it, I wonder why Dad never did advance to a capo's rank. If Silvano saw him as inferior due to his job and hasty marriage, that could explain it. It's a question I've never considered, but now, the need for an answer feels imperative.

"It's strange to think I could have been so wrong about people. Your dad was always kind to me, and I thought he and my father were friends, but I'm starting to wonder if I knew anything at all."

Your intentional ignorance keeps you from seeing life's truths. Is that what Zeno had meant when he'd said those words?

That I was turning a blind eye to reality in regard to our stations in life?

"Dad wasn't all bad, but he wasn't always a good man, either. Now that he's gone, I hope his influence will fade. He's the one who set in motion the plan for Zeno to marry the boss's daughter. Although Z will probably go through with it to honor Dad." He shakes his head incredulously.

My steps falter. "Christiano? *That* boss?" It's a stupid question—there's no other boss to speak of—but I'm so surprised that the words tumble from my lips.

"That's the one."

"Huh." The news is so shocking that I have no emotional response. None. Only confusion. What did it mean that there was a *plan* for him to marry someone? Was there an actual arrangement, or was it more of a matter of vague hopefulness? Surely, the two aren't in a relationship. She would have been at his father's funeral, and I never saw him with a woman—not in that way.

"Yeah. I can't say I envy him. I wouldn't want Christiano breathing down my neck every day of my life."

"The only time I've ever met him was briefly yesterday at the funeral." I didn't form the greatest initial impression, but I've tried not to let a quick conversation at a funeral color my perceptions.

"Consider yourself lucky. He's one ruthless bastard."

"Nevio! He's your *boss*. You can't talk about him like that." I can't help smiling a little, though. It's just like him not to care about protocol and speak his mind.

"It's the truth." He grins. "So, are you working at the house today?"

"No, I just need to talk to Gia. Any idea where she was when you left?" The reminder of my original purpose drops a wet blanket on any light-heartedness I'd found on our walk over. My steps are suddenly leaden as we walk up to the side entrance nearest the kitchen.

"No clue, but I'm happy to help you look."

My lips thin as he opens the door for me. "Actually, I need to talk to her in private. It's sort of a family matter."

He raises his hand. "Say no more. I don't need to intrude."

I appreciate his understanding and am relieved to find Gia in the kitchen, irradicating any need to go searching for her.

"Hey, you two," she says warmly. "What's up?"

"Mom here?" She tends to spend her work hours talking with Cecelia in the kitchen, so I'm surprised to find Gia instead. Her absence makes me wonder where Livia and Marca are as well since they weren't at home when I woke up. I'd been too inundated with chaos to question the matter until now.

"Dad had some appointment to go to, and Mom dropped the girls at the mall before going to lunch with a friend."

The mall. Great. I'm freaking out about how to pay Mom's debts, and the girls are at the mall.

"Gotcha." My eyes cut to Nevio, who gives the back of my neck a gentle squeeze.

"I'm going to make a couple of calls, but I'll see you later, right?"

"Yeah, sure." I smile half-heartedly, and when my gaze drifts from his retreating form to Gia's bulging eyes, I shrug. "It's been a seriously crazy morning."

She dries her hands on a dish towel and removes her apron. "I need details."

"Oh, you'll get details, but not the kind you're hoping for. Where can we go where we won't be overheard?"

"I know the perfect place. Come on."

She leads me to the old chapel—a tiny prayer room that's rarely ever visited. Two small benches are centered in front of a podium holding a gold cross backlit by a vibrant stained glass window. The room is good for the devout Catholic or a game of hide-and-seek, but that's about it. The air is musty, and only one of two lights flicker on when we enter.

Gia closes the door behind us and stares at me expectantly. "Start talking, lady."

"I needed to talk to you, but it's not about Nevio. I have no clue what's going on there. He indicated he had feelings for me when we were growing up, and they've come back. I'm not sure what to think, but none of that is important at the moment."

"It's not?" she gawks, confused.

"You know how you were worried about Mom selling stuff?"

Her lips thin, and wariness hardens her gaze. "Yeah?"

"Well, a guy showed up at the house earlier demanding money. She owes ten freaking grand to a bookie," I hiss the last part, my anger reigniting.

Gia's jaw falls open. "No," she breathes. "Please tell me you're joking."

I shake my head sadly. "I wish. She knew he was in town for the funeral and was avoiding him. He wants his money. I told him I'd help find a way to get it paid if he'd give me until the end of the week."

"Luisa, where the hell are you going to find that kind of cash?"

"That's why I needed to talk to you! I've got some, but I was hoping you could help too. This guy is a Mafia bookie. If we can't find a way to pay him, the debt falls on Dad."

My sister visibly deflates, overcome with dismay. "What do we do?" she whispers, eyes searching mine for answers. "I don't have that kind of money, Isa."

"You don't have anything saved?" She lives at home with hardly any bills. How could she not have any money?

She chews on the inside of her cheek, eyes dropping to the floor. "I used a bunch of my savings when I bought my car a year ago. Then there was an incident. Mom told me their credit card got hacked, and someone had spent a bunch of money on it. She said the credit company was demanding they pay for it and was going to file criminal charges. I had the money, so I gave it to her. I'm wondering now if she may have lied. I've barely put anything away since then."

"What's barely?"

"I have two thousand in savings." She grimaces. "I could sell my car, I guess."

She'd do it, too, but I can tell how much the idea pains her. She needs her vehicle just as much as Mom and Dad need their 4Runner, maybe even more because that's her sole source of freedom. And my parents' old SUV wouldn't help—I doubt we could get a solid five grand for it. Plus, if we sold the car, we'd have to tell Dad, and I'm not even sure we could sell it before the end of the week. Gia didn't say how much she gave to Mom, but it had to be sizable to empty her accounts. She's done so much; the last thing I want to do is ask her to forfeit the car she spent years saving to buy. Livia and Marca don't have any money, and I can't think of anything else to sell.

No matter how I look at it, I'm left with only one option.

My eyes close, heavy with the weight of my decision. "You've already helped her enough. I'll handle it." The hollowness of my voice is an outward reflection of the emptiness I feel inside. Too many emotions war for dominance—rage, desperation, anguish. I can't process them all at once, leaving me in a vacuous darkness.

"What does that mean, Isa?"

I open my eyes and meet her concerned gaze with resignation. "I'm going to use my school money to pay her debt. I have just enough saved to cover what she owes. Then I'm telling Mom we're done bailing her out."

"Should we tell Dad? I feel like he should know."

"He would be humiliated if he knew we'd been covering for her, but I don't want him hurt because of her either. If he doesn't know what's going on, he can't protect himself." A pounding headache starts to pulse at my temples. "We have a little time to think it through. Let's not make any decisions on that yet."

Gia pulls me into her arms, but I can't hug her back. A tidal wave of emotion threatens to drown me, and her affection will only draw it closer.

"What does that mean for you and school? Will you still be able to finish?"

I pull away and shrug. "It's taken me forever to get this far. What's one more year?" I put on a strong front because I have no other choice. On the inside, a part of me wants to scream and rage about the unfairness. "I'm going to head out and let you get back to work." I need to be alone. I need a moment to come to terms with my decision because that's what it is—a choice. I don't have to pay off Mom's debt. It's my choice, and that means I can't blame anyone but myself. That won't be easy, but it's necessary. I don't want to carry a chip on my shoulder for the rest of my life, and the only way to be free of that is if I believe the decision was mine.

"Okay, honey. We can talk more this evening."

I offer a broken smile before walking numbly from the room. I'm halfway to the lake before I even realize where I'm going. Nevio had talked about hanging out, and I have his number, but that's not an option at the moment. I have no capacity to even think about Nevio or Zeno when my entire life is in the process of derailing.

I have twelve thousand in savings—some from student loans, and some I've stashed away from each paycheck I've earned waitressing. Without that money, all my earnings would have to go toward rent, leaving me nothing for school. I would need all of my savings plus the three months of summer earnings in order to cover school and living expenses. There's no way I can make ends meet now. I could look into getting more student aid, but I've tried so hard to keep my loans at a minimum and already stress about repayment. Not only would this add more debt to my total but I'd have to take out my standard amount plus a bunch more to cover the money I'd earned at work. I'd have to spend an entire year working to replenish my savings enough to take classes.

The serene waterfront comes into view as something my sister said the first day I arrived plays in my mind.

I could get used to working with you. With Anna gone, we'll need to take on someone new.

If I moved back home and worked at Hardwick, I'd be able to save up twice as quickly. I could take a single semester off and be back in classes by January. But at what cost? I'd lose my fucking sanity living with Mom and Livia, not to mention I'd run into Zeno on a regular basis and have to deal with his infuriating arrogance.

Isn't finishing school worth it? It's not forever.

I heave out a breath, my shoulders slumping.

My internal monologue leads me to the only logical decision. I have to suck it up and do what is needed to get me back on track as quickly as possible.

I have to make Hardwick a part of my life again.

CHAPTER 13

THE GLASSY SURFACE OF THE DARK BROWN WATER SHINES WITH sunlight, reminding me of a storm cloud's silver lining. The water isn't crystal clear like the shores of the Caribbean. There's moss and silt, and the fish within wouldn't wow any children with their lackluster scales if displayed in an aquarium. But the lake is beautiful in its own way. The tall trees standing watch at its borders protect the water's edge like soldiers out front of Buckingham Palace. They seem to recognize the intrinsic pricelessness of the water, though they have no eyes with which to experience its beauty.

I lose myself pondering the wonders around me in an intentional effort to focus on the good parts of life so that I will not sink deep in the quicksand of despondency. Its spindly claws tug at my body each time my mind drifts back to my situation. Each time I think of calling my would-be roommate and letting her know I have to back out of my promise to sublet the room in her apartment. Each time I consider calling the school registrar and asking for a hold on my status as an active student. Each time I resolve to ring my boss and inform her that I won't be coming back.

Disappointment lives and breathes inside me, but I will not let it take over.

Something about the permanence of the lake gives me a wealth of reassurance. These few months that I'm stressing about are but a single season of rainfall to a body of water that has existed for possibly centuries. It's a welcome reminder that a handful of months out of what I hope will be a long and happy life will hardly be memorable in the long run.

Performing mental gymnastics to keep the proper perspective helps to some extent. I have assured myself that the world isn't ending, but I'm still not in a great headspace.

"Please, don't."

The rumbling command startles me for the hundredth time today. If this keeps up, I'm going to need a pacemaker to keep my heart from giving out.

I whip around to find Zeno standing not ten feet behind me. "What?" He's clearly talking to me, as there's no one else around, but I have no idea what he means.

"If I didn't know better, I'd say you were contemplating drowning yourself in the lake."

My eyes drift back to the surface of the water. "I'm surprised you wouldn't cheer me on," I mutter.

"Why would you say that?"

The frustration I'd had on a leash is suddenly wriggling free, hissing at me to say brash, hurtful things.

"Because every time I'm near you, I get the sense you wish I'd disappear." Tears burn at the back of my eyes. I try to regain the control I thought I'd mastered minutes before, but

I'm swimming out of my depths with no idea where the shore has gone. "I'm sorry," I clip, attempting to minimize the damage I'm doing. "I've got a lot going on."

Why is he suddenly interested in starting a conversation? Of all the times to play nice and talk civilly, he has to choose the moment I'm at my lowest. I can sense the heat of his gaze studying me—assessing and analyzing—when all I want is to be invisible.

"Is everything all right, Luisa?"

Do I detect a note of genuine concern in the mellow hum of his voice? I look back at him, but his face is stoic as ever. Why is he even here? I can't imagine he was walking by the lake in the middle of the day and just happened by me, though no *other* explanation appears any more or less probable.

"I'm fine." I wave him off, then peer back at him. "But since you're here, I have something to ask you." Might as well hit him up for a job while he's in a relatively decent mood. "My plans have recently changed, and I'll be staying with my parents a while longer than expected. Gia mentioned that Anna would need to be replaced, so I was wondering, if you're okay with it, if I could take the job. It wouldn't be forever, but I could really use the money until the end of the year." I struggle to hold his gaze. It shouldn't matter what he thinks, but it does. I hate for him to see me moving back with my parents and groveling for a job.

Z steps closer; his position uphill from me magnifies his already imposing height. Light reflects off the water, making his cobalt eyes almost cerulean. His irises have always had a touch more green than mine, and the effect in this light is breathtaking.

"Has something happened?" His assertive nature urges

me to spill my guts. It's tempting, but word of my mother's debt getting out is exactly what I'm trying to avoid.

"No, it's nothing to worry about. Some things didn't line up as I'd expected." Maybe I'm reading into it, but I swear his face is lined with conflict, as though he's torn about helping me. The resistance I detect raises my defenses. "Look, you don't need to feel obligated. It's not a big deal. I can find a job somewhere else."

"*Stop.*"

Zeno's barked command silences me instantly.

"Don't assume to know what I'm thinking because you don't. I want to help you, but I'm concerned about my brother."

"What about him?" Is it true? Is he worried Nevio might form an attachment to me and shame his family?

Z moves even closer until only a foot of space remains between us. His nearness sucks up all the oxygen in the area, leaving me breathless and dizzy.

"I've seen the way he watches you. His track record with women is … let's say he's not great at sticking around. I don't want you to get swept up in that." He wants me to think he's protecting me, but is that the truth? Or are his motives more selfish?

"I appreciate you trying to protect me, or whatever this is, but your concern is unnecessary." And unwanted. "Nevio is a friend, and that's it. But even more importantly, I'm an adult who can make relationship decisions on my own."

The slight furrow of his brows and pursing of his lips tell me he's not convinced. My threadbare patience unravels along with my hold over my emotions. I sense tears threatening on the horizon and know I need to get away from him before the storm hits.

"Look, you can trust my judgment and give me the job or

not, but whether I do something with your brother is none of your damn business."

Zeno stiffens at my rebuke. "He's my brother and a soldier under my command. I don't need you to tell me what is and isn't my business."

My lips snap shut. "You're right. He's your family, despite how you treat him."

"Do you want the job or not?" Each word is clipped and sharp, spoken between clenched teeth.

I hold my ground, not allowing my gaze to waver, but I realize I'm jeopardizing the plan that will get me back to school the quickest. With that in mind, I inhale slowly before speaking calmly. "I do."

"I'll tell my mother you're staying on." The bitter cold of his reply stings, though I brought it on myself. I can't be angry because it achieves what I need. Our conversation is over.

I hold perfectly still as he turns and walks away. A sob is clawing its way up my throat from deep inside me, and if I make the tiniest move, it will burst free while he is near enough to hear. Using the last of my mental energy, I hold tight to my reins until I'm certain he's gone, then I allow the emotions to drag me under.

Hiding my face in my hands, I attempt to suffocate the sound from my uncontrollable weeping. Heaving breaths wrack my chest, and my shoulders curve in as my legs threaten to give out. For long minutes, I come undone.

Six years of hard work, and I was so close to being done. So close to achieving my goals. It's only a delay, but no matter how much I try to package the turn of events in shiny paper and colorful bows, it still sucks. And no matter how many times I tell myself this is my choice and it's what I want, I'm still heartbroken over it. Someone has extended the finish line of my marathon, and after all the running I've already done, those last few meters feel like an eternity.

I cry—long, and hard, and ugly.

The cleansing wash of emotions leaves me ragged and bleary-eyed. I do my best to wipe away the snot and tears before making the slow trek back to the cottage. I give myself the afternoon to wallow in bed, only leaving my room for bathroom breaks and a single stop in the kitchen. I don't want to eat, but after not having anything all day, my stomach insists.

When Gia returns from work in the evening, she comes straight to our room and curls up with me in bed. She doesn't ask questions. She doesn't give empty assurances. Gia's most innate skill is intuiting how to provide the perfect form of support and comfort to those she loves.

"I'm so sorry, Lulu," she whispers.

"I know, G. Me, too."

A few sounds filter in from downstairs, but otherwise, the room is quiet. My sister's presence is enough to give me more mental strength than I've had in hours, enough that I can pretend to function for the evening.

"I made arrangements with Z to stay on and work."

"Have you told Mom?"

I shake my head. "Tomorrow. I'm not up for it today."

"Totally understandable. You know, maybe she still has some cash stashed away. If we used my money and hers, maybe you could still swing school." The hopefulness in her voice is why it's impossible not to love her. Gia will always hope for the best and explain away the worst.

"No, G. She already paid what she could."

My sister lifts her head to look at me in surprise. "If she already paid some, how much was the debt to start with?"

"Fifteen," I say dryly.

She falls back down onto the soft mattress. "Jesus," she breathes.

"Yeah."

"Well, on a totally selfish note, a part of me is glad I'll get to see more of you. I know that sounds awful, but it's true."

It's probably the most selfish thing I've ever heard my sister say, and it makes me smile. "I love you, too, G. And I'm glad we'll get to spend some time together."

We're both quiet for several long minutes before Gia speaks again.

"How was talking to Zeno?"

I huff out a dry laugh. "I might have been a little short with him. He didn't catch me at the best time." I tell her all about our conversation and what I'd learned earlier in the day from Nevio.

"I'm not sure what to think of all that—any of it," she muses, staring blankly at the wall.

"You and me both."

"So, Zeno followed you down to the lake—"

"We don't know that," I cut her off.

She shoots me a critical look from the side of her eye. "Right. He just *happens* by you at the lake—the same as he just happened by you in the kitchen the other night. Are you sure Zeno doesn't have a thing for you? Maybe that's why he doesn't want Nevio around you."

"Gia, you know Zeno as well as I do. Do you really believe he's so shy he couldn't make a move on a woman if he wanted her? That he's wanted me all this time but was so meek he couldn't find a way to tell me? I'll admit that his behavior is confusing, but I'm not about to read into it."

"Now you sound like me," she teases. She's right, and it draws a reluctant smile from me.

"Oh, G. You're the only reason these next few months are

going to be remotely tolerable." I pick up my phone after ignoring it all afternoon and find I have a missed text from Grace.

Grace: The Bishops want to have you all and the De Rossis over tomorrow night for dinner. That work?

I shoot a sly grin at my sister. "Looks like we're all having dinner at the Bishops' tomorrow night."

As I'd hoped, her face lights up like a kid at Christmas.

Realization dawns that I have a secondary purpose for my stay here at the Hardwick estate. I'll do my best while I'm here to help my sister make a move on her crush. Considering how into each other they both are, it shouldn't be all that hard. Helping her find her happily ever after would make every minute here worth it.

Me: Sounds wonderful! We'll see you then.

Gia and I both get up to go downstairs for dinner, and as I freshen up after a day in bed, I start to wonder if fate has kept me here for a reason. I'm still not thrilled with delaying my graduation, but my perspective begins to shift. I have the next six months to play matchmaker for Gia, guidance counselor for Livia, and spend some precious time with my father. Knowing my sacrifice serves more than one purpose is gratifying enough that I'm able to refrain from strangling my mother at dinner. That alone is proof that miracles happen.

The next morning, I find myself alone with my mom in the kitchen and decide it's time to have a talk. Gia is finishing in the bathroom, and the younger girls were still asleep when I came down, so I've got some time before we're interrupted.

I walk to the coffee maker, right next to where she's peeling an orange.

"Aldo came by yesterday while you guys were out." I impart the information with perfect calm and quiet enough that we can't be overheard, just in case.

Mom drops her orange.

"He wasn't going to give you more time, but I told him I'd get it paid, so he's giving me until the end of the week." I place a mug under the coffee spout, not meeting her stare, though I can feel her wide eyes gaping at me. "I understand Gia has already helped you recently. You've cleaned her out, so she has no more to give. I'm doing my part to help this *one* time. You hear that?" I finally lock eyes with her. "Once, Mom. That's it. After this, you will be on your own. Gia and I have agreed."

Mom flings her arms around me, crushing me in a hug that I want no part of. I stiffen, but she doesn't catch on to my irritation. All she can focus on is how she's miraculously escaped yet another shit situation.

"Oh, sweetheart, thank you so much. I swear, it won't happen again." She pulls back and looks at me with earnest hazel eyes that I don't trust for a second.

"Don't thank me. I'm not doing it for you. I'm doing it for Dad. You know damn well what they'd do to him if we don't get this paid."

She finally shows a hint of the remorse that should be eating her from the inside out. "Are you going to tell him?"

I lift my now full coffee mug up and breathe in the caffeine-laden steam. "Probably, but not until this has all settled down. In the meantime, I suggest you find a new damn hobby besides gambling and shopping."

"I will—I am," she stutters. "I swear."

I'll believe it when I see it.

"In order to make this happen, I'm moving back home for a while. I already talked to Zeno, and he said I can take Anna's place."

"Oh! Well, doesn't that work perfectly!" She grins, tossing her orange peel scraps in the trash. "Gia will be especially happy to have you here. And your dad. You stay as long as you need, honey."

Who cares about the life I'm putting on hold, so long as you get your debt paid? So much for mothers putting their children first.

"Hopefully, it won't be too long. A few months, maybe more."

"Are you starting today?"

"I suppose I will, but I have to make a few calls first. You and Gia can go on without me, and I'll catch up." I make myself comfortable at the kitchen table and pull out my phone.

"No problem, I'll leave you to it, then. See you at the house!" She wiggles her fingers at me, and I flash a thin smile to get her to leave.

I spend the next thirty minutes making arrangements to put my life in the city on hold. I'll need to retrieve some of my belongings from storage at some point, but I have a little time. The girl I'd planned to live with is clearly upset when I inform her that I'm backing out, and rightly so. I hadn't signed a lease yet, so I could legally back out, but it was a shit thing to do when she counted on me. I feel horrible, but my family comes first.

"What's this I hear about you not going back to the city?" Dad is leaning against the doorframe behind me, studying me curiously.

"Morning, Daddy. I figured you'd gone to the house with the others." I get up and give him a hug, loving how my head rests at the perfect place over his heart.

"I was down by the water when they left, then I over-heard the tail end of your call there. What's going on, Lulu?"

"I ran into a bit of a snag with my job and decided it would be best to stay here for a bit and save up before jumping into my last year of school." I try to weave in as much honesty as I can so that the lie feels real. I *will* tell him the truth, and soon. Just not quite yet.

He pulls back, and while there's happiness in his sloping brown eyes, there's also a touch of hesitation. "You sure everything's okay?"

"Absolutely! And don't you worry, I one-hundred-percent will finish school."

"No worryin' here—not about you. If you tell me you're okay, I believe you. And I certainly won't complain about having you around." He lightly pinches my chin and grins proudly. The sight fills me with conviction that I'm doing the right thing. My dad is unquestionably worth whatever sacrifice I have to make.

"I told Mom earlier that Zeno is letting me take Anna's position. I thought I'd spend the day getting acquainted with what I'll be doing. If you can wait a minute for me to throw on some clothes, I'll head over to the house with you."

He waves a hand and strolls to the coffee maker. "I'm in no hurry. Take your time."

My first day goes as smoothly as I possibly could have hoped. Cecelia is thrilled to have a dedicated hand back in the kitchen rather than relying on my mother when she happens to be around. We discuss my duties, gossip about the gardener having an affair with a maid from another house, and I help her plan the meals for the following week. Gia stops in several times to visit along with Laney, Mom, and even Nevio, who pokes his head in after hearing of my change of plans.

The one person I don't see is Zeno.

Overall, I'm relieved because my day was emotionally draining enough as it was. However, a niggling seed of guilt has sprouted in my mind over the way I'd spoken to him the day before. I need to apologize and plan to do so when we're at the Bishops' for dinner. Cecelia told me earlier in the day that the De Rossis would all be attending, but she and Laney already had prior engagements. Zeno would be present and hopefully receptive to an apology. He's my boss, and no matter how much he frustrates me, it's the right thing to do.

We are able to get home in time from work to clean up before going to the neighboring estate. Grace has assured us that dinner won't be formal, but I can't imagine dining as a guest at one of these magnificent homes and not stepping up for the occasion. She may be used to the house and its family, but I've never been to the Bishop home.

I straighten out the frizz that has blossomed around the crown of my head and give my hair a controlled wave with a flat iron. I've always been grateful that I didn't get Mom's kinky red curls. Livia is the only one who got the full brunt of Mom's genetic blessings. Marca's hair is similar to mine in texture, but the color is a deep auburn. Sometimes, Liv tries to tame the curl with a flat iron, but it takes ages, and if there's any humidity at all, the resulting frizz is hardly worth her effort.

I hadn't put on any makeup in the morning since Dad was waiting on me, so I remedy that with some eye shadow and mascara. I rarely mess with foundation. I'm fortunate enough to have good skin and am fine with a few imperfections showing.

After asking Gia what she's going to wear, I choose a sundress appropriate for dinner. It's a soft cotton fabric, green with small yellow flowers, and wraps in the front in a way that teases at my cleavage and the side of my leg when I walk or sit. It's feminine and classy, yet sexy at the same time. I add hoop earrings and a delicate gold chain with my favorite pendant—a golden rose in full bloom.

We drive to the house even though it's not far. None of us care to walk home in the dark. There is a third row of seats, but no one wants to climb over the back seat, so Marca sits on

Gia's lap for the short ride. The sun is still out when we arrive, though settling low enough on the horizon to soften the evening light. Carter Bishop's home is much newer than the Hardwick mansion, so it doesn't have the same majestic feel, but it is impressive in its own way. A huge fountain in front of the house welcomes visitors as they enter the circle drive. The landscaping is perfectly manicured, thanks to Mr. Larson, and the home itself is stunning—three stories of cream-colored stucco with cornerstones cut at alternating lengths lining each corner. It's a beautiful example of architectural design, and while it's larger than anything I could ever imagine owning, it's quaint compared to Hardwick's sprawling thirty-five thousand square feet.

"Hello, everyone!" Carter greets us at the front door. "I'm so pleased you could join us. It's been such a trying week."

Dad extends his hand to shake Carter's. "We appreciate the invitation."

Carter smiles broadly before his eyes are drawn over our shoulders to the driveway. "Ah, it looks like the rest of our party has arrived as well."

We all turn as Zeno drives up in a black Range Rover with Elena in the passenger seat. The two exit and join us at the front door, everyone greeting one another.

"Will Nevio be joining us?" Carter asks Zeno as we make our way inside.

I wave to Grace, who approaches from the living area, but my attention is focused on hearing Zeno's answer.

"No, I apologize for the late notice. He had something come up." He doesn't sound particularly upset about Nevio's failure to attend, making me wonder if he played a role in his brother's change of plans.

I hate to think Nevio can't enjoy an evening with his family and friends because his brother is so impossible to be around. When I saw him earlier in the day, he'd sounded like he fully intended to be present at dinner. In fact, he had sounded excited enough about seeing me that I'm surprised he didn't text to tell me he wouldn't be here.

Grace and her father join us at the door while her younger sister and mother are back in the kitchen. Cora is also present, but she keeps herself apart, only offering cordial smiles from a distance.

"Not a problem at all. This wasn't meant to be anything formal, simply a friendly gathering after a trying week." He leads us into the elegantly arranged dining room, despite his assurances of a casual affair. "I believe Mrs. Larson has dinner ready, so have a seat."

Carter sits at the head of the table with Cora at the opposite end with the two children.

"Livia, Marca, you can sit with Boston and Emily," Mom says.

Liv gapes at her. "I'm twenty-three, Mom. Did you really just put me with the kids?"

Marca stills while holding the back of one of the chairs as though she were going to sit until her sister balked at the suggestion.

"I don't mind sitting down there," Gia offers.

"Oh, but I'd love to have your company on this end," Carter says hopefully.

Irritated that Livia is acting like the child she claims she isn't, I hiss at her under my breath. "*Sit*, Livia."

She rolls her eyes at the indignity but does as she's told. Mom, Dad, and the Larsons fill the middle of the long table. I find myself sandwiched between Grace and Gia, who has been encouraged to sit on the end next to Carter, across from Elena.

The arrangement suits me perfectly, except that Zeno is

seated directly across from me, making it almost impossible not to accidentally meet his gaze. He's left his suit jacket at home and rolled up the sleeves of his light gray dress shirt to expose his tanned forearms. His right wrist is adorned with a platinum watch, accenting his deep olive skin tone. Over the course of dinner, I practically memorize the contours of his strong hands in an attempt to avoid meeting his eyes. Every time my eyes raise from my plate, they snag on his hands or the buttons of his shirt instead of risking an inadvertently awkward collision of our gazes. The only times I openly peer at him is when Carter speaks, and I'm assured Z's eyes will not stray to mine. I study him during those brief moments, especially the way he watches Carter interact with Gia. His eyes shift back and forth between them, and I wonder what he's thinking, especially when his gaze wanders over to his mother before he appears to grimace and shift in his seat.

Curious if I missed something that would have caused such a response, I attempt to jump back into the conversation. I wasn't paying a lick of attention, so now I struggle to catch up.

Gia is laughing after Elena commented on something she said.

Carter wears an enchanted smile. "I'd say that's a perfectly reasonable response. Just the other day, I held an entire conversation with someone talking on a Bluetooth earpiece. I thought she was talking to me. It took a full three minutes before I realized."

"Well, I couldn't believe I'd done that." Gia blushes softly. "But now I know."

"That's one of the best things about our Gia," Mom cuts in. "She can brush things off when they don't go as planned. She'll make a wonderful mother someday. Don't you agree, Mr. Bishop?" The meaningful glint in her eyes leaves no one to guess at her insinuation that it's *his* children Mom has in mind.

I'm hideously embarrassed, but poor Gia looks like she wishes the floor would swallow her whole.

"*Mother!*" I hiss around Grace, who flattens herself wide-eyed against the back of her chair to stay clear of my rebuke.

"It's the truth." Mom shrugs with a smirk. "There's nothing wrong with being honest." She looks back at Carter and grins. "This has been such a lovely evening. We'll have to do this again but at Hardwick next time." She turns an expectant gaze to the De Rossis, and I can't bear to witness their expressions at her presumptive offer.

"Yes!" Livia cheers from the other end of the table. "And maybe we could invite a few others. Zeno did say the other day that it would be good to entertain some more." She grins, totally oblivious of the imposing nature of her request.

It's as if Livia and Mom have launched an all-out smear campaign to embarrass us until our family is left without a shred of dignity.

Elena smiles graciously as ever. "I think that can be arranged."

I look over to offer her an apologetic smile. Fortunately, she's known Mom forever and can't be too shocked at the behavior. Elena is an exceedingly patient woman, which is the only explanation I can find for her enduring tolerance of my mother.

"Wonderful!" Mom cheers while Liv silently claps her hands together. I take a giant swig of my wine and pray that the worst is over.

The remainder of dinner goes relatively smoothly. The food is delicious, and I'm able to tell Grace about my plans to stay, keeping to the massaged truth I told my dad. Even if I was going to tell her about Mom, which I'm not sure I will, I certainly can't do it at dinner in front of everyone. Much like Gia, Grace expresses how sorry she is that my school is delayed but can't hide her pleasure at having a friend nearby.

After dinner, Carter turns on the speaker system to play some light pop music while everyone takes their wineglasses onto the back veranda. Gia helps the kids set up a backyard game where participants throw two balls connected by a thin rope at a ladder and try to get the rope to wrap around one of the rungs. Carter plays with them, and everyone laughs heartily at their attempts.

About thirty minutes in, I notice Zeno slip back inside, and I decide to take the opportunity to apologize. Two over-sized glasses of wine and plenty of laughing have relaxed me enough to take the leap. He's in the bathroom when I step inside, so I refill my glass and wander to the adjacent sitting room to admire the artwork while I wait.

"Did you need something?" Z asks when he reappears.

"Not exactly. I, uh … I wanted to tell you I'm sorry for how I acted by the lake yesterday. You caught me at a rough moment. I really do appreciate you letting me work, especially when I was so short with you."

He stares at me for agonizing seconds that stretch an eternity, wreaking havoc on my nerves.

Not a word. Not a hint of emotion.

"This is where you tell me it's fine. No need to worry," I tease with an uneasy smile, giving into the pressure to fill the silence.

"And what if it's not fine?" he finally asks, his voice coarse as volcanic stone. Affected and raw. "What if none of it's fine—your anger at me or your prolonged stay at Hardwick?"

I'm so stunned by his words that I nearly spill my glass of wine as I lower it to the table next to me. "I'd ask for an explanation." I can't fathom why my presence would be so damn upsetting to him.

"And if I refuse?" He steps closer so that I have to crane my neck to keep my eyes on his.

I don't understand this game he's playing, but I won't let him win either. "Then I'd say *you're* the one with a problem."

Before I know what's happened, he's spun me around to face the wall behind me. He keeps his strong fingers firm around my waist, holding me in place when his mouth lowers to my ear. "What if I make it your problem as well? I see the way you look at me, Luisa. I'm not the only one who's torn."

I place my hands on the wall to ground myself. His grip assures he won't let me fall, but the world suddenly tilts on its axis. "I wouldn't be torn if you wouldn't be such an ass." My words are breathy, more so than I'd like, but his nearness has made my entire system unsteady.

I have no idea where any of this is coming from.

Why, after so many years of stilted encounters, is he changing the rules?

"I wouldn't have to be an ass if you weren't so *fucking* beautiful." He spits the words with savage hostility. An admission ripped from deep within him against his will. "This … *this* is what you do to me." His right hand snakes farther around toward my belly, his palm pressing flat against me and tugging me flush against his rigid frame.

The length of his impossibly hard cock molds itself into the soft flesh of my backside. Words escape me. My lungs no longer expand and contract in a proper rhythm. Every ounce of blood in my body rushes to my core for a mindless moment. A handful of seconds when need consumes me, but my thoughts begin to return after the initial rush.

Zeno wants me, but he's conflicted. Why? Why does his desire make him so angry?

Because you are nothing but the help. Always have been, always will be.

I flinch at the sting of my own thoughts because I know they're right. Despite his attraction, Zeno wouldn't want me because he thinks I'm unworthy. Between my family's behavior, economic situation, and Mafia rank, I am nothing but a pretty face and potential disgrace.

In a matter of seconds, I run an emotional gambit that leaves me spinning. Anxiety, shock, desire, elation, confusion, then blinding fury. I would be hurt if there were any room left for the emotion, but my skin is now tight with righteous anger.

I press off the wall in one swift motion, forcing him to release me and stumble back a step. When I whip around to face him, my eyes impale him with shards of jagged ice.

"Thank you for making your *uncomfortable* situation so clear. I had no idea my presence was such a problem for you."

He scowls with irritation. "You're putting words in my mouth, yet again."

"Only because you haven't done any explaining of your own. But then again, I don't know why I expect civility from you when you can't even be kind to your own brother. Did you keep him from coming tonight just so you wouldn't have to be near him?"

A mask of indifference settles over Zeno's face. The swift and complete change at the mention of his brother causes goose bumps to dance along my arms.

"I didn't say a word to him," he clips. "But I would have if he hadn't backed out of his own accord."

"You know, in a twisted way, I get why you push me away. I think it's shitty, but there's logic to it. Nevio is your *brother*, though. He's kind and decent, and there's no excuse for hurting him like you have."

"I lost all respect for my brother long ago, and he has failed time and again to earn it back. Any rift between us lies squarely on *his* shoulders, not mine."

I scoff on a dry, humorless laugh. "I'd say your refusal to even entertain a relationship reveals that you're equally as flawed. He's your *brother*."

"Exactly," he barks. "He's *my* brother, and our relationship is none of your damn business."

"You make it my business when you try to keep Nevio and me from being friends. If you had your way, he wouldn't get within six feet of me."

"You're *goddamn* right he wouldn't." He slams his hand on the table beside us, rattling my wineglass.

The sound of his palm slapping against the wood resounds in my head long after the room has stilled. We stand in that vacuum of time, our eyes locked in an unspoken battle until my heart begins to ache.

"I don't understand what's happened to you … to the boy I used to know." My confession slips quietly from my lips on a wisp of uncertain air.

It's a final plea that goes unanswered.

"Life happened." The arctic touch of his voice stings my skin.

Zeno leaves the room without another word.

Tears sting at the back of my eyes for the second time in two days. This time, I'm able to use my anger to successfully ward off the threat, but I can still sense the emotion fighting for release.

I say little more than a word the rest of the evening. Zeno is equally withdrawn, though his quiet nature makes the change harder to discern. I don't want to discuss the incident, and fortunately, Gia is so wrapped up in Carter that she fails to notice my silence. Dad, however, has a keen eye, especially where I am concerned. He pulls me aside not long before we call it a night.

"You all right, Lulu? I noticed you and Z were both inside for a while. Neither of you seemed very upbeat when you returned."

I try to smile reassuringly, but judging by his expression, I fail miserably. "Yeah, it's fine. We had a bit of an argument, but it was nothing. All we do is butt heads anymore."

"Zeno is complicated. Unlike Carter, Zeno has a role to play in a demanding organization. He can't be relaxed and friendly, but that doesn't mean he isn't a good man underneath."

"I'm not so sure, Daddy. He's definitely not the same person I used to know."

Dad wraps his arm around my shoulder and pulls me in for a side hug. "Well, at least this is only a pit stop in your journey. You won't have to be around him for long."

Even less if he avoids me as I suspect he will now.

That should be a good thing, so why do I feel like I have an ice pick buried deep in my chest?

Zeno, Age 19
Luisa, Age 17

If Elena hadn't offered up her house as an escape, I might have strangled one of my sisters by now. Not Gia, of course, but a thirteen-year-old Livia is more than I can take. It's only early July, but I'm certain I wouldn't have survived the summer if it wasn't for Elena and Hardwick. Thanks to her generous offer, I find myself tucked away in the TV room most weekends with my nose buried in a book. The comfy sectional sofa is hardly ever used now that Zeno and Nevio are both gone.

It felt strange at first to be here alone. Nevio has been away at school for almost a year. I thought he'd come home for the summer, but he didn't. Poor Elena practically begged me to come over and keep the house from feeling so empty. It works for me. I'm away from my family, out of the heat, and free to read uninterrupted—

Saturday afternoons don't get any better than this. If I'm not working at the local library, which is the summer job I was lucky enough to score, then I'm usually here. The Hardwick library would be a fabulous place to read, but that's Elena's space. Faced with choosing another hideaway, I naturally gravitated to the media room. I suppose it felt the most comfortable after so many years spent playing in here with the boys. The smell alone fills me with warm familiarity.

After an hour or so of reading, I slip away to the bathroom. The house is silent, but that's nothing new. Even when the boys and I were little, the stately mansion was a vacuum of sound. Elena and Silvano are here, somewhere, along with Cecelia and one of the housekeepers, but the place is so large that sound doesn't travel, and it's easy to feel alone.

I find the solitude cathartic.

In the month since I started coming here to read, I've learned to embrace the seclusion, which is why I squeak in surprise when I return to the media room and find a half-naked man holding my book.

Not a man.

Zeno.

I've hardly seen him in a year, and he's done a lot of growing in that time.

My mouth fills with cotton at the sight of him. Broad, sculpted shoulders glisten with droplets of sweat that run down muscular arms. Arms now adorned with artfully drawn black ink. I desperately wish I could move closer and study the details of his tattoos. Explore the thin trail of hair leading down beneath the low-slung waistband of his athletic shorts. Lose myself in the aquamarine eyes now staring me down.

Zeno is absolutely breathtaking, and I might be mesmerized enough to tell him if I thought my confession wouldn't make him angry.

"Were you reading here?" he finally asks while I still openly gawk at him.

"Yes ... um, your mom said I could. I didn't know you were here." As the shock of seeing him settles, a sense of unease creeps beneath my skin. Zeno made it perfectly clear in the past that he didn't want me in his house. I try to squash the self-doubt. I am an invited guest, whether he likes it or not.

"I got in this morning. Just went out for a run."

"I see that." I swallow at my own semi-admission that I've been ogling him.

Z's hypnotic gaze holds me captive until he peers down at the book in his hand. That's when I remember what it was I'd been reading. Of all the books he possibly could have caught me with, and I cruise through nearly one a day, it had to be the one time I was scratching an itch for a historical romance. The book is the epitome of bodice-ripping, virgin-snatching, rake-filled smut, complete with a shirtless man on the cover. The novel is every stereotype and cliché in one printed paperback, and I was loving every word.

That is, until the book found its way into Zeno's hand.

Now, I'm utterly mortified. I rush over and try to take it from him, but he stubbornly refuses to hand it over.

"Just give me the book, Z, and I'll get out of here."

His head tilts to the side a fraction. "Is there a reason you need to leave?"

My lips part, then snap shut before repeating the process. "Are you serious?" I've felt unwelcome in his presence for nearly two years, and he wonders why I'd run the second he shows up? Is he screwing with me? I have no idea what to think.

Zeno's full lips thin and brows knot while his eyes sweep the room. "Why are you reading here?"

I stand a little taller, raising my chin. "It's a hell of a lot more quiet than my house. When I mentioned to Elena ... to your mom ... that I never had any peace and quiet at home, she suggested I come here." I pause before adding, "I think she likes the company, even if we aren't hanging out together."

His eyes drop from me to the book still clasped in his hand before he gently tosses it onto the sofa. "I suppose there's no harm in you reading." He steps around me, but before he's out of reach, he pauses and turns back. I get the sense he's about to say something when his father's voice booms up from the stairwell.

"Z, I've made arrangements for dinner at seven. It's your birthday, son. Are you sure there isn't anyone you'd like to invite?"

His birthday, of course. How could I have forgotten? That's why he's come home.

Zeno stares at me as though his father had never spoken, though a barrage of questions quickly pass behind his ocean eyes. Their meaning is completely lost on me.

Instead of pushing for answers, I offer him an uneasy smile. "Happy Birthday, Z." The words drift between us, a white flag raised in the air, only to hang limp when Zeno's thunderous look sucks all the oxygen from the room.

His brow looms heavier, and the cut of his jaw sharpens like a knife's edge. "Seven is good," he calls out to his father. "And no extras."

He doesn't tell me I need to leave, but he doesn't have to. I feel his sudden animosity in every fiber of my being. His dismissal cuts open the old wound, especially when seconds before, I'd started to wonder if we might have a normal conversation. If maybe, just maybe, we might work toward being friends again.

But I'd been delusional.

Zeno De Rossi wants nothing to do with me, and I'm only too happy to comply.

CHAPTER 16

Rain falls in sheets on Saturday. It's the perfect excuse to hide at home and do nothing. However, my day is less than ideal, considering six of us live in this small cottage. Solitude is hard to come by.

I try not to dwell on my exchange with Zeno at the Bishops' house, but the scene plays over in my head the second my mind wanders. Even reading doesn't hold my attention. Watching television would require me to join whoever is in the living room, and I'm not in the mood to be around anyone.

A brief reprieve in the afternoon weather allows Gia the chance to run some errands. She drags me with her, and I'm surly about it, but I appreciate the chance to get away from the house. The outing lifts my spirits enough that I agree to play a game when we get home. The four of us girls get out our old Sorry board game and sit around the kitchen table.

For a precious hour, we are girls again. Gia doesn't mother anyone, and Livia has no reason to act out. Marca giggles at all of us while I fall into my natural place as the ringleader. We are a team, enjoying our time together, despite the battle of our game pieces. With every laugh between us, the bond of sisterhood reforms and solidifies. Livy and I may never be close, but I appreciate these times when we can connect. She needs that. I need that.

"Who's going to Mass with us tomorrow?" Mom asks from the doorway behind me after Gia steals the win, and we pack up the game.

"I'm about to go to Claudia's house for the night, so I won't be here," Livia responds.

"Do you need a ride?"

"Nah, she's coming to get me." She checks her phone and stands. "Damn, it's later than I thought. I better go up and get ready."

Mom's eyes fall on me. I find it ironic that she goes to church since I'm not sure she lives by any of the principles, but it's one of the few rituals she has clung to over the years.

"Luisa, what about you? Gia and Marca will be going. You want to come with us?"

If they're all going to church and Liv is out, that means the house will be empty. I would have the place to myself—it's too good an opportunity to pass up.

"Sorry, I'm going to pass. Maybe next week."

She shrugs. "Suit yourself."

I will, thank you.

I wake when Gia does the next morning, but I don't budge until she and the others bound out of the house. They go to the late service, so it's a good time to get up—I never could sleep in very long.

The rain has subsided since yesterday, but the sky is

overcast, and the air is still and peaceful. It's the perfect morning to recalibrate myself after the week from hell. I take out a journal I brought with me and open it to a fresh page. I title the page *New Goals*. Number one is, "Save all the money I can." Next to the number two, I write, "Enroll in school for the spring semester." I'm not certain this is attainable, but these are goals, not blood oaths. The third is, "Commit to a first novel plotline by the end of summer." I've considered so many ideas over the years that it's hard to know where I should start. It's time to get over that fear and go for it.

Three things. That's it. And all three should be feasible.

It reassures me to see my plans in black and white.

Feeling empowered, I jump in the shower. I don't want to waste precious alone time in the bathroom, so I make it quick. Once I'm dry and dressed, I feel like a new woman. Downstairs, I brew a cup of coffee and admire the scene from the kitchen window. The leaves and grass are all still damp, making them look even greener than normal. Moisture is heavy in the air, at least, until the rich scent of coffee permeates the house. Then all I can smell is encouragement and optimism. For a moment, I'm confident things are going to be okay. Like really, truly believe that things will work out for the best.

Then there's a knock on the door.

My heart lurches in my chest, but I admonish myself for being paranoid. The chances are slim that Aldo has found his way back to our house. He told me he'd give me until later this week for the money. And besides, it's Sunday morning. Surely, even bookies take off Sundays.

To be safe, I sneak to the window beside the door and peek past the edge of the curtain. The chances weren't slim enough, apparently, because Aldo, dressed in a leather jacket and a ridiculous chain draped from his pants' pocket, is standing on our front porch.

Blood races through my veins until my pulse pounds in my ears.

"Little Miss Banetti, open up. I see you in there." His sing-song voice mocks me, helping me regain clarity through my anger.

I debate not opening the door, but I don't want him to think I am reneging on our deal and go after my dad. With a slight tremble to my fingers, I undo the deadbolt and open the door a few inches.

"What are you doing here, Aldo?"

His arms splay wide, and one corner of his lips smirk while the other holds a toothpick in place. "Jesus, that's some fucking hospitality you got here. I just came to talk to you about easing your burden." His foot scoots backward as if to steady himself.

I take a more scrutinizing look at his face and note his bloodshot eyes. Is he drunk? He may be slightly unsteady, but he's not totally trashed. Maybe he's still riding a binge from last night. Whatever is going on, I want no part of it.

"You shouldn't be here. My dad could have seen you."

"I saw the rest of you Banettis get out at St. Luke's, so relax. That's why I'm here. I wanted to talk to you because I know you're in a rough place." He steps closer until his face is only a foot or so from the door.

I don't want to retreat from my position against the door because it gives me leverage to slam it shut if needed, but I hate his face being so close for many reasons, the least of which is the stench of liquor wafting from him. I pull my face away as much as I can without conceding my position.

"I told you I'd get you the money. I'm going to the bank tomorrow."

"Yeah, but what if I made a deal with you to ease the terms? I can be a real generous guy, you know." His voice drops to what I suspect he intends to be soothing, but it's only that much more grotesque.

I can't stop my lip from lifting in a snarl. "No, *thanks*," I grit, then go to slam the door, but nothing happens.

My eyes widen, and a vile grin creeps across his face. We both peer down to where his foot has wedged its way between the door and its frame.

In one swift move, he lunges forward on the leg, flinging the door open. I stumble back against the hall closet door with a gasp.

"There's no reason we can't talk. I never got to tell you about my discount program. And since your delay is keeping me from getting back home, it's only fair that you give me a little of your … time."

"I don't need a discount. I have the money … I'll have it to you tomorrow, every cent." I don't want to sound scared, but I'm terrified. I'm no match for his strength, even in his inebriated state.

Aldo places his hands on the door beside my head, caging me in. "How do you know what you want when you haven't heard the terms? Maybe you'd like it a whole lot."

His noxious breath makes me sick to my stomach. The walls close in around me, and adrenaline floods my veins with the need to fight for my life. I know down to my bones that if I don't do something, this man will take what he wants. He'll take a part of me that I won't ever be able to get back. I'm no virgin, but what he wants would tear my soul to shreds. I can't let that happen, not without a fight.

I don't plan my actions. They simply happen.

My knee flies upward with every ounce of my strength, smashing up into his crotch. He instantly folds over, giving me the leverage I need to shove him out the front door and slam it behind him, deadbolt clicking into place.

"*You fucking* cunt!" His enraged scream chases me back to my parents' bedroom, where my father keeps his guns. I grab a nine millimeter and take off the safety as I rush back to the front of the house.

Aldo raises himself enough to pound a fist against the door before catching sight of me in the side window, gun raised.

"I'll have the money tomorrow, asshole," I call through the window. "You can come back at three in the afternoon, no earlier. You'll take your money and get the fuck out of here."

"You think you can fucking *threaten* me?" He pounds a fist against the door. "Your debt just went up twenty fucking percent, you *bitch*. Have every dime in cash, or I take your dad with me when I leave." He hawks up a loogie and spits it at the glass.

I blink, but I don't flinch, so I take that as a win.

Aldo walks away, his body still curved in on itself despite his efforts to disguise his pain. Again, there's no car in the driveway. He disappears behind the thick brush by the street, but I can still feel him all over me.

I shudder and hurry to the kitchen, where I set the gun on the counter and scrub my hands, splashing water on my face as well. My body begins to shake uncontrollably. I lean my hands on the counter and bend at the waist, hanging my head to catch my breath. When the world slows its spin, I put the safety back on the gun and pour myself two fingers of my father's scotch to settle my system. I down it in one breath, the burn giving me focus.

Holy shit, I can't believe that just happened.

I sit at the kitchen table and thank God I used to love target practice with my dad and am comfortable with guns.

I'm not sure I could have pulled that off without the confidence that I could shoot if I needed to. I roll the black gun around in my hands, appreciating its heavy weight. The security.

Heading back to my parents' room, I open the drawer where Dad's guns are kept and swap the nine millimeter for a small thirty-eight. He rarely carries a gun on a daily basis anymore—there's no need at Hardwick—so I don't think he'll notice it's missing. Even if he does, I'll make up an excuse. Until things are settled with Aldo, and maybe for a while after, I'll feel safer with protection.

I breathe deep, in through my nose and out through my mouth.

It's over. Everything is going to be okay.

I would tell my mom what happened, but I'm not sure it would make a difference. I'm not sure anything will push her to change until she has to face her consequences. And she will … next time. Once Dad is safe from the effects of her fuckups.

———

THAT EVENING, Dad and I sit on the porch together. I've spent days thinking about my parents, and after witnessing first-hand the nightmarish culmination of my mother's carelessness, I have questions that have to be asked. My dad may not know about Aldo, but he sure as hell knows who my mother is at this point. He sees the way she behaves, and I can tell he doesn't approve. I'm not even sure he likes her all that much. So, why? Why continue to put up with her?

"Daddy, can I talk to you a little more about Mom?"

His smile bears a sadness even his dimples can't erase. "Of course, sweetheart. You can always talk to me about anything."

"I can't help but ask myself why you stick around. Don't you think, if you guys aren't happy together, that you'd be better off separating?" I'd love for my parents to be a happy couple, but that's simply not the case. It serves no purpose to pretend otherwise.

"It's complicated, Lulu. And I don't hate your mother. If I was miserable, that'd be different. This is simply how things played out for us." His complacency baffles me, but that's my father. Dad is so much more laid-back than I am. I could never have tolerated Mom's hot mess express.

"You know she spends way too much money." I decide to extend feelers and test the waters.

"I do, but she's a grown woman."

"Yeah, but her spending impacts you too. What will you do when you can't work anymore if she's blown all your savings?"

Dad smirks. "Fortunately, the family doesn't exactly force us into retirement." He's laughing off my concerns, and while I'm glad he's not overly burdened, I wish he'd take the matter more seriously.

"It's not just money—she has responsibilities. Livia and Marca need a good role model."

"Your mom did fine with you and Gia. I can't imagine two more perfect girls."

I nudge his chest with my shoulder. "Daddy, stop. You know Livia especially is a whole other monster. She's following in Mom's footsteps, and I hate to see that."

"As you get older, Lulu, you come to accept that you can only do so much for people. Even your children. We've done the best we can, and at some point, a parent has to let their kids lead their own lives. Livia will find a man who thinks she walks on water. He'll provide for her, and even though they may not have a relationship you would find fulfilling, it'll work for Livy. She'll be fine, you'll see."

I hear the truth in his words, but I'm not totally sold. At only eighteen, Marca is still malleable. Mom's and Livia's influences are still shaping my youngest sister, and I hate to imagine where that will leave her. I don't want Livia to think she has to rely on a man. I don't want Mom to put my parents in the poorhouse. But like my dad says, if I can't change any of it, getting upset over it is pointless.

Ughhh.

I sigh deeply and lean back against his warm chest. Once I get the debt paid, I'll find a way to tell Dad about it, and maybe then he'll change his tune.

Please, God, let him see reason.

CHAPTER 17

First thing Monday morning, I arrange to take a late lunch and borrow the car. I tell Mom my plans and enlist her help making sure Dad doesn't wander back home while I'm at the house. When it comes time to leave, I grab a canvas tote bag to take to the bank and make sure the gun is in my purse. I won't take it into the bank with me, but with Aldo keeping tabs on us, I want to at least have it in the car.

Walking into the bank with a tote for money and a gun in the car is the strangest feeling I've ever experienced. I have to actively remind myself I'm not robbing anyone. I explain to the teller that I'm buying a car, feeding her the story because I am self-conscious about cashing out so much money. I have no clue how often this kind of thing goes on at banks. Would a twelve-thousand-dollar cash withdrawal raise any flags, or is that an ordinary Monday for them? It feels like a ton of money to me, but I'm guessing it's not as much as I think.

My hunch is confirmed when the teller hands over a stack of bills about an inch tall, and that's being generous. She counts out the hundreds, and I realize my tote bag was a gross miscalculation. Clearly, I watch too much television because I was envisioning stacks of cash in a duffel bag like in one of the *Ocean's* movies or something.

It's actually kind of sad when I think about it. A year of savings—enough money to get me through my last year of school—and it fits in a damn greeting card envelope.

I take the cash and toss it in my purse, clutching the leather bag against my chest when I step outside. With my luck, some giant bird of prey might swoop down and mistake my Coach knockoff for lunch, and I'll be screwed. I'm not taking any chances.

Once I'm back in the car, a tiny trickle of relief eases the vise clenched around my chest. I drive extra slowly the whole way home. I should get there with another twenty minutes before Aldo is supposed to arrive. As I drive, I decide to sit out front and wait for him. I'm done with surprises.

The ironic part is, I keep expecting to have some semblance of control when fate is hell-bent on stealing the reins. I might as well sit back and enjoy the ride like Dad suggested because I clearly am nothing but a passenger in this shit show my life has become.

When I pull up at the house, Aldo is already there, and he's with Grace. Sweet, unsuspecting Grace, who smiles at the wolf in sheep's clothing as though his claws are not hanging out for everyone to see.

Frantic to get him away from her, I toss the gun back in my purse and rush from the car.

"Hey, Grace. What are you doing over here?" My greeting is less than cordial, and her face registers the surprise.

"Um, your mom borrowed my mom's sewing scissors a

while back. Mom is trying to mend one of the drapes that got sucked up in the vacuum and sent me over to get her scissors back."

"Yeah, no problem. Let me look for them, and I'll bring them over in a few minutes, okay?" My eyes cut over to Aldo, who is openly enjoying my discomfort.

Grace smiles politely at him. "It was good meeting you, Aldo."

"It's been a pleasure." His gaze follows her as she leaves, making my fists clench with the need to claw those black eyes right out of his skull.

I pull the money from my bag, leaving my right hand in my purse, gripping the gun. "Here's your money," I hiss, tossing the thick envelope at his feet. I'm not letting my manners put me within ten feet of him. Not again.

Aldo's eyes cut down to the money before flicking back up at me. He stares, the hint of a snarl rippling his lips. He's trying to intimidate me, and it's working, but I try not to show it. Eventually, he bends and retrieves the money.

"It better all be here."

"It is. The ten plus twenty percent, like you said. Now, take it and leave."

His beady eyes narrow. "You got a real fuckin' attitude problem. You know that?"

I purse my lips as I remove my hand from my purse, clicking off the gun's safety without taking my eyes from Aldo.

A slow Cheshire grin spreads across his face as he slides a toothpick back in the corner of his mouth. He raises the money to use in a salute at his temple. "So long, Banetti. It's been a pleasure doing business with you."

I keep his retreating form in my sights so long as I am able. Only after he disappears onto the main road do I hurry onto the porch and nearly break off my key trying to get inside, suddenly wishing I hadn't locked the door when I left.

It's over. You can breathe now.

I rush inside when the lock gives, then re-lock the deadbolt and fall back against the wood door. I take in several lungfuls of air with my eyes pressed shut to calm myself. Once my heart has slowed from its sprint, I get out my phone and text Mom that I'm back and tell her about the scissors. She offers a guess as to where she may have left them, which is enough for me to track them down. I put the safety back on the gun but leave it in my purse, then head out to find Grace.

I meet up with her at the rear entrance of the Bishop house. "Grace, I'm so sorry about that. I know I was rude, but that guy gives me the creeps, and I didn't want him bothering you."

"He was definitely on the slimy side, but he wasn't being rude or anything."

"Well, you're lucky then because he's a real asshole. If you happen to see him around again, please stay away from him."

Her brow furrows, and she glances around before responding. "He said something about you guys owing him a little money. Is everything okay?"

That cocksucker has a big mouth.

"Yeah," I assure her. "Just a little loan, but I got him all paid off. It's nothing to worry about. And look! I found your mom's scissors." I hold up the heavy silver sheers.

"Perfect! Thanks for bringing them by."

"Not a problem at all, but I better get back to Hardwick. Maybe we can hang out later this week—Wednesday evening or something?"

"Sure! That would be great. Shoot me a text, and we'll figure it out." Grace waves with a smile.

I return the gesture and begin my walk back to work. The

sun is sweltering, so I do my best to stay in the shade. I walk straight past our house and continue toward Hardwick. As I near the open clearing of the main grounds, I spot Nevio walking toward me.

"Where are you headed?" I ask once we're close enough to talk without yelling.

He squints in the sunlight, narrowing his already hooded eyes to nothing but slits. I have no idea how he even sees out of them. He gives me a beaming grin, his half-dimpled smile causing a flutter to stir in my chest.

"I was just out getting some air. What about you?" He directs me back beneath the shade of a large tree. "It's too damn hot to stand in the sun."

"Welcome to summer." I wink. "I had to run an errand, so I took a late lunch. We missed you at dinner on Friday."

He flashes a lighthearted grimace. "Yeah, I'd thought I could stomach going, but then I reconsidered. I know what it's like to spend an evening with Zeno and have him constantly remind me that my presence is unwanted. I couldn't do it. We'd had a bit of an argument earlier in the day, so I knew spending any time around him would be extra miserable."

Nevio would have had enormous fun playing lawn games and chatting with everyone over wine, and I feel awful that his brother took that from him. That Zeno makes him feel like an exile in his own home.

"I'm so sorry, Nev," I offer softly. "I hate that he acts that way around you." I lean back against the wide tree trunk behind me and peer up at my childhood friend. "My sisters may drive me crazy, but I'd never treat them the way he treats you."

He eases closer and places a hand on the trunk above me so that he's leaning beside me. It's a position of familiarity that could easily morph into something more intimate, and I'm not sure how I feel about it. My pulse kicks up with uncertainty, but being near him doesn't light a fire inside me the same way being near his brother does. The realization is disappointing. Why on earth does the jerk turn me on more than the nice guy?

"I don't have to worry about him for a little while," Nevio continues, unaware of my internal conflict. "Z left for the city yesterday."

My suspicions had been correct. Maybe it's presumptive to think I'm the reason he left, but I had a feeling he'd avoid me after our confrontation at the Bishops'. His retreat to the city is remarkably coincidental.

"When's he coming back?" I ask absently. When I peer up at Nevio, he's studying me.

"I can't say. He doesn't tell me his plans, that's for sure. What I do know is that I've arranged to stick around for a while." He lifts his free hand and traces the angle of my jaw with a touch as gentle as a butterfly's wing. "Have dinner with me, Luisa. You name the night, any night this week, and I'll be there."

I don't know what to say at first. I enjoy being around him, but I remember his playboy history. I don't want to be just another good time.

Am I not willing to give Nevio the opportunity to prove he's changed?

Ten years is a lot of time to mature.

"Yeah, that would be great. How about Friday?"

Nevio's smitten gaze is so unguarded and pure that I'm mesmerized. He smiles as though I've offered him the world on a platter. I can't help but smile back, and when I do, his eyes darken. Ever so slowly, he leans down, one millimeter at a time as though I'm a fawn who might startle away at any moment. My eyes drift to his slightly parted lips, and I can almost taste him on my tongue when the crash of glass shattering pierces the air around us.

We both turn to the house where one of the windows on the main floor has been broken. Laney appears in the opening, and though she's some distance from us, I can see the whites of her wide eyes. She mouths what I'm guessing is a curse, then disappears into the shadows, undoubtedly cleaning up after herself.

Nevio and I exchange a look of surprise.

"I'd better go help her." I smile awkwardly.

He nods with a hint of irritation. "I suppose so."

He raises a hand toward the house to lead the way. We don't openly acknowledge what passed between us, but I can sense a shift in our dynamic. The ease of old friendship to the uncertainty of something new. Am I truly open to being with Nevio? He's everything his brother is not—exciting and doting and easy to talk to. I'm so angry with Zeno for so many reasons that it's easy to lean into my relationship with Nevio, but is that what's best? The two brothers are so overwhelming, it's hard to see beyond their enigmatic shadows. Is there light on the other side or just more darkness?

last long. I find my mother talking to Elena Wednesday morning and learn my aunt and uncle are coming from the city to visit. Emanual Gravina is my mother's older brother, and his wife, Chiara, is my favorite aunt. She's clever and loves a good laugh. Their five kids are close in age to me and my sisters, so we all grew up visiting each other frequently. I never got the sense Uncle E was overly fond of his sister, but he maintained the relationship for the sake of his wife and kids. Aunt Chiara gets along well with Mom, and us cousins always had fun playing together when we were little. Now that we are older, however, gatherings mostly consist of the two sets of parents.

"When are they coming?" I ask Mom.

She's sitting with Elena in the library, which is Elena's favorite haunt. She's managed well since Silvano's death, but her eyes don't light up the way they used to. I'm glad Mom is here to keep her distracted, something my mother excels at. The two have a friendly working relationship. They aren't best friends or anything, but they often talk about more than household affairs and even go to lunch occasionally. Elena has never displayed any hang-up over our disparate stations in life the way Zeno has. If Silvano was, in fact, the source of that mindset, it appears his eldest son was the only member of their family to subscribe to his beliefs.

"They'll get here on Friday. I thought I'd make a lasagna. It's such a process that I haven't done one in forever. Having them over will make the effort worth it."

I begin to chew absently on my cheek as I consider the fact that I've made plans with Nevio for Friday night. Dinner with him would be fun, but there's something about the first night when company arrives. Everyone is excited and catching up with drinks and laughter. I don't want to miss that.

"What?" Mom blurts. "Is there a problem?"

"No, it's just that I'd actually made plans for Friday."

"With who? Grace? She'll understand."

I glance at Elena with a touch of embarrassment. I'm not sure why. Nevio and I are adults, but I feel awkward admitting to our date in front of his mother. "Actually, I had dinner set up with Nevio. I'm sure I can reschedule, though."

When I peek at my mother, her eyebrows have launched into space. For once in her life, though, she keeps her mouth shut, which I greatly appreciate. I have no doubt she'll grill me about it later.

"Of course, you can," Elena chimes in. "My Nevio is always understanding. You should definitely spend time with your family—you can see him around anytime now that he's staying for a bit."

I nod and smile. "You're absolutely right. Any idea where he's at this morning?"

"Oh, I don't think he's even up yet. He's always out late."

"No problem, I'll shoot him a text. You two have a good morning!" I offer a parting wave with a smile and flee from the room before there can be any more discussion about why Nevio and I would have dinner together.

I text him as I walk back to the kitchen, and once he gets back to me, we decide to move up our dinner by a night. That means we have our first date tomorrow.

My stomach dips and swerves, but I'm not sure if it's out of excitement or trepidation. It's hard to suss out my feelings for him when there's history between us. Not romantic history, but still enough of a past that it complicates everything.

I don't see him at all while I'm working. I keep busy, and he doesn't seek me out. I try not to read into any of it and am now incredibly relieved that I made plans with Grace for the evening. Hanging out with her will be the perfect distraction.

I go home at five to change out of my dirty work clothes, then walk the familiar path over to her family's cottage. When I arrive, she hauls me up to her bedroom. Since it's only her and her younger sister, they each have their own rooms. I used to be jealous as a kid. Maybe I still am a teensy bit, but I also know that Grace has her own issues. No one's life is perfect.

"What's with the rush?" I ask teasingly, making myself comfortable on her bed next to her. "You didn't even let me say hi to your mom."

"I didn't want to risk her saying something before I got a chance to tell you."

"Tell me what?"

Grace flashes me with a smile so bright it could power the

city for a week. "I'm making the move. I've got enough stashed away that I can get my own place in the city."

"That's amazing! I'm so freaking excited for you!" I give her a tight hug, and my heart fills with joy for my dear friend. Getting away from Tuxedo Park will be the best thing she could do for herself. "From the way you talked a few days ago, I thought you were looking at another six months or more." I sit back and look at her, ready to hear all the exciting details, but Grace's gaze has trouble finding mine.

"I wasn't sure myself, but I managed to scrape together a bit more than I expected."

I study her, really examine each of her movements and words. The result forms a knot of unease in the pit of my stomach. "Gracie, where did you get the extra money?"

"I'm twenty-seven, Luisa, and I still live with my parents. Your dad was able to help you when you left home. We don't all have parents who can afford to do something like that. If I didn't find a way myself, I'd never escape Tuxedo Park and make a life of my own."

Her defensiveness surprises me and solidifies my suspicion that something big has changed since we last talked about her plans. This is no adjustment in her budgeting plans. She's come up with new money somehow, and she's embarrassed to tell me the source.

An image of her talking to Aldo flashes in my mind.

No. She wouldn't … couldn't have. They were only together for a handful of minutes.

He's a bookie—did he moonlight as a loan shark too? My eyelids drift shut with defeat because it makes perfect sense. She'd never be defensive about getting a loan with a bank or taking a second job. I know where she got the money, and it terrifies me.

"Please tell me you didn't borrow money from Aldo." The

reality of her situation sucks all the joy from hearing she is moving to the city. Doing business with someone as dangerous as Aldo is no reason to celebrate.

Her chin is raised defiantly when I open my eyes. "You guys borrowed money from him, too. He can't be *that* bad."

Fuck! God-fucking-*dammit!*

I want to pound my fist into something so bad my fingers ache. "Grace! He *is* that bad! He's the reason I'm having to move back home. I had to get him paid off for my mom before he hurt my dad. I used all my savings—paying him off cleaned me out, but it was worth it because he's *that bad.*"

A hint of worry softens her posture. I don't want to scare her, but it has to happen. She needs to understand what she's gotten herself into.

"I appreciate your concern," she responds, "but I've got it all sorted out."

Until Aldo changes the terms.

"I know you want to hurry things along and move, but you'd be so much better off not relying on his money. Is there any way you can give it back?"

She visibly flinches at the suggestion. "Look, you're pretty and smart, and your family has enough money that you'll never know what it's like to be in my situation. I was hoping you could be happy for me, but maybe that was too much to ask."

I clasp one of her hands in mine, pleading in my eyes. "I know how much you want this, and aside from the Aldo part, I'm absolutely thrilled for you. I just want you to be safe, Gracie." I don't want to lose my oldest friend by pushing her away, but I can't ignore the mistake she's making. "Your life could be in danger."

"I appreciate you looking out for me." Her lips form the thin line of a forced smile, and she squeezes my hand. "But what's done is done. You can accept that and help me pick out a neighborhood to live in, or you can go. I'd prefer we didn't argue and for you to stay, but I understand if you need to leave."

Leaving her to manage the situation alone would only put her in more danger. Plus, I'd never forgive myself if something happened to her while my back was turned.

"You can't get rid of me that easily. We'll figure it out together."

A cautious smile tugs at the corners of her lips. "I'd really like that."

"Do you have any particular areas in mind?" I do my best to look excited when, in reality, my heart is weeping.

We spend the evening talking about apartments and where to look for work. I mention the possibility of her taking over the sublease I had to back out of, but the rent is more than she can afford. We talk budgets and expenses until well after dark. Painting a smile on my face for so long is exhausting. By the time I step outside to walk home, I welcome the blanket of darkness that wraps itself around me. Clouds choke out the moonlight, and the area is far enough removed from any city that light pollution doesn't cast its invasive glow. I am invisible in the night. No worries or expectations. No witnesses to my shortcomings. No need to laugh when all I want to do is cry.

My feels weighed down by the time I collapse onto my bed back home. Gia is already under the covers, but she's left the bedside lamp on for me. I slip off my shoes, then grab my pajama shirt before creeping to the bathroom. Light beams from beneath the door of the younger girls' room, telling me they are still wide-awake. It shouldn't surprise me. Without school or jobs, they can do whatever they like. It must be nice.

Once I've mechanically performed my bedtime routine, I

return to our room and crawl under the covers. Something about sinking into bed is incredibly cathartic, as though the light blue duvet is an impenetrable barrier to the outside world. Beneath these down feathers, all is safe and warm and perfect … until I hear a sniffle from beside me.

"Gia, you okay?" I whisper into the dark.

My words are met with silence for several long seconds.

"I made cookies this afternoon to have on hand for when Uncle E and Aunt Chiara come. I thought I'd take a few over to Boston and Emily, but … but they're gone." Emotions choke the sound from her words.

"What do you mean, honey?" I move in close, spooning my body around hers.

"Cora was there packing up some of her things. She said Carter and the kids had already left for the city and that…" Her breathing catches on a sob that guts me. "That Carter decided to leave because certain *situations* had made him uncomfortable lately. She made it clear that … that it's *me* … he needed to escape." My sister has never spoken with such heartbreak, and in an instant, I am ready to ravage the world on her behalf.

"Oh, Gia. That's terrible, honey. I'm so, so sorry." I hold her tightly while she struggles to maintain her composure. I wish she'd let herself come undone, but that's not her way. Not even in front of me.

"I just thought … but I must have imagined it. I mean, of course he wouldn't…"

"Gia, don't you dare doubt your feelings. That man was *clearly* into you, plain as day. You weren't misreading anything." I'd bet my life on the fact that his departure had everything to do with that bitchy sister of his. I'm not sure what her motivation might be, but she has to be behind this. "And maybe you misunderstood, and they're just leaving town for a long weekend. They aren't going to sell their house because of you." I try to assure her, but my sister rarely over-reacts. If she understood they were leaving for good, she's probably right.

"I'm so embarrassed, Isa. I don't understand how I could have been so confused."

"Because you weren't. For once, I'm telling *you* that there's been a misunderstanding, and we'll find a way to fix it. I've seen the way that man looks at you. He is totally smitten."

She doesn't deny my claim, nor does she grasp at the hope I've placed before her. Instead, Gia lies silent in my arms as we both listen to the gentle murmur of Livia's and Marca's voices passing through the thin walls. After a while, I start to think she's fallen asleep when her voice carries back to me.

"How was your night with Grace?" It's just like Gia to ask about me when her world is collapsing around her. I've never met a more selfless person than my older sister. If Carter is dumb enough to walk away from that, then he's a bigger fool than I could have imagined.

"That depends. You've already had a rough day, so I hate to burden you."

Gia adjusts herself so that we are now lying eye to eye. "What happened?"

I sigh deeply, a practice that is quickly becoming a habit lately.

"The other day, when Aldo came to get the money from me, Grace happened to come by the house. They got to talk-ing, and I guess he told her about Mom owing him money. Grace got it in her head that she could borrow money from him and be able to move to the city rather than having to wait to save more. She borrowed money from him, Gia. I can't believe she'd go and do something so reckless. I get that she wants to get out of her parents' house, but that's not the way to do it."

"I admit, it's not the safest route, but I'm not sure we can say what's best for her. We don't know what goes on under their roof. I'd like to believe the Larsons are kind people, but only Grace can decide what's best for her."

I sigh, yet again, at Gia's response because it's so completely *her*. "I cannot comprehend how borrowing money from a guy who may rape or kill her is ever the right move."

Gia props herself up on an elbow. "Rape or kill her? What on earth makes you say that?"

I realize I never told Gia about my close encounter with Aldo. I peer into her already swollen eyes and consider telling her, but I can't do it. She's already so broken up that burdening her further feels wrong.

"I just get a bad feeling from him, and it worries me."

She eases back down and pulls me into her arms. "It's hard to watch people struggle, but she'll be okay. Grace is a grown woman, and unlike Mom, she'll get this guy paid off."

I nod, but I don't believe it one bit.

"WHERE IS HE TAKING YOU?" Gia asks the next evening as she watches me put the finishing touches on my makeup.

"Stella's. Have you heard of it?"

"Of course! It's delicious, and they always have live music in the evenings. Makes it a little hard to talk over dinner, but the music is always excellent."

I shrug. "I guess we can talk anytime since we live next door to one another."

Gia's eyes fall to a loose thread she's toying with on the

duvet, and I realize my comment has made her think of her own romantic estrangement with our other neighbor.

"Did you try to reach out to Carter today?" I ask softly.

She smiles and shakes her head. "No, not yet. Like you said, he may come home in a few days, and I'll have worried over nothing." Her tone isn't totally convincing, but I'm glad she's trying to stay positive. I'm also glad our aunt and uncle will be here to distract her.

"Luisa, Nevio is here for you," Mom calls up the stairs.

My face breaks out in a goofy grin. "Wish me luck!"

Gia gives me a warm hug before I clatter in my heels down the wood stairs. Nevio is standing in the front entry, dressed in slacks and a button-down shirt with the sleeves rolled up. He is incredibly handsome, and the grin he flashes me bathes me in adoration.

"Don't you two look lovely," Mom beams. "Don't worry about needing to be up tomorrow, Luisa. You guys stay out and have as much fun as you want." And then she does the unthinkable. My mother winks at Nevio suggestively.

If a person could die of embarrassment, I'd be six feet under.

"Thanks, Mom." I grab Nevio's hand and drag him out the door. At least my dad was absent to miss the absurd innuendo.

"Hey, hold up." Nevio chuckles, trying to slow me down. "I didn't even get a chance to tell you how incredible you look tonight."

"You can do it in the car where my family isn't watching."

He tugs me backward a smidge before I reach the passenger door of his car. "Let me." Reaching across my body, he opens the door and helps me inside, pausing to lean forward and catch my gaze. "You look radiant, Luisa."

I'm hidden from the view of my family, but I'm still a little embarrassed. My cheeks warm, and I drop my eyes. "Thank you. You don't look so bad yourself."

He smirks and closes the door. Our ride to the restaurant goes smoothly, if not a touch awkward. Like any first date, I'm hyper focused on every element of our time together. His choice of sensual music on the radio. The way his voice lowers to a rumbling purr in the confines of his car. The possessive feel of his hand resting on my lower back as we approach the hostess station in the restaurant. Every nuance of Nevio's being is crafted for seduction, and it puts me on edge. I don't even think he means to do it. In the same way charisma is a natural part of his personality, seduction is the way he shows interest in a woman. I have no doubt every other female on the planet must fall helplessly into his capable hands, and it makes me uncomfortable.

I'm able to ignore my unease during most of dinner. We sit at a small table across from one another, and the live music that Gia had mentioned fills the air around us. I limit myself to one glass of wine. Nevio does the same. We catch up on our years apart, talking straight through dinner and long after about school, concerts, friends, and all other aspects of our lives. At the candlelit table in a crowded restaurant, we are merely friends talking, and I'm able to relax, though the nerves resurface the second we stand to leave.

Nevio walks me to the passenger door of his car, but instead of opening it, he stills, eyes seeking mine. "I would invite you back to my place, but it's not exactly private."

I gnaw on my bottom lip and smile awkwardly. "That's okay. I'm not quite ready for that."

"I didn't mean to pressure you. I just hate for our evening to end already."

"We do live next door to one another. I have a feeling I'll

see you around plenty, although that might be more difficult when Zeno returns home."

He lifts his hands to cup my cheeks and pierces me with his stare. "I'm not afraid of Z. In fact, let him see us together. I'd love for him to face the fact he can't control everything."

His words snag in my ears, unraveling a thread of concern.

"That's not what this is about, though. Right?" I pull back enough to escape his touch. "You're not going out with me just to piss him off, are you?" It hadn't occurred to me before, especially when Nevio is so convincing with his admiration, but now that the idea has taken root, it makes sense.

"Of course, not!" he says adamantly. "I was only trying to say that I let you slip away once, and I'm not doing it again." His eyes soften before he leans in to place a gentle kiss on my forehead. "You are worth so much more than Z's petty wrath." His words are murmured against my skin, their heated promise coaxing goose bumps to line my arms.

I nod shakily, all the blood from my head rushing southward.

Nevio finally opens the door to the sleek black Mercedes. Our ride home is quiet, and I wonder what he's thinking. Mainly to distract me from my own confused thoughts. When we pull up at my house, he tells me to wait so that he can help me from the car. I let him because I recognize that the gesture has little to do with my actual need for assistance. This is about him showing me respect, and I appreciate his thoughtfulness.

His hand holds firmly to mine once I'm out of the car. "Tonight was absolutely perfect," he says quietly, chirping night insects providing a chorus to his murmured words.

"It was pretty great, thank you." I smile and drop my

gaze, unable to overcome a shyness that creeps up in his presence.

Nevio doesn't seem to mind. If anything, the display of my demure side encourages him. He begins to move closer when the porch light flicks on, startling me. For the briefest second, my father's face peeks from behind the curtains in the side window. Despite my age and years of living away from home, I'm instantly transported back to my youth and take a lunging step away from Nevio.

"Looks like Dad is still up." I bite on my lips to hold in a laugh. I feel like I've been caught stealing from my parents' liquor cabinet as a minor. The absurdity of my response is endlessly funny to me.

Nevio smirks, seeing the humor, but I sense his disappointment at being thwarted. He lifts my hand and places a kiss on my knuckles. "Good night, Luisa. Sleep well."

"You, too. And thanks again for a lovely evening."

I slip away and hurry up the porch steps. Inside, the downstairs is now empty. I'm a little surprised Dad didn't stick around to ask about my date, but it's late, and we all have to work in the morning. He probably waited up to make sure I was alive and had already fallen into bed. I'm a little envious. The date has given me so much to think about, and it's going to take me ages to fall asleep. I'll survive, though I don't handle sleepless nights as well as I used to.

Maybe I should have indulged in another glass of wine or two.

I picture Nevio's sultry stare and know immediately that I made the right choice. I'm not ready to crawl into bed with him, but with a little more alcohol and his persuasive abilities, there's no telling what would have happened. I'd rather suffer insomnia than get carried away and make things even more complicated than they already are. Taking a friendship to the next level is one thing; getting drunk and fucking a friend is another.

In a moment of weakness, I picture Z as I walk up the stairs. If things hadn't fallen apart at the Bishops' house, would more have happened between us? I can't deny the searing lust I felt when his body was pressed against mine. If I'd been on a date with him, and he'd said the things Nevio had said, would my night have ended alone?

I shiver at the answer resounding in every fiber of my being.

I would have given myself to him completely, but that scenario would never have happened. It's not even a possibility because Zeno is not like his brother. Not even close.

CHAPTER 19

UNCLE E AND AUNT CHIARA ARRIVE MIDAFTERNOON ON FRIDAY, but I don't get to see them until I'm off work at five. By the time Gia and I get home, the house is filled with the delicious aroma of lasagna and the chatter of excited voices.

"There are my girls!" Aunt Chiara and my uncle, along with Mom and Marca, are sitting at the kitchen table with music drifting in from the living room.

I go straight to my aunt and wrap her in a hug. "It's so good to see you!"

"You, too! It's been ages. Come sit down and tell us what's going on with you two."

I swap with Gia to give Uncle E a hug, then retrieve one of the extra chairs Mom keeps in the living room. "Dad not home yet?"

"You know your father," Mom shoots back while scooting her chair around to make room for us. "It's just like him not to pay attention to what's going on in this family. He knows I'm making lasagna, so he'll show up eventually."

Chiara ignores Mom's fussing and places a hand over mine to get my attention. "Your mom says you're staying here for a while?"

"Only for a few months. I got a little short on cash, so I'm going to save up before finishing out my last year at school."

"Always so responsible and determined. We are so proud of you!"

"Thank you." I grin shyly because praise from her truly does mean the world to me. "Tell me what's been going on with you guys. I want to hear everything I've missed."

Aunt Chiara dives into a quick update on each of her children—three boys and two girls, all grown and living on their own. Gia and I contribute what we can about our own lives, but there's little to tell. Eventually, Dad and Livia both show up, and we all move to the dining room table and stuff ourselves with a delicious dinner. With food in our bellies and wine in our veins, we sit back and continue to talk through the evening.

About an hour after dinner, Mom slips away to the restroom, and Aunt Chiara turns to Gia with concern lining her face.

"Gia, sweetie, are you okay? I get the feeling something's off."

"Oh, I'm fine. Just tired. It's been such a busy couple of weeks!" She attempts to infuse her smile with reassurance, but it doesn't reach her eyes.

"You know what you need?" Chiara perks up in her seat. "A vacation. When's the last time you got away from here?"

Gia chuckles. "It *has* been a while, but Luisa just got here. I'd hate to leave."

"I'm not going anywhere for a while," I remind her.

"See!" our aunt cries. "There's no reason you shouldn't come back with us and spend a week in the city. Everyone needs to get away from home every now and then. You'll feel so much better once you do."

This is perfect. If Gia goes to the city, she can find Carter and talk to him. In-person conversations are so much more effective than texting or even phone calls.

"Absolutely," I chime in. "You should definitely go. There's at least one friend you'd like to catch up with, and this would be the perfect opportunity." I infuse my stare with meaning to make sure she knows who I'm talking about.

"I don't know, Isa. Surprising someone out of the blue isn't always a great idea."

"Sure it is, especially when that person adores seeing you."

"What if you're wrong, and they don't feel that way?"

"G, you won't know until you try. Maybe you lost touch because of a miscommunication. This is the perfect chance to find out for sure and reconnect." More than likely, Carter's absence is owed to his sister, but arguing a miscommunication has a better chance of gaining Gia's favor. And I'm hoping that seeing her will snap him out of whatever brain-washing Cora has used on him.

Aunt Chiara's gaze ping-pongs between us with curiosity. "Who exactly…?"

I place my hand on hers and look at where Mom exited the room. "G can tell you all about it on your way into the city." It's not that Mom can't know what's going on with Gia, but Gia would prefer if Mom didn't end up in the middle of her business.

She nods with understanding. "I look forward to it."

"I'd like to go to the city," Livia cuts in. "Can I come, too?"

"Come where?" Mom asks as she enters the room.

Aunt Chiara sits tall and grins at Mom. "Gia is going to come back with us to the city. And as for you, Livy, maybe next time. This trip is for your sister."

Liv is unimpressed, setting her wineglass down with more force than necessary. "Gia and Luisa always get everything," she mutters.

Everyone ignores her, as usual.

"That sounds like a lovely idea," Mom says. "With Luisa here, we can definitely manage for a few days."

We spend the next thirty minutes planning Gia's upcoming getaway—how long she'll stay, activities to do, and people she might visit. I'm absorbed in the conversation when my phone buzzes in the back pocket of my jeans. I pull it out, expecting to see a text from a city friend but find an unknown number.

Unknown: Did you enjoy your dinner last night?

Heat blazes across my face as if I've been caught doing something I'm not supposed to, and I have no clue why. I don't even know who is behind the text.

Me: Who is this?

Unknown: The man who had you panting against a wall less than a week ago.

Zeno. It wouldn't have been all that hard for him to get my number, but why would he want it? He acts like he hates me. I have no doubt he can get any woman he wants with a single look, so why is he texting me? Why flirt then push me away?

Me: Enormously. Enjoying your escape to the city? Irritated, I have to make a dig at his sudden disappearance.

Zeno: No. Not even a little. His admission catches me off guard. Considering how pompous he can be, I assumed he wouldn't admit to emotions that might hint at an error on his part. That might hint he regrets leaving Hardwick.

Maybe he's more self-aware than I thought.

Or maybe not. He's so damn adamant Nevio is at fault for the rift between them that he won't even entertain the idea he played a role as well, so it makes sense that he would believe our own tense exchanges are no fault of his own. Hell, maybe I'm reading into his meaning, and his remorse about leaving has nothing to do with me. Maybe he had a shitty meeting or was in a car accident. There's no way to know what this is about unless I ask.

Me: Why did you leave?

It takes three whole minutes for his response to come.

Zeno: I needed time to think. Not everyone manages their emotions as well as you do.

What does that mean? It's not exactly an apology, but it hints at reconsideration.

I'm not sure what to say in response. I feel a need to keep the channel of communication open, but I don't want to say the wrong thing.

Me: I'm not so sure. Sometimes, my head is messed up like anyone else's.

Sometimes, I crave the man I hate.

Me: Why are you texting me, Z?

Zeno: Because I can't stop thinking of the way you felt against me.

Zeno: Hearing about your date made me furious.

I'm speechless.

I glance around at my family, still talking about God knows what. "Um, I'm wiped out. Sorry to bail so early, but I'm going to head to bed so I have the energy to hang out tomorrow." I have to get away because they'll ask me why I'm so distracted, and I don't want to lie. Fortunately, Gia and I still have our bedroom, whereas Livia and Marca have been moved to the pullout sofa to give Uncle E and Aunt Chiara their room.

As I hurry upstairs, I wonder how Zeno found out about the date.

Me: How did you know we went out?

Zeno: Are you alone?

I close the door to my bedroom and turn on the bedside lamp, then sit on the edge of the bed, staring at his question.

Me: Yes, why?

Zeno: In your bedroom?

My chest stirs with a surge of tingling anticipation that radiates out to my fingertips. I should stop this—tell him it's none of his business—but I don't want to. I want to see where he's taking me. I want to get burned by the fire he stokes.

Me: Yes.

Zeno: Lie back on the bed.

Zeno: Imagine I'm pressed up against you like we were on Friday.

My breath escapes my lips on shallow pants. Just as he said I'd been breathing that night.

I know the second I do as he says, the sensation will swarm me because it won't be the first time I've sought out the feeling. Drawn it forth from my memories.

I start to move, then pause. My fingers tremble as I type.

Me: How did you know? Did Nevio tell you? Nevio said his pursuit of me wasn't derived from spite for his brother, but if he reached out to rub our night in Zeno's face, I'd have to wonder if he was lying. Why else would he intentionally anger his brother?

Zeno: Do you really want me to answer that?

Me: Yes.

Zeno: I keep tabs on everything Nevio does.

He keeps tabs on Nevio? What does that mean? Does he have his brother followed? Or does he just watch his credit card receipts and use GPS to track his location?

I couldn't be more surprised if Z had announced he was gay and carrying on a secret relationship in the city. I'm at a loss. Why the hell would Zeno need to monitor his brother's every action? Clearly, there's a lack of trust between the two, but tracking him? That takes things to another level. I'm not sure what to think.

Me: Why?

Zeno: Because it's my job.

As a brother? As Nevio's Mafia superior? What does he mean it's his job? Every text between us only makes me more confused.

Zeno: Are you going to do as I said? Because my cock is hard just reading the words you write.

Zeno: I need to know you feel the same.

If he only knew how his words were affecting me. I can't breathe or think. My thoughts are in shambles, and I don't know how I feel except that I want—I want him to want me. It's absurd and dangerous. He probably only wants me in order to keep me from Nevio, but here in the dim lighting of my bedroom, where only the walls can see me, I don't seem to care.

I want to be desired by him.

I need to feel that connection.

Glancing around the room, I slowly scoot back on the bed. My family will be downstairs talking for hours, so I don't have to worry about interruptions. I lean back on the pillows and soak in the nervous excitement lighting my veins on fire before I tap out an answer.

Me: Yes.

Zeno: Good girl.

Zeno: I want you to free your breasts. Expose those

beautiful nipples, then give them a sharp tug because I wouldn't be gentle if I were there.

Jesus Christ.

I shudder with a wave of crippling hunger elicited from his words alone. He does something to me that no other man can do. Speaks to a primal side of me that I never knew existed.

I do as he says, moaning quietly when the sensation sparks a fire in my belly.

Me: Please tell me I'm not doing this alone.

I need to hear he's there with me, drowning in an ocean of desire as deep as the one pulling me under.

Zeno: I'm right here with you.

Zeno: My cock is in my hand, so angry and red. My fist can't grip tight enough.

Zeno: Are your nipples peaked and sensitive? Have you given them plenty of attention?

Me: Yes. God, yes.

Zeno: Fuck, I wish I could see you.

Zeno: Take your hand slowly down to your slit. Dip your fingers into your wetness, then roll them gently around your perfect clit.

Even if he hadn't instructed me to do it, I would have done it on my own. I'm so damn turned on I'm blind with need—that mindless place where nothing else matters but chasing the pinnacle of pleasure.

I use dictate to text him back now that one hand is occupied. Without having to text out each word, my messages become less guarded. Words tumble from my lips without fully thinking them through.

Me: Why are we doing this, Z?

Zeno: Because we want to—we want one another—and because it feels good. Doesn't it feel good, Luisa?

Fuck, yes.

I start to lose myself in the sensation and forget to text him back until my phone buzzes again.

Zeno: Don't you dare finish without me, Isa. You hear me?

Me: Z, I need to come. I'm so close.

Zeno: WAIT.

Zeno: Imagine we're back against that wall, but this time, my hand slips down beneath the waist of your pants. Imagine my teeth grazing the skin of your neck and my other hand claiming your perfect breast.

Me: Z!

Zeno: NOT. YET.

Zeno: Feel my cock, hard and desperate to be inside you.

Zeno: Hear the way my breath shudders with each of your moans.

Me: I can't...

Zeno: NOW, Luisa. Come all over your hand for me.

I held off as long as I could so that when I read his text and release the flood of sensation, I'm completely swept away. In fact, I'm so lost in the cascade of pleasure that I don't realize I hit the text record button. Panting and moaning through the crescendo of physical bliss, I record the sounds of my release, and when my finger slips from the button, the recording is automatically sent to Zeno. I don't even realize what I've done until I regain my bearings and look at my phone again.

Zeno: Jesus Christ, you're killing me.

Me: Oh my God. I didn't mean to record and send that. I accidentally hit the button.

Zeno: Sexiest sounds I've ever heard. I only wish I was there to lick your fingers clean.

My mouth falls open in awe of his words and everything that passed between us.

I just sexted with Zeno De Rossi, the man who treats me like shit and makes me totally crazy. The man whose *brother* I went on a date with. What in the actual fuck was I thinking?

Me: I have to go.

I type the words as panic overrides my post-orgasmic chill.

Zeno: Luisa

Me: I'm sorry, I have to go.

I turn off my phone and bury my face in my hands, but that's even worse because I can smell the evidence of what I've done on my fingers. Needing to escape and clear my head, I right my clothes and hurry to the shower. I hope that getting the scent off me will help, but touching my naked body only reminds me of the way his words made me feel.

Zeno has injected himself into my bloodstream like a poison I can't escape.

I was confused before, but now, I'm utterly lost.

It takes me hours to go to sleep, and when I finally do, cobalt eyes are there waiting for me, feeding me dirty commands I don't hesitate to obey.

Zeno doesn't text the rest of the weekend, and I'm hesitant to admit how forlorn that makes me. I try not to let it show—my confusion and distress, longing and duality. Instead, I spend time with my family. We get in some shopping and play a few board games before Sunday rolls around, and it's time to say goodbye. I don't want them to leave, partially because I enjoy their company, but also because I'll have more time to think. About Nevio. About Zeno. About everything.

I keep Gia company while she packs Sunday morning. The Bishop house is still empty, making it look less and less likely that the family took a quick trip to the city. I catch her looking toward the house when she thinks no one will notice. The spear that pierces her heart with every glance passes straight through her and into me. Her pain is my pain. Maybe not to the same degree, but I abhor knowing she's so heartbroken.

"It'll all work out, G. You'll see," I assure her and myself. I desperately hope I'm right. Surely, Carter wouldn't be stupid enough to let his snobby sister keep him from someone as perfect as Gia.

"I suppose you're right, one way or another. I appreciate you encouraging me, though. It'll be good to at least get it over with."

"And if for some reason he's a total jackass, then I want you to spend some time thinking about moving to the city with me. Liv is a grown woman, and Marca is out of school now. Without Carter or the girls, there's no real reason for you to stay."

She starts to say something, but I cut her off.

"Just think about it. That's all I'm asking."

Gia shakes her head with a smile. "Okay, Miss Bossy Pants. Now, help me carry this thing downstairs. Uncle E wants to head out as soon as possible."

I give my sister an extra big hug before she gets in the car and make her promise to be in constant contact. Everyone else goes back inside when the car disappears around the corner, except for me. I turn and gaze at the trees in the direction of the Bishop house and swear to myself that if Gia can't resolve things with Carter, then I'll step up and have words with him myself. If he truly doesn't have feelings for her, I want to hear him say it with my own ears.

"Do you stare at the trees like that often?" Nevio's voice startles me from my reprieve.

"Hey! Um, no. Gia just left for the city with my aunt and uncle for a little time away. I guess I got distracted by the view. What are you doing over here?"

"It looks like your sister isn't the only one headed to the city for a bit. Zeno has insisted I join him for a few days, but I'll get back out here as soon as I can. I wanted to tell you in person."

Nevio has no idea, but I'd bet my life this is about Zeno keeping his brother away from me. But somehow, this time, I'm not as upset. I don't like that he's manipulating his brother's life to serve his own purposes, yet I'm also kind of flattered. Coming between Nevio and me to keep us apart is one thing, but pushing his brother out of the picture because he has feelings for me—that's very different. Surreal. Shocking, even. But not totally unwanted.

"That's sweet of you. It should be a quiet week, so you won't miss much." I smile, but it falters when I meet his steady gaze, full of desire.

"I'll miss *you*, and that's all that matters."

How did I end up in this dangerous dance between two brothers?

I don't want to lead them on, nor do I know exactly what I want. Who I want. They're both alluring in their own ways, though the two are complete opposites. If I'm going to entertain a relationship with one, I'll need to pick soon or risk losing both of them.

Nevio detects the swell of emotion I'm battling and mistakes it for passion. He's not totally wrong, but the feelings are far more complicated than that. He only sees what he wants to see and places his hands on either side of my face, bringing our lips together in a delicate first kiss rife with tenderness.

"Promise you'll keep in touch while I'm gone. I want to hear about everything I'm missing."

I nod, words escaping me.

Just when I think he's going to close in for another kiss, the front door barrels open.

"Oh, damn. Excuse me, I didn't realize anyone was out here." Dad waves a hand in the air, and I leap away from Nevio as though I've been electrocuted by his touch.

"It's okay, Dad. Nevio was just stopping by on his way out of town." The shrillness in my voice makes it clear that I would make a terrible criminal. The slightest hint of guilt, and I crumple completely.

Nevio grins at me, finding my reaction enormously funny. "I'll be in touch, gorgeous." He winks, waves to my dad, then heads back toward Hardwick without the slightest indication of discomfort. Either he's damn good at hiding embarrassment, or he isn't the slightest bit fazed at getting caught by my father.

"Sorry, Dad. Didn't mean to make things awkward." I join him on the front porch, expecting him to tease me and laugh off the situation, but instead, an unusual wariness darkens his already umber eyes.

"I heard about your date the other night. I didn't say anything at the time, but I don't think Nevio is a good idea." Daddy's caution speaks louder in my ears than most. I'm surprised to hear him say anything against Nevio.

"I thought you liked him."

"I do. Nevio is a good man, but—" He looks around as if searching the trees for the right thing to say. "That doesn't mean I think he's good *for* you. I may not be an active part of the Giordano family, but I still hear things."

"You've heard something bad about Nevio?" He's always so pleasant and laid-back. It's hard to imagine he's capable of doing something my father would deem unworthy.

Daddy frowns, his eyes tracing soft lines across my face. "Would it be enough if I simply asked you to trust me?" He doesn't want to say, and though I'm endlessly curious, I adore my dad too much to refuse him.

"Of course, Daddy. I know you're only looking out for me," I say softly. After two days of uncertainty wavering between the two brothers and wondering what I should do, Dad's request is almost a relief. I'm even a little surprised at how easy I'm able to mentally set Nevio aside, at least as far as my feelings are concerned. Putting the brakes on a relationship between us will be a tad more difficult.

Dad's face melts with relief and pride. "That's my girl." He pulls me into a hug, filling my heart with joy. When he begins to release me, he pauses and stares deep into my eyes, down into the depths of my soul. "On the topic of looking out for you, I need to ask a question. And Luisa, I want to know the truth. Why are you moving back home? You're too responsible to have spent your school money. I want you to tell me why you're actually staying."

Shit. Shitshitshit. I'm not ready for this conversation.

I may not ever be ready, but I need to tell him at some point. Might as well be now.

"How about we walk for a minute?"

He nods, and I lead us down the porch steps.

"You're not going to like what I tell you, so just listen and try to understand. When I arrived home a week ago, Gia told me that Mom had been acting weird lately—selling things and behaving funny. I didn't think anything of it, but then a bookie came by when I was at the house one day. Mom owed him a lot of money. A *family* bookie. I was so worried about them hurting you and your reputation that I decided I wanted to take care of it."

Dad's gait becomes so stiff, I can sense his agitation without even looking at him. "Are you telling me you paid my fucking debt?" Never once in all my years has my father spoken to me with such disdain. His anger is a punch to the gut, but I keep going in an attempt to explain.

"It wasn't your debt. It was Mom's. And yes, I *chose* to pay it. My choice. And before you get even more upset, let me finish. I didn't tell you about it because I knew you wouldn't let me do it. But the reason I'm saying something now is because I won't step in again, and I agree that you need to know what she's been doing. You need to protect yourself because Gia and I won't help Mom again—or at least, I won't. I guess I can't control what Gia does. I don't know if you can tell the family not to deal with her or if you have to … if you have to divorce her, but I don't want you getting hurt." Each word is harder to say than the last until my emotions have stolen my voice completely.

"And where does Gia fit into all this? Did she contribute as well?"

"Not this time, but it turns out Mom was in trouble about six months ago."

We walk for several minutes in silence. I feel like there are eggshells under each step I take, my shoulders tense with worry. Eventually, I give in and continue pleading for his understanding.

"I know it kills you to hear all this, but as much as you can't stand to hear that your daughter took on a burden you feel should have been yours, it would have killed *me* if you were hurt when I could have prevented it. Don't begrudge me for what I did. You would have done the same."

Dad stops and stares at me. His eyes are bloodshot and

suspiciously glassy, piercing me with a flood of emotion. Once again, he pulls me into his chest. "Christ, I don't know what I did to deserve you." His pained words wrap themselves around my heart the same way his arms cradle my body.

"I love you, Daddy."

"Love you, too, Lulu. And you don't need to worry about me. I'll take care of everything."

CHAPTER 20

I DON'T HEAR FROM ANYONE FOR A DAY AND A HALF. NOT UNTIL Gia calls after lunch on Tuesday. I can't wait to find out how her trip is going, so I answer with an enormous grin.

"Hey, G! How's the city?"

"Not so great." Her broken whisper barely traverses the distance between us.

My heart crumbles to rubble at my feet. "Oh, Gia, honey. What happened?"

"I wasn't sure how to reach out to Carter, but I had his city address, so I wandered that way while I was thinking this morning. I ordered a latte at the coffee shop in the lobby of his building and sat down to get the courage to call him when Cora happened by." Her words grow unbearably full of emotion, making them thin and brittle. "She came straight over and accused me of stalking her brother. Isa, I've never been more embarrassed in my life. I never was crazy about her, but the things she said … they were so hateful. I can't figure out what I did to deserve being treated like that."

If Cora Bishop were here right now, I'd break that snooty nose of hers and laugh while she bled all over her designer shoes. I'm so fucking mad that I'm shaking.

"You didn't do anything at all. She's a wretched, hateful human being. Please tell me you aren't going to let her win—that you'll keep trying."

"I can't possibly risk him thinking I'm stalking him like a crazy person. I've been praying all morning that she doesn't tell him. God, how embarrassing."

I want to fuss at her not to let Cora intimidate her, but Gia is too upset to see reason. "Maybe once things settle down, you can talk to him and explain. You two were friends, and at the very least, it's reasonable for friends to talk things over before they end a friendship. He can't leave without a word and expect you not to be upset. That's especially unfair to his kids—they adore you!"

"I'm not making any decisions right now. I just want to finish my trip and pretend none of this ever happened. I was almost too embarrassed to even tell you, but I knew you'd force it out of me."

I smile at the tiny ray of love warming her words, so grateful I can give her that when she's hurting. "Never in a million years. I'd make you tell me everything."

"I know, and since I had to call you anyway, I knew keeping it a secret was pointless."

"Why else did you have to call?"

Gia's voice drops to a whisper again, but in a different way than before. This is a whisper rife with secrecy. "I was looking to distract myself earlier and decided to go to a restaurant for lunch over in Little Italy that Anna used to rave about before she up and disappeared. It's owned by someone her parents know. I didn't end up going in, though, because I saw her inside through the window."

"The woman who used to work in the kitchen at Hardwick? The one who's job I took over?"

"*Yes!*"

"If she disappeared so suddenly, why didn't you go in and check on her?"

"*Because* … she was inside with *Zeno*. They were standing together, almost intimately. His hands were holding her face while he talked to her, and she was nodding intently. It looked pretty serious, but I have no idea what could have been going on. Maybe he happened to see her as well and decided to confront her about leaving so abruptly?"

The food I ate for lunch solidifies in my stomach. I don't buy into coincidences. In a city of millions, what are the chances that he happened to run into his missing housekeeper? Practically zero. But what does that mean? Did he know from the beginning where she was, or did he track her down? And if so, why?

"That *is* strange." It shouldn't unsettle me, but it does. He owes me nothing and may have only been talking to the woman, yet I feel deceived. Or at least, I'm worried about being deceived.

I don't trust Zeno. That much is clear.

He hurt me years ago, and a part of me fears he'll do it again. Am I willing to take that risk?

"It's not like he was asking her to come back. Now that you're working at the house, they don't need any more staff. It was so intriguing."

Would Zeno seek out Anna to hire her back in order to get me away from Nevio? That would be crazy. It couldn't be … could it?

"Yeah," I say distractedly. "Hey, I actually need to get back to work, but I'm glad you called."

"I'm glad I did, too. Just hearing your voice makes me feel better."

"Love you, G."

"You too, Isa."

We hang up, but I don't hurry back inside. I had stepped out the side door when Gia called, but now, I need a minute alone. Only, there are two dueling brothers who don't get that memo because two texts ping on my phone simultaneously.

Zeno: What's wrong?

Nevio: How has your week started out?

Zeno's unusual text draws my attention first.

Me to Zeno: Why would you think something's wrong?

Zeno: Because I'm watching you on the security cameras.

My heart leaps into my throat as my eyes dart up to the eves of the house. Of course, there are cameras. I knew that, but it never occurred to me he'd be watching. I slip back into the kitchen to escape his view.

Me to Nevio: All is quiet here. How about you?

Me to Zeno: Stop watching me! Everything is fine.

Don't you have meetings with other women to attend to? My insecurities flare to life in my head, begging me to lash out. I'm able to keep them caged, for the moment.

Nevio: This trip is a waste of my time, but I knew it would be. It's Zeno's way of exerting his power over me. He can call me to the city, but that won't keep me from you forever. 😉

Zeno: How else do you expect me to know what's going on when you never texted me back?

I scroll up to look at his messages and realize he's right. Technically, there was one last text from him telling me not to ignore him. I had ignored it.

I switch back to my conversation with Nevio and start to reply only to come up short. I don't know what to say to him. I want to keep things light because I don't want to lead him on. Judging by his comment, though, he already thinks we're … together.

Me to Nevio: When do you think you'll be back?

That implies I'm here waiting for him.

Me to Nevio: 😬 At least the city is never boring!

Perfect. Neutral yet engaging. I'll deal with him later. Back to Zeno.

I imagine him with Anna. I remember the months of hurt and worry after he quit talking to me when we were younger, then I hear all the harsh words he spoke to me in the years since. He suddenly wants to connect with me, but only after years of pushing me away. He has no right to expect anything from me. Maybe I'd be better off walking away from both brothers—God knows it would be easier.

Me to Zeno: I don't have to tell you anything. It was phone sex between two people who had an itch to scratch. That's it.

Harsh but necessary. I'm tired of being blown around like a leaf caught in his turbulent winds.

Nevio: I'd still rather be with you. I'm coming back no matter what on Friday. Will I be able to see you?

I can picture his dimpled grin coaxing me to say yes, but I respect my father too much to ignore his warning. I don't understand it, but I don't have to.

Me to Nevio: I should be around. *That sounds vague enough.*

Zeno: Is that what you think?

Me to Zeno: What have you done over the years to suggest anything different?

Nevio: Knowing I get to see you once I'm back makes this trip tolerable.

Me to Nevio: See you soon!

Shit. Was an exclamation point too much?

Zeno: Nothing. I've done everything I could to push you away.

His words cut deeper than I'd like. So deep, my hand plants against my stomach to keep the bleeding at bay. The only consolation is that I now know he recognizes the way he's acted toward me. He knows exactly what he's done.

I stare at the screen of my phone for several agonizing minutes. Tears blur my vision, then retreat, but I can't force myself to text a reply. There is nothing left to say. Zeno must feel the same because my phone falls silent.

I force myself back to work, but I'm lethargic at best. Between the prospect of hurting Nevio and the pain of Zeno's confession, I fall deep into a melancholy haze. I find places to work in the house where I'm guaranteed to be alone. I'm even hesitant to answer the phone when Grace calls well into the afternoon, but I worry she could be in trouble, so I force myself to take the call.

"Hey, Grace. What's up?"

"I'm planning a trip into the city to look at apartments and wanted to ask if you'd come with me."

"When were you thinking of going?"

"I was hoping to leave Thursday and come back Sunday."

"I would, but I can't ask for time off when I've only been working a week." Although, having a break from the incessant drama here would be a welcome relief.

"I know it's a big ask, but I really need your help. I've never done this before, and I don't know anyone else who could help guide me through the process."

I don't have to hear the concern in her voice to feel

compelled to help her. She is a fish out of water in the city, and if she doesn't have experienced help, she might end up in an even worse situation than she's already in. And I'm the reason she's in that situation—I invited Aldo to meet me at our house. If I hadn't done that, she'd never have run into him.

"Okay, let me find Elena and talk to her. I'll let you know what she says." It can't hurt to ask. And after all, this isn't my forever job.

"Thank you so much, Luisa! You don't know how much this means to me."

"Don't thank me until I get the thumbs-up. I'll text you in a bit."

Grace will be on pins and needles until I text with an answer, so I go straight in search of Elena. I'm not worried about her being upset. I'm almost certain she'll agree, but I feel bad taking advantage of my situation. She's been so kind to give me a job on short notice, and now I'm asking for more.

I find her alone in the library, scrolling on her phone. "Hey, Elena. Do you have a second?"

She's a stunning woman, even in her fifties. With blond waving hair and green eyes that change in the light, she could be a model. Her cheeks are smooth and full above perfectly shaped lips that almost curve upward without her even smiling. Her hair is blond, which hides any sneaky gray hairs, and the few creases she's gained through the years are minimal. She's absolutely gorgeous, inside and out.

"Of course, come sit down." She motions for me to sit in the armchair across from hers.

"Thank you. I just got a call from Grace—the Larson's daughter."

"Of course, Grace is such a sweet girl."

I smile in agreement. "She's making the big move to the

city and needs to find an apartment, but she knows nothing about the process or where to look. I know I just started, and I feel terrible for asking, but if it wouldn't be a huge inconvenience, I'd like to go to the city Thursday to help her. I'm worried if someone isn't with her, she'll end up in a bad neighborhood or a terrible lease."

"Oh! Of course! I can't imagine how overwhelming that would be." Her brows knit together, a sign that her beauty is a product of excellent genes and not buckets of Botox.

"I really appreciate it and want to assure you that I'm not going to run off every weekend."

Elena puts her hand over my knee and smiles warmly. "Life happens sometimes. And not always when we expect it."

"No kidding," I murmur with an apologetic smile.

I expect this to end our conversation, but Elena's head tilts to the side, and she peers at me questioningly.

"Luisa, would you be willing to talk to me about why you ended up back here?"

The silence in the library is suddenly deafening.

I'm not sure why everyone insists on pushing this issue when I have no desire to talk about it. However, I asked for a huge favor from my new boss, and I hate to deny her a simple request for understanding.

I look down at my hands pressed flat together, tucked between my thighs. "I just hit a bump in the road. I'm not thrilled to have to move home, but it's not forever."

"That's right. You know, life rarely goes as expected. I don't talk much about it, but many years ago, I had a miscarriage. I hadn't told anyone about the pregnancy, but I was *so* excited. That baby was a new life—a new beginning. I was devastated over the loss." The lingering sorrow in her voice is unmistakable.

"I'm so sorry, I had no idea."

"No one did. And the only reason I tell you now is because I want you to know you aren't alone. Just because people don't talk about problems doesn't mean they don't have them. I hated feeling like I was going through that alone, and I recognized the turmoil in your eyes. It may not be a lost baby you're dealing with, but life interruptions can be difficult no matter the source."

I nod because words escape me. I'm so touched by her sincerity and vulnerability. She didn't have to put herself out there, but she could see I was struggling and decided to forge a connection.

"More specifically," she continues, "if money is the reason you had to leave the city, I want to help. You are so close to your goal—your parents are always telling me about all your accomplishments. I have the means to get you back on track, and I'd like to do that."

I list backward as though the power of her words has physically moved me. Shock doesn't even begin to describe how I feel. Dumbfounded. Awestruck. Humbled.

"Elena, I don't know what to say."

"Just tell me how much   that's the only thing you need to say."

And it would be that easy. Her sincerity is plain in her loving green eyes. But I'm not the type of person who could take a handout like that. Maybe it's my father's teachings that nothing free comes without a price, but I can't do it.

I shake my head slowly. "You are giving me the money I need by paying me to work. It won't take but a few months, and I'll have what I need without owing you or anyone else. I am incredibly grateful for the chance to work at Hardwick, and right now, that's all I need."

Elena smiles affectionately, but there's a glimmer of

sadness in her eyes. "You're an independent young woman, and I suppose I should have expected nothing less. However, in a world where women need to stick together, I hope you'll reconsider. My offer has no expiration."

Her generosity and solidarity nearly bring me to tears. It's true that as women in Mafia families, we are our own best allies, yet there is often pettiness and rivalry among us. And as the matriarch of such a powerful family, she could easily be guarded and wary of outsiders. But that's not Elena. The harsh reality of our world hasn't touched her—or maybe it has, but only in the best way. She recognizes the ugliness around her and chooses to be a light in the darkness.

I push forward and wrap my arms around her. "Thank you, Elena. Your support means so much to me."

"I adore my boys, yet having a daughter would have been a special blessing. That wasn't in the cards for me, but I've been lucky enough to watch you girls grow up and want the best for you. If you ever need me, all you have to do is ask."

It's been easy to become overwhelmed by the chaos of my current life, yet a single outreach from a friend leaves me feeling centered and stable when I return to work. In part because I now technically have options, but also because compassion feeds the soul.

Elena is a special woman. I see her generosity and friendliness reflected in Nevio's eyes. I can't help but wonder what happened to Zeno. At one point, the two brothers were both playful and innocent, then something changed. Zeno changed. And I wonder if I'll ever learn the truth behind that transformation.

CHAPTER 21

"Grace texted. The Uber is on the way." I set my ridiculously overstuffed bag by the front door. Without knowing what exactly we'll be doing while in the city, I end up packing most of what I originally brought to my parents' house.

I give my parents hugs in the kitchen. They usually come home for lunch anyway, but today, they both got here early to make sure they saw me off. I suppose some things never change. And even though my mom makes me crazy, I appreciate that she's present and tries the best she can.

"You two have a wonderful time." Dad engulfs me in one of his perfect hugs before I move to give Mom a quick hug as well.

"We'll be pretty busy checking out apartments, but we'll have a great time together no matter what we're doing." I've successfully avoided Nevio and will have several more days to put off discussions with him, which is a relief. This will be an escape from him and all the rest of my troubles, at least for a few days. "A friend of mine is taking us in for the weekend, so we'll also get to hang out with her."

"Damn!" Dad says suddenly. "I totally forgot to give you this." He digs in his pocket and pulls out a folded sticky note. "That's the address to Z's apartment in the city."

I take the paper and peer at it warily. "What's it for?"

Dad grins. "I told him what you were up to, and he insisted you stay there. That way, you have your own space and don't have to crash with your friend."

"But isn't *he* staying at his place?"

"No, I don't think so. He made it sound like the place was empty. It's a gorgeous apartment. You should take advantage of the offer!"

I nod and slip the address into my pocket, but I'm confused. Why would Zeno offer up his place? We haven't talked or texted in two days. Considering our last exchange, I figured we were on shaky ground. Had he truly meant to let us stay in his home, or was he simply being respectful to my father? Like offering a part of your lunch to someone when you're crazy hungry and prefer to eat it all yourself.

I don't know the answer, but I'll find out before we roll up at his apartment.

The car arrives within minutes, picking me up first, then Grace. We talk excitedly for a while before I explain the possible change in arrangements.

"That would be so incredibly awesome!" Grace is practically vibrating in her seat.

"Before you get too excited, I need to text him and hear for myself that he's good with it and wasn't just being polite."

"I totally understand. I need to make a quick call to check in with my real estate agent anyway."

We both pull out our phones and get to work. When I open my text conversation with Z, my eyes graze the last words he wrote, carving out my insides a little further.

I've done everything I could to push you away.

I hate that he can make me feel so empty with a few careless words. Gritting my teeth, I swear to myself that I will not give him that kind of power over me.

Me: Dad says you offered your apartment to Grace and me. Are you sure about that?

Simple. Straightforward. Unbothered. Not the text of a woman who can't find herself beneath a landslide of emotions.

Zeno: It's just an apartment, Luisa. You might as well use it if it's empty.

It doesn't feel like *just* an apartment. It feels personal—staying at someone's home when they aren't there. Especially for someone as private as Zeno.

Me: Where are you staying?

Zeno: I won't be at the apartment.

Shit. Why did I ask when I really don't want to know? Now, all I can think about is whether Z is staying with a woman in the city. I stare at the screen of my phone long enough that the phone begins to ring before I can respond. Zeno is calling me.

"Hello?" I answer awkwardly as though I'm a child answering a call on my mother's phone.

"The mayor's place is up in Lincoln Square. We've been working on some negotiations this week, and I didn't want to deal with commuting, so I got a hotel room here. Take the apartment, Luisa."

"Okay," I breathe. The vibrations of his voice short-circuit my brain, especially when he says my name. I don't know why. It's not the first time I've heard him speak, but it's the first time I imagine the words he texted coming from those lips. Sexy, dirty words abrading my skin with their gravelly need.

Get a grip, woman!

"Um … key. Do I—will I need a key?"

"I'll text you the code, and I've already informed security of your arrival. There are three bedrooms—you're welcome to take your pick. Use whatever you need."

I still don't understand why he's doing this when he admitted days ago that he didn't want me around. I don't understand, but I'm also not going to reject his offer. Taking thousands of dollars from Elena is too much, but a weekend in an upscale apartment … *that* I can do.

"Thank you, Z."

His voice drops to a velvet caress. "Be safe, Isa."

I'm breathless when the line goes dead. My mouth is dry, and there's a nagging ache in my chest. It takes Grace's excited chatter to stir me from my Zeno hangover. I tell her the good news about the apartment and give the address to the driver. The rest of our ride goes smoothly, though I remain somewhat lost in my own confused thoughts.

The apartment is jaw-droppingly gorgeous. The concierge escorts us up to make sure we get in safely, and we wait until he leaves to squeal with excitement. Or at least, Grace squeals. I am too overwhelmed—with the extent of his wealth and the fact I'm surrounded in Zeno. It's so different than being in Hardwick. The old mansion brings memories of childhood in a setting steeped with history. Pieces of Z are present there, but not like this. The apartment is where he lived for years until his father's death. Everything about the understated elegance of the place screams *Zeno*, from the sweeping panoramic views to the clean, modern lines and the pristine mix of wood and concrete. A custom light fixture of overlapping rectangles hangs over the dining room table from the two-story ceiling. The apartment is stately, bold yet reserved, and undeniably masculine. Zeno is here in every muted fabric and stoic painting gracing the walls.

"I can*not* believe we get to stay here. This is *incredible!*" Grace spins around, eyes wide and her jaw hanging open. "We have to check out the bedrooms." She scurries away, and I am right behind her. Z's bedroom is too tempting to resist. Another woman in my position might respect his privacy, but the opportunity is too great, and my curiosity about him is endless.

First, we come across a bedroom accented in reds with rich walnut furniture before peeking at a similarly outfitted second bedroom utilizing a deep royal blue for its pop of color. Each is equipped with an en-suite bathroom complete with a soaker tub.

"Which do you want?" Grace asks.

"Oh, I don't care. You pick."

"I guess I'll go with red. Let's check out the master before we unpack, though. I'm sure it's amazing." She leads us to the other side of the apartment, where a hallway cordons off a private entrance to the master. The bedroom is cozier than I expected. The ceiling is vaulted about a foot with lights tucked away to illuminate the recessed top. There are four windows, tall but not particularly wide. They are each outfitted with heavy rolling shades currently halfway lowered. Opposite the king-sized bed is a large fireplace bumped out from the wall with bench seats on either side and a window above each. The space is soothing and comfortable —not exactly words I would have used for Zeno.

"Pretty epic," Grace muses. "I can't imagine."

"Me either."

"Come on, let's get settled so I can show you the areas my agent recommended. I want to hear your thoughts."

I unload my things in the blue bedroom, then join Grace on her bed. She pulls up emails, showing me a couple of places the agent suggested. We talk extensively about the city —jobs, apartments, restaurants. Everything. I love sharing all my hard-earned knowledge with her.

After a while, we check out the impressive patio we'd forgone on our first inspection of the home. The day is warm, but the breeze from being up so high helps cut the heat.

"This place is so gorgeous," I muse. "I hate to even leave for dinner."

"I'm right there with you. How about we order in for tonight? We'll be out in the city the next two days and can eat out plenty then."

"Sounds like a plan to me." My grin almost hurts. I'm so pleased we got this chance to spend time together. Grace truly is a great person and a wonderful friend.

We order pizza and make ourselves comfortable on the large sectional in the living room. Of course, Zeno has every TV channel imaginable, so we spend ages scrolling through options before we land on a classic.

"*Clueless*! I love this movie, and it just started a few minutes ago." Grace claps her hands, making me giggle.

"It's pretty much perfect. *Rollin' with the homies*," I sing, and we both wave our hands like Brittany Murphy does in the movie, then we burst into a fit of giggles.

"Man, did Paul Rudd age well. I mean … yum." She smacks her lips, and we both laugh again.

"No kidding. He can play such goofy characters, but those eyes."

"And that body—did you see him in *Ant-Man*?" She fans herself. "You know who else is crazy gorgeous?"

I look at her quizzically.

A mischievous grin lights up her face. "Zeno."

I try to shake my head to tell her not to go there, but she quiets me.

"No way. You went on a date with Nevio, and now Zeno is letting you use his apartment? This warrants a little more information."

"There's nothing to tell. I won't be going on a second date with Nevio, and absolutely nothing is going on with Z." Nothing real. Nothing of substance.

"What happened with Nevio to warrant a one-and-done?"

"He's a great guy, but you remember how he was when we were younger. I'm not interested in being with a playboy." Telling her that is easier than describing my father's vague warning. She'd probably argue Dad is being overprotective, and I'm not in the mood for that conversation.

"I guess I do. I didn't hang out with him in high school the way you did. What about Z? I find it hard to believe he'd offer his place to just anyone."

"I honestly can't tell you what he's thinking. You know how impossible he can be." *And mysterious, and alluring, and totally consuming.* "He wants to be the next underboss of the Giordano family, maybe even the boss, and that's all that matters to him. Ambition. Reputation."

"Yeah, but look what he has to offer." She motions to the room around us. "You'd never have to worry about rent or insurance or anything again."

"There are more important things than money," I murmur, that hollow feeling returning. "Z may seem enticing from the outside, but he's done some pretty awful things."

"Like what?" Grace sobers along with me.

"Well, who knows what he's done as part of his job, but there's also the way he treats his brother. He's practically exiled him from the family. That's why Nevio didn't come to dinner at the Bishops' the other night. The two don't get along for some reason, and Z uses his power and position to lord over his younger brother."

Disbelief mottles her features. "You're kidding?"

I shake my head gravely.

"I had no idea."

"I knew they didn't get along, but until I came back home, I didn't have a clue how bad it was. It's heartbreaking, and I feel especially bad for Nevio. Z told me he knew Nevio and I had gone on a date. When I asked him how he knew, he said he *keeps tabs* on his brother. It's so strange. Sometimes, I wonder if he's jealous of Nevio's easy nature, but I hate to believe he could be that petty."

A sly smile creeps back on her face. "Nevio is *extremely* likable."

I chuckle. "You're terrible." I'm about to continue chastising her when a knock sounds at the door.

Grace and I both stand stock-still, eyes locked on each other before I snap out of my shock and scramble for the front door.

Holy crap, who's here? Surely, it's not Zeno. But who else stops by unannounced? Please, God, please don't let it be a woman.

I close my eyes and take a single deep breath before opening the door. As if I wasn't shocked enough, Christiano De Bellis stands impatiently in the hallway. A hulking man in a suit that strains around his biceps stands off to the side, eyes cast away.

"Hello, can I help you?" I don't acknowledge that I know the man because I'm certain he won't remember me—I am nothing to him—but I won't soon forget the sight of the Giordano family boss.

He lifts his chin, studying me with a quick flick of his eyes before glancing back to where Grace is cowering in the living room behind me. "I was looking for Zeno. Is he home?"

"No, I'm afraid not. He was kind enough to let us stay for a couple of nights while we're in the city."

Did the heat in here just kick on? Am I sweating? Oh, God. Please don't sweat in front of this man.

"I see. They told me downstairs that someone was occupying the apartment, and I thought perhaps Zeno had come back early." Christiano's eyes narrow. "I'm surprised to find you here, I must say. I'm not sure I've ever known Zeno to host guests while he's away."

"Well, my family works for his. We've known each other all our lives." I try to explain.

He doesn't look convinced, and I'm not sure what part of our situation he questions.

"You look familiar. We met at the funeral, did we not?"

I smile gently, hoping our connection will help me find my way into his good graces. "Yes, I'm Luisa Banetti. My father is Antonio Banetti. He worked for Silvano for decades."

Recognition registers, but I don't feel any less scrutinized.

"If Zeno calls you family, then I do as well. Join me for dinner tomorrow night at seven, you and your friend. I own the penthouse upstairs. You can ring security from the elevator, and they will clear your arrival." This was not a request or an invitation.

"Yes, sir. We would be honored." I smile and tuck my chin to show the proper deference.

Christiano gives a tiny bow of his head. "I look forward to seeing you again. Enjoy your evening."

My legs almost give out after I close the door.

"Who the hell was that?" Grace hisses across the room.

Trouble. That was trouble.

I have no idea why Christiano would deign it necessary to

invite us to his home, but I had no way to refuse. I couldn't say no to one of the most powerful, dangerous men in the world. A man to whom my father swore an oath of allegiance.

"That was Christiano De Bellis, boss of the Giordano family, and he's invited us to his place for dinner tomorrow."

"Oh, shit," she breathes.

You said it.

CHAPTER 22

WE SPEND THE BULK OF FRIDAY HOPPING AROUND THE CITY looking at apartments. After our last stop, we swing by my storage facility. I need to extend my rental agreement and retrieve more of my clothes. There's not much else I need while living with my parents, and I don't own all that much, anyway. It's hard to accumulate things when you've been living in a five-hundred-square-foot studio with a roommate.

Grace helps me lug back the two boxes of clothes and shoes. When we finally stumble back to Zeno's apartment, we're exhausted.

"Let's leave the boxes by the door. I can deal with them later," I tell Grace.

"Oh, thank *God*." Her box crashes to the ground next to mine. "I have to go sit."

We both melt onto the sectional sofa like a pair of wilting flowers.

"Why is it that in summer, I can't wait for winter's cooler temps, but come January, I wonder why we don't all move to Florida?" Grace muses absently.

"Ain't that the truth."

"Hey, what are you wearing tonight for dinner?"

"Ugh, I have no idea. Probably a dress, assuming I can stop sweating. Otherwise, I may have to go in a swimsuit."

"At least you have your whole closet here. I should have shopped for a dress today."

"Please," I scoff. "What does it matter what he thinks of our clothes? I'm going out of respect, but I don't need to impress Christiano De Bellis." If he doesn't like what I wear, he doesn't have to invite me back.

Please, don't invite me back.

"That's easy for you to say. You look good in *everything*." She says it teasingly, but the statement is rooted in insecurity.

"Grace, you are stunning with all that dark hair and ivory skin. I don't know how you don't see it. Come on." I drag myself from the sofa. "Let's get showered. We'll feel so much better once we do our hair and makeup."

"I suppose scraping off these sweat-soaked clothes can't hurt. What an interesting evening we're going to have. At the very least, it'll be a great story for later."

I shoot her a thin smile but grimace on the inside. I can only hope our evening is so uneventful, outside of the company we'll share, that it is never, ever worth mentioning again. My father will ask me about it, but that's only because I called him this morning to tell him what had happened. I felt like he needed to know. Chances were slim that Christiano was going to toss me in the river, but still. Crazier things have happened. Dad assured me we'd be fine but insisted I text him after dinner.

I get myself ready relatively quickly, then help Grace with

her makeup to give her what she calls "a city look." I'm assuming that means a heavier application of shadow than usual. I'm pleased with how it turns out, and when she rounds the corner after putting on the clubbing outfit she'd tried to hide from me, she looks downright dangerous. She'd be better off not joining me tonight, but the selfish side of me demands her presence for moral support. Seeing her all decked out, I'm glad she has a reason to dress up.

"Holy shit, Grace! You look gorgeous. Why on *earth* wouldn't you want to wear that outfit?" Her black cropped pants are formfitting, showing off her curves to their fullest. Instead of hiding her hourglass figure with an oversized shirt, she wears a fitted sequin camisole in a rich forest green. With the littlest bit of confidence, she would be unstoppable.

"I don't know. I got it on a whim, not expecting to actually ever wear it."

"Well, my friend, you're wearing it tonight, and you're going to own it. You look fabulous."

Her makeup isn't so heavy that I can't detect the blush that creeps across her smiling cheeks. "Come on, let's get going before I change my mind."

I wipe my suddenly sweaty palms on the bed before I stand and straighten my own dress. I had to give it a little steam treatment in the bathroom while I did my hair because it was buried in one of the boxes we retrieved. It's gunmetal gray in a stretchy fabric that bunches from my waist down to where it stops at my knees. I debated about wearing it because of the top—it's sexy as hell. The fabric pulls diagonal across my chest, outlining my breasts and leaving my right arm bare. The left arm is covered in a three-quarters sleeve, and the overall look is edgy but classy. I'm hoping it will give me the confidence I need to survive the night.

Inside the elevator, I press the button labeled for the penthouse. A masculine voice crackles from the speaker.

"Yeah?"

"This is Luisa Banetti. Mr. De Bellis invited us for dinner tonight?" I can't help the uncertainty that transforms my statement into a question.

In response, the elevator lurches into motion. My wide gaze locks with Grace's as we rise to the top of the building. The doors open onto a luxurious landing area where a very large, very serious man in a suit with an earpiece studies us. He eventually extends a hand to direct us inside. I shoot him a tight smile and try to look like I belong when, in truth, I only want to avoid his eyes and scurry away.

Grace shadows each of my steps, staying strictly behind me as we take in the magnificence of the penthouse residence. Glossy marble floors and twenty-foot ceilings make the space bright and airy, if not a touch institutional. Where Zeno's apartment showcases an earthy, modern design, Christiano's place is ultra-contemporary. White on white with the occasional splash of black or red or silver. The simple palette enables the sweeping New York skyline to serve as the focal point, visible through enormous plate glass windows the full length of the main living area and curving around toward the kitchen, making the dining room appear suspended over the city.

"You must be Luisa. I'm Arianna De Bellis, but you're welcome to call me Ari." A beautiful young woman with black hair and striking blue eyes joins us from the kitchen. She extends a hand, and I'm struck by the memory of Nevio telling me that Zeno is expected to marry Christiano's daughter. The realization that this goddess is probably her chafes at my skin.

I brush the confusing emotion aside and smile. "Hey, Ari. It's lovely to meet you. This is my good friend, Grace."

"Grace," Ari says as if to test the word on her lips. "It's a pleasure to meet you." The two shake hands, and I'd almost swear something passes between them. Something about the sensual quirk of Ari's lips and the way Grace's cheeks blossom with color.

When Ari turns back to me without any sign of awkwardness or unease, I wonder if my imagination is acting up.

"Would either of you like a drink while we wait? My father is still back in his office."

"That sounds great. What would you suggest?"

"I was about to throw together a gin and tonic, but I can get you whatever you'd like. Maybe some wine? Dad will want a glass when he comes out."

"That sounds perfect." I smile and amble after her toward a minibar next to the kitchen, where an older woman is finishing the preparations for dinner. Ari doesn't introduce her, so I simply smile when our eyes meet, then peer back at the grand living area. "I'd tell you that your home is lovely, but words don't do it justice."

Ari smiles as she pulls out bottles from the cabinets. "Thanks. It's definitely something. A little much for me. None of this is really my style, but it suits Dad to a T." She's wearing a snug collared blouse that comes to a plunging V below her breasts and stylish pleated slacks with stilettos. Her sleek, glossy hair is slicked back into a long ponytail, and the smoky shadow she's wearing makes her eyes almost glow. Altogether, she's a warrior queen—her beauty only outdone by the strong sense of confidence she radiates.

"I don't know. I'd say you fit in just fine."

She lifts her eyes, peering at me from beneath a forest of

lashes. "Looks can be deceiving." She then pours a glass of wine, lifts it to her nose, and sniffs gently as she swirls the liquid, then casts her gaze at my silent friend. "I think you'll like this one, Grace. Not too dry and just sweet enough to tease your taste-buds." She hands the glass to Grace and waits to watch while my wide-eyed friend samples the selection. "What do you think?"

"It's excellent," Grace breathes. "Are you sure you don't want a glass?"

A devilish smile spreads on Ari's face. "Oh, no. I have to have something stronger if I'm going to tolerate my father all evening. He's not exactly the nurturing type." Ari winks to make light of her comment, but in reality, having Christiano for a father had to be difficult. If his austere exterior is any indication of what he's like behind closed doors, I doubt he played Uno with Ari or took her to the zoo as a kid.

"Don't say that," Grace hisses playfully, regaining a touch of her normal self. "I'm already nervous as hell."

"I believe he's more interested in this one." Ari nods in my direction. "So you shouldn't have anything to worry about."

"Why me?" I gape at her. "I can't even figure out why we're here."

Ari shrugs. "That's my father. He likes to keep people guessing. I was invited on short notice and only just told that you would be joining us, so I'm of no help."

"Well, it was a good excuse to get dressed up. I just hope I don't say the wrong thing, whatever that might be."

"You'll be fine." She hands me my glass. I'm grateful for the liquid courage, especially when footsteps hail the approach of our intimidating host.

I don't fully understand why he makes me so anxious. My father's been in the Mafia all my life, though I rarely witness that aspect of his world. But I've heard rumors. Whispers about the ruthless Giordano boss and his endless influence and power. The thought of pissing off a man like him is terrifying.

"Ladies, I'm glad you've had a chance to meet. How is the wine selection this evening?" Christiano is dressed in a dark navy suit, and though he's older, he's fit and handsome enough to be featured on an upscale cologne ad. I shouldn't have been surprised at Ari's good looks—she came from incredible genes.

"It's delicious," I offer.

"I happen to be particularly fond of acquiring a broad range of vintages. I've been told my collection is incomparable." He lifts the open bottle to examine the label. "Yes, this one is direct from Tuscany and not a bad year, though I prefer the Pinot Noir from that lot."

"I'm afraid I don't know much about wines besides whether I like one or not, but this one is excellent."

Christiano eyes me as he slowly pours himself a glass. "If you're not into wine, what do you enjoy, Miss Banetti?"

I get the sense his opinion of me hinges on how I answer the next series of questions. No pressure.

"I enjoy reading. I'm actually close to finishing up my degree in English literature at St. Joseph's."

"Is that so? I was under the impression you were living with your parents at Hardwick."

I sip from my glass to help dilute the bitterness of my next words. "I encountered a small hiccup recently and had to postpone my final year of classes."

He leans his hip against the counter and feigns a look of remorse. "That's too bad. It seems it's already taken you a while to get this far, so further delays have to be most unwelcome."

I'm not sure if he's implying I'm slow or old or both, but

it's undoubtedly an insult, no matter how I examine the statement.

"Life is about the journey, not the destination." I force a smile, and my eyes slice over to Ari, who has been surprisingly silent. I expected more engagement from someone so confident. Her suave nonchalance has been replaced with bristling irritation kept in tight check with restraint more hardened than tempered steel. When her eyes find mine, they are brimming with apology and frustration before falling to examine the glass of ice in her hand—the glass that had been full minutes before when her father joined us. If I were to guess, I'd say Ari's father is her Achilles' heel—the thorn beneath her armor.

The catlike grin Christiano flashes me makes me wonder if I've stepped into some invisible trap. As though he'd hoped I'd respond exactly as I had.

"A trite phrase used by the underprivileged to assuage their lack of accomplishment."

Oh, yeah. He's definitely putting me down. What the actual hell?

He's crafty. Calculating. If I didn't know better, I'd say he was hunting for opportunities to belittle me. But why? And if he acted like that around everyone, how had some hothead not killed him years ago? Ari may feel caged by her father, but I suffer no such afflictions.

"I suppose I'd rather be underprivileged and content than wealthy and unsatisfied."

The look on his face is smug, as though only he knows what a great fool I am, and I'm only too happy to let him think what he will. His opinion of me is totally irrelevant to my life.

A murmur of deep voices saves us like the proverbial bell as they echo in from the front entry. I glance at the dining table and realize that there are five place settings. I'd admired the artfully arranged settings when we entered, but I'd been too distracted to notice the number. I turn back to wonder at our fifth guest when not one but two men step into view, and one of them snares me in his piercing blue gaze. Zeno is *here*, and the shock paralyzes me. Did he know I would be here? If he did, why didn't he tell me he was coming? Is he upset that I'm having dinner at his boss's home?

I have no answers, and his austere façade gives no clues.

The man at his side is familiar. I recall Christiano introducing him at the funeral as his nephew, but I don't remember his name. He's handsome with a heavy shadow of hair on his face that accents his square jaw structure. Unlike Zeno, this man's posture is more relaxed. I get the sense he's easygoing—somewhat unusual in the Mafia world. My father fits that mold, but he hasn't had much to do with the business since his youth. I would expect someone vying for the under-boss position to be more fierce. More intimidating. Someone more like Zeno. But I guess if you're the boss's nephew, that changes things.

"Savio, I see you brought a guest." Christiano doesn't sound particularly thrilled with Zeno's arrival. Nor does he sound like he knew Zeno was coming. That would mean Savio was our fifth. So, why was Zeno here if he wasn't invited?

The new arrivals both approach and shake hands with their boss while Savio explains himself.

"I was telling Z that I had plans to join you for dinner, and he said he'd wrapped up his business early, so I invited him to join us. I hope that's not a problem."

Wrapped up his business early? Did that mean he planned to stay at his apartment? I try to focus on the conversation, but my thoughts are reeling.

"Of course, not," Christiano says dryly. "Let me introduce you to our other guests. Savio, this is Luisa Banetti and her friend Grace. I happened to learn of their stay at Zeno's place and invited them up. Zeno hadn't told me he had such lovely guests occupying his home." Christiano looks at Z with a challenge, making me increasingly uncomfortable. I don't know what I've stepped into the middle of, but something is definitely going on. Fortunately, he continues with the introductions. "Ladies, this is Savio Fiore, my nephew, and I assume you know Zeno, as you are all neighbors … of sorts."

We all smile and say hello.

"Luisa here was just telling us about her love of literature —something we could all probably use a little more of. With social media becoming so pervasive, the finer arts seem to be dwindling." Christiano's complimentary presentation of my interests surprise me when he'd been openly critical minutes before.

"Do you teach?" Savio asks, his gaze intent as though he's genuinely interested.

"No, I'm still finishing up my degree. I got a late start and have paid for school myself, so it's been a bit of a process."

"Dedicated *and* independent—very impressive." Savio turns his raised brows to his uncle. "I can understand why you'd lure her up here to enlighten our otherwise brutish dinner plans." He grins, glancing at Zeno, who isn't remotely entertained.

"She should be here in the city finishing that degree rather than working back at Hardwick. It makes me wonder what could possibly be problematic enough to interrupt her when she is so close to the finish line." Zeno stares at me as if he hadn't just spoken about me while I am standing in front of him.

My spine lengthens as I flash my most brilliant smile, trying not to falter when the sight makes him visibly flinch.

"I would have told you all about it if it hadn't been a personal matter." I hold my head high, but his behavior makes every cell inside me want to retreat.

"Well," Savio cuts in, tossing me a lifeline. "I have no doubt that someone as devoted to her passions as you are will follow through at the first opportunity." He smiles warmly at me then turns to Grace. "And your lovely friend, Grace, was it? You've been awfully neglected over here. Tell us about yourself."

Grace blanches momentarily before responding. "There's not a whole lot to tell. I'm in the process of moving to the city. That's actually why Luisa and I are here. To look at apartments for me."

"How exciting!" Savio is a natural conversationalist. He may not be intimidating, but he would make an excellent spokesperson. "I was born and raised in the city, so I can't imagine living anywhere else."

"When your livelihood depends upon the people you know," Christiano inserts, "you might find a more suburban home like mine a necessity." The older man turns to look at me for his next comment. "I have a home on the opposite side of the lake as Zeno. The networking in our area is incomparable." He turns back to his nephew. "One of these days, you'll embrace the notion."

"Only time will tell." Savio smiles, but his lips are stretched thin. "It looks as though dinner is ready. I don't know about everyone else, but I'm starved."

We all make our way to the table, Christiano in the host's seat at the end, Grace and Ari slip back to the far side, leaving me between Savio and Zeno. My stomach seizes so tightly that I have no idea how I'll eat a single bite. We distribute the food from elegant serving ware that the cook places on the table. Once our plates are full and we begin to eat, Savio resumes our conversation.

"How long are you ladies in town?"

"A couple of nights," I answer. "We'll head back to Hardwick on Sunday." I set down my fork as my eyes peer to the broodingly silent man on my other side. "If your business has finished early, we can stay somewhere else," I say softly, hoping to keep the discussion between us.

Savio kindly takes the hint and engages Ari in a discussion about her most recent trip abroad. I'm mildly curious about where she visited but more interested in Zeno's response. Every ounce of my attention is concentrated on him.

"That isn't necessary," he assures me quietly but brusquely. "I'd already made arrangements to stay with Savio. That's why I'd called him in the first place. When I heard you'd been invited to dinner, I knew I had to join."

"I hope you know that I never meant to intrude in your life. He showed up at the door, and—" I lean in to make sure I'm not overheard. "I didn't feel like I could refuse."

"I'm not upset, Luisa. At least, not about that."

Then what are you upset about? Why did you feel like you had to come here?

I peer over at him, and our gazes lock. The questions inherent in my stare collide with his impenetrable walls and clatter to the ground, unanswered.

He's the first to sever our connection. I turn my attention to the table conversation and try to look engaged despite the frustration gnawing away at my insides.

Dinner goes better than expected. We discuss a number of random subjects, primarily led by Savio. Ari even contributes to matters not instigated by her father. Where he is concerned, she is quiet—withdrawn, even. It amazes me that such a vibrant, strong woman could so visibly change herself to fit a mold imposed by someone else. I want to reach across the table and shake her shoulders, insisting that she not clip her own wings for his approval, but I know nothing about their situation. It would be presumptive to assume otherwise.

When our evening comes to a close, Christiano shocks me by insisting we come together again once he's back at his lakeside house. I smile and nod, thanking him for his hospitality and pray his invitation was mere politeness. One dinner with the Mafia boss was enough for me.

The second the elevator doors close, signaling the end of our night, Grace slumps back against the wall and opens her mouth to speak, but I quickly silence her with a finger to my lips and direct her gaze to the speaker system. I'm not sure if anyone would be listening, but better safe than sorry.

Once we are back at Zeno's apartment, I finally let down my guard. The release of my coiled muscles and piqued awareness makes me feel like a vine without its trellis, swaying in the wind.

"Holy shit, that was exhausting." I drop my purse on the console by the door and step out of my heels.

"It was something, that's for sure. I felt like I'd stepped onto the set of *Dallas*—rich people stirring up drama for no reason—none of it felt real. The intensity and passive dueling? Incredible."

I huff out a laugh. "Yeah, it was. If Savio hadn't been there to keep things flowing and upbeat, dinner would have been downright oppressive."

"He was definitely personable." Grace slips off her own shoes and dangles them from the fingers of her right hand. Her eyes wander to the entryway mirror, where she appears to assess her own reflection.

"You know who else was interesting? Ari." I watch Grace carefully for her reaction. "I wish we could have gotten to know her better without her dad there."

"Yeah," she says absently. "She sure was … unexpected."

With my eyes still glued to my friend, I join her at the mirror. "Call me crazy, but I could have sworn you two had a bit of a … connection."

Grace's eyes widen when they collide with mine. "What do you mean?"

"I mean, I could have been wrong, but I thought you two clicked. It wouldn't matter to me at all if you were interested in her … or other women, for that matter. She seemed really into you as far as I could tell. I was excited for you, but maybe that's not your thing." I shrug, trying not to put her on the spot.

She sucks her bottom lip between her teeth and moseys into the living area. "I hadn't thought about that kind of thing before … as you know, I don't have much relationship experience at all. I'm not sure what to think, but she is one of the most beautiful people I've ever met. And I felt this warmth in my chest when our eyes met." She turns apprehensively toward me, her trepidation constricting my heart. "Ari asked for my number before we left."

Unadulterated joy is a shot of adrenaline to my weary psyche. "Oh, Grace! That's so exciting! Did you give it to her?" Being involved with the De Bellis family isn't ideal, but nothing would make me happier than for Grace to find her place in this world.

She nods, an anxious smile teasing her lips. "I have no idea what I'm doing. She's so gorgeous and confident, and I'm so … so *me*. And she's a *woman*. If I was into that, I would have thought I'd known, but when she asked me, I just thought, I need to see her again. Is that crazy? Am I crazy?"

"Not at all, honey. You're perfectly normal, and I couldn't be happier for you." We meet halfway in a hug built on years of friendship and acceptance. "However, you absolutely *must* keep me posted on what happens, understood?" I pull back and cock an eyebrow at her.

She chokes on a laugh and reassures me that I'll be the first to know.

"Okay, I'm wiped out. If there's nothing else we need to discuss tonight, I'm going to bed." I need some time to decompress from my day.

"I'm right behind you. My feet haven't hurt this bad since we stood in line for that Taylor Swift concert back in high school."

"Oh, God. Don't remind me," I groan. "We spent all damn night out there."

"Yeah, but it was so worth it."

"Hell yeah, it was. Night, honey. I'll see you in the morning."

"Night, Isa."

When I fall back onto my bed, arms spread wide, my limbs no longer feel as leaden as they did upon exiting Christiano's penthouse apartment. I'm exhausted but encouraged. And when my mind drifts to Zeno and his anticipated bride, the irony draws a humorless chuckle from my belly.

Did any of the men present at dinner realize that Ari is into women? I hate to think her father would know and still want her to marry a man, let alone arrange a marriage for her. I begin to wonder where the notion of an expected engagement came from. Is there any truth to the rumor? Does it matter if there is?

I take in a lungful of the peace and quiet of my bedroom and exhale out tension and anxiety. I'm not up for a shower. Instead, I remove my makeup and change into my pajama top before crawling into bed. The cool sheets against my heated skin incite an army of goose bumps all over my body. I left the blinds raised, washing the room in a soft glow of light. My eyes trace the shadows. For endless minutes, I try to clear my thoughts by examining the way the light bends and shifts depending upon its destination. I try to keep my mind blank, yet every time my eyes linger on the blue accents in the room, I see Zeno's fathomless gaze staring back at me. The soft glow of light brightens the blue the same way his ocean eyes are multilayered with depth and dimension.

After nearly an hour of sleeplessness, I find myself wandering to the kitchen. My throat is scratchy and dry. I snag a bottle of water from the fridge and marvel at the refreshing chill of the liquid as it slides past my lips. Once my thirst is quenched, I start back toward my room but pause to peer at the hallway leading to Zeno's room. Anticipation ignites a firestorm of sparks in my nerves. I haven't consciously decided I'm going to his room, but my body seems to know the script before I do.

My feet move without instruction.

I pad softly in the dark, drifting to Zeno's bedroom as though I've been hypnotized. The draw is unrelenting. Pulling me. Coaxing with silent whispers I can't ignore.

When my feet step on the silky rug under his bed, tingles surge up from my toes and gather at the apex of my thighs. Looking to stem the sensation, I climb onto the bed, but once I'm close to Zeno's pillows, I become engulfed in his scent. Even the detergent can't totally eclipse the remnants of his expensive cologne—the spiced musk of a freshly showered man. One man. And every breath I take is too much, too intimate, too Zeno.

My eyelids flutter shut. I'm high on the smell of him, and it's terrifying, but I don't seem to care. The palm of my hand caresses the surface of the crisp comforter, and similar to my toes on the rug, sparks ignite in my veins. Images of Zeno acting out the words he's texted me flash in my head. It's all too easy to picture him here with me in his bed, his eyes turbulent and unstable as he moves above me.

I slowly roll back onto the pillows, breathing him in, feeding the fantasy. My hand drifts up to my breasts, and I pull on the aching peaks just as he'd instructed.

I've lost all sanity.

What I'm doing is wrong, but I don't care. I need it. I need a taste of *him*.

When my fingers first come in contact with my core, I'm shocked at the moisture already pooling at my entrance. Zeno stirs desires in me beyond comprehension. He doesn't even need to be present to wield his control over my body. My clit is so swollen that a few passes from my trembling fingers are all it takes to coax a moan past my lips. I'm almost there. The anticipation is a drug heightening my sensations, launching me headlong into a rapid-fire release. I speed up my rhythm, circling the pulsing bundle of nerves one direction, then the next, each change reigniting that initial burst of concentrated pleasure.

I can't stop myself, even if I want to, which I don't.

When I turn my face toward the pillow and breathe in his scent, an orgasm sweeps through my body like a tsunami razing the land. I am lifted on its sweeping current and left gasping for air, unable to comprehend anything but the sensations consuming my body.

When nature unleashes her most catastrophic forces, the devastation can't be tallied until the chaos has subsided and the smoke clears. My unraveling is no different. Only after my brain regains function do I realize the extent of my depravity.

The spindly fingers of guilt and shame claw at my body, ravaging me from the inside out.

I nearly fall off the bed in my haste to escape the truth, but when I glance back and see the evidence of my actions, there is no denying it. I masturbated to thoughts of Zeno in his bed, and now his comforter is stained with my arousal. My ultimate shame comes in the form of a wet spot two inches in diameter.

I have to cover my mouth with my clean hand to keep from vomiting.

Shitshitshit. What have I done? What do I do now?

Panic is quick on the heels of regret. There's no way I can get his king-sized comforter in a washing machine. Plus, the luxurious fabric is undoubtedly dry-clean only. I rush to the bathroom and wet a hand towel before attempting to spot clean the bed. After several minutes, a small dab of detergent, and three trips to re-wet the towel, my nerves begin to settle. Once the spot dries, no one will be able to tell anything has happened. And besides, I doubt he examines the comforter before yanking it down the bed each night.

This is going to be okay. You fucked up, but it's okay.

I deposit the used towel in a hamper containing other dirty towels and breathe a sigh of relief before fleeing the master suite. I crawl beneath the covers of my own bed and scrunch my eyes shut to hide from Zeno's blue gaze impaling me from the walls in my room. If he ever finds out what I've done ... I'll never overcome my embarrassment.

I'll never be more ashamed of anything I do in my life than I am of what I did in Zeno's bed.

God strike me down if I'm wrong.

CHAPTER 23

THE NEXT MORNING, I FEEL LIKE I'VE BEEN HIT BY A TRUCK AND am waking from a medicated coma at the hospital. I'm so groggy that I can barely keep my eyes open. I tried all night to sleep, but my mind was on overdrive, unable to quit thinking of Zeno and what I'd done.

Grace gets one look at me and insists I stay in bed. She assures me that she can manage without me for the morning when I argue, and in my weary state, I am no match for her. We come to an agreement that she'll swing by at lunch to grab me after I've had a chance to get a few more hours of rest. I scarf down a cold piece of pizza left over from our first night, then crawl back into bed, making sure to set the alarm with enough time to get cleaned up.

As soon as my head hits the pillow, my brain succumbs to sleep, and though I'm still tired when the alarm goes off, I'm more functional than before. I force myself into the shower, and by the time I throw on some mascara, I feel halfway human again. I'm not sure when exactly Grace will be back, so I decide to use my time checking in on Gia. I'll see her tomorrow back at home, but I haven't talked to her in a couple of days and need to hear for myself that she's doing better.

I curl up on the couch and dial her number.

"Hey, Isa," Gia answers warmly. "How's your weekend in the city going?"

"It's been good, I think. Everything was pretty standard until we ended up at Christiano De Bellis's penthouse last night for dinner. That was … interesting."

"Holy *crap*! How did that happen?"

I give her a rundown of the events, leaving out my unhinged sexcapades. That little bout of insanity never needs to be shared with another living soul. "Everything about being at Christiano's was wild. We got to meet his daughter, though, and she was pretty cool."

"That's insane. I would have faked malaria if that's what it took to get out of it. There's no way."

I chuckle, envisioning my demure sister going up against Christiano. "I'm just glad it's over. How has the rest of your stay been?" *Did you ever talk to Carter?*

"It's been good. Chiara and I did some shopping, and she convinced me to take her hair appointment yesterday, so I got a trim and some highlights." Gia isn't overly expressive on a regular day, but I can tell she's even more sedate than normal. She's trying to hide it, but I know her too well. She's utterly heartbroken.

"I can't wait to see it!" I pause and steel myself for my next question. "So, no news on the other front?"

"No, and before you fuss at me, I'm not going to force something if it's not meant to be." The sorrow in her voice sits like a boulder on my chest, but I don't want to contribute to her sadness, so I keep my response upbeat.

"No fussing necessary. I'm glad you've had a good visit and got away for a bit, but I'm ready to see you back at home."

"Same. Hey, if we're both going back tomorrow, we can travel together."

"Of course, we can! I don't know why I hadn't thought of it. Grace isn't here, but I'll let you know our plans once she gets back."

"Sounds perfect. What are you two doing today?"

"Grace is supposed to pick me up anytime now to join her and her agent to look at apartments. We've already short-listed a few good options."

"That's great! You'll have to tell me all about them on the way home tomorrow."

"Absolutely. All right, I'll let you go, but I'll be in touch."

"Love you."

"Love you, too, G." I end the call, our talk leaving me with a bittersweet taste in my mouth. Gia has always given more than she received, and all I want is for her to find the happiness she deserves. Melancholy threatens to sour my day, but a knock on the front door keeps me from dwelling too long on my sister's troubles. I leap from the sofa, realizing I never gave Grace the code for the front door. With a smile on my face, I fling open the door, then gasp.

"Zeno! What are you doing here?" I blurt the question without thinking, my brain scrambling to catch up with the unexpected change of circumstances.

Z leisurely steps forward, one prowling step at a time, forcing me to move aside and allow him in. "Last time I checked, this was *my* apartment." He's wearing a button-down with the sleeves rolled up, a silver watch on his wrist accenting the sloping girth of his muscular forearms. Even more distracting, though, is the primal intensity peering out from beneath his heavy brow.

"Of course, it's your place. I only meant I'm surprised you stopped by." I close the door, and when I cross through the space he just occupied, I'm overtaken by a cloud of his masculine scent—a not so gentle reminder of my shameful weakness the night before. My eyes drift shut for a second as panic threatens to overwhelm me.

Deep breath in, then out. I can do this.

Zeno's attention snags on my exaggerated smile, sensing my unease. "I didn't mean to interrupt, but I needed to grab something from my office here."

"No interruption at all. Grace isn't even here."

His eyes return to mine, inciting a raging storm of guilt and desire inside me. The two forces war with one another until I'm sure I won't survive the conflict. My twitching muscles beg me to walk away and escape his scrutiny.

"I'm sorry again about last night," I blurt once I'm in the living area where the air isn't so charged.

"I told you, it's not a problem."

I nod jerkily, and my gaze falls to my phone on the sofa, bringing Gia to mind. Thoughts of her naturally lead to Carter, and I suddenly wonder if Z might be of help sorting that situation. "Hey, have you run into Carter while you've been in town? I understand he's here as well." I'm curious what he might know about his friend's departure. The two seemed close—or as close as Z is with anyone—so Carter may have entrusted him with an explanation for his hasty exit.

"I haven't. We rarely see one another in the city."

"Oh. Well, did you talk to him before you left?"

Z strolls closer, and with each of his steps, the air in the room thins. "Why are you asking me about him?"

"No reason." I'm not comfortable sharing Gia's plight with anyone else. "I think it's great you guys were able to become friends over the years. Especially if you aren't close to your brother." Ugh, I wasn't meaning to pick a fight, but I'm nervous and saying things without thinking them through. "I mean that genuinely. It's good to have friends, even if they aren't family."

Good save, Isa. Not at all awkward. Jesus.

Hypnotic ocean eyes anchor me in place as Z moves closer. "Why are you acting like this?"

"Like what?" I paint on my most convincing expression of innocent confusion.

"Like *that*. You're acting … guilty. It's not like you." He continues to move, pacing a circle around me.

If I don't stop this now, my shame will come oozing out in a messy confession I won't ever be able to bleach from our memories. "I'm like this because of you," I explain with a touch of force because it's true, in part. He makes me crazy. "I never know how you're going to act. What you'll say or what you're thinking. The uncertainty makes it hard to know how to behave around you." My hands wave around as I speak, then fall to my sides in exasperation.

He takes one silent step toward me. Then two.

He's so close now that I have to crane my neck upward to hold his gaze. "Do I make you uncomfortable?" Deep, predatory, and unmistakably lustful, his voice caresses every inch of my skin.

I nod because it's true for a multitude of reasons.

"What if you did know me better?" He lifts his hand to trail his fingers along the edge of my jaw. "Would that help you feel more comfortable?"

My body sways into his touch. My breath trembles with each shallow pant of air my lungs squeeze past my lips.

"What is this, Z? Why are you saying these things?" *Please don't hurt me again.*

"Because I can't … because you aren't…" His lips clamp shut, and lightning flashes in his eyes. "*Fuck!*" The curse explodes in the air before he clamps his hand behind my neck and brings his lips crashing down on mine.

I gasp in shock, inhaling him before melting into his touch. His lips are warm and soft, contrasting harshly with the ferocity of his kiss. His touch devours me. Claims and covets me. And when our tongues tangle with one another, I know I've tasted heaven—spontaneous perfection sugarcoated with desire.

They say some drugs will sink their claws into a person after only one hit. One misstep, and lives are changed forever. An addiction so sudden that there is no going back. This is what I feel as I absorb Zeno into my bloodstream—an inescapable craving for him that will never be slaked by anything but its source.

His touch is demanding, laying siege to my doubts and worries. Commanding my surrender. To him. To this thing that lives and breathes between us. My body is only too ready to comply, flooding my core with blood until the pressure between my legs is unrelenting.

Zeno shifts his hand to fist long fingers in my hair, gently tugging to ease our lips apart. His eyes have gone so dark that they mimic the depths of the sea where it meets the fathomless sky at the midnight horizon. Black and blue and full of cosmic mysteries. Never in my life has anyone looked at me with such ardent concentration.

"Isa…" The word on his lips is so much more than a name. It's a benediction and a curse and turmoil, through and through.

My brows knit together in confusion, misty tendrils of loss

creeping up around me. He's still torn, and I have to know why. I have to know what it is that causes this chasm inside him. But before I can ask, knocking sounds at the door in a playful rhythm. Grace is home with epically bad timing.

My lips part to tell him I need to let her in, but I don't have to say a word. Zeno retreats in an instant, leaving me cold and disoriented. When the knock comes again, I shake away my haze and hurry to the door.

"Sorry about that," I say as Grace steps inside. Her smile falters when she spots Z a few steps behind me. "Hey, Zeno." She waves awkwardly.

"Grace," he murmurs with a nod. "I was just leaving. You two enjoy your afternoon." His gaze only grazes me briefly before he slips away into the hall and disappears into the elevator sitting empty after Grace's arrival.

Had he really come to retrieve something from his office? If he had, he left without it. And if not? Did that mean he'd come to see me?

I stand for long seconds with the door open, bemused over our exchange.

Grace steps forward and slips the knob from my grip, closing the door herself. "What did I miss?"

No matter where my eyes fall in search of answers, none appear. "I have no idea."

"You like him, don't you?" she asks gently.

"He's impossible. Aggravating and pompous. He treats people like crap—his brother and even his *mother* sometimes. I don't understand him at all."

"That would definitely explain it."

"What?"

She smiles softly. "Why you're so conflicted. There's nothing like wanting something we shouldn't to tear us apart inside."

"But that doesn't make any sense." My voice begins to fray at the edges as my emotions catch up with me. "Why would I want something so bad for me?"

She shrugs. "Why does chocolate taste so damn delicious? Nothing is ever so simple as good and bad, black and white."

My lip quivers as I nod. Grace scoops me into her arms, pulling me into a tight hug. "It's going to be okay, sweetie. You'll see. I don't know what's going on between you two, but you'll survive it. I promise."

I may survive, but I'm not sure I'll be okay.

Zeno has the power to devastate me, and every time I'm near him, that possibility becomes more and more certain.

Nevio: I'm looking forward to seeing you. 😊 When will you get back today?

I audibly groan when I read Nevio's text. I feel terrible that he's been treated like an outsider in his own home, but that's no excuse to lead him on. Even if my father hadn't warned me away from him, I can't erase the connection I have with his brother—not that I even know exactly what exists between us. Whatever it is, it's enough. Zeno's kiss has consumed me each waking hour since it happened. Compared to that, what Nevio and I shared couldn't even be called a kiss. But how the hell do I let him down gently after everything he's been through with his family? I would be adding salt to the wound in the most hurtful way possible.

I stare in the bathroom mirror, hair piled haphazardly on my head, and try to recognize the face peering back at me. It isn't an easy feat. This girl is hesitant. Troubled. She struggles to understand what is right, and that is not me. I am decisive and confident and protective of the people I care about. I treat people with respect so that I don't have to question my motives or regret my actions, yet that's exactly where I find myself, lost and unsure.

As though putting school on hold and moving back home wasn't enough, I'm now teetering on the edge of a full-scale identity crisis.

I take a deep breath and rub my eyes until I'm seconds from causing permanent damage, then pick up my phone and finally respond to Nevio's message.

Me: We'll be back by lunchtime.

I pray he won't text back because I don't know what else to say to him. Thankfully, my phone is silent while I make myself somewhat presentable. Grace is still finishing her shower when I poke my head in her room. I holler into the bathroom to tell her I'm grabbing us coffee. Before bed last night, we set up a plan with Gia to meet at the train station at ten, so I have plenty of time to get breakfast before we need to leave.

Stepping onto the elevator reminds me of our evening in the penthouse, which, in turn, reminds me of Zeno. Again. I can't seem to escape him. We haven't spoken since the kiss. He never texted, but neither did I. I'm walking on a tightrope that grows thinner with each step—hundreds of feet in the air with no net to catch me. If I continue forward with him, I will be risking everything.

My stomach climbs up into my throat, and it has nothing to do with the elevator's rapid descent.

By the time the doors open on the ground level, I'm so eager to get away from my thoughts that I rush out and collide with a solid body.

"Oh, God! I'm so sorry," I say in a rush, looking up to find Savio grinning down at me.

"No worries, unless you're late for something."

"Not at all! I was just lost in thought and being careless. How are you?"

We step aside and allow someone else into the elevator. Savio's attention is now fully directed at me.

"No idea. We'll see after I find out what my uncle wants." His lips thin as he slips his hands casually into his pockets. "He's called me over, but I have no idea what it's about."

"Working with family—it's a complicated combination." And one of the reasons I never considered staying at Hardwick.

"There's no escaping it for some of us, I'm afraid. Being a part of my family has its perks, but there are expectations as well."

Savio truly is a beautiful man. He's close to my age, putting him just under thirty. I'm surprised that he isn't married, considering his personality and good looks. It's an intriguing mystery I'd be interested in solving when I'm not so distracted by my own issues.

"At least you have friends who understand. I take it you and Zeno are close?"

"We are. He's a few years older, but we both started working about the same time and ended up doing the same crap jobs that every family man does starting out. We had to watch one another's backs, and that helps you form a certain bond. I've been giving him hell about moving to Hardwick, but I don't think he'll change his mind."

"You could always move out there as well. You'd be close to your friend *and* make your uncle happy." I arch a brow wryly, recalling that Christiano was already badgering Savio to make the move.

He rolls his eyes playfully. "Not you, too."

I shrug. "Hey, you could live in worse places."

"You're absolutely right. It really wouldn't be that bad,

and I guess the estate next to Z might come available soon. He was telling me a friend of his owns it and might be looking to sell."

Adrenaline sends a rush of tingles from my scalp all the way down to my fingers and toes. He's talking about Carter. I have to find out what he knows.

"I'm familiar with the family, though I don't know them well. Did Zeno say why they were leaving?" I try to look casual in my interest. Inside, I'm a jungle cat poised to tackle him for information.

"Relationship trouble of some sort. Isn't that always the case? Guess the guy was seeing some girl who Z thought would be trouble. He implied she was a housekeeper in the area. Z has a lot of respect for the guy and convinced him to put an end to it. Not sure I would stick my nose in someone else's relationship, but that's Zeno. He's the most loyal man I've ever met. He'll always speak up if he thinks a friend is making a mistake. He'd rather piss someone off than stay quiet in order to protect the people he cares about." Savio carries on without any clue that he has shocked me to my core.

I sway where I stand, ready to topple over with the slightest breeze.

I am stunned. Appalled. And as I struggle to regroup, a distant rumble of thunder reverberating off the insides of my skull signals the approach of an apocalyptic storm.

"Zeno advised his friend to leave town?" I ask calmly.

"I believe so, though he didn't go into detail. I just know the place might be available, and if I was going to placate my uncle, that would at least put me next door to a friend." Savio glances down at his watch. "Speaking of my uncle, I shouldn't keep him waiting."

"Of course. You should head up," I say quickly. "I'm so

glad we ran into each other, though. Hopefully, I'll see you around again."

"I'm certain you will." Savio's gaze lingers.

I cannot deal with any more drama, and especially no more men, so I wave awkwardly and bolt into the lobby. I have to get away before the angry tears set in.

It was never Cora that separated Carter and Gia.

Zeno was the only one to blame.

He'd thought my sister wasn't good enough for his friend. Thought she'd be *trouble*, whatever the fuck that means, and had convinced Carter to walk away. From the beginning, I wasn't pleased that Carter would allow anyone to have sway over his relationships. This new information changes little in regard to him. But Zeno. How could I ever look at him the same way? He'd ripped out Gia's heart and shredded it. And for what? Because she wasn't *good* enough? She may not have money, but there is no better, more deserving soul on this planet than my older sister.

Yesterday, I was kissing the man who had crushed Gia's spirit.

I feel sick.

Disgusted.

How could I have ever thought someone who had pushed me away and alienated his brother could ever be truly decent? That he would ever think of anyone but himself and his own ambitions?

Tears mark my cheeks like war paint as I storm down the sidewalk. I don't see where I'm going. I just walk. Once around the block. Twice. I have to do something to settle the rage blistering under my skin, or Gia will know something is wrong when I see her.

I want to scream until my throat bleeds.

I want to burn something to the ground and dance in the embers.

I am the embodiment of righteous fury, and I will not be satisfied until justice is served. But there is nothing I can do right now. Zeno's transgression deserves more than an angry text or phone call. This kind of grievance must be addressed in person, and I will do so the minute I am able. In the meantime, I have to pretend Athena, Goddess of War, hasn't taken up residence in my veins.

By my third trip around the block, I've managed to contain my tears and reroute myself to the coffee shop as I'd originally intended. I order an iced coffee and a bagel for Grace. I'm not hungry for anything but blood.

GIA IS SILENT NEARLY THE ENTIRE RIDE HOME. I DON'T PUSH FOR conversation because pretending to be happy takes too much energy when all my focus is tied up in anger.

We drop off Grace first and pass by the Bishops' house in the process. I glare at the estate with such sharp intensity that I'm surprised the car window doesn't shatter. I only pause my visual assault long enough to note that Gia keeps her eyes strictly glued to her hands folded in her lap, avoiding the house at all costs.

It shouldn't be that way.

If Zeno had minded his own damn business, Gia would still be looking at the Bishops' home like heaven itself. I resolve to do everything in my power to make that true again.

Once we're home, Gia and I pick and choose pieces of our trips to share with our family—the lighter moments that aren't so personal. She leaves out her run-in with Cora, and I don't say a word about Zeno. We paint a pretty picture enough to satisfy their curiosity, then retreat to our room, where we unpack in silence. Nevio texts, asking to get together, but I'm in no mood for company. However, I also don't want to turn him down, so I simply leave his message unanswered.

I spend the afternoon stuck in my head, replaying pretend scenarios where I tell Zeno what I think of him. I want the conversation to take place in person, but I don't have any idea when he'll return to Hardwick. The wait might kill me.

I can't think of anything else, and every distraction I attempt falls painfully short of its purpose. When the sun finally concedes the sky to the cloak of darkness, I escape outside to sit on the back porch.

The approach of night is soothing.

Its obscurity and gloom reflect my mental state. An ocean of negativity—I'm weighed down by the sticky substance until even a smile is a laborious endeavor. And the worst part of it all is the disappointment. I'd carved out a place in my heart for hope. Despite my own warnings, I'd clung to hope that Zeno could be the man I'd imagined in my head. I'd started to fall for his potential, blinding myself to the harshness of reality. Conceit. Selfishness. Cruelty.

When a footfall crunches in the grass near the trees, my bleak mood prevents me from startling. Instead, my gaze cuts toward the sound, and I calmly watch a male figure emerge from the shadows. Both Nevio and Zeno are of a similar build, but their energies are too different to ever confuse them.

This determined march can only be Zeno.

I've wished dozens of times over today that he were here so that I could yell at him and get it over with, but now that the time's come, emotion clogs my throat. My sinuses burn, and my chin quivers as I stand and begin to walk toward him.

"I wasn't expecting you to be out," he says in quiet greeting.

"I'm sorry to disappoint."

He shakes his head. "No, that's not what I meant. Not at all. I'm actually relieved because I need to talk to you."

"I need to talk to you, too." Relief washes over me that we are doing this in the dark because I can sense a scalding flush rising in my cheeks. Night will provide the veil that I need to keep my emotions from him. The last thing I want is for him to see how deeply he's wounded me.

"Just let me say what I need to say before it eats me alive," he commands softly. "I thought keeping you away would diminish my desire for you, but having you here has made me realize that I'm only fooling myself. It's so obvious every time I'm near you, yet I fight it. The pull. My desire. It's always been you for me—always will be—no matter how hard that is for me to accept. No matter the disrespect to my father or the disgrace I will earn among the family, I can't deny that you are the only woman I could ever want at my side. You are worth whatever the struggle. Your strength and loyalty. Your beauty and grace. There is no other woman for me, and the thought of losing you to someone else sends me into a violent rage. I want so much more than a stolen kiss or a heated exchange of words. I want *you*—your body. Your soul. And I want the world to know you're mine. I know you feel that connection between us. I just need to hear you say the words. Tell me … tell me you'll be mine." His voice is almost unrecognizable with emotion—cracked and raw. He has laid himself bare, thinking he has done me an honor, but instead, he has only stoked the flames of my anger to towering heights.

"I had no idea the hardships you've had to overcome. How insensitive of me not to realize that desire for me could cause you such agony. What will people think if you attach yourself to such a pariah?" It takes all my will not to spit the words in his face.

"Pariah? What the hell are you talking about?"

"You're the one who just told me you want me despite the myriad of reasons you shouldn't—none of which even touched on the fact that you're expected to marry another woman. That might at least have been something I could understand, but a disrespect to your father? A disgrace to the family? I'm surprised you'll risk being seen with me even in the darkness of night. Every word you said was a back-handed compliment inflicted with the same double-edged sword you use for all our encounters. And if your approach wasn't insulting enough to keep me at bay, there's always the fact that you shattered my sister's heart. I *know* you were the one who drove Gia and Carter apart, so don't try to deny it. And for what? Because she's a measly housekeeper? Because she's not rich enough for your wealthy friend?" Angry tears well in my eyes.

Zeno's spine has gone as rigid as the trees around us. "I have no reason to deny that I interfered. I explained my perspective to him about the complications of such a relation-ship. He decided my concerns had merit and opted to get away to the city before anyone could be further injured."

"How very *thoughtful* of you," I say with saccharine sweetness. "I suppose a similar kindness was your motiva-tion for alienating your poor brother from his family? For asking him not to come to his own father's funeral? Who exactly were you helping in that situation besides yourself? Because I fail to understand how exiling him could possibly benefit anyone else."

The air around him shivers with an arctic plunge in temperature. "How is it everything always comes back to Nevio? Still to this day, his influence is a plague I cannot eradicate."

"Listen to you! That's your *brother*!" I hiss. "You made a pledge to honor family above all else as a Giordano and a De Bellis, yet you break that vow *every single day*. You treat your brother like shit out of petty jealousy. You're not loyal; you're arrogant and pathetic."

"Please, don't hold back on my account." His voice is devoid of emotion, so much so that a chill shivers down my spine. "I have tried my best to be honest with you. I would think you might respect that honesty rather than lash out in injury, but clearly, I was wrong. Everything about this was a mistake."

There is a knife in my belly, and his words twist it even deeper. "Your indifference to the harm you cause others is the source of my anger, not some poorly scripted confession of your feelings. You have been rude to me since the day you threw me out of your house. You've pushed away your brother and ruined my sister's chances for happiness. You couldn't flatter me enough to convince me to be with you. Not after everything you've done." My venomous blow strikes its target with perfect accuracy.

Zeno raises his chin, his eyes now too shadowed for me to see. "In that case, I won't insult you with my presence a second longer." He whips around and marches back toward Hardwick, the darkness quickly enveloping him into its folds.

CHAPTER 25

My eyes drain themselves dry of tears in the night, one drop of sorrow at a time melting into the welcoming embrace of my pillow. I don't make a sound. There is no evidence of my turmoil, save for the remnants of salt collected among the cotton fibers of my sheets. I lie awake most of the night. Perfectly still. Irrevocably shattered.

I still struggle to accept the degree of Zeno's callousness. It's hard to believe what he did, but he admitted it, and I hate him for it. But I also hate myself for what I said. I shouldn't. Though he deserved every word, his pain had been palpable, and no matter how justified I was, hurting him hurt me too. Every verbal blow unleashed by either of us was another slash by an invisible dagger, slicing through our insides until there were too many wounds to bandage. All I can do is let the bleeding ebb and hope that I am strong enough to build myself back up.

The anger that had shot me full of adrenaline has abandoned me. I can't summon its infallible strength to lift myself out of this abyss of despair. I wish it would return because anger is so much easier than what comes after. But there is no escaping my current situation.

Words cannot be unsaid.

Deeds cannot be undone.

Assuming I still have a job, I must get up and go to work. I've already taken off two days more than I should have. I must keep going.

A scalding shower unlocks my muscles, tight from a night of clenching. It also helps relieve some of the puffiness under my eyes. By the time I'm ready to head to the main house, my heartbreak is sufficiently camouflaged to prevent a barrage of questions from my family.

I get started working in the kitchen at Hardwick, mechanically moving through the motions of my duties, hardly aware of the world around me. Elena has to call my name twice before her voice breaks through the haze.

"What? I'm sorry, I was lost in my head."

She smiles, but her emerald eyes are riddled with sadness. "Zeno wanted me to give this to you." She hands me a sealed envelope. On the front is my name penned in his writing. "I'm not sure what's going on between you two, but I hate to see you at odds."

"Thank you," I say, unable to form any other words. Emotions rise up and obliterate the numbness, clogging my throat.

She nods gravely and leaves me alone to read his letter. Cecelia is nearby, and I don't want an audience, so I slip around the corner to the formal dining room. My fingers tremble as I tear through the envelope's seal. I sink into a chair when my legs threaten to give out. His edgy script summons a new swell of tears without having to read a word. There are several pages, and I have to wonder why he didn't call or email or text. Paper and pen feel so official. So final.

I close my eyes and take a shaky breath before absorbing his words.

DEAR LUISA,

I've spent hours thinking through what happened last night and have decided a number of explanations are in order. The things I'm about to tell you are things I never thought to tell another living soul, and I trust that you will respect the confidentiality of the matter.

I want to address your sister first. I know how important her happiness is to you. It may be hard to understand, but I was trying to look out for her as well as Carter when I raised my concerns. My parents did not have the happy marriage others may have thought. Mom was eleven years younger than my dad, and I always got the sense that the age difference was a wedge between them. When Carter began to show interest in Gia, I grew concerned that two people in such different phases of life could never truly relate to one another. I expressed that view to Carter. It was my understanding there was nothing formal between them, so I didn't think there was attachment enough to cause injury. I never urged him to leave or said any slight against your sister. I've never known her to be anything but kind and honorable. If she's been hurt because of my actions, then I am sorry. It wasn't my intent.

As for the implication that I am in some way bound to marry someone else, it is purely a case of wishful thinking on the part of my boss. He would like to see his family positioned to continue rule of the Giordano organization. I have never consented to any arrangement, nor will I. I have dedicated my life to the family, but I'm only willing to give so much of myself.

That leaves us with the issue of my brother. We have had a strained relationship for many years. First, I assure you that I never attempted to keep him from our father's funeral. In fact, I was upset that he didn't arrive sooner when I first told him about Dad's passing. He originally told me he wasn't coming at all, so when he changed his mind, I'd already promised his room to guests. I asked him to stay at a hotel. He refused.

The reasons for our disdain of one another are complicated. Primarily, it's a product of the same type of behavior that he has exhibited in leading you to believe I kept him away when that wasn't the truth. He is a master of manipulation, and I have no room for that in my life.

I will own that some of the strain between us is my fault. It is the same reason I have struggled with my feelings for you and why I have steadfastly attempted to keep you and Nevio apart through the years. Jealousy may have been a factor, but the main reason is that Nevio is your half brother.

I STOP READING, my eyes staring unseeing at the paper as his last words roll around and around in my head. They are awkward and unfamiliar.

Half brother.

Nevio my brother? Why would Zeno say such a thing?

I can't make sense of his statement, so I force myself to continue reading.

WHEN I WAS FOURTEEN, I accidentally saw my mother kissing your father. I felt horrifically betrayed, but I never said a word out of fear for what my father might do. I watched them through the years. Saw the stolen glances between them and the many ways they found to be together. I was angry with my mother, but as a child, it was easiest to blame your father. I hated him with a passion. In my eyes, he lured my mother away. Of course, now, I understand that these things aren't so simple. As I mentioned above, my parents' ages and different focuses in life were more to blame than anything. But it's still hard for me to look at your father and not think of all those years of turmoil. And when you smile, it's his dimples I see. I could never imagine despising and adoring something at the same time, but that's what I felt every time you smiled at me. When I looked at you, I saw the man who had torn my family apart. Especially when you smile and those dimples come out. The same dimple Nevio wears.

After learning about my mother's affair, I began to wonder about Nevio. We are so drastically different in looks and personality—something entirely possible, even with the same parents, but taking the affair into consideration, I started to wonder. The Christmas before I graduated and moved out, I decided to learn the truth. I discreetly collected DNA samples from your father and my brother. Even though I had anticipated the results correctly, I was still gutted when they confirmed that Nevio was Antonio's son. And if that wasn't hard enough to deal with, I watched you two that week. I saw the way Nevio stared at you and listened to him talk about you when you weren't around. He was falling for you.

I was faced with a horrific choice. I could spill my family's secret and cause irreparable damage to my parents' lives, or I could find a way to keep you and Nevio apart. If you two couldn't be together anyway, that seemed the less destructive option. It meant sending him away and keeping you at arm's length, which wasn't overly difficult when I was already struggling with my anger toward you.

My plan fell into place two months later when I found reason enough to convince my parents to send Nevio to boarding school. It may appear harsh in your eyes, but I stand by my decision. I did the best I could in the circumstances I was given. My father didn't deserve to be disgraced, and despite what Mom had done, I didn't want to hurt her either by telling the world what she'd done. As for Nevio, he needed that time away more than you could know.

Years later, I found myself continuing to push you away even after I'd matured beyond my anger for fear that Nevio, who was then an adult living his own life, might reconnect with you should you cross paths at Hardwick. None of it was fair to you, but I knew of no other way. I felt compelled to keep my family's secret, and though my father has now passed, I feel it's more important than ever to protect his honor when he isn't here to do it himself.

I've never put my family at risk as I've done by giving you this information. All I ask is that you respect my need for secrecy. In fact, I'd prefer if you burned this letter as soon as possible. It pained me to even put the words on paper, but you needed to hear the truth.

I needed you to know the truth.

I have spent a lifetime keeping secrets and covering for people, but I'm glad to share this with you, even if only for your own protection. None of this absolves me of the wrongs I've committed, but I hope it helps you understand. My treatment of you has been unforgivable, and for that, I will forever be sorry.

You will be happy to hear that I've left for the city. I understand that you, for undisclosed reasons, are in need of your job at Hardwick. I won't deprive you of that or make you endure my presence against your will.

I wish you the best.

Z

MY FATHER AND ELENA. An affair.

How had I never noticed? I scour my memory to examine their interactions, but I've never paid close attention to recall enough detail. Nevio does have a single dimple, where Dad and I have a matching set, but that's hardly proof of anything. Loads of people have dimples. I envision the two men, and it's their matching sad, brown eyes that make me want to kick myself. They aren't exactly the same, but it's enough that I can't deny the similarity. Not when examined under the light of this new information.

Nevio is my half brother.

And I kissed him.

I drop the letter and slap my hand over my mouth when my stomach threatens to revolt. Beads of sweat dot my forehead, and I can't get enough air. I rush to the closest bathroom and brace my hands on the counter over the sink. Slowing my breathing, I coerce my stomach to settle, then splash water on my face.

When I stare at my reflection, I wonder if I know anything at all. Twenty-four hours ago, I'd looked in a mirror and thought myself unrecognizable, but now, the entire world is foreign and strange.

Nevio is my half brother.

Does my father know? He must. Is that why he urged me to stay away from Nevio? I don't know of any other reason to explain his warning. And I would imagine Elena knows, but does she know that Zeno figured out her secret? What about Nevio himself? He has no idea that he's the product of an affair. Z may have been trying to protect his parents, but his actions caused Nevio to feel alienated from his own family. If he'd been told the truth, Nevio never would have needed to be sent away—something that pains him to this day. And for what? So that people wouldn't whisper that Silvano's marriage was a sham? No matter how I look at it, I can't condone how Zeno handled the matter. But if this revelation has taught me one thing at all, it's that I shouldn't presume to know anything. He was doing what he thought was best. Protecting his family.

My family.

Nevio is my half brother.

I recall all the wretched things I said to Z, and a sob claws its way up my throat, shattering the quiet. I have to go. I have to leave this place and everything it represents. I have to get away from all the heartache and secrets and shame before they drown out all the light in the world.

I rush from the bathroom, grabbing the letter before I go, and race to the closest exit. I don't tell my mother or Cecelia that I'm leaving. I just run. Down toward the lake to the water's edge. I run along the rocky shore until my lungs scream and my legs quiver in protest, and then I run some more.

I don't relent from my punishing pace until I step awkwardly on a rock, and a searing pain shoots up my ankle. Stumbling to the ground, I collapse in a sweaty heap, my heart thundering in my ears and my breaths wheezing from the effort.

As I suspected, the second I stop, my sobs catch up with me. Howling, inhuman cries echo off the water's surface. I have so many reasons to cry that I'm not even sure what cause or which emotion has me the most upset. Perhaps it's the powerlessness of it all that gets me the most. One thing after another, life continues to prove to me how little control I have over anything. How little I know about anything.

And in yet one more display of my sheer helplessness, life throws me one more curveball. With the snap of a twig, I discover that I'm not alone. No matter how fast or far I run, I can never escape the truth.

Nevio is my half brother.

"Isa." The single gasping utterance possesses a world of worry and fear. The same as his sad brown eyes.

Nevio has chased me down, and I have no idea what to say.

PART TWO

To Rah Rah:
There's no one I'd rather tease, argue, or debate with because every word between us is spoken from a place of love.
Romance can be fleeting, but soul sisters are forever.

CHAPTER 1

"WHAT THE HELL HAPPENED?" NEVIO ASKS BETWEEN HEAVING breaths. "I thought I'd catch up and see why you were running off, but you were like a thing possessed."

You should have let me run.

I want to scream at him. Take out all my frustrations and anger on him for imposing on my moment of crisis. He would be an easy target. The man who has no idea he's my brother.

None of this is his fault.

It's true. He doesn't deserve my wrath. He was only trying to help by coming after me, and lashing out would only make me feel worse.

I close my eyes and inhale a slow, long breath, keeping my jaw wired shut.

Nevio bends at the waist and leans his hands on his knees to steady his breathing. "My first thought was that my brother said something to upset you, but then I remembered he left for the city early this morning. Was it your mom? You gotta tell me what happened, Isa. I can tell you're upset."

His instinct is accurate, but not in the way he might imagine. Zeno wasn't heartless or condescending.

He told me the truth for once.

A truth that's even harder to swallow than the years of muttered slights. So hard that I felt no choice but to run from that truth. Literally. I raced from Hardwick with no destination in mind and now find myself exhausted with a twisted ankle, collapsed into a hopeless heap on the shore of Tuxedo Lake. I would happily wallow in pain if I were alone, but that's not the case. Nevio chased me down, and I had to give him some semblance of an explanation.

I study the man standing fifteen feet away and try to wrap my brain around the knowledge that he is my brother. My half brother. I think of our kiss and the handful of daydreams I'd entertained when I'd considered having a relationship with him—a sexual relationship—and my stomach convulses violently. This time, I can't keep it held in. I lean to the side and throw up my breakfast. Thankfully, I didn't eat much, but it's all there.

Nevio starts to rush over. I frantically wave him off, desperate for him to stay away. Having him close will just make the nausea worse. There'd been no way for me to know that Nevio was my half brother, but it doesn't lessen my disgust when I consider where things might have gone between us. It's too grotesque to consider. I shut those thoughts securely into a concrete vault where they can never see the light of day again.

"I'm fine. I'm fine." I wipe at my mouth with the back of my hand. "Guess I ran a little too much right after eating."

He takes one more step closer. I keep my eyes locked on

his feet, avoiding his questioning gaze and the sight of my father's sad eyes.

"Isa, you're scaring me here. What the hell is going on?"

Tears stream from my eyes like rain down a windshield. I can't fathom where it's all coming from, but there's no end in sight.

Nevio's kindness and distress make it all so much harder because, on top of everything else, a part of me grieves for the loss of a brother I never knew I had. So many years down the drain when we could have been such close friends. Had we known, we would never have lost touch. I feel it with a certainty deep in my bones. That unique bond formed between siblings would have kept us close, but that opportunity was robbed from us. Not only did we miss out on years of connection, but I may never know Nevio as a brother. Zeno confessed the truth in his letter, but he also begged me to keep Nevio's paternity a secret.

Can I honor such a burdensome request?

I'm not the only person to consider when trying to answer that question. No matter how aggrieved I may feel, my injuries are fractional compared to Nevio's. He is the most obvious victim of this charade between our families, and he has no idea. I firmly believe he deserves to know the truth. But who am I to divulge such a secret? I can disagree all I want with Elena's choice to keep her affair a secret, but that doesn't give me the right to come between mother and son. I certainly shouldn't go off half-cocked in a fit of my own raging emotions and rip his world to shreds. This is not the time or place. I have to keep my mouth shut, no matter what it costs me, at least for now.

"It was my mom," I blurt. "You know how she gets under my skin. And it's even worse now that I'm older."

"Whatever she did must have been pretty bad, considering we're halfway around the lake and your tears are still falling." He's not sure he believes me, and his suspicion is reasonable. I've never been an emotional person, so I can only imagine how shocked he must have been to see me bolt for the trees.

I have to find a way to explain away my actions. If I don't, he'll become suspicious.

While I hadn't wanted anyone outside our family to know about my mother's gambling problem, telling Nevio was my best way out of this situation. It's the one thing I can give him that could genuinely justify my outburst of emotion, so I take a deep breath and surrender a secret of my own.

"I decided to stay with my parents instead of going back to the city and finishing school because I discovered that my mother got into financial trouble. She has developed a problem with gambling that I wasn't aware of until I came home. I didn't tell you or anyone else because the bookie she owed was a Giordano family bookie, and I was worried my father's name would be smeared by her actions. I paid off her debt, and it's all over now, but putting my life on hold to rebuild my college savings has been hard on me. I was almost done with school, and now I won't be able to finish for another year. I lost the new apartment I was going to move into and had to quit my job so I could stay with my parents and save. It's been a difficult couple of weeks. Mom said something insensitive this morning, and it set me off. All the emotions hit me at once, and I had to get out of there. And with my shit luck, I twisted my ankle right before you caught up with me." I rub at the offending appendage, which has begun to swell, though the pain has eased to a dull throb. "That's why I was so upset."

"Shit, Isa." He hurries over to inspect the injury. "You should have told me about your mom. I could have helped."

I breathe deeply with relief at successfully dodging further interrogation but stiffen at his nearness. "I didn't need help."

"Maybe, but there's also no reason for you to deal with something like that alone. You know I'd keep a secret for you. Hell, there's plenty I don't tell my family." He gingerly lifts my ankle and rolls the joint in a small circle. "It's definitely sprained, but I don't think anything's broken."

"Yeah, it's already starting to feel better."

Nevio peers back in the direction we came with a frown. "That may be, but there's no way you're walking all the way home on it." Nodding to himself, he slips an arm beneath my knees and tries to scoop me up in a bridal carry, but I screech and flail.

"What the hell are you doing?" My response is a gross overreaction, but it can't be helped. I'm petrified of him thinking there's something between us or doing anything that he might interpret as encouragement.

He releases me to my feet and gapes at me as though I've gone batshit crazy. "I *was* going to carry you to the road, but I suppose you can walk in pain if you'd prefer that to being near me."

"No! It's not that. I just..." *God*, how do I explain this? "You just surprised me." I hold out my arm to urge him closer. "If you'll let me lean on you, that should be plenty of support."

Doubt twists his lips, but he returns to my side. "I figured someone could bring a car around to pick us up from there."

I nod and slide my left hand around to cup his shoulder from behind, using his solid mass as a crutch. His right arm supports me from behind, keeping me pressed against his side. We take a few steps to test our system, and I minimize my hobbling so that he doesn't insist on carrying me.

"My mom could probably come pick us up," he offers while we ease over the uneven terrain. "But if you'd rather try to get ahold of someone from your house, we can do that instead."

"No, your mom would be great if she's available." I need to be alone to process everything, and that'll never happen if my family gets wind of my panicked flight. The questions would be endless.

We make it to the road in less time than I expect. I suppose I'm owed at least one shred of good fortune in the midst of my nuclear meltdown of a life.

Elena brings the car around and studies me with curious eyes but doesn't pry for answers. She drives me to my parents' cottage and agrees to tell my mom that I went home with a headache. They will be far less curious about me going home sick than if they knew I'd twisted my ankle after freaking out and sprinting down to the lake. Yet again, Elena is my saving grace. A beacon of kindness and understanding piercing the darkness. I may not agree with her choices in life, but I find it hard to fault her. Each of her thoughts and deeds is motivated by the purest of intentions.

I offer her a genuine thanks before allowing Nevio to help me to the cottage door.

"You need me to get you set up inside? I can put together an ice pack and grab you some ibuprofen."

I smile and make sure to leave a buffer of space between us. "Thank you, Nev, but I'm really okay."

He lifts his chin and peers down at me skeptically. "If you say so. Make sure to rest, and we can talk more about your mom later. Don't think I'm letting that slide." He leans in before I can stop him and drops a kiss on my forehead. "Text me if you need anything."

The touch of his lips on my skin is like a scarlet letter

condemning me. A brother's kiss isn't necessarily inappropriate, but in this instance, anything at all between us is too much because he doesn't know. He doesn't intend his touch in a brotherly fashion, and it makes my skin crawl.

He glides down the front steps without a clue.

My eyes seek out Elena, who watches us from the car. Her face is inscrutable, keeping me in the dark about what she might think of Nevio's affection toward me.

Does it bother her to see us together? Would she consider telling Nevio about her affair in light of his renewed interest in me? Or will she concoct another reason to send him away and maintain the masquerade she's constructed? I have no answers, but one thing is certain. I absolutely must shut down his advances immediately. It's crucial that he have no lingering hope about anything forming between us.

If he simply knew the truth, everything would be so much easier, but Zeno was clear on that point. If I break his trust and share a secret he's guarded for half his life, I'll risk losing him forever. I'm not sure he'd ever forgive me. Twenty-four hours earlier, that might not have bothered me. But now? Everything has changed.

ONCE I'M ALONE INSIDE, I grab a bag of frozen broccoli from the freezer because I don't have the mental or physical energy for a baggie and ice. The running wore me out, but it's the emotional exhaustion that leaves me bone-weary. Each step up to my bedroom requires a pep talk and burst of energy that I can only summon with a sheer force of will. A desperation to hide myself away.

After closing the bedroom door behind me, I crawl onto the bed and prop myself against the pillows Gia has artfully arranged against the headboard. She makes the bed each morning like clockwork. Mom never required us to make our beds, so I'm not sure why Gia does it. Routine? A sense of order? Whatever the reason, the bed is made, and I don't feel like undoing it. I toss the bag of broccoli over my ankle and allow my body to sink into the blue and white quilted bedding.

I wish my thoughts were so easily subdued.

My eyes lose focus as I stare out the window and think of my father. The man I've idolized my entire life has been the measuring stick I compare all others to. I've only recently learned how loveless my parents' marriage has been, and now I have to adjust my image of him again to include the taint of infidelity.

I'm old enough to understand that no one is perfect, but this is my daddy. The pedestal I've crafted for him is exceptionally tall. Leaving Mom would have been one thing, but cheating on her is another. I wouldn't wish that on anyone. Nevio and I are not even six months apart in age. No matter how things went down, that fact doesn't paint my father in a flattering light. Mom may make me crazy, but even she doesn't deserve that kind of betrayal.

And what does the affair say about sweet Elena? She had to have known my mother was pregnant with me when she was intimate with my father. Did that bother her? What did her infidelity say about her own marriage? I don't know how to reconcile what I've learned with what I thought to be true.

No matter how much we think we know people, the truth is, we see what they want us to see.

There will always be parts of ourselves we keep hidden from everyone. The darkest parts that we hope will never see the light of day. But all it takes is the smallest deviation from routine to pull open the curtains and shine a glaring spotlight on our transgressions. That's what happened the day Zeno went to look for his old Game Boy after I'd whined about the game he and his brother were playing. He discovered our parents' secret affair but chose to keep it in the dark until today. Until he offered me a look behind the curtain at a sight I cannot ever unsee.

The knowledge is hard enough for me to process as an adult. I knew my parents were no longer in love, but an affair? That's so much harder to comprehend. I can't imagine how hard it must have been on Zeno to carry that burden as a child. In a way, I understand why he hated my family. My heart aches for him, but at the same time, his justification doesn't erase the hurt he caused for so many years with each slighted insult and cold shoulder.

My emotions have split into two opposing camps. Empathy and remorse war with anger and blame, and I can't tell which is the dominant force. Do I want to scream at Zeno for hurting me or beg his forgiveness for assuming the worst of him?

He'd so consistently dismissed me in all our exchanges that I'd given in and labeled him arrogant and heartless. I'd written off my suspicions that something major had happened to change him, even though I'd been there the day the change came about. I knew something was wrong that had nothing to do with me, but he'd worn me down with his arctic confrontations, and I eventually abandoned my faith in him.

You're not loyal; you're arrogant and pathetic.

My own hate-filled words come back to haunt me. I had a valid reason for my venomous attack, not unlike his own reasons for his treatment of me, but that doesn't make me feel any better about what I said.

We've both been wrong.

Both said awful, spiteful things to one another over the years.

So where does that leave us?

And what about Nevio? As far as I can tell, he's been the greatest victim of the whole charade. Mom and Silvano were cheated on, but if the De Rossi marriage was anything like my parents', Silvano had to have known his marriage was less than perfect. It's not an excuse for cheating, but they were adults willingly staying in compromised relationships.

Nevio had been an innocent child.

He'd had no control over his parentage, nor was he given the decency of an explanation to help him understand the situation. To know why he was sent away and why his brother grew so distant. Instead, Nevio was made to feel like an outsider in his own home. I can't imagine how painful that was. No secret is worth that kind of damage.

I slip my hand into the back pocket of my jeans and pull out Zeno's folded letter. The previously crisp pages are now supple with a hint of moisture from my run. My eyes trace over his flowing script. I can envision him at his father's desk, bent with intensity as he pours out his deepest, darkest secrets for me.

It pained me to even put the words on paper, but you needed to hear the truth.

I needed you to know the truth.

I have spent a lifetime keeping secrets and covering for people, but I'm glad to share this with you, even if only for your own protection.

As I read over the last paragraphs for a second time, I get a sense of finality as realization dawns. The primary reason his letter broke me into pieces wasn't the secret he conveyed. The greatest source of my turmoil is in the underlying message. It is the same reason he wrote instead of telling me in person and the reason he left Hardwick for the city.

Zeno De Rossi's letter is his way of saying goodbye.

I told him that he was the last man I'd ever want to be with, and he respected my wishes by walking away. It's an honorable response to my anger, yet my heart feels like it's been wrapped in barbed wire, tangled and bleeding with no way to break free.

After so many years of hurt, I should be glad that he's told me the truth, but somehow, I only feel worse. For the suffering all around me. For the lost years and needless tears. For the man who has always been just out of my reach.

They say the truth sets you free, but it can't undo the past.

So, I ask again, where does that leave us?

I spend hours staring out my bedroom window without arriving at an answer. Sounds filter upstairs as my family returns home. Gia checks on me briefly, disposing of the soggy bag of broccoli. She doesn't push me to talk, though she can tell something has happened. The smell of garlic and pasta wafts upstairs, but not even the tempting aromas can lure me from my solitude. Eventually, golden streaks of sunset cast the trees in stark relief. The light shifts and fades as the sun descends, immersing me in a darkness I welcome with open arms.

W HEN I WAKE THE NEXT MORNING, MY HAND IMMEDIATELY reaches for my phone. I'm not sure why. I have no reason to expect a message from Zeno, but I look for one anyway. My breathing hitches when a notification shows a missed message, but it's only Grace telling me she's chosen an apartment in the city. I can't summon even feigned interest, so I drop the phone back on my nightstand without responding.

Gia stirs behind me. Her hand lifts to run comforting fingers through my hair. "You want to talk about it?" she asks softly.

If only I could.

Even if Zeno hadn't asked for my silence, my emotions are still so jagged and raw that spilling them aloud would be more than I could bear. However, should I decide to divulge what I learned at a later point in time, Gia would be the first person I'd turn to. I trust her absolutely.

But for now, I shake my head and feel grateful that Gia is so patient. Had I found her nearly catatonic in our bed last night as she'd found me, I would have demanded an explanation. My worry would have trampled her need for space, but my sister is hypersensitive to those around her. She is able to shelf her concerns and give a wealth of grace with a simple hug.

She offers the perfect support with one arm draped over me and her body curved around mine. Once I've absorbed all the love I can handle without summoning more tears, I sit up and give her a weary smile. "Thank you, G."

"I'm here for you whenever you're ready."

I give her arm a squeeze and stand, noting that my ankle has improved greatly in the night. It's stiff but not terribly sore. I grab a change of clothes, walking gingerly so as not to risk further injury, and head for the bathroom. The entire time, I keep my right fist tightly clasped around the letter I held throughout the night. I don't release the crumpled paper until I'm safely locked in the bathroom. It's time to respect Zeno's wishes and dispose of his message before it's accidentally discovered.

I open it one last time, only pausing from my task briefly to note my filthy reflection. I didn't even put on pajamas last night, let alone shower. I didn't care then, and I don't care now. My attention is solely focused on the pages suspended between my trembling fingers.

I turn on the shower to start the water warming and to drown out the sounds I'm about to make. Turning to the last page, I tear away the bottom portion containing his final words.

I wish you the best.

Z

I set the small scrap of paper aside before shredding the

rest of the letter and depositing the strips into the toilet. One flush later, the letter is gone—all but his parting words. Those, I tuck into the pocket of the clean leggings I plan to wear. I'm not sure why I've kept the shred of paper. I'm still upset with Zeno in a number of ways, but I'm also a little scared he'll never be a part of my life again. Even when he was an ass, he was still there, asking my dad about me or giving condescending advice. All I know is that if this is where our paths permanently diverge, then I want to take a piece of him with me.

I shower longer than normal, scrubbing away thoughts and emotions until I'm adequately numb for my day. Working at Hardwick will be a challenge when everything around me serves as a reminder of thoughts I wish to ignore. To stay strong and unaffected, I'll need to ensure my defenses remain intact. I promise myself I'll avoid people whenever possible, keep busy at all times, and stay far, far away from all things Zeno.

I'm remarkably successful throughout the morning, maintaining a machine-like trance until lunch. I'm so diligent in my earnest attempt to keep my mind preoccupied that I don't notice Nevio watching me until his playful voice snags my attention.

"It's twelve thirty, Isa. Even if you don't want lunch, that ankle could probably use a rest." He smirks at me lightheartedly from where he leans against the dining room doorframe.

I pull out my phone and confirm that he's right. "I didn't realize it'd gotten so late." I toss my polishing rag onto the tray I'd been working on and survey my progress. Cecelia mentioned polishing the silver when I started working at Hardwick, and I figured today was an ideal day to begin the mammoth undertaking.

Nevio closes the distance between us and reaches for my hand. "Let's grab a sandwich."

I pull back and raise my hands for him to see. "Careful, I'm covered in silver polish." In truth, I don't want him touching me in any way, but the sticky polish is an easy excuse.

"I'll survive," he says wryly, clasping my hand and tugging me away from the table. "That ankle feeling better, I take it?"

So much for avoiding touching him. I've got to say something. This can't continue.

He's still courting the idea of a relationship between us. I don't want to lead him on, but I'm not sure how to pull away without hurting him. He's been nothing but sweet to me since he returned home.

"Yeah. I made sure to ice and rest it," I answer.

Come on, Isa. Put your big girl panties on and set him straight.

"Good, but just to be safe, I want you to have a seat, and I'll get us lunch." Nevio pulls out a chair at the kitchen table and motions for me to sit. "I believe there's pastrami and turkey—one of those sound better than the other?"

"Pastrami sounds good." I'm not hungry, but I'll eat anyway. I don't want him asking questions.

"Same, that makes it easy." He winks.

My stomach cinches even tighter. My only consolation is that his lighthearted mood might make this a tiny bit easier. I open my mouth to shatter his hopes of a relationship between us, but the words don't come forth.

"Am I allowed to get us drinks?" I say instead. "Or would that get me in trouble?" My tone is playful purely from awkwardness, but I know he'll misinterpret and think I'm flirting. *God, what a mess.*

"You stay put. I've got it covered."

"If you say so."

"I do say so. I need you to be better by Thursday."

My heart rate kicks into a jog. "Oh, yeah? Why's that?"

"Because a friend of mine is having a party, and I want you to go with me. It's hard to dance with a bad ankle. We have never danced together, and there's nothing I'd like more." He cuts a glance at me briefly between layering the pastrami on Kaiser rolls.

Shit. This is exactly what I wanted to avoid. I've been gently giving him the slip even before I found out the truth, but he's still in pursuit. My desire to avoid conflict is urging me to keep making excuses until he gives up. I'm tongue-tied and obliging despite the crucial importance of putting distance between us. But it's disrespectful to leave him guessing and toy with his emotions. Haven't I spent the past twenty-four hours judging others for not being honest with him? How am I any better if I take the coward's way out instead of being up front and telling him truthfully that a relationship between us isn't meant to be?

I sit in silence as I debate my next move. My lack of response is enough to put him on guard. He brings over a plate for each of us and joins me at the table but makes no move to eat.

"You have something against parties?"

"No, it's just that … I want to make sure we're on the same page."

"And what page is that?"

Here goes nothing.

I meet his deep mahogany gaze. His eyes narrow at the apology he must see in my eyes. "I enjoy hanging out with you—I always have—but I don't want you to get the wrong impression."

"Wrong impression? What impression am I supposed to

get when you leaned into our kiss? You went to dinner with me, and your face lights up whenever I see you. Exactly what impression did you mean to send?"

Goddammit. He's not wrong, but things have changed.

"My head has been a mess with my mom's stuff, and I know I've sent some mixed signals, which is why I wanted to clear things up. I don't want to hurt you, and I'm so glad we've gotten back in touch. I don't want to lose that."

Nevio slowly crosses his arms over his chest, ramping up the tension surrounding us. "This has to do with Zeno, doesn't it?" His hushed question drips with disgust.

"No," I urge quickly. "This has nothing to do with him." I lean forward and place my hand flat against the table halfway between us. A plea. A bid for understanding.

My words bounce right off him like rain on a tin roof. "Mom told me she thought something was going on between you two. I didn't believe her because I've seen the way he's treated you. I knew you had too much self-respect to demean yourself like that." His lips lift in a snarl, and I pull back, growing defensive as his response morphs into a personal attack.

"I'm telling you my decision has nothing to do with him. If you don't believe me, that's *your* problem."

Cruelty twists his lips into a vicious scowl. "My only problem was finding a way to loosen that vise around your puritanical knees. We've known each other our whole lives, and it's taken weeks to get a fucking kiss. As far as I'm concerned, I should thank you for saving me the headache of going any further. Besides, I have no interest in my brother's leftovers."

My mouth hangs open as Nevio strolls from the room as though he didn't just spit in my face. Never in a million years would I have expected his reaction. A bruised ego is one thing. His calculated attack came deep from a cesspool of bitterness I'd never dreamed lay inside him. Was the animosity a product of the lies he'd been subjected to? Nevio claimed Z had treated him poorly, but I'd never been witness to any behavior by him or their parents to justify such residual hatred. Where had such spite come from? The mere hint that I'd chosen his brother over him had eliminated all rational thought.

I shake my head, finally hinging my jaw shut as my shock wears off.

I'm disappointed that he could say such awful things, but mostly I'm just sad for him. Nevio is more damaged than I realized. I hate that for him, but it also helps ease the sting of his attack. His reaction is a reflection of his own issues, making me wonder what made him so bitter.

My father had warned me about him. It would make sense that Dad was trying to keep me from dating my own brother, but maybe there was more to his warning. Zeno and my dad both hinted that Nevio was trouble. I'd told myself both men had been overreacting for one reason or another. I'd known Nevio so well when we were children, and it seemed like he hadn't changed a bit. His charm does a remarkable job of hiding the scars that mar his personality, but they're still there beneath the surface, mottled and raw.

I think back to Zeno's letter. He indicated that Nevio had lied about Zeno asking him not to come to their father's funeral. Such a falsehood isn't so hard to imagine anymore. I have to wonder how else Nevio might have massaged the truth to paint himself in a better light.

It's no wonder the two brothers are no longer close.

And to think of how accusatory I'd been about the way Zeno treated his brother. Neither man is faultless, but I had no business inserting my own misguided opinions. My self-righteous judgments. In that regard, at the very least, I owe Z an apology.

Slipping my phone from my back pocket, I check for missed messages.

Nothing.

My emotions are only slightly more settled than they were when I woke up this morning, but it's enough to give me direction. I need to know whether Zeno is still willing to talk to me.

When I open our text thread, I expect to type a short apology, but that's not what comes out. I try not to overthink the three simple words because while they're not an apology, they need to be said. I'm starting a conversation with him. That's the important part—that and speaking from my heart. Everything else is out of my hands, so there's no point in worrying over it.

Me: You hurt me.

I hit send and only have to wait a minute for his reply.

Zeno: That is my one greatest regret in life.

And with those few simple words, a bandage wraps gently over the wounds scattered across my heart. They've been unable to fully heal since he first kicked me out of Hardwick so many years ago. His remorse without caveat or explanation means more to me than he could ever know.

In addition, the tiny thread of communication between us reassures me that all is not lost. I may not know what else to say or where we go from here, but I know there is hope.

Hope for clarity and honesty.

Hope for trust and maybe even reconciliation.

To what end, I don't know, but the prospect is enticing. And if the mere possibility of a connection with Zeno brings me joy, then I should do what I can to explore that outcome. Considering our rocky past, any kind of relationship between us would be a challenge—friendship or otherwise. We are both lugging around enough baggage to ground a jetliner. But is a challenge necessarily bad? What if he and I could reach a place beyond our past? Wouldn't that be worth the obstacles we might encounter? When I think of the Zeno I used to look up to—the boy who befriended and protected me—the answer is a resounding yes.

I DON'T SEE NEVIO AGAIN BEFORE LEAVING WORK. MY afternoon is spent elbow-deep in silver polish, but the thoughts that accompany me are noticeably improved. When Gia informs me that we received a dinner invitation from the Larsons the day prior, I initially consider declining simply to avoid the burden of conversation. But by quitting time, I'm relieved to find that the prospect of socializing isn't as overwhelming as it had felt earlier in the day. I'm much improved, despite my tiff with Nevio. When I first lumbered from bed with the weight of the world on my shoulders, I would have thought it would take far more than a single text to shift my mood. But Zeno has always had that effect on me. No matter how securely I anchor myself, I will always feel the pull of his current.

After stopping home for a few minutes to freshen up, we all make our way to the Larson cottage. All of us except for

Livia, who is yet again missing in action. Fine by me. My tolerance for drama is at an all-time low. And dinner with the Larsons isn't a grand occasion. Our families have hosted one another at least once a month for as long as I can remember. My parents sometimes host, but dinner is often at the Larson's house. Considering neither of my parents is particularly fond of cooking, and the house is usually a mess, our reciprocity is somewhat lopsided. Fortunately, Mrs. Larson adores having company.

Their family welcomes us with warm greetings and the delicious aroma of a slow-cooked pot roast. Grace is all smiles. She's even wearing a touch of makeup, which is unusual for her.

"You look gorgeous, Gracy! You'll have to tell me all about the apartment you picked." My joy for her is genuine, and I do everything I can to suppress my fears that her house of cards will come crashing down. I don't ask her about Aldo, the disgusting bookie/loan shark who helped finance her move to the city. I don't want to think about him at all, so I don't.

"Absolutely, but I have even more good news to share! I got a job!" she squeals quietly, hands clapping together with excitement.

"Oh, my God, that's *wonderful*! Where will you be working?"

"It was kind of a long shot, so I can't believe I got it, but I'll be ushering at Broadway plays! I put in applications for all kinds of positions, and I may still need to do some waitressing as well, but this kind of job was what I was really hoping for. I'll get discounted tickets for most shows and can watch the shows when I'm working for free. The head ushers who run everything actually make decent money. I'd love to work toward that someday."

"That sounds incredible, Grace. I'm so happy for you!" I give her a hug with a wide grin. Her optimism is infectious, and it nurtures my ravaged psyche. "When do you start?"

"They want me as soon as I'm able, and the apartment is already available, so I'll be moving this weekend. It's all come together so fast that my head is spinning. That's why we're having dinner during the week instead of Friday or Saturday. Dad is going to help me move this weekend. It shouldn't be too bad, though. I don't have all that much stuff to move." She proceeds to tell me all about her studio apartment and her plans to make her transition as smooth as possible. "I suppose it's good I'm leaving since we don't know if the Bishops will be coming back. Mom and Dad may be looking for new work as well."

I hadn't even thought about them. I'd been so focused on Gia's heartbreak that I hadn't considered how the Bishops' departure would affect the Larsons.

"That would be awful—they've been working at the estate forever. Has Carter not given them any hint at his intentions?" It's a question I should have asked ages ago. If anyone knew what Bishop was doing, it would be his estate manager.

She shakes her head. "No. He told them he wasn't sure when or if he'd be back, but there's been no word since. Dad keeps assuring Mom that it'll be fine, but I can tell he's worried, too."

I wonder if Zeno realizes his interference in Gia and Carter's budding relationship has affected so many lives. And for what? His fear that the couple would end up like his parents? He may have been right regarding his warning about Nevio, but he overstepped his bounds where Carter Bishop was concerned. He should never have meddled in their relationship, and I have an urge to tell him so, but it will have to wait.

Dinner passes quickly in the company of longtime friends. Grace's parents share their excitement for their firstborn, leading to stories from everyone about first venturing from home. The food is delicious, as always. Ordinarily, we would stay until at least ten, but with work the next morning, we head home at a reasonable hour. Everyone else heads inside to start getting ready for bed, but I linger on the back porch and take out my phone. Enjoying my evening didn't diminish my need to tell him how upset I am over his role in Carter leaving. He explained his perspective about warning Carter away from Gia in his letter, but I need him to know that I still disagree with what he did.

Me: We had dinner at the Larson's tonight.

It's a bit random, but I'm not sure how else to introduce the subject.

Zeno: How was it?

Me: Good except they're worried about their jobs.

Me: It wasn't your place to come between Carter and my sister. They aren't your parents.

The conversation dots appear then quickly disappear before my phone buzzes with an incoming call. Zeno's name flashes on the screen, and I swipe to answer.

"Hey," I say softly. "You didn't have to call."

"I did. This subject is too complicated for text. I take it your sister is still upset?" His voice is warm molasses heating me from the inside out. It's my turn to talk, but I wish I could sit back and listen all night to the honey-tipped tenor of his words instead.

"She is, but there's so much more to consider. They're really worried about whether Carter will come back and if they'll lose their jobs if he sells the place."

A deep swell of breath comes across the line. "Sometimes, there are unfortunate consequences to our actions. I was concerned for a friend and voiced that concern. I don't regret that decision. There are many things to apologize for, but I still don't believe that's one of them. If his affection for her was delicate enough to be doused by our brief conversation, then that is an issue all its own."

"That's not entirely true. Carter and Gia aren't like you or me. We're headstrong and stubborn, and for the most part, confident in our actions. They're different. Shyness and reserve make it harder for them to form attachments, especially with someone as equally timid. People like them struggle to make lasting relationships. While they're steadfast and loyal once a connection is forged, those early days are exceedingly fragile."

"Yet you're convinced that they suit one another?"

"I am. They would be considerate and uniquely devoted to each other if given that chance."

"I didn't think you knew Carter so well to make that kind of call."

"I know enough, and I trust my sister's judgment. She's never been so attached to anyone."

"I'll have to take your word for it. She never seems overly interested in him from my perspective," he admits warily.

"She's reserved with her emotions. Even I sometimes struggle to interpret how she's feeling, and I've known her since birth."

Zeno huffs. "I suppose I should admire her reserve, but it sure makes reading her difficult."

"You're one to talk," I tease softly, then take a deep breath as the direction of our conversation shifts. I hadn't expected to text him about my exchange with Nevio, but now that he's on the phone, I feel the words need to be said. "I spoke with Nevio today."

Z is quiet for several long seconds. "And what did you discuss?"

"He wanted me to go to a party with him. I'd already decided before your letter that I wasn't interested, but with my new perspective, I knew that I needed to be up front with him. He's been very … attentive, and I didn't want to lead him on."

"I'd like to think he'd respect your decision, but I doubt it."

"It was awful, Z." My voice grows thin and small as I recall the hurtful words Nevio spat at me.

The line is dead silent before Zeno's ragged growl touches my ear. "Did he fucking touch you?"

I shake my head, though he can't see me. "No, but the things he said—they were terrible. It was like he became a complete stranger all of a sudden, spewing such hateful things. I knew he used his charm on people, but I had no idea … I had no clue that the person underneath had become so ugly."

"He's not who you think he is, Luisa."

"I can see that now." I stand and begin to pace on the back porch as awkwardness sets in. "Anyway, I just wanted you to know, and … I want to say that … I'm sorry. I should have apologized already, but it's been a lot to take in. I said some really awful things to you when I didn't know the whole picture. I assumed the worst of you, and though the truth hasn't erased all my anger and hurt, it helps to understand."

"You couldn't have known why I behaved the way I did," he says fervently. "The whole thing has been a shit situation for too long. You have every right to be upset."

I don't know what to say. Zeno is being considerate and civil, and even though I want to gobble up his attention, a part of me is still waiting for the other shoe to drop. For him to snap out of his temporary insanity and remember that he wants nothing to do with me.

Will I ever be able to trust him again like I did when we were young? Only time will tell. That type of faith and connection would have to be reforged, and a new bond created.

"I know you don't want the affair to get out," I say, broaching a sensitive subject. "But do you think it would help Nevio to know? To understand?"

"Knowing about that would only make things worse."

I can't imagine how that could be right, but he knows Nevio's issues and past better than I do. My pious assumptions have already gotten me into trouble once, so I'm not about to make that same mistake again so soon. "That's too bad, but I guess at this point, there are no easy fixes."

"Unfortunately, no."

The phone line hums with an awkward silence as our discussion wanes, though neither of us seems eager to end the call.

"Well, I better get going," I finally concede. "It's getting late."

"Of course, you should get some rest."

"Good night, Z," I whisper.

"Isa…" He pauses, and I wait with bated breath to hear his next words. "I'm glad we talked."

"Me, too."

"Sleep well. I'll be in touch."

I end the call with a blossoming smile sprouting straight from my heart. I feel like we've taken the first step down a new path. A thrilling and promising new path that is so unexpected, it's also a little terrifying. Do I dare get my hopes up? Could I quash them even if I wanted to? I doubt it, judging by the electric energy now thrumming in my veins. My train is already headed down the tracks. All I can do now is proceed with caution.

Inside, my dad is watching TV alone in the living room. I tell him good night and head upstairs to find Gia cuddled under the covers, playing a mindless game on her phone.

"Hey there." My smile grows as I join her on the bed.

Her face lights up, clearly relieved at my improved mood. "Hey! You feeling better?"

"I'm getting there. It's been a crazy couple of days. Hell, it's been a crazy few weeks." I lie down next to her, and she follows suit, turning on her side to face me.

"You want to tell me about it?"

I do, but I deliberate for a moment before going forward. I know by telling Gia this secret, I'm technically breaking Zeno's trust. However, I can guarantee with absolute certainty that she will go to her grave before she tells anyone. I need to be able to talk to someone about what I've learned, and there is no better secret-keeper than Gia. And after all, this secret involves her, too.

"What I'm about to tell you cannot be breathed to another living soul. I was told under the strictest of confidences."

Surprise widens her eyes. "Maybe you shouldn't say anything, then. I don't want you to break anyone's trust."

"It's not that simple. This involves all of us, and I need to talk about it with *someone*."

"Okay." She nods for me to go on.

"After we got back from the city, Zeno came by the house."

"He did?"

"I was on the back porch, so he didn't come inside. We talked, and it didn't go well. Actually, it was more like a fight. The next day, he left a letter for me finally explaining what happened when we were kids and why he's been so distant ever since."

"What happened?" She lifts onto her elbow expectantly. "What could possibly justify the way he's behaved?"

"You're not going to believe this." I lean in and speak on a hushed breath. *"Dad had an affair with Elena, and Nevio is their son. He's not technically a De Rossi. He's our half brother."*

Gia drifts slowly back down to her pillow, wide eyes turning to the ceiling. "Holy shit."

I have to bite down on my lips to keep from laughing. Gia rarely cusses. And though this is a serious matter, hearing her swear always tickles me.

I've pulled the rug out from under her. I know the feeling well. Only, she wasn't embroiled with the brothers like I was. For her, the news may be a little distressing, but it's more fascinating than anything.

"That's why Zeno tried to keep Nevio away from me," I continue. "It's also why he's been so rude. He said that for the longest time that I reminded him of Dad, who he blamed for tearing apart his family."

"Oh, Isa. That's terrible. I mean, I can see why he'd feel that way, but the whole thing is just awful."

"He's known all this time but never told anyone. Fourteen years."

Her brows draw together over compassionate brown eyes. "That had to be so hard on Z to carry that burden as a child."

"Yeah, but not telling anyone meant Nevio was sent away in high school solely because he had a crush on me, though he wasn't told as much. He felt like he was being cast out. That hurt him so much, and now … Gia, he's terribly bitter. I didn't realize, but today when I told him I wasn't interested in a relationship, he showed his true colors. It would have broken your heart. He's so angry with the world."

"I imagine Z did the best he could at the time. We can't expect a young teenager to know how to navigate something like that." Always compassionate, that's my sister.

"I know. I hate for someone who was so good-natured to become twisted with spite, especially if simple honesty could have prevented it."

"You don't know if that would have helped. Some people become bitter for no reason at all, and others have all the reason in the world but choose to remain unjaded by life's misfortunes."

God, I love my sister. I may begrudge her perspective at times, but for the most part, she is insightful beyond belief. I hadn't considered that Zeno's secret isn't necessarily the sole cause of Nevio's issues. The two seem so naturally connected, but I have no proof that's the case.

I pull her into a hug. "You're the best, G. I'm sorry I wasn't up for talking yesterday. I needed a chance to process things."

"You know I'm always here for you. And don't worry about the secret. I won't tell a soul."

When I ease away, Gia shakes her head dazedly.

"Dad and Elena. Who would have thought?"

"Crazy, right? Guess I can cross Ancestry.com off the Christmas gift list." I cut my eyes over to her, and we both burst into laughter—a cathartic, healing, hysterical laughter totally inappropriate for the moment but exactly what we need.

I drift into a peaceful sleep that night, my heart lighter than it's felt in weeks. Things are looking up, and I can only hope that my luck has turned a corner. Before I know it, I'll be finishing school, and this chaotic summer will be a distant memory.

Gia and I talk again on Wednesday once she's had a chance to digest what she learned. Other than our discussions, the day is blessedly free of drama. Thursday follows in a similar fashion, except when evening rolls around, I'm surprised by a text from Zeno.

Zeno: I was hoping we could talk in person this weekend, but Christiano asked me to join him in the Hamptons for a meeting.

I smile at his text. He didn't have to tell me his plans, especially where Christiano was concerned. He's the boss of the Giordano crime family—Zeno's boss—and I know better than to expect Z to tell me anything about that aspect of his life.

As I begin to type, a trickle of doubt creeps into my mind. Does Z actually have a reason to stay away, or is he avoiding me? If that was the case, why reach out at all? Maybe he's reconsidering his feelings and trying to slowly back away.

I try to calm the doubts and take him at his word, but years of discord between us makes that difficult.

Me: We can always talk next week. It's been good to have time to think.

Zeno: Just so you know, I've ordered Nevio to the city. He shouldn't be back at Hardwick anytime soon.

I'm not sure how to respond, verbally or emotionally. I hate for Nevio to be kept from his home, but I can't deny the relief of knowing I won't run into him at the house. That possibility hung in the back of my mind over the past two days and kept me slightly on edge. Nevio wouldn't hurt me —not physically, anyway—but I don't want to argue with him either. Not if he's going to turn ugly. I assume the reason he hasn't reached out to apologize is that he's still upset. I'd hoped he'd come to his senses by now, but that doesn't appear to be the case.

Me: I haven't heard from him. Not sure if that's good or bad.

Zeno: It's good, trust me.

Me: Will you tell me what happened to him?

I may be butting in, but if Z wants open communication between us, then I need to be free to ask questions.

Zeno: Some things are better left in the dark, but if you really want to know, I'll tell you next time I see you.

Me: I would appreciate that. *For the information and for not being upset that I asked.*

Zeno: Anything, Isa. All you ever need to do is ask.

What I wouldn't give to feel the rumble of those words spoken against my skin. To see the veracity on his face and truly believe his declaration. As it is, I stare at the digital screen like a child pining for the toys in a store window, unsure how to make it happen. To truly believe all of it could be mine.

Fortunately, Z saves me the uncertain task of coming up with a response.

Zeno: I'm having dinner with some colleagues, so I have to go, but text if you need me.

Text if you need me. It's like he's reading my mind, saying all the things I've always wanted to hear from him. It feels too good to be true, except it is true, if I can find the courage to believe him. To step off that ledge and trust that he'll catch me.

Me: I will. Enjoy dinner.

Zeno: Good night, Isa.

And I do have a good night, that is until a noise wakes me around three o'clock. Gia is still sleeping soundly beside me, but my brain is whirring like the blades of a fan as I lay in the dark, waiting for the noise again. When a thud resounds from the bathroom, I realize that Livia has most likely woken me, yet again, after one of her not-so-stealthy returns from a night out. The last time she woke me, she was drunk and hardly able to undress.

I groan quietly and roll from bed. No matter how annoying she may be, she's still my little sister, and I feel the need to check on her. She hasn't locked the door, which is helpful, and I'm pleased to discover that she isn't completely trashed.

"Hey, Isa. Did I wake you?" Her hair is a mess and makeup smudged, but her smile is genuine as she sits on the edge of the tub. She's had a good night.

"Yeah, you're not the quietest drunk," I tease her.

"I'm not even drunk—not anymore, at least. Nevio made sure I drank my water this time." She slips one of her wedge sandals off, eyeing me coyly for my response. She thinks she's teased me with a juicy nugget of gossip, not realizing what she's actually done is drop an atomic-sized bomb on the vinyl bathroom floor.

My heart thunders in my ears as I momentarily forget to breathe. "Livy, you have to listen to me. You *cannot* date Nevio." I move close and drop to my knees so that I'm at eye level with her. The pain in my kneecaps is nothing compared to the overwhelming panic surging in my veins. I have to find a way to make her listen, but I know my sister, and my warning will only make her want him more.

As expected, her initial surprise quickly fades to irritation. "Why the hell not?"

Livia would be the absolute worst person to tell about Nevio's paternity. Everyone in New York would know within the hour. And besides, I already told one more person than I was supposed to. There's no way I can tell her the truth. How can I possibly convince her without telling her that she's dating her own brother?

Shit. Shit. SHIT!

"I know he's charming and seems like the perfect catch, but Liv, you have to believe me. Nevio has issues. He's not who you think he is, and I don't want you to get hurt."

"No, you don't want me to land the hottie next door that you couldn't get for yourself. You're just jealous." She stands and tries to maneuver around me, but I'm on my feet in an instant.

"I'm not jealous, Liv. If I'd wanted a relationship with Nevio, I could have pursued that years ago. I'm trying to protect you as a sister. I'd love for you to be deliriously happy and marry a wealthy man, but Nevio will not give you that. *Please*, listen to me." I clasp her arms and plead with her green eyes, ringed in gold just like our mother's.

She shakes off my hold but avoids my gaze. I've managed to inject a sliver of doubt into her plans.

"I'm not sure any of it matters anyway. He's staying in the city now, so I'm not sure when I'll see him again." She wipes at her eyes with a makeup removing cloth as though she doesn't care one way or another.

I see right through her. Liv would never be so nonchalant about a relationship with a wealthy man.

"He's not trustworthy, and I don't want to be hurt. Did you know he asked me to the party you were at tonight? Hell, he probably asked you in some twisted attempt to get back at me. When I told him the other day that I wasn't interested in going out again, he said some awful things to me. Even if he is truly interested in you, surely you don't want to be with someone who's that two-faced."

"You want me to end up stuck in this house forever, don't you? Whatever happened between you two is irrelevant and only tainting the way you see him. I should have known you wouldn't be happy for me." She tosses the dirty wipe in the trash and turns cold, unfeeling eyes on me. "It's late. I'm going to bed now."

My bumbling attempt at reasoning with her is abruptly shut down when she walks away. I don't sleep the rest of the night. My mind is too busy concocting horrific ways for Livia's new crush to end in disaster. I brainstorm every possible solution I can devise and measure the probability of success. By the time the sun finally peeks through the blinds in our room, I've come to the conclusion that I need help. And not just anyone's help. I need my dad.

I may not be able to tell anyone the secret, but that doesn't stop me from talking to someone who already knows. And it's a safe assumption that Dad knows he's Nevio's biological father. He'll recognize how urgent it is to keep the two of them apart and help without me having to bring up Nevio's paternity. I'll get my help and still mostly keep my promise to Zeno.

I go downstairs early, hoping to catch him before Mom or Gia show up for breakfast. Coffee is my first priority after lying awake for hours. I turn on the Keurig and wish I had access to an espresso. I'm going to need all the caffeine I can get today.

A few sips into my first cup, Dad strolls in from his bedroom with a grin.

"How come you're up so early?"

"Actually, I wanted to talk to you. Can you come outside with me for a minute?"

His face sobers. "Lead the way." He opens the door for me, and I step out into the grass a few feet from the porch. Far enough that we shouldn't be overheard.

"You know how you warned me about Nevio?"

"Yeah?" he asks warily.

"Well, I shut that down, but last night, I learned that Livia went out with him." I watch closely for his reaction. If I tell him outright that I know about his affair, I will have had to explain how I acquired that information. Word would likely travel to Elena that Zeno knows, and he might not want that. I need to play this carefully.

"She's seeing him?"

"They went to a party last night, and she hinted that it wasn't the first time they've gone out." *Read between the lines, Dad. Please, see what I'm getting at without me having to spell it out.*

He kicks at a stick and gives me a smirk. "You know how Livy is. She thinks every man with money is her golden goose. Neither of the De Rossi boys is interested in her.

They've known Liv her whole life and never paid her one bit of attention."

"Daddy, things can change. Aren't you worried about her?"

"Not really. You know how she is. She probably begged to go with him hoping to meet friends of his, and he let her tag along."

I gape at him incredulously. How can he be so dismissive about the possible dangers? He has to know, doesn't he? How could he not? Even if Elena didn't tell him Nevio was his, surely, he could see his own eyes looking back at him—the same way Zeno figured it out. Once a person knows of the affair, the resemblance between father and son is hard to miss.

But then again, if he *did* know, how could he blow off a potentially incestuous relationship between his children? There's no way he'd be so casual about it.

A stream of curses vulgar enough to make a sailor blush fires through my mind.

Dad won't be assisting me as I'd hoped. His hands-off approach to parenting was always a little annoying where my younger sisters were concerned, but this is plain maddening. With Livia still living at home, Dad's leverage over her would be enormously helpful. All I can do now is hope that Nevio returning to the city will limit their interaction, but it's not a guarantee.

I meet my dad's sad eyes pleadingly. "I get that you're not worried, but I am, and it would mean a lot to me if you'd help me discourage her from hanging around him."

Dad cups his hands around my upper arms and gives them a gentle squeeze. "Of course, Lulu, if you're that worried about it. Your mom mentioned wanting to hit Macy's on Saturday, and I had somewhere I wanted to stop in as well. What if she and I take the girls and spend a weekend in the city? We'll keep them busy, and you and Gia can have a little time alone. It's not a permanent solution, but it's a start."

I fling myself into his arms, relieved to have any help I can get. "Thank you, Daddy."

"Don't mention it. It's been ages since I've been out of here. It'll do me some good."

The back door opens, and I pull away to see Mom watching us curiously.

"What's all this about?"

"Just hugging my daughter," Dad answers. "I'm allowed to do that, aren't I?"

"Sure, you are, but you two look suspicious doing it out here in the yard when the sun's hardly up."

"I was telling Luisa that I thought I'd take you and the younger girls into the city this weekend. We can leave after work this evening."

Mom's face lights up, all her nosy curiosity forgotten. "I'll get Chiara on the phone and let her know we're coming!" She dashes inside to call her sister-in-law. Dad and I follow her inside and resume our morning routines, my shoulders already feeling lighter. It's not a permanent fix, but it's a start. Between Gia, Dad, Zeno, and myself, surely we can keep them from disaster.

While Gia and I walk to Hardwick some thirty minutes later, I tell her about Livia and Nevio.

"You think Mom and Dad will be vigilant with her this weekend?" Gia asks. "If he's in the city, there's a chance she'll try to slip away and meet up with him. Dad doesn't have a great track record of keeping tabs on her, and Mom would cheer her on. If Dad doesn't know the real reason you're worried, he won't be overly strict."

"That's crossed my mind as well. I'd like to think Dad won't let her go off on her own, but I'm not certain."

"One of us who knows the truth needs to be near her at all times until her infatuation wears off. I should go with them and make sure nothing happens." Gia's offer is a huge relief. I'd been contemplating whether I should go with them but was selfishly reluctant.

"Are you sure?" I ask only half-heartedly.

"Yeah. We can check in on Grace, and I'm sure Chiara will have plenty for us to do."

"I really appreciate you doing that. When you get back, we can come up with a monitoring system. I don't think we can trust her an inch."

"Agreed," Gia sighs. "At least this business has taken my mind off Carter." She shrugs, and the hopelessness of it hurts my heart.

"Maybe you can use the trip to take another shot at talking to him." I doubt she'll do it, but I have to suggest it.

Gia just smiles placidly and continues walking.

"I'm supposed to talk to Z on Sunday," I continue. "I can enlist his help as well."

She peers at me from the corner of her eye. "You guys talking?"

This time, I shrug. "A couple of times. We're slowly wading through everything."

"If it means anything, I think you're doing the right thing. I know how much you always adored him growing up and how much it hurt when he pushed you away. It's about time things got worked out between you."

"Let's hope it's a good thing and not more heartbreak waiting to happen. Because if he bails on me again, I might need help disposing of a body." I raise a brow at her playfully.

Gia grins mischievously. "He hurts you again, and I'll gladly bring the shovel."

CHAPTER 5

Friday night, the house is quiet, and I'm blissfully alone. I thought I would read once everyone left, but I do something unexpected once the house is empty. I get out my idea notebook. I've been jotting down book ideas for years, so an extensive collection of story tidbits is scribbled on the pages. I read through each until I come to my notes from nearly a decade before, when I still spent time wondering why Z pushed me away. The change in him had been so abrupt, I'd channeled the trending *Twilight* books to develop a fanciful theory about what had happened. I hypothesized that he'd been transformed into a vampire and was pushing me away to protect me from himself. It had been a childish escape from the truth, but the story idea suddenly intrigues me and takes on new life now that our story has further unfolded.

Before I know it, my stomach is growling, and I've written

ten pages outlining a vampire romance that captures my soul. The story materialized before my eyes. The basic plot is the same as I'd first envisioned, but I'm able to add depth and complexity now that my imagination has the benefit of experience.

I adore the alternate reality I've created.

When I finally head to bed, I go to sleep with the satisfaction of believing for the first time that I might actually make my publishing dreams a reality. I have never felt so damn proud of myself.

I wake early with enthusiasm the next morning, excited to dive back into the creative process. I spend hours on the couch developing my characters and the fantasy world in which their story unfolds. Normally, stress inhibits my creativity, but the chaos of my life has somehow inspired me. The release of ideas is invigorating, and the escape from reality is more than welcome.

When my phone rings close to noon, I grumble until I see Grace's face flash on the screen.

"Hey!" I greet her excitedly. "How's the new apartment coming along?"

"It's the size of a shoebox, but it's mine, and I love it!"

"That's awesome!"

"Yeah, but there's more. I didn't want to say anything until I knew how it went, but Ari called last week. We went to dinner last night." A radiant smile colors her words with happiness. I don't have to see it to know it's there.

"Oh my God, Grace! That's wonderful! I take it the evening went well?"

"It was perfect. I told her that the whole scene was new to me, and she was happy to take things slow. We had such a great time together. She's coming by tomorrow to help me finish setting up the apartment. There's not actually that much to do, but she offered, and I like the idea of showing her my new place."

"Honey, I'm so incredibly happy for you. So many exciting new adventures!"

"It's a lot at once, but I'm so happy about everything. I have two months until I'm supposed to have Aldo paid, and I don't think that will be an issue since I got that job already. Everything has come together perfectly."

"I'll offer one bit of advice. It may sound paranoid, but take someone with you when you give him the money. I'm even happy to come to the city if you need me." I can't help but warn her again. She seems to have everything under control, but I worry.

"Okay, I'll make sure to do that. Sorry to keep this short and sweet, but I'm meeting Gia for lunch. I just wanted to keep you posted on the Ari situation as I promised."

"I'm so glad you did! Enjoy your lunch!"

We say our goodbyes, and I end the call with a buoyancy in my chest that I haven't felt in ages. There are still plenty of worries I could dwell upon if I was so inclined but also an equal number of reasons to be optimistic for the future. Grace, my budding career as an author, and even the fragile reconstruction of a relationship I had thought was irreparable.

I choose to be optimistic and focus on the rays of light peeking through the clouds.

By the time the sun has set on my Saturday, I'm two glasses into a bottle of rosé and dancing around the living room to Britney Spears's "Toxic." I have a dance-off with myself, drowning in a release of endorphins like I haven't felt in months. Even once I give into fatigue and slump onto the couch, the pulsing strains of music from my youth keep my spirits floating high. Eyes closed. Hand waving in the air. I am the embodiment of contentment. I am the music that fills my ears, keeping me from hearing when my little party of one doubles in size. It's not until I open my eyes to skip a song that I realize I'm no longer alone.

I see his reflection first.

Outlined against the black television screen, the form of a man leaning against the entry wall behind me catches my eye. I instantly snap from my tipsy state of relaxation and bolt from the sofa. My motion jars the coffee table, knocking over my half-full glass of wine, but I pay it no mind. Every ounce of my attention is glued to the menacing man who has broken into my house and now stares at me with a drunken gleam in his eye. A vulgar, depraved look that I remember all too well from the last time I chased him from my house.

Aldo Consoli smirks when my rounded eyes meet his.

"Get the fuck out of my house." My limbs are frozen in fear, but I force as much bravado into my voice as possible. Blood thunders against my eardrums, but it's not enough to drown out the music, its energetic beat suddenly as out of place as the shrill tunes of an ice cream truck driving past a funeral.

"Come on, now. You don't expect me to hear your little party from the street and not come pay you a visit." He holds himself up against the wall, his wrinkled clothes disheveled and dirty.

I refuse to argue with him. No matter how loud I play my music, or how revealing my clothes, or how pleasant I act, I am not extending an invitation to invade my personal space. And no amount of arguing will justify that conclusion. "Get out. You have no right to be here."

I had thought my troubles with this man were over. Mom's debt had been paid. I'd assumed I was free of him and had even tucked Dad's pistol back where it belongs in his room. I couldn't have known Aldo would come back, but I berate myself regardless. How could I have been so careless?

Aldo raises himself upright off the wall with a lewd grin.

Sticky nausea fills my belly, curdling with fear and desperation. He's not going to leave. I know it in my gut. He's come back to take what he didn't get the first time, and if I can't find a way to escape, he's going to succeed.

I try not to be obvious as I consider what I can use as a weapon within reach.

"I stopped by to check on your little friend," he says, his speech slightly slurred. "But no one's home. When I heard your music and saw you dancing by yourself, I knew it was fate giving us a second chance." He steps toward the back of the sofa, inching closer to me.

I retreat, taking a wobbly step to the side, my calves pressed against the coffee table. I consider breaking my wineglass and using it as a weapon, but that seems so unreliable. What if I cut myself in the process? I need something heavy. A lamp. Or a fireplace poker. *Something.*

"She said her loan wasn't due for two more months." I don't care about the details of their deal. I just have to keep him talking so my frantic brain has a chance to figure a way out of this.

He shrugs. "Who's to say? There's nothing in writing."

Fucking asshole. I knew he'd pull something shady.

"If you touch me, my father will find out. You'll be crucified for hurting a family man's daughter."

The icy grin that splits his face is dripping with superiority. "I have permission to be here, and when you wanted to help work off a friend's debt, who's to say otherwise?"

Permission? Who else knew about Aldo's visits to Tuxedo Park? I try to peel apart his words, but before I can get the chance, he launches himself over the back of the couch. I spring toward the kitchen, hoping to make it to the back door, but searing pain lances through my scalp when he grabs my ponytail and yanks me backward.

My body ricochets off his. Before I can use the momentum to pull away, arms wrap like steel bands around me. I cry out, my throat burning with the effort, but it's pointless. The music is too loud for anyone to hear, even if we did have neighbors close enough to help me. I'm trapped in my own home with a deranged sociopath intent on raping me. His cock is already hard against my backside. The unwelcome feel of it makes me thrash viciously against his hold.

"That's it, little girl," Aldo hisses joyously. "Fight me. Make me want it." His caustic words grate against my ear, the moisture from his breath clinging to the skin of my neck.

I want to dip myself in acid to cleanse away the feel of him.

Bending forward as much as I can, I suddenly snap backward and slam my head into his nose.

"*Fuck*!" His curse booms over the music as he releases me momentarily.

I try to run again, but he grabs my hand and whips me around. Using my own momentum against me, he cracks his fist against my cheek, sending me stumbling to the ground.

The blaring music finally fades into the background while the world dips and weaves in slow motion. My thoughts are hazy and confused, but the fear never retreats. I know in every cell of my being that I'm in danger. That I have to move.

Blinking, I try to clear my thoughts. When I look behind me, I see Aldo assessing his bleeding nose in the living room mirror.

I did that.

He's trying to hurt me, and I busted his nose.

I have to get out of here.

"You little cunt. I think you broke my fucking nose."

Ignoring him, I pull myself up against the doorway into the kitchen. I have two options. I can make another attempt for the back door, or I can lunge for the block of cooking knives on the counter. I have only seconds to decide.

My left eye is quickly swelling, and my thoughts are frayed at the edges.

He may be drunk, but I'm no match for him in this state.

I'm not sure if it's resignation or determination or an overload of adrenaline, but an unnatural stillness settles over me as I lock eyes with my attacker.

Blue colliding with black.

Feral desperation warring with malicious psychosis.

Any debate about my next move becomes moot as I recognize that Aldo Consoli will never let me get away. Madness and alcohol have consumed him with the need to conquer me, and if I have any hope of escaping, it's in the form of an attack and not retreat.

I don't give him time to read my thoughts.

Lunging to the side, I dive into the kitchen and wrap my fingers around the handle of a knife just as he grabs my other hand and whips me around.

The next few seconds pass in a blur. As if time skips from one point to another.

First, I've got my hand outstretched to reach for the knife, and before I know how what's happened, I'm facing Aldo, his features contorted in astonishment as he looks down to where my knife is buried deep in his belly.

Point A to point B with no in-between.

We are both silent.

The world stills around us, all except for the damn music

still blaring from the living room speakers. My eyes lift slowly to his. His seething hatred claws at my skin.

I need to get away, but I'm unwilling to part with my weapon, so I yank back harshly, pulling the blade from his body and stumbling backward.

Aldo's lips round on a silent gasp, his hands quickly clutching at the growing wetness blossoming across his black shirt. The fabric is so dark that the stain doesn't even look like blood. But his shaking hand comes away crimson, and there's no denying the viscous substance dripping from my knife.

I don't think. I just run.

Out the back door. Knife in hand. Feet winged as I fly through the tall grass between my house and Hardwick.

It's late, so I go to the front of the house. The property is flooded with lights, enabling me to glance back and check that I wasn't followed. I bang on the door and ring the bell before doubling over, my lungs screaming with exertion.

I have to ring the bell a second time before Elena's rattled voice comes over the intercom.

"Can I help you?"

I look up toward the camera in the corner. "Elena, it's me, Luisa. There was a man at my house, and I may have killed him. I don't know. Please, I need your help." My voice is shrill and shaky. And as if hearing the trauma in my own voice makes it that much more real, all the muscles in my body begin to quiver and quake.

The locks quickly turn, and Elena flings open the door to usher me inside.

"Oh, God. Sweet girl, are you okay?" She secures the door behind me then wraps a comforting arm around my shoulders.

The hand still gripping the knife lifts before us, trembling. "I didn't know what else to do. He was going to hurt me.

And … and I grabbed the knife, and then it was in him. I don't even know how."

Elena moves in front of me to gain my attention. "Stay right here for just a second. I'm coming right back, okay?"

I nod.

She's only gone for a handful of seconds, but in that time, my chest begins to shake with the threat of sobs. Elena wraps a hand towel around my fist, coaxing my fingers to release their grip. She rolls the knife into the towel and sets it on a table.

"Let's get you upstairs and cleaned up."

She takes my hand in hers and leads me to the nearest guest bedroom. I follow in a haze. My brain is so overwhelmed with shock, I can't manage even basic thoughts. While Elena starts a hot shower in the on-suite bathroom, I stare blankly at the wall.

Then her eyes are in front of me, blue pools of worry.

She places her gentle hands on my cheeks. "I know you're scared, sweet Luisa, but everything is going to be okay. You shower and try to calm down."

I nod because that's what I'm supposed to do.

"I'll be right outside the door if you need me. We'll take care of everything, sweet girl, I promise."

Once she slips from the room, I dazedly remove my blood-spattered clothes. I can't look at them. The fabric is discarded into a pile on the floor. The heat of the shower spray warms my skin, but it can't touch the permafrost coating my bones. When I lift my hands to the water, I see the blood staining my fingers. Under the nails. Blotching my skin. Filling each crease and crevice.

My shaking amplifies until I have to sink to the shower floor.

What have I done? Did I just kill a man? If he isn't dead,

will he come after me? What about my family? Would he report me to the police? The Mafia usually doesn't involve the cops, but if he takes himself to a hospital, they might report the incident.

If he's alive.

If he's not, will I be in trouble with the Giordano family? The law would deem my actions self-defense, but would the Mafia be so understanding?

I had to do what I did. I don't regret it, but what consequences will it bring?

The uncertainty is terrifying.

Reaching for the bar of soap, I scrub at my skin as sobs wrack my body. I try to stay quiet. I'm not even sure why. Maybe because a part of me still feels unsafe. As though my cries will alert the world to what I've done.

I scour my flesh until I can't tell if I'm red from blood stains or excessive scrubbing. Eventually, I force myself to turn off the water. Silence awaits me. I used to love time alone —time for my mind to be free—but now, the silence is a petri dish for toxic thoughts and fears.

As I towel off, a soft knock sounds on the door. "Luisa, dear, I've got a change of clothes for you. Can I come in?"

I open the door and accept the stack of clothes she offers. "Thank you," I whisper hoarsely, my throat raw from crying.

"Of course. I've got a small tray of food along with some juice out here on the vanity. Help yourself. It might calm your nerves. Will you be okay up here tonight? I can stay in the room next door if you're more comfortable having someone close."

The world doesn't deserve Elena De Rossi. Her kindness and generosity are without reproach, and I have a sudden epiphany that a woman like her wouldn't stray from her husband except in the most desperate of circumstances. If she found companionship in the arms of my father, it was for a good reason. Zeno may idolize his father, but I would bet money his parents' marriage wasn't what he thought. That Silvano De Rossi wasn't who Zeno thought he was.

"Thank you so much, Elena. I'll be fine up here until I can sort things in the morning." In the light of day, once the monsters are gone.

"You're always welcome here. We'll get this all sorted tomorrow, I promise. For now, you take care of yourself. Get some rest and know that you're safe at Hardwick." She pulls me in for a motherly hug despite the stray droplets of water dotting my skin.

I cling to her and the assurances she offers. I've handled my own problems for a long time. I had to. My mother wasn't the type of mom I could turn to for help. Dad was always there for me, but there's something different about a mother's love. A generosity that I never experienced. Elena isn't my mother, but at this moment, her maternal love for me is unquestionable.

When I pull back, emotions lodge in my throat. I can't speak, but I hope she can see the gratitude and love I have for her through my tear-filled eyes.

Once she leaves, I put on the clothes she provided and slip beneath the covers of the king-sized bed. I leave the light on in the bathroom. I'm not ready to face the dark and the images it will summon. I would play music if I had my phone, but it got left behind at the cottage. There is nothing in the stately room to distract my mind save for the intricate chandelier above me. I start at the top and count the crystals, dull in the dim lighting. There are three hundred and twenty-five. I make it to one-hundred and thirty-two on my third count before exhaustion finally pulls me under.

I HAVEN'T BEEN ASLEEP LONG WHEN I WAKE, CURLED INTO A BALL in the middle of the bed. I don't know why I've woken until I sense a presence in the room. Terror floods my veins in an instant, but when I jerk upright, it's Zeno I see sitting in the corner of the room.

He lifts his hand to calm me. "It's okay, Isa. It's just me." The gentle purr of his voice instantly soothes my thundering pulse back from near cardiac arrest.

"Z." It's the only word I can squeeze past my constricting throat, but it's all he needs to hear. Every bit of my fear and vulnerability is there in that one syllable. Zeno came when I needed him most, and my relief is instantaneous.

He swiftly rises from his chair and joins me on the bed. I crawl onto his lap without hesitation, my body trembling from the comfort of his arms wrapping securely around me, as though I'd been holding in my fear and anxiety coiled tight in each muscle while I slept, but the presence of this mercurial man is all I need to release that tension.

"Jesus, you had me worried," he murmurs into my hair. "I've never driven so fast in my life."

His admission makes me recall that he was in the Hamptons this weekend. That's a three-and-a-half-hour drive. Assuming Elena called him, he must have jumped in his car before he even hung up the phone.

"I'd say I'm sorry to pull you away from work, but I'm not," I whisper.

Z gently eases back, coaxing me to lift my face toward his. When I do, his eyes dilate with murderous intent as he examines my bruised cheek. I'd been too tucked away beneath the covers for him to see before, but with the bathroom light still on, my discolored cheek is now visible. His fingertips raise to trace a delicate circle around the outer edge of my swelling.

His touch is reverent. An apology and a promise.

Never again.

"I need you to tell me every way he hurt you." His eyes light with pain, and I realize what he's asking.

I shake my head. "He didn't touch me like that. He wanted to, but I got away before he could."

Zeno's chest expands with air, but his features never soften. His relief will not grant Aldo any leniency, should the man still be alive.

At that moment, I feel the full impact of what I mean to Zeno De Rossi.

Every caustic comment and brutal rebuff from the past melt away as concrete understanding settles in my bones. He would slaughter the city for me. Raise the dead and give his own life for me. The enormity of his feelings is there in his eyes, waiting to be seen. Waiting for me to look hard enough to see the truth.

I am the center of Zeno's world. Always have been. Always will be.

I don't need to understand the man to know that one simple truth.

My lips beg for his touch. I readjust until I'm straddling his lap, my eyes never leaving his. His strong arms hold me against him with one hand firmly at the back of my neck. Once we're face-to-face, I rest my forehead gently against his.

Zeno's body is stiff with uncertainty and restraint. For once, I don't presume to know his reasons. It's not my place to project my own interpretations. Instead, I bring my lips to his hesitantly and allow fate to take us where it will.

My lungs steal his shuddered breath before his mouth seizes mine.

A primal moan rattles his chest and buries itself deep in my heart. Our tongues taste one another with the urgency of starvation. Years of deprivation and need are released all at once. Barriers drop, and bridles rip free. For the first time in our adult lives, we give ourselves over to the connection that has always lived and breathed between us. Nothing else exists. No families or duties. No past or future. We are two people fully engaged in our present need for one another.

"Fuck, I don't deserve this." His hand kneads my ass cheek while his teeth graze against my bottom lip.

"No talking about the past." I shake my head. "We can deal with it later. Right now, we need this. *I* need this."

"Tell me exactly what you need because I want to fuck you. If that's not what you mean, say it now." His words are ragged, taut with restraint.

"That's exactly what I want. I need to feel you inside me."

Without another word, Zeno rolls our bodies back onto the mattress until he's looming over me. Possessive yet tender, ardent desire burning in his eyes. Our hips align, and my knees raise to align my center fully against his hard length. The relief from his touch where I most need him steals the air from my lungs.

His kiss is savage. Feral in its intensity but absolute in its reverence. He makes me feel cherished with the simplest touch, and I devour every delectable bite.

Eventually, Zeno lifts himself long enough to remove his shirt, then slips mine up over my head. I want to study every inch of him, worship and memorize his breathtaking body, but he doesn't give me the opportunity. Consumed with his own ravaging desires, he descends to the column of my neck, trailing kisses down to my chest. I wasn't wearing my bra when I'd gone to bed, so I'm bare to him. My body as naked as my emotions, raw and exposed and utterly his in every way.

While he showers my breasts with attention, I drift my hands over his broad shoulders. The muscles flex and coil beneath my fingers. He's so solid. So strong and masculine. Yet I've never felt so safe with a man. As if his strength is an extension of my own. His body mine to command.

I cry out when his teeth tug at my nipple. The jolt is the perfect marriage of pleasure and pain. Zeno makes my body sing with desire until my core weeps, and a sheen of perspiration coats my skin.

"How many times have I dreamed of tasting you? Hundreds. Thousands." His body lowers until his head is positioned at the apex of my thighs. Eyes locked on mine, his tongue takes a slow, languorous lick along my slit. "Not once did my imagination live up to this. You're fucking *divine*."

I moan his name as he devours me. Fingers kneading at my breast, tongue relentlessly circling my swollen bundle of nerves, Zeno unravels the fabric of my being. I am nothing but pleasure and writhing greed, relentlessly chasing that perfect moment of carnal bliss.

When his finger slips past my entrance and finds its way to that perfect spot inside me, I don't have to chase anything. Release crashes over me like the torrential downpour of a summer storm. My throat burns from a scream I can't hear. I'm too lost in the liquid elation coursing through the highways and byways of my body. He coaxes every possible shudder and shiver from my body like an artist crafting the perfect portrait.

"Zeno." I breathe his name to remind myself that this is real. He's here, and for the moment, he's mine.

The loss of his touch draws open my eyes. I watch raptly as he unbuttons his pants and allows them to pool on the floor. His naked, tattooed form is on full display, and I have never laid eyes on anything so flawless. Models and actors are sculpted with muscle, but Zeno's body is more than an aesthetic. He is the embodiment of power and strength, and I have no doubt he knows how to wield both.

He rolls on a condom, and I'm not sure what's more erotic: his straining cock, or his broad hand fisting that hard length. His abs ripple with his movements, and I feel each twitch of his muscles deep in my belly. I know it's safer to use protection, so I don't object, but damn if I don't crave the unobstructed feel of him. I'm tired of things coming between us. Even the thin rubber barrier is a burden after so many years of conflict and strain.

But we aren't there yet. For now, I'll savor what I can.

When his body aligns with mine, my breaths become shallow with anticipation. The scalding heat of his cock radiates through the condom and soothes my aching clit, but only for a second. With one arch of his hips, he's at my entrance, pressing inside me. Once, twice, three thrusts find him fully sheathed within me. My jaw drops at the fullness, and my eyes stray up toward the ceiling.

"Eyes on me, Isa." Strain tugs at Zeno's voice. A vein bulges in his neck, and his triceps bunch with effort.

I do as he says, and only when our gazes are locked does he resume his movements. One quick thrust, then a slow retreat before surging back inside me. He speaks a million words in those ocean eyes of his, but there's only one I hear. One word can be discerned without interpretation.

Mine.

I respond in kind with the only thing left for me to say.

Yours.

Zeno rewards me with an increase in his pace, pounding into me with the intensity of a holy man seeking God. My core is still sensitive from release, each of his movements re-igniting the fire in my belly. I move my body in tandem with his. A push and pull as natural as waves crashing on the shore. Over and over, we melt together in pleasure.

My body is alight with sensation, but when Zeno finds his release inside me, it's my heart that seizes with feeling. Emotions threaten to overwhelm me. To consume and destroy me. Being with Zeno is something I've only ever let myself imagine in my darkest moments. Times of great weakness when I sacrificed my pride to give my heart a taste of the impossible.

Or so I thought.

I never believed something like this could happen, but it has, and I've never experienced sex bound with such intense emotion. All my past escapades shrivel and pale in light of what exists between Zeno and me.

He clutches me tight, my name wrenched from his lips, over and over, his cock pulsing deep within me. Once his movements still, he brings his lips to mine one last time in a kiss fraught with tenderness and devotion. He then slips away to the bathroom. This is his house, so I wonder for the briefest second if he'll leave now to go to his own room, but that thought is banished when he joins me back in bed. He spoons his body around mine, pulling me against him with a strong arm around my middle. We lie on our sides, bodies molded together, lungs expanding and contracting in sync with one another.

I trail my fingers absently over the ridges of his knuckles, not wanting to move and burst the bubble keeping us safe from reality. I note the dusting of hair on the back of his hand and a few smooth slivers of skin that I attribute to scar tissue. There is something alluring about a man's hands —the embodiment of masculinity and physical strength. They are a roadmap of a person's aptitudes and experiences, and Zeno's hands reveal that he's no stranger to hard work.

"I don't want to upset you by forcing the subject," Zeno says softly. "But I need to know what happened. Did you recognize the man who broke in?"

I breathe deeply through my nose. My mother's problems can no longer be kept a secret. I'm not sure how Z will respond to the truth, but I have to tell him.

"The reason I had to move back home is because I discovered that my mom has been gambling, and she got herself into debt with a family bookie. I knew what that would mean for Dad, so I used my school savings to pay off her debt. After, I told my dad what was going on. He was pissed, but I knew he didn't have the money to handle the matter himself, and there was no way in hell I was letting the family label him a deadbeat and possibly hurt him."

Z is silent for several seconds as he absorbs the information. "I would tell you that you should have come to me, but I understand why you didn't. I'm fucking pissed at myself, though. You should never have been in that situation."

I squeeze his hand, holding his arm tight against my chest to let him know I appreciate his remorse. "None of it was a problem until the bookie came to the house drunk one day while everyone else was gone."

Zeno's body goes inhumanly still. "This has happened more than once?" His guttural words are infused with lethal calm.

"Not as bad," I whisper. "But, yeah. I was able to escape and get one of my dad's guns."

"Jesus *Christ*!" Z rolls away from me and surges from the bed, a hand stabbing through his hair as he paces back and forth before turning a wall of fury in my direction. "His name." The two clipped words hiss between clenched teeth.

"Aldo Consoli." My voice is small. I know Z isn't mad at me, and I'm certain he'd never hurt me, but I've never witnessed this side of him. Not to this extent. He is the embodiment of righteous vengeance. If anything, I'm scared for anyone who stumbles into his path.

Z grabs his clothes and begins to hastily redress.

"What are you doing?" I blurt.

"I have to go. This is all my fault, and I need to fix it."

"*Stop*." My command is strong enough to snag his attention. "You haven't slept, and there's nothing that can be done at three in the morning. Please, stay until the sun is up so I don't spend the rest of the night worrying."

His piercing stare holds firm, but I know I've won when the tension in his shoulders eases. Slowly, he strips his clothes back off and returns to the bed. This time, he lies on his back and pulls me into his side. His body is still, but the press of my ear to his chest reveals a thundering pulse.

"Tell me the rest," he instructs with a forced calm.

"I got him paid off, but when he came to collect the money, Grace happened to come by our house to get her mom's sewing scissors. The two talked, and when Grace heard that Aldo had loaned Mom money, she decided borrowing from him would help get her moved to the city sooner rather than later. When I learned what she'd done, I was terrified. I tried to get her to return the money and back out, but she refused. I've been so worried for her, but I didn't think I personally had anything to worry about anymore. Last night, I was listening to music, and I guess he heard it on his way to pay a visit to Grace. I guess that's what he does—get drunk, then seek out female customers to offer discounts for … services. That or change the terms of his loans to coerce an *exchange*. I hate him with every fiber of my being."

"How did he get inside the house?"

"I don't know exactly. The music was loud, and he was suddenly there. I tried to get away, and we fought. That's how I got this." I motion to my cheek. "Then he was so angry, I knew I'd never get away. That I had to find a weapon." My voice begins to quiver.

Zeno's arm holds me tighter against him while his other hand cradles my head. "You don't have to say any more," he whispers. "I'm so proud of you, Isa. You did exactly as you should have, and I'll take care of everything else. I promise."

I nod and try to take a calming breath. "There's something else you should know about last night," I tell him. "When I threatened Aldo with the probability that he'd get in trouble for hurting me, he said he had permission to be here in the Park. I never saw him drive a car, so as far as I know, he could have been climbing the wall to get in. He could have been lying, but I figure you should know."

Zeno trails his fingers through my hair. "No permission will exonerate him from what he's done. Coming onto my fucking property to hurt anyone on my estate. As I said, you don't need to worry about any of it again. I'm here, and for now, all you need to do is get some rest."

"Okay."

My head still rests above his heart. I don't expect to sleep, considering everything that's happened, but nestled safely against Z's warm body, lulled by his gentle caress, my thoughts drift to unconsciousness. I slip into a deep, cathartic sleep and don't wake again until the sun is well into the sky.

When I come to, I don't have one of those moments when everything comes rushing back to me in a flash of memory. Between the pulsing pain in my left cheekbone and Zeno's scent blanketed around me, my conscious mind is all too aware of all that's happened in the past twelve hours. Even the fact that I'm now alone in the bed doesn't come as a surprise. Considering how urgently Z wanted to start his manhunt, I doubt he waited five minutes after I'd fallen asleep to leave.

I sit up and scan the room around me, unsure what to do next. Do I go home? Is Aldo dead on my kitchen floor?

Did I kill a man last night?

The possibilities make me want to retreat beneath the covers and never leave this room. I have so many questions, but that one worries me the most. I'm desperate to know the answer but equally terrified. I don't want to have killed anyone, but I also hate to think of Aldo alive and hungry for my blood. Regardless of my aversion, I have to know.

If he did survive, could he be at the house waiting for my return? Surely, his need for vengeance wouldn't overrule his need to save himself and get medical attention. I can safely assume that Z has stopped by the cottage to assess things for himself, but I'm not going over until I know for sure. That's when I notice my phone on the nightstand. I left it at the house when I ran. Zeno must have brought my phone back after checking out the scene.

I could call and ask Z what he found at my house, but he won't want to discuss it over the phone. If he came back to Hardwick with my phone, he might still be here. My best bet for answers is to go in search of him and hope he hasn't left.

I'm up and dressed in an instant. Aside from my need to know what's going on, my family will be back from the city anytime. I don't have the luxury of burying my head in the sand. I've got to get home and clean the blood out of the kitchen. I'm not sure why, but I don't want them to know what happened. I don't want them to see our family home the way I am now feeling about it. Unsafe. Tainted.

While I'm in the bathroom, I examine the bruise on my cheek. It doesn't look as bad as I expected, but there will be no hiding it from my family. I'll have to decide what I'm willing to tell them. Maybe once I know more myself, the answer will come to me.

When I reach the bottom of the stairs, Elena is sipping coffee in the sitting area right off the main entry. Her face lights up when our gazes meet.

"Isa," she says my name with relieved affection and hurries over. "Were you able to get some sleep?"

"Yes, thank you." I glance in the direction of Zeno's office. "Is Z still here?"

"No, but he did let me know on his way out that you were safe to go home, if that's what you want. Of course, you're welcome to stay here as well."

Safe to go home—what does that mean? Was Aldo dead? Surely not, or Zeno would have come to tell me himself, right? Is he out dealing with my attack, or is his disappearance part of an awkward morning after? I have no idea where our night leaves us. Will he text me on his own? Am I supposed to reach out? If he told his mom to pass along a message, I should probably assume that's the extent of what he needs to say at the moment. It's not particularly informative, but it's at least something to go on.

I smile and nod. "That's good to hear. I ought to get back before my family gets home."

"Would you like a cup of coffee before you go?"

"If I can take it to go, then sure. But I really need to get going."

She places a gentle hand on my arm. "Of course, let me get you a travel mug."

I follow her back to the kitchen, where she loads me up with a ton of coffee, and I give her a hearty thanks before slipping out the back exit. I've been given the all clear to return home, but even in the bright light of day, my nerves have me searching the shadows for hidden dangers. Elena offered to walk with me, but my silly pride insisted I'd be fine.

I would pick up my pace to a healthy stroll if I wasn't somewhat dreading what I'd find at the house. I'm not in an outright panic because Zeno wouldn't have told me the place was safe if it wasn't. When I reach the back door, I find it unlocked. Slowly, I ease open the door. My eyes immediately cut to the block of knives on the counter across the room. Every slot is filled. Each knife handle is in place.

Confused, I tiptoe around the small island to discover the floor on the other side is immaculate. There's not a drop of blood. No sign of a struggle at all.

I'm stunned. The incident already feels like a living nightmare. To see my kitchen looking as though nothing ever happened is surreal. If I didn't know better, I'd say Aldo's attack had never even happened, but the sticky memories I can't escape are too real to be a product of my imagination.

I walk around the corner to the living room. Everything

looks to be in order, but when I place my hand on the carpet where my glass of wine spilled, the area is wet. Either Zeno cleaned the place himself, or he had someone else do it. That is the only explanation.

I have to know what happened—what Z found when he arrived at the house. I have to know if I killed Aldo Consoli. I don't have the patience to worry about upsetting Z by calling. I don't care about dating protocols or anything else. I need answers.

I open my phone and dial his number.

"Everything okay?" Zeno answers his phone with an urgency to his voice.

"Yes, everything's fine. I just got over to my parents' house. Z, I need to know if I … k—"

Before I can say more, he cuts me off. "Not over the phone, Isa. I'll be back later today. We can talk in person."

"Oh, yeah. Okay." My eyes scrunch shut in annoyance at myself. Of course, I shouldn't be saying something incriminating over the phone. "Just answer one question. Was there anyone here when you got here?"

"No."

The sound echoes in my ears. The word bears such finality, but in this case, it births a world of uncertainty. Aldo left the house alive, but what happened after? Where is he now? Will he come after me?

"Alright, then," I respond, my voice thin and reed-like. "Well, thank you, again, for your help."

"Isa," Zeno calls to me, his voice a gentle caress. "I told you I'll handle it. He won't touch you again, understand?"

"Yeah, okay," I whisper.

"I'll see you soon, sweet girl." His murmured words melt my heart like warm butter.

"Bye, Z." I end the call and breathe deeply.

I don't want to panic about Aldo, so I give myself over to thoughts of Z instead. I'd rather overthink that situation than dwell on the possible dangers around me.

After so many years at odds with him, having Z back in my life feels like a dream. A glorious, intoxicating, ethereal dream. It's hard for me to comprehend that it's happening. I suppose the real test will come when I see him again. Will I sense cool restraint in his presence, or will he seal his place in my heart? I didn't get the sense last night that Zeno's interest in me had been transient, but our history makes it hard to wash away the uncertainty. Enough uncertainty that I have plenty to contemplate until my family shows up a half hour later.

They parade through the front door like any other day but stop short when they get a glimpse of my face. The only one who doesn't gape and pepper me with questions is my father. He doesn't say a single word. Not out loud. But his remorseful stare speaks volumes.

Zeno has informed him of the situation. It's the only explanation.

I have no doubt my father now knows all about Aldo. It's there in the murderous cut to his jaw and slow intervals of his measured breaths. He's a powder keg of emotions waiting to ignite.

I assure everyone that my injury was a product of my own doing—too much wine at my impromptu dance party and a sneaky coffee table wanting in on the action. I point out the wet carpet as evidence of my shenanigans and breathe a sigh of relief when Mom and my sisters accept my excuse as the truth. Mom chatters airily about their outings with my aunt while Livia rolls her eyes and charges upstairs without saying hello. For once, I encourage Mom's incessant blathering with feigned interest until I notice the effervescent smile on Gia's face. It hasn't faded an ounce since she walked in the door, aside from a few moments of concern over my black eye.

When she slips upstairs to unpack, I sneak away from Mom to follow her. "You sure look happy to be home," I say once we're alone in our room.

The joy shining in her eyes warms my chest.

"Carter reached out yesterday. I thought about calling you but decided to wait and tell you in person. He and the kids will be back today and have invited all of us over to celebrate Zeno's birthday this evening. He was so sweet, Isa. I don't know what all happened in the last couple of weeks, but I think he may have sorted his feelings. I'm just so happy he's coming back." A healthy flush has returned to her porcelain skin, and I'm reassured that her heart is well on its way to full repair.

A tidal swell of relief makes my sinuses burn with the threat of tears. "Oh, Gia. I'm so thrilled for you." I pull my sister into a hug, and when we pull away from one another, her eyes are glassy.

"Who knows what will happen. I'm just glad there's a chance. I missed him and the kids so much."

"I know you did, honey."

Did Zeno play a role in Carter's return? If he did, he took the initiative before our night together. He'd listened to my perspective when we spoke, that I can say for certain. I don't know for sure whether he took corrective action, but my gut insists that he did. That all his barriers between us have dropped, and it's changing him.

He's changing me, too. Making me realize how quick I've been to jump to conclusions. There are so many things in this world that I know nothing about. How incredibly brazen I've been to judge what I don't know.

"We're supposed to go over for dinner at six. I thought I'd

make cookies to take with us. I'm sure Mrs. Larson will have a cake, but the kids love iced sugar cookies."

"I'm sure they'd appreciate that." I grin, so incredibly happy for my sister.

I debate telling her about Zeno and me, but I'm not sure what to say. I don't want to scare her about Aldo, and otherwise, it's a bit odd to explain how Z and I came together. Plus, I want to see him in person and put to rest the last of my fears before I go professing my feelings for him. If there's any chance he's going to regret sleeping with me, that should be obvious by this evening once he's had plenty of time to consider what he's done. Until then, I'll wait anxiously to learn my future.

CHAPTER 7

DAD INSISTS WE DRIVE TO THE BISHOPS' RATHER THAN WALK. No one argues, but my mother gives him an odd look, and I understand why. The evening is unusually temperate. Dad loves the outdoors and would normally be the first to suggest we all walk and take full advantage of the weather. It's out of character, but no one says anything. I suspect he has finally decided to err on the side of caution in light of recent events.

Livia has gone to a friend's house, leaving Gia, Marca, and me in the back seat of the car, along with Gia's tray of cookies. Zeno and Elena are already at the house when we arrive. My insides twist and flutter at the sight of him, unable to decide if they are more nervous or excited.

I'd completely forgotten about his birthday. I feel bad not having a gift or even a card, but we were hardly even speaking to one another a week ago. So much has changed in such a short span of time.

He and Elena join Carter at the door to welcome us. I pay special attention to Zeno's interaction with my father. Dad is stiff and reserved, adding to my suspicions that the two have spoken recently. I wonder what was said and desperately hope Zeno isn't angry with my father. Dad's discomfort seems to be one-sided, which makes me think any blame he's feeling is likely self-imposed.

My mother croons when Z places a welcoming kiss on her cheek. He is surprisingly attentive to her and even gives Marca a special hello when he normally sticks to a stoic nod or a raised glass in lieu of a greeting. When it's my turn to pass before him at the tail end of our little procession, his eyes soften as his fingers weave through my hair to cup the back of my head. He pulls me close to place a kiss on my forehead as though it's a ritual gesture we share frequently.

I momentarily forget how to breathe.

Gia pauses from her cheerful reunion with Carter to shoot me a bulging stare. I give her an innocent shrug as Carter's two kids come rushing in. They wrap Gia in hugs and excitedly survey the cookies she made. The foursome is a Hallmark movie come to life, and I can't help but grin at their happiness. Curious at its origin, I glance back at Zeno with a questioning look, but he merely raises a single quizzical brow and ushers me forward with a hand at the small of my back.

As we walk toward the living area, I realize Cora is nowhere to be seen. It doesn't necessarily mean anything, but one can only hope her absence is permanent. Even if she wasn't solely responsible for Carter's hasty exit, her snobby attitude couldn't have helped.

Without Cora's snide comments or Livia's whining, our gathering is perfectly crafted for the lighthearted enjoyment of a summer evening. Carter grills burgers. Gia and Marca play a card game with Boston and Emily. I sip on a Michelob Ultra and try not to stare at Z while he chats with Carter by the grill. It's a storybook evening, aside from being asked several times what happened to my eye. I'd prefer not to be reminded of the homicidal lunatic who tried to rape me but cannot escape the questions about something as noticeable as a shiner. I pass along the same made-up story I'd told my family, and no one raises any doubts. They laugh along with me as I regale my clumsiness, and the subject moves on to safer waters.

Not long after we finish eating, Zeno steps into the yard to take a quick phone call. When he returns, he's all business. Every ounce of birthday levity from minutes before has been erased.

"Carter, I hate to do this, but I've been called to the city on urgent business."

"Oh … well, I hope everything is all right."

"Yeah, but I have to head out earlier than I would have liked." Zeno's eyes slide briefly to mine.

"You want us to package up a slice of cake for you? I'd hate for you to miss your own birthday cake."

"How about you send a piece home with my mother? Antonio, would you mind giving her a ride back to Hardwick?"

Dad nods gravely. "Of course. I'll make sure she gets home safely."

"I appreciate that," Zeno says, turning his attention back to Carter. "And sorry again to run. We'll have to return the favor at my place next."

"Absolutely. Be safe on your way out."

Z smiles and nods his appreciation at a chorus of happy birthdays before making a hasty exit inside the house. I can't let him leave without knowing if the call was about Aldo. I jump up with a muttered, "Excuse me," and dash for the back door.

"Z, wait!" I call out through the house as the front door clicks shut. When I reach the door and fling it open, I'm able to flag him down before he's in his car. "Wait! I need to talk to you, just for a minute."

He closes the car door, and in several long strides, meets me on the other side of the black Range Rover. "I need to get going, Isa."

"I know, but the uncertainty is killing me. You have to tell me what's going on. Do you know where Aldo went? Is he still alive?" *Will he come after me?*

Flyaway hairs pull free from my messy bun when the evening breeze blows past. Zeno's fingers coax them back behind my ears, then trail down to cup either side of my neck. His thumbs on my jaw angle my chin up to receive his kiss. A sensual caress filled with assurance, apology, and promise.

"The less you know, the better, but be assured that I'm handling it." His voice is as coarse as the gravel at our feet. He turns his head to the side and lets out a sharp whistle that startles me but not as much as seeing two men materialize from the bushes not twenty feet from us.

I instinctively reach for Zeno. "What the hell?"

"Easy, Isa. They're with me. I wanted you to know that I've had eyes on you since the moment you left my house this morning. You have nothing to worry about."

"Is Aldo the reason you're leaving?" I can't help but push for more. I want to know what's happening.

He takes a slow step back without offering an answer, spoken or otherwise. When he takes a second step and starts to turn away, I call out one last question. He may be adamant about refusing to discuss Aldo, but there's one topic he can't deny me.

"What is this, Z? What's happening with us?"

He pauses, his inscrutable gaze coming back to mine. "This is whatever you want it to be. I've told you how I feel—it's been the same since we were teens. What comes next is up to you."

His admission winds me. Baffles and bemuses me.

I don't say another word as he slips into his car and disappears into the night. I am speechless. A part of me genuinely expected him to be distant this evening and show some sign of second thoughts, but that couldn't be farther from the truth. Zeno De Rossi cares for me. He still wants me, despite the horrific things I said. The insults. The accusations.

And if I'm honest with myself, I want him too.

It's like Gia said weeks ago. Some people we simply never get over—no matter the time or distance that spans between us. That has always been Zeno for me. It's the reason his insults continued to hurt, and it was my motivation for never giving up on him.

Z is that one person who will always live in my heart and own a piece of my soul.

I never dared to dream the opposite might be true—that I might be that person for him as well. Who am I to reject that kind of divine connection? I couldn't even if I wanted to. And I don't. Even now, I'm anxious for him to return. Now that I've had a taste of what we could share, I'm ravenous for more.

I take a lungful of the mild, humid air to ground myself.

The sentries Zeno summoned have sunken back into the shadows and are no longer visible. I appreciate knowing they are watching, but their invisibility is an unsettling reminder of how easy it would be for an enemy to approach unseen. I hurry back inside, locking the door behind me, and wind my way to the back of the house, where I happen to spot Carter in the kitchen. When I step closer, I discover he's alone and decide to seize the opportunity.

"Hey, Carter. Do you have a minute to chat?"

He whips around from the fridge, a bottle of water in hand. "Sure! I was just grabbing some water. Want a bottle?"

"No, thanks. I'm good."

He closes the door and strolls toward me. "What can I help you with?"

"I wanted to talk to you about Gia," I say softly. Both because it's a sensitive subject and because I don't want to be overheard.

His lips thin, and his blond eyebrows knot together. "Is she okay?"

"She is now, but your stint in the city was hard on her. I would normally never butt into someone's life like this, but this is important. Gia isn't like most people. She keeps her emotions guarded, so it can be hard to tell what she's feeling. I want you to know that she adores you and the kids. If there is any doubt in your mind, please know that it's unfounded. I've never seen her so happy as when she learned you were returning." Lord forgive me, but it needed to be said. If I leave it up to Gia, Carter might never feel confident enough in her affection to pursue her.

Carter toys with the lid on his water bottle, eyes cast downward. "She's come to mean a great deal to us. The last few weeks weren't easy on me either, and we won't be leaving again anytime soon." When his eyes lift to mine, they glow with love and conviction.

I give his forearm a gentle squeeze. "That's so wonderful to hear. I guess we better get back outside before they devour the cake without us."

"They wouldn't dare." He gives me a scandalous look.

"Wouldn't they?" I tease back.

We start for the back patio, and I can't help but dig for information on his sister. "Did Cora decide to stay in the city a while longer?"

"We decided it was best for everyone if she spent a little less time here." He glances back at me with a cryptic glint in his eye.

"Ah, well. They say absence makes the heart grow fonder."

"Indeed." Carter opens the glass patio door and motions for me to go first with a smirk.

The rest of our night passes without further disruption. Dad takes Elena home before coming back to chauffeur us to the cottage.

"Liv texted that she's back home," Mom informs no one in particular. "She said she was going to bed early because she wasn't feeling well. Hopefully, she hasn't picked up a stomach bug. We'll all end up with it."

Dad parks out front of the house, ignoring Mom's comment. "Isa, why don't you come around to the front for a minute. I'd like to have a private word."

Mom, Gia, and Marca all turn to stare at me. I widen my eyes with a look that says, "What? You know as much as me," then exit the back seat. Talks with my dad are rarely heavy, so it's easy to make like of his request in front of the others, but on the inside, I know this talk will be different. This isn't our normal subject matter, and I can sense how upset he is.

Once we're alone, the car becomes saturated with tension. It radiates from my father like heat from a flame, and I begin to realize how much he's been holding back since they returned home. Since he learned what his willful ignorance has enabled.

"Did Zeno call you?" I ask quietly.

"He did. First thing this morning. He told me what happened last night. You can't imagine how upset I was." Dad pauses, his eyes unseeing out the front windshield. "But when … when he informed me that it wasn't the first time Aldo had gone after you, I thought my skin would blister my anger burned so bad. At myself and Aldo, but also you." His words are brutally honest and spoken with painstaking calm. They slowly drive a stake into my heart and wrench my chest wide open.

My lips part to speak, but no sound emerges. Emotion squeezes down on my throat.

"Do you have any idea what it's like to find out my baby was—" his words catch, and he has to take a deep breath before continuing. "My baby was *attacked* right in our own home, and she didn't trust me enough to tell me? To let me know so I could make sure it didn't happen again?" Dad clenches the steering wheel in both hands, his knuckles bleeding to white. "I know none of it was your fault and that you're innocent in all this. I'm not trying to blame you. I just always thought that of my four girls, you'd be the one who would trust me with anything. Yet, somehow, I fucked up enough that even my Lulu thought she had to take on a monster by herself."

Tears tumble down my cheeks as I watch my daddy's chin quiver with regret.

Regardless of what he said at the start, he's not mad at me. He's furious with himself. But as much as I hate for him to be upset, there's a part of me realizing for the first time that he's right. I don't fully trust him, and that breaks my heart even more than witnessing his self-loathing.

Where Aldo is concerned, I had a variety of reasons for not speaking up about his first assault attempt that didn't necessarily involve my father. But in addition, I was also reluctant to go to my father with my problems because he can be dismissive that any real trouble exists. How many times have I gone to him with concerns about Mom and my sisters? And how many excuses has he made on their behalf? I adore my father, but he isn't a man of action. As much as it hurts to admit, Dad is just as flawed as any other person, no matter how much I've idolized him.

"Why don't you ever confront her?" I ask with a shaky breath. If we're going to talk about what happened, we're going to address the cause, not the result. Mom has been dragging our family down for years while Dad stands by and turns a blind eye. If we're going to talk about trust, then we'll go straight to the root of the matter.

"Because I didn't realize how destructive she'd become."

"You didn't want to see it, and I can understand that. I adore you, Daddy, always have and always will, but we needed you to step in and be the parent Mom couldn't be. Marca *still* needs that." I try to speak with tenderness because I know what I'm saying has to hurt. Confronting his short-comings isn't easy, but that's one area where he's better than most. Dad's not afraid to be wrong.

He turns his bloodshot eyes in my direction. "I'm so sorry, baby girl. I just … I never thought…"

I lean forward swiftly and wrap my arms around him, assuring him of my love. "It's okay, Daddy. I know you never meant anything bad to happen."

His body hitches with a shuddered breath that matches my own, and his arms clutch me tightly. As tough as it is to have such a difficult conversation and to see my father so distraught, I'm relieved it happened. That I voiced the things needing to be said, and that for once, Dad heard me.

He pulls back eventually, after we've both settled, and

wipes at his eyes. "I want you to know things are going to change. *I'm* going to change."

"As long as you're still you," I say softly. "You mean the world to me, Daddy, just as you are."

He gives me a sad smile and kisses my cheek. "Enough with the waterworks. Let's get inside."

I'm happy to oblige. It's been one hell of a day.

I sleep like the dead, but only after giving Gia a doctored summary of my evolved relationship with Zeno. From the looks of it, she'd been busting at the seams to find out what had happened between us. I also told her about my talk with Dad. By the time the lights clicked off, mental and emotional exhaustion carried me straight to dreamland.

When our alarm first sounds the next morning, I feel like I'm being drawn awake from a medically induced coma. I'm disoriented, and my movements are clumsy and sluggish.

"God, I could sleep for a week," I moan to the universe, in case it's listening and cares to comply.

Gia chuckles and sits up, seemingly unencumbered by my affliction. "Do you need a quick shower to wake you up? You can jump in the bathroom first if you need to."

"Nah, you go ahead. The only thing that's going to help me is sweet caffeine." I fling the covers off me and slouch ogre-like on the edge of the bed. Once I've summoned the energy to stand, I slide on some lounge pants and plod down the stairs in search of liquid energy.

When the Keurig kicks into gear, the rich aroma alone is enough to prick at my sense and liven me up. I take my full mug to the kitchen table, surprised when Livia breezes into the room.

"Morning, Isa," she says cheerily.

"You're up early. You have somewhere to be today?"

"No," she says innocently while rummaging through the fridge. "Not really."

Okaaaay. My spidey senses tell me something is up, but it's awfully early for her games. I sip my coffee instead and focus on waking up.

"Don't we have any orange juice in here?"

"Juice? You always have coffee in the morning."

Liv turns to grin at me and places a hand over her flat abdomen. "I don't think I'm supposed to have coffee now."

"Oh, yeah. Mom said you weren't feeling great last night."

She sucks her lips between her teeth, fighting a grin. "That's not what I meant. I'm pretty sure you aren't supposed to have caffeine … when you're pregnant."

For the briefest moment, I convince myself that I've had a stroke. It explains my exaggerated weariness and Livia's outlandish admission—I'm clearly suffering from brain damage and delusions.

It has to be.

I dazedly sip from my mug, burn my tongue, then startle enough to slosh hot coffee onto my fingers. "Goddammit!" I set down the mug and shake my hand to ease the sting.

Livia giggles and offers me a paper towel. I look between her and the coffee, a horrible surety settling in that this is real. My tongue really is burned, and Livia really did just tell me she's pregnant. I've never been so disappointed in my own good health.

"Please, tell me you're joking," I breathe.

Annoyance flashes behind her eyes. "Well, that's *rude,*" she mutters. "I wasn't certain until this morning, but I took a test, and it's positive!" She stretches her arms wide and beams like the happiest woman in the world.

"Liv, you don't even have a boyfriend. How can you be so happy? Who is the father?"

"It's Nevio, of course." Her grin is eerily calculating. "I told you everything would be fine. That I'd marry someone rich and wouldn't have to scrub toilets all my life."

I'm going to be sick.

This can't be happening. If Liv is pregnant with Nevio's child, that would mean they've been having sex since … practically since he came home for the funeral. I think back to her disappearing from the lunch that day and recall all the times since that she wasn't around. When she said she'd gone out with Nevio, it never occurred to me she'd been hanging out with him for weeks already. It certainly never registered that they might have already been having sex.

Holy shit. She has no idea she's pregnant with her half brother's child.

I place my hand over my mouth to keep back the bile as Mom joins us in the kitchen.

"You look awfully pale, Isa," Mom says. "Did you get a touch of Livy's stomach bug?"

"That would be tough to do, considering it's not a stomach bug," Liv says proudly. She waits dramatically for Mom to give her full attention. "I'm pregnant, Mama. Nevio and I are going to have a baby." My sister grins exultantly.

Mom's jaw drops, and for a second, I wonder if she knows the implications. Then she's jumping up and down and crushing Livia in a congratulatory hug. She has no idea.

So many fucking secrets, and now look where we are.

Anger and adrenaline buzz through my veins. I have to do something. I have to tell *someone*.

I could call Zeno. He definitely needs to know, but this has snowballed beyond the point of return. This isn't just about protecting his family's honor anymore—this is beyond catastrophic—and it's past time for my father to know the truth. If that angers Z, then I'll deal with him later.

"Where's Dad?" I blurt harshly, dousing their reverie.

Mom and Livia look at me quizzically.

"Why?" Mom asks. "What's gotten into you?"

"Just tell me where the fuck Dad is!" I scream, slapping my hand on the table.

I've completely lost my mind, and I don't have a single fuck to give.

My sister is pregnant with our brother's child.

There is only so much a person can take, and I have pushed well beyond that limit.

CHAPTER 8

Mom's eyes bulge at my outburst. "He was meeting the gardener this morning. He left a half hour ago."

I run upstairs, grab my phone, and slide on my tennis shoes. I don't mess with socks or take time to put on my bra. Instead, I bolt down the stairs and out the back door, completely ignoring Mom's and Livia's gaping stares. The morning dew permeates my thin lounge pants as I jog through the knee-high grass on my way to Hardwick. There's a narrow path worn into the dirt where we always walk, but the tall blades of grass still arc over to graze across my shins.

Once I'm on the open lawn where the grass becomes manicured and free of trees, I run for the front of the house. Dad is talking to a younger man near one of the many flower beds. His face hardens the second he sees me running over, and he quickly ends his conversation, striding toward me to close the distance between us.

"What's wrong? Are you okay?"

I glance at the gardener, my chest heaving with exertion. The man is out of earshot, but to be safe, I lean close and speak as softly as my screaming lungs will allow. "I didn't want to tell you that I knew because Zeno asked me not to tell anyone, but Livia just announced that she's pregnant, Daddy, and I don't know what to do." As soon as the words tumble out, I know they don't make sense.

Dad's brow furrows, his eyes growing impossibly squinty. "You're going to have to slow down and explain. I'm not following you. Livy's … pregnant?"

I take a deep breath and try to calm myself. "I know that you and Elena had an affair and that Nevio is your son. I found out that day last week when I went home sick. I wasn't so much sick as upset—not at you," I hurry to explain. "Just about everything. I said some awful things to Zeno, but we're mending that. It's beside the point. The point is, Livia announced that she's pregnant *with Nevio's baby*. Daddy, what do we do? She has no idea he's her *brother*."

Dad's eyes drift sadly toward the stone fortress that is Hardwick. "That boy always was too clever for his own good," he muses quietly before turning back to me. "I'm sorry you had to find out like this, Lulu. We've already talked about how my relationship with your mother hasn't been all that great. Not long after Gia was born, I started spending time with Elena. She was so lonely. Their relationship was primarily entered into for strategic reasons—a sort of marriage of convenience. He needed a wife and family, but the two were never truly in love. His devotion was always to the organization. He'd spend weeks at a time in the city, and poor Elena was so young and lost. We connected in a way I've never experienced with anyone else."

His voice is tender when he speaks of her, and I wonder if

he's still in love with her. Could that adoration for her be the reason he's never left Hardwick? I try to be patient as I listen. The information is fascinating, but it doesn't change the catastrophe we're facing.

"I have no good excuse for what happened next. There was a brief time when I was torn between two houses. When I learned that I was expecting children from two women at the same time, I was so ashamed. After that, I tried to keep my relationship with Elena platonic, though I wasn't perfect by any means. The one thing I did right was going to the doctor before you were even born to get a vasectomy. I didn't know where life would take me, but one thing was for certain, I wasn't having any more children. I went back to the doctor three times to make sure it wasn't a possibility. For a time, Elena made a push to strengthen her relationship with Silvano, so I did the same with your mother. When she became pregnant with Livy, though, I knew that I wasn't the only one who had strayed. I never told her that I knew. Who was I to judge her? And besides, there was no point confronting her. Elena would never divorce Silvano, and I didn't ever want to leave Elena. If your mother and I separated, she likely would have had to find another place to live, taking you girls with her. That wasn't an option. And as a single man, spending time with Elena would be inappropriate. The way things evolved sounds messy, but it worked. At least, I thought it did. I'm starting to realize how wrong I've been." He peers at me warily as if waiting for me to condemn him.

I'm dumbfounded.

Nothing in my life was what it seemed. I would think at some point I'd stop being surprised, but each new revelation blindsides me.

"So, Liv and Marca aren't yours? Who's their biological

father?" I know it's not particularly relevant, but my brain is struggling to keep up.

Dad shrugs. "Don't know and don't really care. I've always considered them mine, though I'm embarrassed to say I never felt quite as invested in them as I did you and Gia. I love them. I do. But my bond with them isn't the same."

"So, that's why you weren't worried about Liv dating Nevio?"

"Exactly. While the situation isn't ideal, it's not as bad as you were thinking. Not like when you set your sights on Nevio. That was a problem on so many levels."

They aren't related. Livia may be pregnant, but she's not in an incestual relationship.

Oh, thank God!

I reach forward and wrap my arms around Dad's middle. "It's okay. Everything's going to be okay," I murmur, mostly for my own benefit.

Dad chuckles. "Yeah, baby girl. Everything's going to be just fine."

"Okay." I nod and pull back. "I need to talk to Zeno, though. He needs to know what's going on."

"So, he knows about me and his mom?"

"Yeah, he's known since we were kids. He saw you guys. That's why we stopped being friends, but he only explained himself recently. He was pretty upset with you for a while." I say the last part gently because I know my dad will feel awful.

He frowns and has trouble meeting my eyes. "I can't say enough how sorry I am."

"It's in the past, Daddy. I promise. Though, I need you to pretend you don't know that Zeno knows. I wasn't supposed to tell anyone, but the whole Livy thing freaked me out." Zeno's secret is escaping like water through my fingers. I can't say for certain if Dad will tell Elena. I just don't know, but the more people I tell, the higher the chances. I don't want to break Z's trust, but I felt I had no choice. The possibility of upsetting him pulls at my already frayed nerves.

"You have nothing to worry about. I won't say a thing. Now, you better go home and get dressed. Don't think you want to show up for work in wet pajamas." For once, I know the sadness in his eyes is genuine, and it makes my heart hurt. He never wanted to hurt anyone. And how could I possibly begrudge him pursuing the woman he loves. I can't, and I don't want him to feel down on himself, so I smile and keep things light.

"You're absolutely right. Thanks, Dad. I know none of this is easy, but we'll figure it out."

I wave and head back toward the cottage. As I walk, I give Zeno a call on my phone.

"Hey there." His masculine purr sends a zing straight from my ear down to my belly.

"Hey. I hope I didn't wake you." I can imagine he had a late night since he didn't leave for the city until after dark.

"Not at all. I'm actually headed to the house."

"Oh, good. We need to talk." The line is dead silent for long seconds, and I realize how that sounds. "Nothing bad, not exactly. I just need to tell you some stuff that's happened."

"I'm not sure I'm any less worried."

I huff out a laugh. "Sorry about that. Try not to stress, and I'll come find you once I'm back at the house."

"Back? Have you already been to Hardwick this morning?"

"It's a long story. I'll tell you everything when I see you."

"How could it be a long story? We haven't been apart for twelve hours yet."

Again, he has me laughing. "Things happen fast around here. Try to keep up."

He grunts and hangs up. I walk back home with renewed hope that the world isn't ending—at least, not today.

"JESUS CHRIST. SHE'S FUCKING *PREGNANT*?" Zeno paces in front of the windows in his office while I sit on the sofa. I've just finished detailing everything I learned from my father and am surprised to find Z is more upset than I expected him to be.

"At least they aren't related. That would have been a disaster. And I know you didn't want my dad to know that you knew about the affair, but under the circumstances, I had to talk to him. I hope you're not upset." After thinking things through, I decided I had to admit to Z that I'd told my dad. There was no other way for me to explain knowing that Livia wasn't Dad's biological child. Besides, it's time for the secrets to come to an end. I feel better knowing I've been honest.

"I don't care about what your father knows, but I'm going to wring Nevio's fucking neck. How many *fucking* times do we have to go through this?"

His venomous words crawl along my skin like angry ants. How many times has Nevio gotten someone pregnant? This has happened before? Does Nevio have other children out there in the world?

"Z, what's going on?" I dread hearing his explanation, but I have to know the truth.

He stops and looks at me with trepidation—a worrisome emotion to see on a man like Zeno.

"My brother ... *our* brother ... is a sex addict. I didn't tell you about his issues because regardless of what you and others may think, I don't want to hurt Nevio. People with gambling or alcohol addictions aren't looked at the same as someone whose weakness is sex. At least as a man, he isn't condemned like he would be if he were a woman with the same problem. That is his only saving grace. He cheats and manipulates everyone in his life, and I know that's the addiction poisoning him, but it's hard to separate the two. He's been in and out of rehab. He has a counselor and resources, but celibacy rarely lasts long, and once he has sex, the cycle starts all over again. Sex in moderation has been beyond his reach."

I slowly list backward against the back couch cushions as I try to grasp what Zeno is telling me. I've always known Nevio was a playboy, but that's a far cry from sex addiction. When did it develop? Why? Can that type of addiction evolve out of nowhere, or did something tragic happen to trigger his disfunction?

No matter the cause, I'm devastated to hear that Nevio's issues are even worse than I'd thought. "Z, I feel terrible for him. How did this happen?"

Zeno joins me on the sofa, leaving enough space that we can face one another. "If you'll recall, I told you that we found reason to send him away after his sophomore year of school. The truth is, he had an inappropriate relationship with a teacher. According to the law, he was too young to consent, but he swore he was the one who seduced her. You know how he is—how he's always been. I don't doubt he could have been very persuasive, and the girl was in her second year of teaching, hardly older than him. It was an incredibly challenging time. My parents decided to remove him from the situation and get him counseling. While he was away, he proceeded to have sex with every female he could get close to. I'm not sure if the addiction came first or if the first relationship created the addiction. I'm not sure if he even knows. Regardless, his struggle has been a pervasive problem in his life. One he can't seem to escape." Z pauses, his gaze distant. "The one thing he didn't allow his addiction to stain was his love for you. I think the reason he never tried to get you back in his life after school is because he wanted to protect you. He adored you—we both did—but he knew he'd only hurt you. As he suspected, once you two were together here at the estate, the craving was too much. He had to try to get with you."

Surely, the universe can only dole out so much heartbreak to one person. Have I not reached my quota? Isn't it time to sprinkle the gloom and doom on some other unsuspecting sap? I want to be angry with Nevio, but how can I be when he's clearly so broken? Instead, I'm left with an abundance of sorrow.

"He made it sound like you guys ganged up against him and sent him away out of spite."

"Sometimes, he's more honest with himself than others. When his issues are at their worst, he blames us exclusively. When he's doing better, he accepts responsibility. But I wouldn't expect him to ever reveal his darkest secrets to you voluntarily. The shame would be immeasurable."

What a horrible way to live. Every relationship is shallow at best, if not toxic and manipulative. And now, Livia has bound herself to him for life.

I close my eyes and take a deep breath. "How many children does he have out there?"

"Not as many as I might expect. There are two that I know of, and now two more are on the way. I do my best to keep apprised of his ... activities. Before Livia, he got the housekeeper, Anna, pregnant on a visit home. I'm embarrassed to admit, but he tried to coerce her into aborting the baby. When she disappeared, I worried it had something to do with him. I confronted him, and he admitted what had happened. I tracked her down as quickly as I could. I needed her to know that he didn't speak for the family and that her child was safe and would be provided for."

His explanation aligns perfectly with what Gia witnessed in the city. Poor Anna. She had to have been terrified if she thought the Mafia wanted her unborn baby dead.

Z scoots closer on the couch and angles my face with gentle fingers to get a look at my eye. "It's looking better. How does it feel?"

"Fine. It doesn't hurt too bad unless I press on the bruising." I glance down at his hand and notice for the first time that his knuckles are mottled with dried blood. My fingers drift to his wounds and ghost over the broken skin. "What happened, Z? Did you fight with someone?" I stare deep into his kaleidoscopic eyes and search for the truth, but he is an expert at concealment.

"I did what I said I'd do—I took care of things."

Aldo. That's why his knuckles are bloody.

A flutter stirs in my chest from a surge of adrenaline. "What does that mean? You can't just kill him if he worked for the family, right? I don't want him coming after me, but I don't want you to get in trouble either—with the family or the law." My heart skips into a run, pitter-pattering against the confines of my chest.

Zeno brings our foreheads together, his hands cupping my face as he seems fond of doing. I'm pretty fond of it as well. His intoxicating scent fills my lungs when we're this close. It's delicious and distracting and is zero help in calming my frantic heartbeat.

"It means he's not an issue. You'll have to leave it at that.

He won't bother you again, and Grace's debt has been cleared. Forget the name Aldo Consoli ever existed."

And that's how I know Zeno De Rossi killed a man for me.

He didn't admit to it, but he doesn't have to. I know in my bones he would never allow such a threat to exist in the world. Does it bother me to know he's capable of murder?

I picture Aldo's beady eyes and shiver at the thought of his lecherous hands reaching for me. He was a disgusting excuse for a man, and I have no reservations about his death. In fact, I'm touched that Z would risk his own life and freedom to protect me in that way.

The answer is no. I'm not at all bothered by what he's done.

"Thank you, Z." I can only whisper because another set of words—three very special words—has wedged its way in my throat, but I'm not ready to release them. Not yet.

Instead, I bring my lips to his. It's meant to be a tender kiss of gratitude and affection, but it quickly morphs into something heated and carnal. He pulls me onto his lap, hands kneading firmly into my backside. Breathless, mindless minutes go by until Zeno draws his lips from mine and allows us both to settle our racing hearts.

"I'm taking you to dinner tonight."

"You are?" I smirk.

"Yeah."

"Is that your way of asking me on a date?"

"You can call it whatever you like, as long as you're there beside me."

My answering grin is effervescent. "When you put it like that, how can a girl say no?"

A satisfied rumble fills his chest while my mind drifts back to my sister.

"What are we going to do about Livy? She's convinced Nevio is going to marry her." I don't want to force them together, but I also don't want her abandoned and alone.

He releases years of frustration in a weary breath. "That is a far more complicated matter."

After work, I take a minute to call Grace and tell her the good news. Her debt has been forgiven.

"So, you and Zeno are together now, and he paid off my loan as like … a gift?" Her tone is incredulous. I don't blame her. It's a fantastical turn of events, and while only partly true, the result is the same.

"I know it sounds crazy, but I've was wrong about Z. We've had a lot of misunderstandings between us and have been sorting through it all. When I told him how worried I was about you, he insisted on repaying the loan. He said it was the least he could do since I'd already paid my family's debt on my own when he could have helped." I can't exactly tell her Z killed Aldo for attacking me, but I figure this makes decent sense instead.

"That is so crazy generous of him." Grace's voice wobbles with the onset of tears. "Please make sure to tell him how grateful I am. I just don't know what to say. I'm stunned. After all those years of trash-talking him … and now … you're together?"

"Well, I don't know exactly what our status is. We're having dinner tonight, so hopefully, we'll have time to talk then. It's all come about so quickly."

"No kidding! I'm hardly gone a week, and chaos erupts. I heard the Bishops are back, too. Mom was so relieved."

"So was Gia. I think she's in love with Carter, and I desperately hope this will be their shot. He seemed very attentive when we were over last night for dinner."

"They'd be perfect for each other," she says wistfully.

"What about you and Ari? Any updates there?"

"She came over, and we had an awesome day together. We've been texting a bunch. She seems so amazing. It scares me a little."

"Why would that scare you?"

"You know what they say about if something seems too good to be true."

"That's not always the case. Just take it slow and keep an open mind." It's advice I should take from myself. "Hey, Gracie, it's been good catching up, but I better get going. I need to get ready for my dinner with Z."

"I know, I know. I'll let you go, but real quick, how would that even work? Would your parents stay on as your employees if you marry him?"

"Holy crap, Grace! Slow down! We haven't even gone on a single date yet."

"Yeah, but you guys have history. It's not like you'd need a lot of time to get to know one another. I'm just saying … there is a lot to think about." She's not wrong, but I've got too many other things on my mind to worry about that now.

"*Bye*, Grace," I say playfully. "Talk to you soon."

"Always."

I end the call with a huge grin. There may be a ton of chaos going on in my life, but it's good to know my drama ended up helping my best friend. She's so upbeat on the phone that she hardly sounds like the same person.

An hour later, Zeno arrives at the house to pick me up. Something eerily similar to love stirs in my chest when he goes out of his way to shake hands with my father. It hasn't been easy for Z to push past his childhood trauma, and I appreciate that he's willing to befriend my father—someone who hurt him, even if the injury was unintentional.

We make our escape from the house with minimal fanfare. As Z reaches to open the passenger door of his car for me, he pauses with our faces inches apart. "You take my breath away, Luisa Banetti."

I'm not wearing anything too crazy—a flowy blouse over a black cotton skirt. It's dinner on a Monday night, after all. But one look from Z makes me feel like the most beautiful woman on the planet. That's the difference between him and his brother. Even before I knew about Nevio's addiction, flattery from him always felt discounted because of its abundance. When someone doles out compliments and attention like candy, it's hard to tell what's genuine and what's simply a habit. With Z, he only ever speaks with honesty when he does deign to comment on a subject.

"Glad I can return the favor," I breathe, my eyes drifting to his lips.

"*Fuck*," he groans before his mouth descends on mine.

His body presses me against the car, teasing my nipples with the warmth of his chest. The kiss is passionate but brief. When he pulls away, I can feel the effort of his restraint.

"I told myself I wouldn't devour you until after dinner … or at least the first course."

My smile has a life of its own. "If there's anyone who has mastered the art of self-restraint, it's you."

"I've never been challenged like this." He reaches for the door handle behind me and maneuvers me to the side to open the door.

"I have faith in you," I say coyly before easing into the passenger seat. I catch Zeno's responding grunt before the door clicks shut and quietly giggle to myself as he walks around to the driver's side.

Our ride to the restaurant is surprisingly pleasant. I'm not as nervous as I expected, and our conversation flows easily. It doesn't take us long to arrive at our destination, but when we do, the parking lot to the small Italian restaurant is nearly empty.

"Are you sure it's open?" I try to peer inside the heavily tinted windows, but it appears the curtains are drawn.

"I'm sure." He turns off the engine and comes around to help me from the car. "I wanted us to have the place to ourselves."

My steps falter. "Wait. What do you mean? You reserved the whole restaurant?" I gape at him.

A small salacious smirk lifts his mouth at one corner. "I own the place, so it wasn't all that hard to do." He takes my hand, and his eyes grow serious. "I missed out on a lot of years with you. I want you to be my sole focus. No distractions."

I'm speechless. I follow his lead in a daze, wondering how I ended up in this dream-like scenario. I try to take in the restaurant's romantic atmosphere and listen to the man who directs us to a table in the center of the room, but I can't stop replaying Zeno's words in my head. It's hard to believe this is real when before, it had only existed in a secret corner of my imagination.

"You're quiet tonight," Zeno notes after we've given our drink orders and are alone again.

I sip from my water glass, giving me a moment to put together the right words. "It's a little hard to wrap my head around how different things suddenly are. You were so … cold toward me for so long, and now you're thoughtful and attentive. It's a lot to process."

"I've always been attentive where you're concerned. You simply never knew it."

Our server brings over the bottle of wine Z selected and pours us each a glass before disappearing.

"You have to explain." I shake my head. "No more secrets or vague innuendoes. Not if I'm going to trust you."

He dips his chin in acquiescence. "Once you moved to the city, and I matured enough to accept that you were innocent in your father's actions, I started to keep eyes on you. I've always felt it was my job to protect you, even if at a distance."

"You had people *watching* me?"

"You weren't being followed or anything—nothing so … invasive. I made sure to look into your roommates … or … *other* people who came into your life. Employers. Professors. Boyfriends. Nothing crazy. I simply made sure the people around you weren't a threat."

"I think you and I have a different definition of crazy." I gape at him, shaking my head. "That's not exactly normal, Zeno."

His voice reverberates deep from his chest. "Who says I'm normal?"

He's right. Nothing about this man is average.

He lifts his wineglass to take a sip, and I'm transfixed by the dichotomy of the delicate glass gently propped between his masculine fingers. I have to force myself to focus on our conversation.

"It would seem you know all about my years in the city, but I don't know much about your life at all."

"What would you like to know?"

Everything.

I shrug. "I spoke with Savio the morning after we all had dinner."

"Did you?"

I detect the tiniest stiffening of his spine and wonder if it's curiosity or a touch of jealousy.

"I did. He told me how you two started working for the family at the same time and indicated you became close."

"We are. He's one of the few people I'd consider a true friend."

"It's a shame Christiano has pitted you two against one another."

"That's his way. He wants his family at the helm, but Savio has no desire to be the face of the organization. He and I decided years ago that I would make a push for boss, and he would be my consigliere."

This is the first I'm hearing directly from Z about his ambitions, and the fact that he's willing to share something so private thrills me, though the rush is tampered with reservation. I knew he was aiming to take over his father's role as underboss, but becoming boss of a Mafia family is a whole other level of responsibility. Of visibility.

"Do you think that'll happen?" I ask, sipping my wine.

"It's hard to say what will happen. Christiano wants Savio to succeed him. He's hell-bent on having his blood in leadership. And Savio is under immense pressure to give his uncle what he wants."

"That's so ridiculous. You'd be a better leader, and if you want the job, giving it to someone else because of their genes is absurd." I'm surprised I'm so defensive on Zeno's behalf. I don't even necessarily want him to be the boss, but I don't want someone stealing away the position if it's something he truly desires.

The corners of his lips quirk upward. "You always did call things like you saw them."

"Yeah, but how I saw it wasn't always right." My eyes trace the tines of the fork at my place setting, unwilling to meet Zeno's gaze when I think of the horrible things I've said to him. "I've been pretty embarrassed about how wrong I've been."

"The only person in this room who should feel any remorse is me. You handled a difficult situation with strength, dignity, and as much empathy as humanly possible. I don't deserve you, Isa, but I'll take every part of you I can get."

Our gazes lock in such a heated, intimate exchange that I'm almost relieved when the server arrives to take our orders. I'm terrified of how quickly my heart is reshaping itself to make room for Z. It's almost as if an echo of him kept his presence alive and allowed him to take up residence as though he were never gone. The seamless transition wouldn't have been possible if my heart hadn't clung to the hope of his return. I hadn't realized it was the case, but I'd never fully given up on our story.

We spend over an hour talking about everything under the sun. Nothing too heavy. Just two old friends getting to know one another again. The food is exceptional, and the candlelit setting enables us to get lost in our own private oasis where none of the drama of reality can touch us. Time slips by without awareness until my bladder insists I step away to the restroom. When I return, the table has been cleared, and Z is leaning back in his chair with a storm brewing in his eyes.

"Everything okay?" I slow as I approach the table. The

melodic strains of an acoustic guitar drift in the air around us, filling the empty room with anticipation.

Zeno stands and stalks around the table to me before I have a chance to sit. "I told myself not to push you—to let you come to me on your own and that you being here was enough—but I want more. I want to hear you say that you're mine."

Maybe it's the wine.

Maybe it's just Z, but I have no reservations about giving him what he wants because it's what I want too.

"I could never be anyone else's," I admit in a quiet but steady voice.

In one swift motion, he scoops me up and sets me on the table. His body presses close, spreading my legs to make room for him and easing my skirt up my thighs. My lips part on a gasp, and Z uses the opportunity to possess me, slanting his lips over mine with ravenous hunger. Fisting a hand in my hair, he tugs my head back to expose my neck. He lays siege to the delicate skin, teeth grazing and tongue laving a path down to my chest. When his knees drop to the floor, eyes burning my face as they drink me in, I realize his plan to devour me was no exaggeration.

"Z, we can't. Someone will see." My breathless objection lacks conviction.

"I sent the others home. It's just you—" His nose grazes my slit through the silk of my thong. "And me." His lips close over my core, coaxing a dizzying rush of blood to my clit.

"No one?" I ask dazedly.

"No one. I don't share what's mine."

My knees spread, spurred by my need for more. I'm about to tell Z to take off my panties when I hear the rip of fabric and feel the warm caress of his breath on my bare center. I moan with anticipation, leaning back on my hands as my eyes roll up to the ceiling. I'm rewarded with languorous licks from his rough tongue. Long, seductive touches that light my body on fire.

"*Yes*, Zeno. That feels so good."

I realize my eyes have drifted shut when cool air signals the loss of Z's delectable mouth. I crack my lids open to see him take a long swig of water. He watches me with predatory awareness. A hunter's warning that he'd be on me if I made the slightest move. So I sit still and wait. Pleasure coiling. Madness looms, and my inner muscles clench with frenzied need as Zeno rolls an ice cube around his mouth.

When his tongue returns to my slit, a burst of cold blasts me with a hunger so intense it clamps down on my lungs. The icy sensation causes a fever to spark through my veins, heating my core and electrifying my nerve endings. An over-whelming, chaotic energy quickly builds between my legs and deep into my belly. It swells and teases, but before it can reach its pinnacle, Zeno pulls away.

He rises to his feet and begins to undo his belt. "Turn around." His coarse, animalistic command licks down my spine. It doesn't just slide over my skin—the demand sinks down into the marrow of my bones, floods my bloodstream, and overwhelms my senses.

I am completely entranced.

Mesmerized and drunk off my need for the enigmatic man before me.

Without hesitation, I slide from the table and turn as I was instructed. Zeno's hands are instantly on my hips, lifting my skirt to fully expose me from the waist down. The heat from his body blankets my back. One hand snakes around to cup the delicate part of my throat while the other drifts down to my core.

"Me being inside you is different from you giving yourself

to me body and soul. Now that you've done that, there's no going back. Do you understand?"

Z waits for me to nod before folding us down, his body pressing my chest onto the white tablecloth. My hands brace against the table on either side of me. The searing heat of his cock settles perfectly in the crease between my cheeks, and I arch my back in invitation. He angles himself at my entrance when I realize I never heard him put on a condom.

"You didn't ask if I'm on birth control," I note absently. I'm on the pill, so I'm not worried about pregnancy, but he doesn't know that, right? Surely, his monitoring activities hadn't been that detailed.

"That's because I don't care," he murmurs against my neck, his cock gliding sensually along my slit. "I'm going to get you pregnant one of these days, and if it happens now, well, then it happens. We're not getting any younger, Isa. Plus, I'm clean, so that's not a concern."

"You don't know if I'm clean."

"Aside from trusting that you would tell me if there was something I should know, I'm going to spend the rest of my life fucking your beautiful body, so whatever you might have will be mine sooner or later. For better—" Z accents his words by slipping his throbbing cock an inch inside me. "Or worse." He thrusts again, voice straining.

I vaguely wonder at his choice of words but only for a second. The fullness inside me is too distracting to hold any thought except for a relentless need for more. He pounds into me from behind, quickly elevating to a merciless rhythm. Zeno manages to make our carnal position feel intimate and connected by keeping his body close to mine, his arms holding me like a precious treasure he can't stand to part with. When one hand lowers to reach between my thighs, I claw at the table beneath me, trying to process the sheer volume of sensation.

Breathless gasps tumble from my lips.

Pleasure commands every inch of me. Sweeps me away and traps me beneath a wave of liquid lightning. My body begins to shudder violently. Thousands of tiny fireworks ignite inside me, bursting from my core out to my fingers and toes as my inner muscles squeeze to the breaking point.

"Jesus, *fuck*," he hisses between labored breaths as his own release crashes over him. He squeezes me until I can't breathe, but I don't care. I don't need air when I'm full of Zeno.

My lungs argue differently, but lucky for them, he eases his hold as our twitching muscles calm in tandem. Our panting breaths slow enough that the gentle strains of music playing in the background return to my awareness.

When Z slides himself slowly in and out of me, his softening length still plenty solid to stir my insides, a purr sounds from deep in my throat.

"That feels so good," I murmur.

"It feels incredible. I've never been in a woman without a condom." His admission stuns me. It would mean either he's never had a girlfriend—which I find hard to believe—or he's never trusted anyone enough to go bare. No one until me.

I twist to meet his eyes. "Are you serious?"

Z lifts off me, helping me up. "I am." He takes a cloth napkin draped over the back of his chair and uses it to wipe the arousal from between my legs. "I watched the destruction that resulted from infidelity, and I wasn't willing to chance permanent ties to someone I wasn't certain about."

"What makes you certain about me?" I ask in a whisper.

He presses his cheek to mine, breathing in my post-orgasmic flush. "You're my Isa. I've never been more certain about anything in my life." He brings our lips together in a kiss that is tender yet passionate and totally intoxicating.

Zeno stuffs the napkin in his back pocket and helps right my clothing.

"Will you come back to Hardwick with me?" he asks after helping me into the car.

His invitation is incredibly tempting. I want to join him, but I also don't want to rush things. To risk losing the incredible feeling I get whenever I'm around him.

"I think I should probably head home. I have to work tomorrow, and there's the whole thing about you being my boss …"

"Is that really going to keep you from sleeping in my bed?"

I shrug. "It's not just that. Our families have a lot of history—*we* have a lot of history—and I don't want to screw things up by rushing."

"I can respect that, but your idea of rushing may be different than mine." He closes the door, a wolfish grin teasing his lips as he disappears from view.

CHAPTER 10

"You're up early again." I find Livia wrapped in a blanket at the kitchen table when I come down the next morning.

"I had to pee, and then my stomach didn't feel so great. Figured I'd try to eat some crackers, but once I got down here, I decided I couldn't eat anything." All her bubbling enthusiasm from the day before is gone. It could be the sickness or her winning morning personality, but I wonder if there's more to it.

"Have you told Nevio the news?"

"Yeah. He was supposed to come out here last night, but something came up." She's so incredibly naïve that my heart hurts for her.

I sit down in the chair next to her. "Livy, honey. You might want to consider the possibility that Nevio could struggle with the news of an unplanned pregnancy. That's a lot for a person to take in." I use my best Gia voice and choose my words with the utmost care. My goal isn't to hurt her, despite her clear and obvious reaction otherwise.

Spine rigid, she glares at me. "You don't know anything. He just doesn't want to come out here because you're so hateful to him. He's *thrilled* about the baby, and I have no doubt we'll be married in no time." She gathers her blanket and leaves the table, storming back upstairs.

That went about as well as could be expected.

Daddy always said you can lead a horse to water, but you can't force it to drink. Livia will always be that horse. She will never learn from others' mistakes or take advice she doesn't want to hear. It's unfortunate, but it's not my problem.

I heave out a sigh and continue with my morning routine. My evening with Zeno was too good for Livia to spoil my bright new outlook.

Once I'm at Hardwick, Elena stops by the kitchen to ask for a word with me. I'm curious but not overly concerned. She doesn't seem upset, and I can't think of a reason for me to be in trouble. I can't imagine she'd have a problem with Zeno and me being together, though stranger things have happened. Lately, strange has become the new normal.

I follow her to the sitting area off the main entry and take a seat in an armchair opposite her. "Is everything all right?"

"Oh, yes." She smiles warmly. "Zeno told me that you know about Nevio's struggles, and I wanted to talk to you about it myself. It hasn't been easy dealing with his issues and being unable to talk to anyone about it for fear of hurting him just adds another degree of difficulty."

"I can't even imagine."

"When we first sent him to boarding school, I cried for days. Silvano assured me that Nevio would be better off in a different environment, but I was so worried. I suppose the thing that helped me cope the most was knowing that Nevio and Silvano were getting space from each other. I always wondered if their strained relationship contributed to Nevio's problems. Silvano was so hard on him. He tried to toughen up Nevio because he thought my gentle boy was too soft." Her words are tortured. What a terrible position to have been in.

I'm endlessly curious about whether Silvano knew Nevio wasn't his and if that contributed to the strain in their relationship. It wasn't Nevio's fault he was the product of an affair. Yet my own father had expressed how the same circumstances had impacted his paternal feelings for my younger sisters. Maybe Silvano had faced a similar challenge.

Poor Nevio. It's no wonder he's a mess.

"There's never any way to know if what we're doing is best. You've always loved Nevio with your whole heart and done everything you can for him. That's all any child can ask of a parent." I try to give her the only assurance I can.

"We both did. Silvano's parenting may have seemed harsh, but he was trying to prepare Nevio for the realities of our world. As you know, we live with dangers other people only experience in the movies."

"Unfortunately, yes. I do know."

Elena nods and takes hold of my hand. "I'm glad Z told you all this. It'll make things easier in the days ahead. He told me about Livia and the baby. I've always wondered if our families might be connected one day, but that wasn't quite what I'd envisioned." Her blue eyes fill with worry. For once, she almost looks her age.

"You never know what the future holds." I smile and squeeze her hand as the doorbell chimes in the entry.

"I wonder who that could be." Elena stands, and I follow suit with plans to return to the kitchen, but when we reach the front door, Zeno is there greeting Christiano De Bellis.

"Come in," Z greets him. "To what do we owe this pleasant surprise?"

Christiano tips his head in an exaggerated bow to Elena and me. "I didn't mean to disturb the entire household, but it's lovely to see you both."

"Always a pleasure, Christiano." Elena gives the older man a hug while I hope my smile and wave suffice as greeting enough. I don't want to come off as rude, but I really don't want to hug him.

"Would you like to come have a seat?" Elena motions toward the sitting area. "I'm happy to get you a drink as well."

"Oh, no. I only stopped by for a moment to invite you all to dinner tonight. Ari will be at the house, and I know how much she enjoys seeing you, Z." He turns his calculating gaze from Zeno to me. His attention crawls across my skin like an army of angry spiders. "And the invitation includes you, Miss Banetti, if you don't already have plans."

I am a deer in headlights. Am I supposed to accept or politely decline?

"Of course, I'd love to come," I stutter my response, quickly defaulting to acceptance where the boss is concerned. He's not the type to extend an invitation if he doesn't want someone present, though I have no clue why he'd want me to join them. Dinner at the De Bellis house is the absolute *last* thing I wanted to do tonight.

"Perfect," he croons.

The little hairs on the back of my neck stand at attention. Something about Christiano gives me the creeps. It's hard to know the exact source when there are so many options to choose from. But it's there in the way he looks at people and his tone of speech. Condescension. Manipulation.

Being in his presence leaves me coated in an oily residue

that not even a good scrubbing can cleanse away. And now I have to spend my evening clogging my pores with his filth.

I shiver from top to bottom the second the front door closes behind him.

***

Christiano's Tuxedo Park home is on the opposite side of the lake and around a bend so that it can't be seen from the De Rossi property. It's traditional compared to his city apartment, but the home isn't a historic masterpiece like Hardwick. Situated closer to the water, Christiano's house is a Spanish-style mansion set upon retaining walls constructed of large river rocks. The home stands out from the landscape, unlike other properties tucked away in the trees. It's not surprising. Christiano doesn't do subtle.

He welcomes us with freshly poured champagne, then offers to give a tour of the estate. His motivation must be his own ego because I know he doesn't care about my opinion of him, and the De Rossis are doubtless already familiar with the home. It's an opportunity to tout his own affluence. It is unnecessary, but I appreciate the show, nonetheless, because it kills time and gives further insight into the man who runs the Giordano family.

I lean in and speak softly to Z as we trail behind Christiano and Elena. "It strikes me as somewhat odd that you guys choose to live out here. Seems like it would be more convenient to live in the city."

"Years ago, the Five Families all went underground in the nineties to escape federal scrutiny—not only our enterprises but also our physical presence. You can't have a target on your back if you're invisible. When the internet enabled the existence of online business, there was even less reason to stay in the city. You won't find made men sitting around tables in Little Italy anymore. Times have changed."

"Your dad spent an awful lot of time in the city. Do you think you'd have to do the same?" I wouldn't want to be left behind like Elena. I'm not sure what went on between her and Silvano, but I would prefer not to live in a separate city than my husband. I'm getting ahead of myself, but it's a topic that needs to be brought up eventually if Zeno and I are considering a life together.

"Time in the city isn't always necessary. I know for my dad, it was a matter of dedication to the family and his work. He was hands-on and wanted to be present rather than rely on a representative to report back to him." His words are infused with respect for his father.

Silvano's choices don't resonate with me the same as they do with Zeno, but I don't want to speak poorly of the dead. Z's father put work above his wife and children. Mafia men may feel like their organization constitutes more than a simple employer, but the truth is, once these men die, they are replaced and forgotten as quickly as any other employee. But Elena and Zeno and Nevio—they'll hold tight to Silvano's memory. They'll love and honor him long after he's gone, which is why they deserved his time while he was alive, not some capitalist organization. I doubt Z would see things in the same light.

When we make our way back to the main living area, Ari is there sipping from a crystal glass.

"Ah, there's my Arianna," Christiano calls with a plastic grin. "I'm sure Zeno has been anxious to see you. Come join us."

Z stiffens then crosses to kiss Ari on each cheek. "You look lovely, as always."

She gives him a thin smile before her eyes flit to mine.

Pink ghosts the smooth skin on the tops of her cheekbones. "Hey, Z. Luisa, Elena, it's great to see you both."

I can't discern what's going on. Is it embarrassment coloring her otherwise flawless complexion? What does she have to be embarrassed about? I'm the obvious fifth wheel in the group.

"Will Savio be joining us this evening?" Zeno asks our host.

"No, I knew you'd want time with Ari, so I decided we'd keep things more intimate. You two should be spending as much time together as possible." He raises his brows and grins, cutting a sly glance in my direction as he turns. "I believe dinner is ready if we'd like to move to the dining room."

Why the over-the-top innuendo about Z and Ari? Does Christiano know that Zeno and I have started seeing one another? What other reason is there for his behavior? I'd swear he's trying to send me a message that Zeno is spoken for, and I shouldn't waste my time. But Z and Ari don't want to marry one another. His intentional ignorance of their interests elsewhere is unsettling. I can't be the only one suffocating in the awkwardness.

When I look at Z, my eyes round with disbelief. He appears totally unaffected. Impassive and even a touch bored. Doesn't it bother him that his boss is still planning his future with another woman? He wouldn't ever agree to a loveless marriage like that, would he? Surely not after watching his parents live separate lives.

Then I recall our discussion the night before about his desire to become boss of the family one day. He and Savio have been planning their ascension for years, strategizing and biding their time. Zeno needs this promotion to underboss in order to make that dream a reality.

Is this how things unfolded for Silvano? Had he fallen in love with a woman unacceptable in the eyes of the family and married for power? Is *that* why he spent so much time in the city? Two homes with two separate lives? It would make sense.

How would Zeno look upon such an arrangement? Would the Mafia culture have molded his perspective in a way that enabled him to justify such a situation? Maybe he's come to believe it wouldn't be so terrible to have his cake and eat it too. He could marry Ari, become boss, and keep me as his dirty little secret in an apartment in the city. Maybe he considers that a normal part of Mafia life.

Is there a chance I had assumed his devotion to me meant marriage while he had assumed something totally different? We haven't been together long enough to have that kind of deep discussion, but it makes sense. It would explain why he would be affectionate with me at the Bishops' house, then cool and distant here in front of his Mafia family. He hasn't made a single move to show any attachment to me. If anything, he's kept a discerning distance between us.

My crystal champagne flute clanks on the table when I lower it distractedly.

I feel sick to my stomach.

I want to run from the house, but I absolutely must keep my composure. I could be blowing things out of proportion. We haven't even been at the house for an hour. Yet I look between Ari and Zeno, two powerful, confident individuals, and watch as they dance to Christiano's manic beat. I've yet to see either of them stand up to the man. Would they ever? What would Christiano do if they did reject his machinations?

I'm not sure I'd like the answer.

The entire train of thought sends me plummeting to a

dark place. My contribution to the dinner conversation is mechanical at best. I chew my food without tasting it. I smile on cue and dance like a good marionette. Like Zeno and Ari and everyone else who surrounds Christiano De Bellis.

By the time we pull away from the table, I'm disgusted with myself. Not for playing my part at dinner because that was necessary. I'm upset that I let myself think I could have Zeno when I knew he was intended for someone else. I let his words assure me, but his actions speak differently, at least when his Mafia family is present. There's been no reassuring kisses or gentle touches. If I'd been a fly on the wall, I would never have suspected he'd been tossing around "for better or worse" twenty-four hours earlier.

When I allow our history to color events, I'm even more ashamed of myself. That I'd jump into his deep waters without the slightest thought for my safety. With his history of brushing me off, how could I have been so careless? I told him I wanted to take things slow, but I'd forgotten to tell my heart the same.

His willingness to kill for me says nothing about his intent to marry me. I don't doubt his devotion. It's his priorities that worry me. Will he place his obligations to Christiano above his feelings for me?

If his behavior tonight is any indication, then I have my answer.

Frustration and hurt threaten to overwhelm me. I need a moment alone to compose myself.

Before I take a seat in the living area where we've gathered for after-dinner drinks, I ask Ari to point me in the direction of the restrooms.

"Let me show you," she offers. "It's a little tucked away—you know these old houses." Once we're in the adjoining room, she presses a panel in the wall, which opens to reveal a well-disguised powder room. "There you go!"

"Ari, wait a sec." I hadn't planned to have a private conversation with her, but now that the opportunity has arisen, I have to seize the moment.

She turns back toward me, expression guarded.

"I want to talk to you about Grace. She's so much more sensitive than either of us. I don't know what your intentions are, and I'm not meaning to imply you're out to hurt her, but I ask that you treat her with compassion. If … *circumstances* … will force you to walk away from her, don't lead her on. She really likes you, and I don't want her to get hurt."

I don't want Grace to be Ari's dirty secret anymore than I want to be Zeno's.

A flash of indignation passes behind her eyes. "My life is complicated," she says stiffly.

My gaze drifts toward the living area where masculine voices carry in the air. "I'm beginning to understand that. It's why I wanted to say something." I meet her arctic stare and brace for my next question. "If it comes to it, would you marry him?" This is the question I most wanted to ask.

Her reaction is visceral. Nostrils flare. Jaw clenches.

She opens her mouth to respond, then clamps her lips shut. With a quick spin and several purposeful strides in her red-bottomed stilettos, she's left me standing alone, no closer to an answer.

I take a shaky breath and wish I could slip out a back door. Instead, I use my trip to the restroom to compose myself and march back to the battlefield.

An hour later, I'm finally granted my freedom when we climb back into the car and head for home. We are all silent on the short drive. My thoughts filter down to a single question. Would I still want to marry Zeno if I knew our marriage would deny him his lifetime ambition? I would love for him to stand up to Christiano, but I would also feel terrible if he lost everything because of me. I keep picturing my father, who chose his commitment to my mother over the family. That didn't play out so well for him. Even if Z was willing to reject Ari, would I want him to be forced to make that kind of decision?

No, I wouldn't. But it's also not my place to steal the choice from him either.

I hate my limited options, no matter how I look at them. And even more so, I hate Christiano De Bellis for imposing his will on other people's lives.

When Z pulls up at my parents' house, I open the back seat door with the last of my strength. The night's mental gymnastics have left me completely drained.

Zeno steps from the car and snags my hand. "Wait, Isa."

I slow, unable to argue.

"I'm sorry about tonight. I know that couldn't have been easy."

I slip my hand from his grasp. "Just tell me now, don't drag it out. Are you going to refuse him or not?" If Zeno and Ari are destined to marry, there's no point in pretending otherwise. A simple yes or no, and we can all move on.

"I'm going to handle it," he barks gruffly.

It's not enough. I need an answer that doesn't leave room for me to become his woman on the side. "Are. You. Going. To. Refuse. Him?"

"It's not that simple, Isa. *Christ*." He rakes his hands through his hair in frustration.

And just like that, my heart splits wide open all over again. As much as I didn't want him to have to choose between me and his ambitions, I still wanted him to pick me. To choose me above our parents' indiscretions and his boss's ploys and all the other obstacles that have come between us.

Tears pool in my eyes. "You're wrong," I whisper, then walk calmly to the house, both relieved and brokenhearted that he makes no move to stop me.

CHAPTER 11

Two days pass without a word from Z.

He left for the city the morning after dinner at Christiano's. I don't reach out to him because he is the only one who can fix this. I made my feelings known, and if he isn't ready to commit to me, then I won't beg him. Granted, a part of me hoped the time apart would help him see things more clearly. Help him realize how much he wants me at his side. But with each passing hour, my hope for such a result dwindles.

I can't say where his mind is at, but our time apart has revealed to me how empty my life feels without him. The realization of how attached I've become is terrifying. What if he doesn't choose me?

Then you'll scrape yourself off the floor and keep going.

I will, but that's not what I want. I want Z. Losing him would hurt dearly. I would have to cut him from my life completely because anything short of calling him mine would be too painful. I've seen a glimpse of what it would feel like to be the center of his world, and I can't accept a casual friendship knowing what could have been. Either he becomes the air I breathe, or I bury a part of myself along with all thoughts of him. There is no in-between.

Livia left for the city the same day as Zeno and hasn't contacted us since, so aside from my troubles with Z, I've worried incessantly about my sister. Mom is convinced Liv and Nevio are off celebrating like blissed-out lovebirds. I wish I could buy into the fantasy, but I know better.

Would Nevio say horrible, hurtful things to her if she pushed for a commitment? How would Livy respond if he did? She's brash and emotional on a good day. I can only imagine how she'd behave with pregnancy hormones flooding her system. Would she feel desperate if he rejects her? Being a young, unwed mother is a long way to fall from landing a rich husband.

Thankfully, Gia's incandescent happiness shines brightly through my gloom and gives my spirits a touch of buoyancy. She flits around the house with boundless energy and is more talkative than I've ever seen her in all our years. In fact, she's been preoccupied enough with her own budding relationship that she hasn't been around enough to ask about mine. I appreciate the distraction because I wouldn't know what to tell her if she did ask questions.

As with the two previous evenings, the second we arrive home from work on Friday, Gia freshens up in record time before heading next door to spend her evening with Carter and the kids. I smile at her retreating form as I check the fridge for dinner options. Mom sits at the table, scrolling through her phone, and Dad has yet to come home. If I want a meal, I'll have to manage on my own.

I'm pulling sausage from the fridge when the front door swings open, and Livy's cheerful greeting carries to the back of the house.

"Hey, everyone! I'm home!" She sweeps into the kitchen and beams at Mom and me. "I've got news," she sings, flattening her palm against her chest to display an enormous diamond ring on her finger.

Mom starts screaming. "You did it, Livy! You did it!" She flings her arms around my sister, and the two begin to jump in tandem.

I'm as floored as my mother but for completely different reasons. He proposed. He actually did it. And now my sister will be married to a philandering, pathological liar. She won't want for money, but I can't imagine she'll ever truly be happy. And the craziest part is, even if I told her the truth about Nevio, I don't think it would change a thing. She'd still walk down that aisle at the end of the day, determined as ever.

So instead of crying the tears that scream to break free, instead of begging and pleading with her to see reason, I plaster on a brittle smile and congratulate my little sister.

"You must be so excited, Livy. I hope you two will be blissfully happy together." I give her a hug and say a prayer that they somehow beat the odds and find happiness. Their start will be even rockier than my parents', which hasn't ended well. But there is always hope, even if only the tiniest sliver.

Liv will get what she wants—to be taken care of—so maybe that's all she truly needs to believe she's happy. Happiness is relative, after all.

"We are over the moon," she croons. "I wish we had time for a proper wedding, though, but I don't want to look all fat in my wedding pictures, and the countdown is on." She rubs her still flat belly with her newly blinged-out hand. "We're thinking only a month or so before we tie the knot." She explains the situation with exaggerated nonchalance. Her expectation is that we'll squawk and fawn over her, and while my mother has no problem falling in line, my generosity will only go so far.

I sit back and watch as the two of them dive into wedding discussions. Rather than thinking of colors and flowers, I contemplate how Zeno managed to accomplish such a feat. The engagement had to have resulted from his influence, and Nevio isn't fond of his brother enough to be guilted into a wedding. He couldn't care less if Zeno was upset with him.

After thinking it over, I'm increasingly curious about Zeno's activities during the past few days.

We all eat dinner together, save for Gia. Dad gives Livy his congratulations, and Marca practically bounces in her seat at the prospect of her sister moving in next door. I know that will never happen, but I'm not about to say anything. As soon as we finish eating, Livia sidesteps cleanup to go show friends her new ring. I force Marca to give me a hand with cleanup, though she disappears the second her duties are completed. I wind up with the living room to myself, grateful for the rare opportunity to zone out while flipping channels until my mother's shrill voice fills my ears.

"Is this some kind of joke?"

My parents' bedroom is right off the living room, so when Mom comes charging out, I'm smack in the middle of their argument. I consider slipping upstairs but am too curious to move when she waves a stack of papers in the air.

"I'm not signing *anything*. You can take these back to your lawyer and ask for your money back." She shoves them into Dad's chest, forcing him to take the papers.

Dad is calm and collected, as always. He isn't letting himself get sucked into Mom's tornado of agitation. "It's your call, but not signing doesn't make them go away. It just means the sheriff will come serve you instead. I'm trying to do this in the least painful way possible. It's time, Gemma."

Papers? Served by the sheriff? Is Dad filing for *divorce*?

I'm stunned. That has to be it, but I never thought he'd go through with it. I'd hoped, but after so many years together, I figured that he'd be reluctant to take the plunge.

"I know no such thing. What about the girls? What about all the years we've been together? You think you can just walk out like we mean *nothing*?" Mom spits at him.

"You think you can go behind my back and put us into debt with the family, then have your fucking bookie show up at our home and threaten our girls? Make them pay for your mistakes?" Seething fury slithers under his skin, a warning as deadly as any rattlesnake. Dad is more upset than I realized. "Of course the past has meaning, but that doesn't change where we're at. We haven't been a couple for a long time, and you know it."

Mom gapes at him for an elongated second before stiffening her spine. "I'm not the only one who's messed up over the years," she hisses, still undeterred by his unexpected show of strength. Mom's been trampling over my father for years without consequence and is unable to understand that his patience has ended. She thinks she can use blackmail to keep him—threaten to tell his secrets if he won't stay. I get the sense she knows about Elena and Nevio and intends to use the information as leverage.

Judging by Daddy's reaction, she should have reconsidered her tactic.

My father goes eerily still. He's only six inches taller than her, but under the weight of his murderous stare, he looks like a giant. "You sure you want to go there, Gemma? Because Liv and Marca might not be happy with how that conversation ends." Ever so slowly, he drags his gaze from Mom to me, drawing her manic stare with him. Dad's not afraid to play dirty either. He's been hoarding his own secrets, and while I already know the truth, Mom doesn't know that.

I gape wide-eyed at the two of them, desperate not to be dragged into the middle but unable to give up my front-row seat to this showdown.

All the blood drains from Mom's face. If she outs Dad, he'll make sure everyone knows Liv and Marca aren't his. Using the girls against her is ugly, but I can't entirely blame him. Mom dragged them both down into the dirt—he's only following her lead.

"Give me a fucking pen," she spits, snagging the papers and a pen from Dad. She scribbles out a signature on the top page, muttering something about not knowing what she's supposed to do all on her own. "Does this mean I have to find a new job? You got me knocked up as a child, and now you're going to throw me out with no job prospects, no education, and no money? This is some *bullshit*, Tony." She tosses the papers at Dad and storms back into their room, slamming the door behind her.

She never did understand that the world didn't owe her anything. That even people who are handed money and power still have to earn respect and deserve the love of the people around them if they want genuine relationships. Mom drains the relationship bank dry then doesn't understand why her balance is zero. Even in her fifties, she still doesn't get it.

Dad lowers himself onto the couch, suddenly moving like a man decades older, sighing as he comes to rest beside me. "I'm sorry you had to witness that, Lulu."

"It's okay, Daddy. I'm proud of you for going through with it. I know it isn't easy."

"I called my lawyer the minute you told me about her debt with the bookie. That's who I went to see while I was in the city with Mom and the girls. Should have done this ages ago."

"Change is hard." I scoot in closer and lay my head on his shoulder.

Dad glances back toward their bedroom. "Doubt this'll be pretty. She has no money for an attorney, so that might help, but she'll find ways to lash out."

"Probably, but you're a good man. I know you won't be unnecessarily harsh on her. She's still our mom."

His cheek comes to rest against my head, and I breathe in the subtle scent of cherry cigars that lingers on his clothes.

"That's the one thing I'll always be grateful for—she gave me you girls. The very best part of my world."

We sit like that for long minutes, each lost in our own thoughts. I wanted to give Zeno time to sort out his feelings, but time is up. Watching my parents' marriage crumble has made me realize the importance of communication. I want us to talk in person, so it will have to wait until tomorrow, but one way or another, we are going to hash out or differences.

Zeno is a special man. I'd be remiss if I didn't work to keep him in my life. My pride had convinced me that fighting for a relationship was groveling and beneath me, but that's not always the case. If I want Zeno to stand up to Christiano for me, I should be willing to make an effort as well—lay my fears aside and do everything in my power to give us a chance at love. He's worth it. *We* are worth it.

CHAPTER 12

THE SMELL OF BACON FRYING ROUSES ME FROM SLEEP THE NEXT morning. When I head downstairs to investigate, I note a pillow and several blankets on the sofa. Dad's new bed for the time being. The sight should make me sad, but more than anything, I think I'm relieved. If there's any sadness in the circumstances, it's that I'll worry less about Dad on his own than I would if he was still married to Mom. It's too bad things couldn't be different, but it is what it is. The door to the master bedroom is shut, and I can only assume Mom won't be coming out anytime soon. It's going to take some time for her to process.

In the kitchen, Dad is stationed at one skillet while Gia flips pancakes at another. Marca and Livia both sit at the table, looking at their phones.

"You guys do know it's Saturday morning, right?" I tease.

My family has never slept super late, but this is a tad unusual, even for us.

Gia grins. "Carter and I are taking the kids to the zoo today, so I had to get an early start." She'd crept in late last night, and I didn't want to keep her awake with news of Dad filing for divorce, so I didn't say anything yet. By the sound of things, the news will have to wait a little longer.

"That sounds like fun. I haven't been to the zoo in ages."

"You're welcome to join us!"

"Maybe another time, but thanks for the invite." I have more pressing matters to deal with.

Livia drops her phone on the table and shoots a look at Marca. "Well, I'd still be asleep if this one had remembered to silence her phone."

"Don't blame me!" Marca shoots back. "You're the one who tossed and turned for fifteen minutes, grumbling about your bladder."

"It wouldn't have been an issue if your phone hadn't woken me in the first place. I don't know what the deal is, but I'm already peeing all the time. This thing isn't big enough to press on my bladder. I even had to make Zeno stop on the way back from the city last night. Can you believe that? I haven't stopped at a gas station to pee on a trip from the city since I was a kid." She shakes her head and resumes scrolling.

"Zeno drove you back home?" That would mean he's at Hardwick.

"Yeah, isn't that sweet of him? I mean, we *are* going to be family soon, but still. Nevio had some things to handle, or he would have brought me back himself."

Right. Sure he would have.

"Who's ready for the first plate?" Gia calls out.

Marca leaps up. Livia groans.

I consider going straight over to find Z but decide it's a little early to surprise him with a heavy conversation. I'd be better off giving him a chance to wake up first, and that would allow me time to eat with my family and get cleaned up.

An hour later, I tread through the grass between our houses like I've done thousands of times before. For years, this walk brought on trepidation and anxiety, but today those emotions are balanced with an equal measure of hope. The sun reflects my optimism as it blankets the landscape in warmth.

My visit is unannounced, so I go to the front of the house and ring the bell.

Elena greets me with a grin. "Good morning, Isa. What brings you over?" She steps aside and welcomes me inside.

"I heard Zeno came back last night and was hoping to talk to him."

"He stayed the night but got up early and left. I'm afraid you've missed him."

Disappointment tugs at my shoulders. "Oh, that's too bad."

"I can try to get him on the phone if you need to speak with him."

"No, thank you." I smile warmly to assure her. I don't want her to worry. "I'll catch up with him later."

"I suppose Livia told everyone the exciting engagement news?" she asks with an admirable degree of artificial excitement.

"She did. I don't suppose you know how that came about? I can only assume Zeno had something to do with it."

She clasps her hands together and takes a slow breath, her voice watered down with embarrassment. "The last I heard, Nevio was insisting on a capo's rank in order to agree to anything."

"But Z is a capo himself. He wouldn't have the power to make Nevio a capo, would he?"

He would if he were underboss.

Surely, he wouldn't agree to marry Ari purely to secure the position so that Nevio would marry Livia. Maybe he did agree to marry but for his own reasons. Could I have pushed him too far the other night? If he thought there was no way to keep me, would that remove the remaining barriers stopping him from marrying Ari?

My pancakes and bacon threaten to make a reappearance.

Elena shrugs helplessly. "I wouldn't think so, but I don't know for sure. He hardly said a word when he got here last night. Whatever is going on, it's consumed him almost as much as losing his father. When I heard him leave early this morning, I was so concerned I couldn't go back to sleep."

I nod shakily. "I'm sure it'll be fine."

Her sad smile tightens the vise around my heart. "Things always have a way of working out."

I say goodbye, and the second she closes the door behind me, I pull out my phone and call Zeno. The call goes directly to voicemail, so I leave a message that I need to talk to him. I don't know what all is going on with him, but I'm starting to wish I hadn't let so much time pass since we parted on uneasy terms.

Turning to walk back home, I only take a few steps when the front door opens again behind me. I glance back to see Nevio and pause. He strolls forward, hands in his pockets, sad eyes glued to me.

"I thought I heard you." His gaze rakes over me. A look of longing tinged with remorse.

"I thought you stayed in the city."

"Drove out this morning." He takes two more slow steps until he's within my reach.

"It's early for a Saturday."

"Orders. Z says jump, and I ask how high." His hand lifts to trace the edge of my face. "You look beautiful, as ever." An apology for the awful things he said? Maybe. Too little too late? Definitely.

I take a step back. "You need to stop, Nevio."

His eyes find mine again. "It was only ever you, you know."

I'm surprised to find I believe him, in part because of what Zeno told me, but I also detect sincere regret. My relationship with him as kids and teens was probably the only genuine female connection he's ever experienced, save for his mother. I suspect he does hold a special fondness for me.

"The problem is, it would never have been *only me.*" No matter how much he cares for me, his addiction would have come between us. As it is, he was having sex with my sister from the day I came back to Hardwick.

His lips pull taut in a remorseful frown. "They told you, didn't they?"

I nod.

He breathes deeply, eyes falling to the ground between us. "I suppose you would have found out eventually."

The defeat in his ragged words is heartbreaking. I want to wrap my arms around him and reassure him that everything will be okay, but that would be a lie. With the challenges he's facing, there are no guarantees, so I keep my hands and my words to myself.

Eventually, he lifts his gaze back to mine, a new earnest conviction in those mocha depths. "I *will* make an effort, though. I want you to know that I'll try to make things work with Liv. I've started back with my counselor."

"That's wonderful, Nevio. I really do wish you both the best."

He nods as though he doesn't want to part but isn't sure what else to say. "I guess I'll let you go then." His statement carries the weight of multiple meanings. He may have held a candle for me through the years, but it's time to extinguish that flame. We'll never be as close as we were as kids, but a part of me will always feel for him.

After raising my hand in goodbye, I turn toward home.

"I'm sorry, Isa," Nevio calls out. "For everything. I'm so sorry."

Twisting to look over my shoulder, I meet his tortured gaze. "I know you are, and if you ever need someone to talk to, I'm happy to listen." I feel a nagging pressure to tell him he's forgiven, but I can't find the words. His addiction doesn't excuse the way he lashed out at me. My wounds from his attack still haven't healed, and I'm not ready to fully absolve him. However, my offer to be a friend is genuine. Knowing his issues go deeper than simple insensitivity makes me want to help him rather than condemn him. I still don't think he and Livia marrying is a great idea. Nevio isn't a lost cause, but marriage to him won't be easy.

With Nevio, even friendship will have its challenges, but he's worth the effort. He's my brother—it's as simple as that.

I'm feeling hopeful when I part ways with him, and if his lopsided grin is any evidence, he feels the same.

One De Rossi relationship on the mend. One more to go.

CHAPTER 13

As I approach home, I catch sight of a black Escalade pulling up at the front of the house. I reroute myself toward the front entry to greet whoever has arrived. I didn't think we were expecting visitors, but with six of us living under one roof, it's hard to keep track.

A glare shines on the windshield, concealing the driver, and the other windows are too tinted to see inside. Once the vehicle comes to a stop, the driver's side back seat door opens. Dressed for the boardroom, Christiano De Bellis exits the car. His steely gaze locks on me instantly like the sight of a gun trained on its target.

He's not here for my father or anyone else.

He's here for me.

Fear rushes through my veins like a river, but I don't let it show. I won't give him the satisfaction.

Forcing my posture to remain relaxed and my chin high, I

do my best to broadcast confidence. If he stands close enough, he'll see the thrum of my frantic pulse at the base of my neck, but that can't be helped.

Whatever the reason for his visit, I must show strength. It's the only way to earn respect in his eyes.

"You're a beautiful woman," Christiano says, hands clasped behind his back casually. "I can understand Zeno's infatuation." He takes two steps, the start of an arcing circle around me. "We all have our dalliances, but your little fling is getting in the way of my plans. I was curious about you at first. Once I saw for myself that you were not worthy of concern, I washed my hands of the matter. However, I've just learned something … disheartening."

I have no idea where he's going with his diatribe, so I keep my mouth shut.

"An associate of mine has gone missing, and it appears Zeno may have been involved in the disappearance. Do you know what that tells me?" He waits for me to shake my head. "That indicates Zeno is taking matters into his own hands. That tells me he's putting other people before the family. Luisa, you've been raised in the family. You must know that we can't have that. If our family is to stay strong—remain united and untouchable—the family itself must *always* come first."

I don't subscribe to his belief, but I won't argue with him. I'm not suicidal. Refusing to show fear doesn't mean I have to put my head on the chopping block. He hasn't technically asked a question, so I remain silent. He seems to prefer the sound of his own voice anyway.

"Surely you can imagine how upsetting it is when one of my top men becomes distracted not only by a woman but by some second-rate soldier's daughter."

I grit my teeth at his sneered comment.

He wants you to lash out, Isa. Don't do it. Just don't.

Christiano studies me as he paces. Taunts and insults me. "I spoke with him and explained my expectations. He's prepared to perform his duties and fall in line. It's time for you to remember your place as well. The question is, are you going to comply on your own, or will you need … convincing? Because this is the only time I will ask politely."

My pulse drives too hard, too fast. I have to fight dizziness and draw a long breath in through my nose.

Would Christiano kill me to get me out of the picture? Unquestionably, yes.

Would Zeno let this man come between us? That I can't answer, and the uncertainty terrifies me. I don't want to give him up, but I'm also not prepared to die today. My only option is to give Christiano what he wants to hear and pray it's not the end of my short-lived relationship.

"I don't need convincing. If Zeno says it's over, then you have nothing to worry about." I've left myself a loophole, and he knows it.

The angry lion charges, clamping his hand around my throat in an instant. "Don't play *fucking* games with me, little girl." Up close, his eyes are black voids—a window into nothingness because there is no soul to be seen.

I gasp and nod as best as I can. "I'm sorry. I didn't mean to." I force the sputtered words past his savage grip, pulling at his hand with frantic fingers.

He watches me squirm for an extra second, giving me one last squeeze before releasing me. I stumble backward, desperately needing space between us, and gasp for air.

Christiano looms over me menacingly. "This is the one and only time I'll tell you in unequivocal terms. Stay *the fuck* away from Zeno."

My hand rests protectively around my neck, doing little to

soothe the burn within or subdue the mutinous fear taking control of me. I am no match for this man, and I hate myself for it. I want to be powerful and imposing. I want men like Christiano to think twice about intimidating me, but my strength of character only gets me so far. I am not enough threat to be of consequence.

I nod, tears heavy on my lashes. A sob claws for release, but I fight it off.

Christiano gives me one last sneer before idly returning to his car and pulling out of the driveway. Once he's gone, my knees give out, and the sobs I'd held at bay wrack my body. I can't even be relieved that he's gone when my heart threatens to collapse. Just when Zeno and I have managed to connect—to set aside our secrets and confess our feelings—the universe is going to steal it all away.

How can our sapling of a relationship ever withstand the mammoth force of Christiano's hurricane winds? He has an entire army of ruthless soldiers at his command. If we went against his orders, we could lose far more than a chance at love.

I'm on the ground, lost to desperation, when my father steps onto the porch.

"Isa? Are you okay? Was that De Bellis?" He races over and collects me in his strong arms. "Lulu, talk to me. What the hell is going on?"

"Christiano … he wants me to stay away from Z," I hiccup through my sobs. "He … threatened me."

"What? Why does he care?"

"He wants Z to … marry Ari."

Dad blows out a long breath and holds me tighter. "Shit," he exhales.

We kneel together for long minutes while I compose myself. Dad is the first to break the silence.

"I need to know the truth, Isa. Do you love him?"

Lifting my gaze to his, I nod without hesitation. "I do."

"Then you need to go tell him what's going on. He needs to know. That man has loved you since you were children. I'm confident he won't let anyone keep you apart."

Not even himself? What if Christiano's threats have already swayed him? Even if they haven't, does he have enough clout of his own to go up against someone so powerful? I don't want Zeno hurt because of me.

But are you truly willing to walk away from him out of fear?

I don't want to let love pass me by because I'm too scared to fight for it. I couldn't live with that possibility. At the very least, I need to talk to Z. I need to see how he feels and make sure he knows what's happened.

"I could try to find him at his place in the city, but he and Christiano live in the same building. If I run into him there, he'll know I'm looking for Zeno and intentionally defying him."

"Then I'll go with you and make sure that doesn't happen."

"Dad, I can't let you get in trouble for me."

"Not your call to make, baby girl, just as I couldn't stop you from paying Mom's debt. Now, go in and get ready. We're going to the city."

WHILE DAD DRIVES, I TRY TO CALL Z. HE DOESN'T ANSWER, SO I text to let him know I'm coming. When we arrive at Zeno's building, Dad and I put on ball caps to hide us from the security cameras—a precaution I insist upon. If Dad is going to risk himself, we will do our best to minimize being seen. Christiano made it clear he doesn't value my father in any way. If he learns Dad enabled me to see Z, the resulting punishment would be merciless.

Heads tucked, we move briskly through the lobby to the elevators. I am only somewhat relieved when we reach Zeno's door without incident because my fate is still undecided.

When I knock on Zeno's door, I'm met with silence. "He's not home, but I have the code to get in."

"You sure you'll be okay here alone?" Dad asks.

"I suppose I'll find out soon enough." I fling myself into my dad's arms. "Thank you, Daddy."

"Anything for you, Lulu. Now get inside and make sure to text me later."

"I will." I give him a weak smile, then enter the code to open the door. Once inside, I call out a hello to make sure I'm alone and set my hat and purse on the entry console. Nerves flutter and flare as I walk into the living room, keeping my lunchtime hunger at bay. I have no idea how long I'll have to wait for him to come home, so I get comfortable on the sofa. Too comfortable. I spend an hour messing around on my phone, and the next thing I know, my sleepy eyes open to the sight of Zeno standing over me.

"Oh, you're here," I murmur, a bolt of adrenaline waking me in an instant. I jump to my feet and attempt to smooth my mussed hair. "I'm sorry to intrude, but I had to talk to you."

His face darkens like a summer storm blackening the sky, sudden and intense. I hold perfectly still, worried my arrival has upset him, but his hand slowly lifts to my neck with a featherlight touch. "Is that bruising around your throat?" His words are stilted from the effort of restrained violence.

I'd been so worried about Christiano's threats, I hadn't given a thought to whether his assault had left a mark. Clearly, it had. "Christiano came by the cottage this morning," I tell him warily. I had wanted him to know, but the terrifying look on his face consumes me with worry. Not for myself. I'm scared of what Zeno might do on my behalf.

"He did this?"

I nod.

"What exactly did he say?"

"He told me to stay away from you. That he has plans for you, and I'm getting in the way." I dive into his ocean eyes and search for the truth. "Is he right, Z? Am I getting in the way? Because I don't want to be the woman who keeps you from your dreams." I don't want him to be punished because of me. "Is that why you've been so quiet? Are you having doubts?"

Z threads his hands into my hair and brings our cheeks together. "*Fuck*, no. That's not it at all. I've been spending every minute of the past few days trying to sort this shit out. Trying to fix everything without making waves. I should have reached out and explained, but I didn't want to make promises before I knew I could keep them." He pulls back and traces his thumb along my neck. "Yet again, I've fucked up. I should never have left you alone." It's a murmur to himself. An admonishment.

I pull back enough to look into his eyes and inwardly cringe at the guilt lining his face. "It's okay. I'm okay," I whisper. "I knew you had a lot to sort out, and considering the engagement news, you'd clearly been busy."

"That's definitely occupied some of my time."

"You didn't have to force the issue. She would have been fine without him."

Z takes a deep, weary breath. "Marriage will give her an easier time collecting child support and give her access to alimony when … *if* they part ways. Nevio has a way of shirking his responsibilities, and I wanted to do what I could to ensure your sister wouldn't fall victim to him more than she already has. Court orders aren't foolproof, but it should help."

I hadn't thought of it that way. "Thank you for looking out for her. I'm not sure she entirely deserves it, but I appreciate it." I recall what Elena said about Nevio's demands, and I have to ask though I'm not sure I want the answer. "Z, how did you get Nevio to agree to the marriage? Your mom said he was asking to be made a capo."

"He would like that to happen, but I don't have the ability to promote him myself and wouldn't even if I could. He's not trustworthy enough. Instead, I gave him the next best thing—control of his finances. After dealing with his issues for years, my dad decided to put Nevio's money in a trust to keep it protected—the money our parents had accrued for him. His own earnings are untouched but fractional compared to the trust. It pissed him off to no end that he wasn't given control over his own assets. The trust was one of the many issues that came between my father and him. Upon Dad's death, I became the trustee with the power to allocate the funds. And the power to dissolve the trust."

"You gave him his money?"

"I did. Or … I will, once he's gone through with the wedding. He may be an addict, but drugs or gambling aren't an issue. I've had to meet with our attorney and the accountant and make plans for the transition. I've also stipulated that Nevio has to continue sessions with his counselor."

"He mentioned that. I ran into him this morning."

His brows rise. "You've had a busy day already."

"I have." The words are but a breath squeezed from seizing lungs. Anticipation unfurls from deep in my chest, launching my pulse into a breakneck rhythm.

It's time to say what I've come here to say.

My eyes follow my trembling fingers as they touch the broad chest before me. An uncertain, tentative touch seeking connection. Strength. Reassurance.

"Z, I came here today to tell you about Christiano, but that's not all. I want you to know—I *need* you to know—that I love you … so much." I can barely speak past the ball of emotion lodged in my throat, but I force myself to go on because my feelings are too important to go unsaid. "I've adored you since I was a little girl with scraped knees. Even our years apart couldn't erase my feelings for you. And the reason I needed to know if you'll refuse Christiano's wishes isn't because I'm impatient or demanding. It's because my love for you is too consuming for me to share you. I could never be the woman on the side, even if a relationship with Ari was purely superficial. I simply couldn't. It would devastate me. So, before my heart is irrevocably bound to you, I need to know if there's a chance for us. A real chance for it to be just you and me."

I'm relieved to have the truth out in the open before he even says a word. I love Zeno. I love him so deeply that my heart beats to his rhythm. I won't degrade that love or myself by relegating either of us to the shadows. I am worth so much more.

Z lifts my chin with the gentle touch of his fingers. "There's more than a chance." His penetrating stare is unflinching. "I'm going to make it happen. You were right to demand an answer, and it wasn't fair of me to put you in that position. The answer should have been yes. Unequivocally, yes. The only reason I didn't say it then was because I didn't know how to make it happen. That's what has taken a majority of my time over the past few days. I want to make things right with you in every way I can so that when I put my ring on your finger, nothing is left to come between us." Z lowers until his lips to ghost over mine. "I love you, Luisa Banetti, down to the darkest depths of my soul."

When our lips finally connect, the kiss sears his name onto the surface of my heart, claiming it as his own. A permanent reminder of the bond that has always existed between us. Not even years or miles or hate could sever the connection. Each has tried and failed. Our need for one another is eternal.

Z lifts me, coaxing my legs around his waist, and walks us back to his bedroom. The shades are lowered with only a small panel of light left at the bottom of each to illuminate the room. Plenty for me to see the inked lines of his tattoos and every dip and swell of his muscled body as I remove his clothes. He does the same for me, taking care to worship each new stretch of exposed skin with his touch.

"I've fucked up with you more times than should be humanly possible, yet here you are, next to me, offering your forgiveness and love. It's beyond my comprehension." Zeno walks us backward until my legs press against the bed, then reaches behind me and yanks the covers down.

I ease back onto the cool sheets, my eyes never leaving his. "We were victim to circumstances beyond our control. That's no one's fault."

He prowls over me, caging my body beneath his. "Not anymore. Now I'm in control, and nothing is going to come between us again." His mouth descends on my nipple, twirling his tongue and grazing the taut peak with his teeth until I'm writhing with need, then he switches to the other side.

Reaching between us, I wrap my hand around the velvety softness of his cock. When I squeeze his length, he hisses with pleasure. The sound adds fuel to my fire, and soon, my core is weeping with need.

Z nips at the side of my breast before pulling upright and reaching for the nightstand. I expect him to come away with a condom, but instead, he rips open a small box and plucks out something small and pink that he slips on his fingers—a vibrator device made specifically for the clit. He then grabs two pillows from where they've scattered around us and has me lift my hips. I watch his every movement with rapt fascination. He hasn't struck me as the type of man who uses toys, but I'm extremely fond of my vibrator, so this new insight has me giddy with anticipation.

Once he has me where he wants me, he squirts gel onto the pink device then brings it to my center, allowing me to adjust to its bumpy texture before turning it on. His eyes devour my every movement. Each gasp and arch. When he clicks on the power, I buck from the sudden blast of sensation.

"Oh, *God*, Zeno." My eyes roll back as I absorb the pleasure coursing through my veins.

I'm used to the intense sensation of a vibrator, but it's different when someone else is controlling the device. Every touch is magnified, and every pause spikes my pulse with anticipation. The vulnerability of my position is intensely erotic. The trust and uncertainty battling one another cause a cataclysmic storm to brew inside me.

"I love to see you splayed open for me, your perfect pink cunt begging for my touch."

Z lifts his fingers away, giving me time to breathe, then resumes his systematic onslaught, sliding the silicon vibrations from one side to the other. He is transfixed at the sight of me. I try to watch him because I'm equally enraptured by the sight of him, but his ministrations are too distracting.

Eventually, he removes his hand to guide himself inside me. He remains upright on his knees, eyes glued to where our bodies become one.

I assume he's done with the toy, but I'm wrong. Once he's sheathed himself fully inside me, muscles straining with need, his fingers return to resume their delicious torture. He uses his free hand to clutch my hip while he thrusts inside me.

I've never felt such a barrage of sensations.

The vibrations.

His pounding cock.

They unite to overwhelm my brain. I can't focus on any

one thing, giving my body over to sensation. I clutch the sheets beneath me as white light threatens the edge of my vision. My breaths become shallow pants. My stomach tightens, and my legs begin to spasm.

"There it is. Z, yes, don't stop."

"Oh, *fuck yes*, Isa. Squeeze me. You feel so fucking good." He thrusts harder and faster, triggering that perfect explosion like liquid jet fuel igniting in my veins. The fiery pleasure swells from my center until it fills every molecule of my being, and I am splitting at the seams.

The orgasm is too violent to contain. It bursts from my throat in a primal scream that leaves me ragged and raw—the discarded shell of a shotgun blast, still scalding from the explosion. I find my breath as I float back to earth. Slowly, my body and mind reunite.

Zeno eases in and out of me, giving me time to soak in the sensation. I hardly notice when he removes the pillows from beneath me—not until his body is flush with mine.

I open my eyes to lock with his. Open my heart to make room for him.

He waits until he sees that I'm back with him, connected and ready. Then he makes love to me.

Face-to-face.

Heart-to-heart.

Each thrust is a promise. Each kiss an oath. I have no remaining reason to question him because his devotion is absolute, and he proves as much by worshiping my body with infinite care. When his release overtakes him, I clutch him against me, swearing an oath of my own to return his love with the same ardent ferocity.

"WHAT MADE YOU DECIDE TO STOP PUSHING ME AWAY?" I lie next to Zeno in the preternatural twilight of his room. He's pulled the sheets over us and drawn me into his side, his arm holding me securely against him. I've tried to keep my thoughts at bay and simply enjoy our moment together, but I've never been good at not thinking.

"I started to realize how much I was hurting the both of us. Through the years, I'd told myself that you saw me as an annoyance and nothing more, so my harsh rebukes were only damaging to me. But seeing you day after day—witnessing the way you reacted to me—I began to wonder if the harm I was doing was outweighed by the good. Yes, I had managed to keep you away from Hardwick and my brother. But what if there was another way I could keep you safe from Nevio? What if you were mine instead? Once the thought took root, I couldn't escape it. I wanted you more than anything, but I knew there was a strong possibility I'd ruined my chances of that ever happening."

"I was so angry with you, especially that night you admitted your feelings."

"I could tell. I was certain after I left that I'd done too much damage to overcome. If there was any hope at all, it lay in the truth. That one sliver of a chance—the hope that a confession might earn your forgiveness—was worth spilling my secrets. Even if we didn't end up together, I hoped to at least keep you from hating me."

I mull over my next words because I'm not sure how they'll be received. "Z, it's not my call to make, but I want you to consider telling your mom and maybe even Nevio the truth. Secrets are insidious. They fester and rot everything they touch. And besides, secrets always end up exposed in the end. Better to control how the information surfaces than clean up after a bomb drops."

Zeno grunts. "I'm not sure I agree, but I'll consider it." He rolls us so that I'm on my back and he's on his side, looming over me. "And what about you? Hmm? Are you going to fess up as well?"

I search his face, relieved to sense an element of playfulness even though I'm unsure what he's getting at. "What do you mean?"

He lowers his mouth to graze his teeth over my jawline. "I mean … this isn't the first time you've had an orgasm in my bed." His voice is liquid caramel, hot and sticky as it coats my skin.

He knows. *Holy shit, he knows.*

My heart jackhammers against my ribs. I'd fingered myself on his bed while I was staying at his apartment, freaking out over what I'd let myself do, but I had convinced myself he'd never know. That my moment of weakness would stay buried forever. How could he know unless … "You have cameras?" I shriek in horror.

"I do," he purrs. "I don't normally check the footage, but after our awkward dinner at Christiano's, I wanted to check in on you. When I saw you creep to my room, I had to keep watching. It was the most erotic, incredible thing I've ever witnessed. That's why I came over the next day. I couldn't think of anything but you. That was the moment I realized I might actually have a chance with you."

"I was out of line," I breathe, my embarrassment transforming to something more seductive. Something sensual and exhilarating.

"You were fucking perfect."

His unabashed desire for me stokes life into body parts that had felt spent minutes before. My breasts feel heavy with need, and my hips flex in search of friction against my now throbbing center.

"Just like that," he murmurs. "I want to know exactly how much you need me."

I lift my eyes to his and smirk. "Oh, yeah? Well, how about this?" In a bout of playfulness, I roll us so that he's on his back, and I'm gleefully on top of him, thighs spread wide on either side of him.

When I raise above him victoriously, Z thrusts his head back into the pillow and howls with laughter. It's the most exultant, incredible thing I've ever heard. His laugh should be memorialized as a national treasure, too rare and precious to waste. Though, if I have any say in the matter, he'll be laughing much more in the future.

While his abs flex and ripple with his laughter, I ease myself lower until my face is inches from the thick head of his shaft. My eyes lift to lock with his, and all levity evaporates. Zeno watches me raptly as my tongue extends. When I make contact and lick his full length, veins already bulging from his renewed erection, his entire body shivers.

I can taste myself on him. That's not something I would have thought I'd like, but with Z, tasting the evidence of our passion means so much more than a bodily fluid. It's the bond of two people who have always belonged to one another.

Taking him into my mouth, I suck him deep into my throat, humming my satisfaction. His moan and staggered breaths are ample reward, spurring me on to see if I can make him mindless with need. When his hand clutches my head, I think I've nearly got him, but instead, he coaxes my lips from his and flips us. He wields his strength with such sudden force that I gasp and am on my back beneath him before I know what's happened.

"My turn," he growls, clasping my wrists in one of his hands.

I am powerless beneath him. A willing victim to whatever sublime torture he wishes to inflict.

Sensing my eagerness, Z flashes a villainous grin before laying siege to my body. We spend hours together in bed, exploring and talking until my stomach growls in protest. I never did eat lunch. Z heats a pasta dish, which we eat out on his balcony, enjoying the sprawling night views of the city. When our stomachs are full, exhaustion descends upon us both. We head back to bed, and I'm asleep in an instant, peacefully engulfed in Zeno's embrace.

WE DON'T ROUSE until well into Sunday morning. Waking next to Z makes my chest flutter with happiness, especially when I feel his hand resting on my forearm. I've rolled away from him in the night, but he's found a way to maintain contact as though he needs that connection even in his sleep.

I shift onto my side. Z's eyelids lift at the movement.

"Morning," I say with a soft smile.

"Mmm…" His chest vibrates with a morning purr. He pulls me against him and nuzzles his face into my hair. "What time is it?"

"Late, I think—maybe around ten. I probably need to have some breakfast and get back home." I don't want to intrude on his day, and I have my own chores to get back to.

"I wasn't planning to go back to Hardwick until tomorrow. Why don't you stay until then?"

"Because I have to work tomorrow?"

"No, you don't. As of this moment, you're fired."

I twist until I can see his face behind me, trying to discern his meaning. "Z, I need that job. It may be awkward for me to work for you, but it's not forever."

Zeno huffs. "Have you checked your accounts lately?"

"No." My face scrunches with confusion. "Why?"

"Because you've got plenty of money. What's mine is yours. Besides, you never should have been put in the position to use your school money. Now you can call St. Joseph's tomorrow morning and change your status back to active. You can start in the fall like you'd planned." He pulls me back snug against him and whispers close to my ear. "You agreed to be mine. That won't always be easy, but there are certain … perks."

I can't say that I'm stunned because it makes sense for him to help me, but I've never expected handouts. With everything so uncertain between us, I hadn't even allowed myself to explore the what-ifs of a happily ever after.

My mind begins to race with possibilities. "I wonder if that girl still needs a roommate." The question is for myself, though I murmur it aloud. If I'm going to return to school, I'll need to find another living situation.

"Fuck, no. You'll live here with me. Once you graduate, you can decide where we go from there."

"Move in?" I balk. "Z, we've been on exactly *one* date. Don't you think that might be rushing things?"

The gorgeous, cryptic man moves on top of me, pressing his hard length into the junction of my thighs. "I told you my definition of rushing might be different than yours. We've known each other too long and been through too much to follow some arbitrary timetable. I'm not missing out on a single opportunity to be near you."

I gasp at the coiling tension stirring in my belly. "I suppose I can manage to wake up like this every morning." The corners of my mouth hook upward playfully. Who am I to say no to such a generous offer?

Logic tells me rushing things could lead to problems, but I can't name one concrete objection aside from shoulds or mights. We're moving fast, but maybe that's the perfect speed for us.

Zeno's victorious grin fills my heart to bursting. Then he slips beneath the covers, his eyes blazing with a desire to fill other parts of me.

By the time we finally make it out to the kitchen, breakfast becomes brunch, and I'm showered but starving. Z cooks pancakes while I cut up a few pieces of fruit. He's wearing a low-slung pair of pajama pants, and from behind, I've got a perfect view of the dimpled indents directly above his ass. I'm amazed at how even the most random of body parts are sexy as hell when it comes to Zeno.

We discuss our plans for the day over breakfast. I agree to spend the day with him if he agrees to get me back to my parents' house by evening. There's only so long a girl can go without a change of underwear. Z has generously kept me underwear-free to help in that cause, but the time has come.

I wipe down the counter as Z loads the last dish into the dishwasher when his doorbell rings. Our gazes collide, mine wide with terror, his steely with determination. There's no guarantee that it's Christiano at the door, but we both know the odds are good.

"He can't know I'm here," I hiss quietly.

Zeno nods. "Agreed. Go back to the bedroom, and I'll take care of it."

He doesn't have to tell me twice. I take off for the hallway, screeching to a stop when I spot my cap and purse in the front entry. Padding on the balls of my feet as quietly as possible, I detour to snag my things, then disappear around the corner. A voice in my head urges me to hide in the closet, but I don't give in to the temptation. Instead, I plaster myself to the hallway wall and strain my ears to hear what's being said.

"…decided to take the day off." Zeno's voice echoes back to me.

My pulse is so loud in my ears that I have to make a concentrated effort to calm myself just so I can hear.

"We all need a day here and there." Christiano's voice comes closer as though he's slowly wandering into the living area. "I won't interrupt you for long, but I need to have a quick word."

"You know you're welcome anytime." Z's tone is easy, but he doesn't invite his boss to stay. I wonder if that's normal. I don't want Christiano around any longer than necessary, but I don't want to make him suspicious either.

"The time has come for me to name a successor to your father. You know I've always had high hopes for you, yet lately, you've given me a reason for concern. I'm done dancing around the subject and watching you piss on my generosity." His comment makes me think that his claim about already talking to Zeno was garbage, as I'd suspected. He was posturing and only now bringing up the subject.

"I'm sorry to hear you feel that way. I've never meant to upset you."

"It's been understood for years that you and Ari are the future of this organization. You know it, and so does everyone of any importance. How do you think it makes me look when you disrespect my wishes and reject my daughter for some penniless housekeeper whose father couldn't muster more than a soldier's rank? You say you didn't mean to upset me, but how else am I to receive such a slight?"

Several heartbeats pass before Zeno responds. "Would you really want that type of marriage for Ari or myself when neither of us desires a relationship with one another?" His voice is tight but respectful. He's trying his best to reason with Christiano.

"What is this? *The* fucking *Bachelor*? We're not in the business of fucking love connections, Zeno. Surely, you're not that deluded."

"Surely, our organization has moved past the dark ages when a man has to bind himself to a woman he doesn't love out of obligation." Z's clipped response is unquestionably aggressive, and it terrifies me.

Why the hell had I ever wanted Z to stand up to his boss? Now that the conversation is unfolding, I'm reconsidering everything I said. I want our freedom to be together, but can that be achieved without the risk of death?

Judging by Christiano's vicious reply, the threat is very real.

"You need to grow the fuck up and learn how this world works," he spits. "Status is everything. Marriage has never been anything but a strategy for survival, and that's just as true today as it was then. If you can't see that, then you're a greater fool than I realized." He pauses, and I envision the two men locked in a vicious stare. "You want to run this family one day? You know my terms. Either put the family first like you swore to do, or watch as you lose everything. I want a final answer by the end of the week." Clacking footsteps charge toward the door, which slams upon his departure.

I melt against the wall. The flood of adrenaline leaving my system drains all the strength from my body. When I'm finally steady enough to go in search of Z, I find him staring out the living room windows. I approach from behind and wrap my arms around his middle, pressing my cheek to his bare back.

"What are we going to do?" I ask weakly.

"We're going to throw an engagement party for Nevio and Livia."

Confused, I peer around him and study his reflection in the plate glass. Not an ounce of worry, only resolute determination. I desperately wish I shared his confidence. If it were only our lives at stake, I could possibly dredge up more bravado, but our choices will affect everyone we care about. Christiano isn't the type of man to forgive and forget. If we jump in the ring with him, we have to be prepared for a fight to the death.

"ENGAGED?" I GAPE AT MY OLDER SISTER, WHOSE TEAR-FILLED brown eyes are as joyful as I've ever seen them. "I was only gone for one night!" I came upstairs in search of Gia the minute Zeno dropped me off at home. I'd wanted to tell her everything that had gone on, but it turns out she had news to share as well.

Gia laughs with a sniffle and gazes down at the exquisite diamond on her finger. "I know! It's all happened so quickly."

"I suppose you've sorted out the whole debacle with him disappearing then?" I hadn't pushed for an explanation. I'd been preoccupied, and she'd hardly been home since Carter came back from the city.

"Definitely. He explained everything—that his feelings for me were growing, but he was worried he would be strapping me down with kids when I'm younger than him. He thought he would be doing me a favor to leave and admitted that he didn't handle the situation well. When I told him how heartbroken I was to think of losing him *and* the kids, that sealed everything." She smiles at me with a grin that could end wars and heal the sick.

"Gia, honey, I'm so happy for you!" I hug my sister close.

"I better go down and tell the others. I wanted to tell you first."

"You haven't told them yet? Mom is going to wet herself. Come on, let's do this."

Finding out yet another daughter will be marrying money manages to bring Mom out of her divorce-laden funk. While she doesn't actually wet herself, she does spill half a glass of rosé down her shirt. We spend the next hour sitting at the table daydreaming about wedding plans and giggling over wine. It's the perfect release after an emotionally exhausting weekend. When we finally crawl into bed, I'm asleep within minutes.

THE FOLLOWING week is spent making arrangements for the engagement party to be held Saturday night. The event is larger than I initially expected. Z's guest list includes about forty people—the Bishops, Larsons, and several important families from work. Of course, Savio, Christiano, and Ari have been invited as well. I don't know what exactly Z has planned for Christiano or how an engagement party plays into those plans. I also haven't pushed for answers. Hell, maybe the party has nothing to do with Christiano. I have no idea. Even if I did ask, I get the sense Zeno wouldn't give me any answers. All I know is the planning keeps me busy, and I appreciate not having time to worry.

I try to explain to Mom about my new relationship with Zeno and how I'll no longer be working at Hardwick without her jumping to conclusions, but I might as well try to contain the ocean. She is ecstatic and loses all pretense of worry over her divorce. Mom can't imagine a scenario where she struggles when three of her daughters will be wealthy even though she has no claim to any money. I have too much going on to force the subject at the moment. It's a bridge we'll cross when the time comes. For now, I let her have her excitement. It'll make things easier for Dad to get his freedom.

Each day I work on party plans, and each night I spend in Zeno's bed. Elena's room is on the opposite end of the house, so that isn't an issue. I find that mornings with her brighten my days. She is more discreet with her emotions than my mother, but even she can't hide her joy at seeing Zeno and me together. And the more I learn about Elena and the De Rossi family, the more happiness I think she deserves. It's easy to assume someone with so much money must lead an enchanted life, but that isn't always the case. Elena's been handed her fair share of struggles. I'm pleased that her tides have turned.

When Saturday finally arrives, I can't shake the nerves that constrict my muscles into angry knots. The mere anticipation of Christiano's presence drives my pulse to a breaking point. He doesn't want me anywhere near Zeno, and I'll be seated next to the man at a Hardwick dinner party. I can't imagine a scenario where that goes down well, no matter how many times Z assures me everything will be fine.

To combat those insidious insecurities and fears, I select a black halter dress that makes me feel invincible. Thick smoky eye shadow is my war paint, and chandelier earrings that dangle over my bare shoulders act as my armor. Blood-red patent heels serve as my weapon in this battle of power. I want every advantage I can get when going up against someone as ruthless and powerful as Christiano De Bellis.

The party invitation stated seven, though a cocktail hour will precede the actual dinner. Savio shows up early and begins the parade of arrivals at half after six. I'm delighted to see Grace arrive with her parents and learn that she decided to make an unexpected visit home for the weekend. When I ask if she knew Ari would be here, she looks genuinely surprised.

"She told me she was doing something with her dad, but I didn't realize they would be here at Hardwick. That's part of the reason I came home because she was going to be busy all weekend." She looks a touch hurt. I imagine she's wondering why Ari wouldn't tell her she'd be at a Hardwick dinner party, and I have no answers for her.

"I'm sure she just didn't consider that your parents might also be invited. This probably feels like any other work function for her."

"You're probably right." She smiles and nods without much conviction. "Mom told me about Gia's engagement as well. I can't believe how fast everything is happening, but I'm so happy for her."

"She is beside herself. At least that's one engagement I can truly celebrate."

Grace leans in conspiratorially, though no one is standing close. "How is Livia? Has she been to a doctor yet?"

"No, she hasn't. She's doing well, though, aside from a nasty case of morning sickness that makes it hard to gloat about her engagement. I don't feel as bad for her as I probably should. So far, she seems fine tonight. She's been waving her hand around since she arrived, making sure her ring is prominently displayed."

"And Nevio?" Her eyes cut to where the couple stands talking to some of Zeno's associates.

"He's playing his part well enough." And anyone who knows him well can see his act for exactly what it is. Nevio wears his heart on his sleeve. If he felt any true joy, the room would glow from the energy he'd radiate.

When I turn my eyes back to Grace, she's eyeing me curiously.

"And what about you? How are things with Z?"

My gaze drifts to him. In less than a second, his eyes are on me as well, as though he can sense my attention. "Things are good," I say with a grin, turning back to Grace. "Things are really good."

Assuming Christiano doesn't murder us both.

Grace takes my hand and squeezes. "That's so wonderful to hear." Her smile wavers at the sight of something over my shoulder.

I turn to see Ari enter the room.

They're here. Oh, God. They're here.

Except, they're not. Ari is alone.

I stare at the front door and wait for Christiano to make his appearance, but it doesn't happen.

"Um, I'm going to chat with Ari, okay?" Grace asks distractedly.

"Of course, you go." I couldn't possibly concentrate anyway.

Minutes tick by until seven has come and gone. Christiano is noticeably absent.

"Excuse me, everyone," Zeno calls out above the din of voices. "Now that the sun isn't beating down so heavily, I invite you out to the plaza in the back where we will be dining. I have a quick matter to attend to, and then I'll join you shortly." He nods to Savio, and the two start in the direction of Zeno's office.

I'm curious about their conference and whether it has anything to do with Christiano's absence, but an answer will have to wait. I join everyone outside and use the opportunity to ask Ari about her father. She assures me he's coming and was held up in a meeting with someone.

I don't know if I feel better or worse. The uncertainty of him not showing made me anxious, yet I don't want him here either.

Sounds like it's time for a cocktail.

I mosey toward the drink table and spy Z through his office window. He's pacing but not in an overly agitated manner. I can't see his face because a dark screen is halfway down the window to ward off the afternoon sun. His expression might have helped me discern what's going on, but it's hidden from view. Instead, I down a large gulp of wine and return to visiting with friends.

Elena hired a company to create an elegant dinner setting complete with white lights crisscrossing overhead and bouquets of white flowers all around. Five round tables are fully set in the center of the flagstone plaza covered in crisp white tablecloths reaching down to the ground. It's a touch warm out but not insufferable. Had the weather not cooperated, we would have changed plans and hosted inside, but the plaza is preferrable with its lake views.

I mingle with the guests, spending most of my time talking to people I know and leave Elena and my dad to schmooze with those I don't. A half hour later, Zeno and Savio emerge from the house and join the party. I make my way to Z as quickly as I can without drawing suspicion.

"Is everything okay?"

His hand cups the back of my neck, bringing me close to kiss my temple. "Everything is just fine."

The gears in my brain spring free of their mechanism and clatter to the floor, leaving me speechless. I'd been fully prepared for Zeno to treat me like a casual acquaintance in front of his Mafia associates. Never in a million years did I think he'd make such an overtly possessive gesture in front of everyone. In front of Christiano's cronies. His touch … that kiss … everyone will know, and I get the sense that's his plan. He's claiming me for everyone to see, and for those who weren't here, word will quickly spread.

I'm terrified and thrilled all at once.

I search for my voice as Zeno's hand drifts down to the small of my back. His branding touch sears my skin in the best way imaginable.

"I suppose you've noticed that Christiano hasn't arrived?" I ask breathlessly.

Z draws my gaze to his. "You have nothing to worry about. I promise. Now, let me introduce you to some of my associates."

I nod and allow him to lead the way. We mingle together for a short while longer before Zeno announces the start of dinner, and everyone takes their seats. Z and I sit with Elena, Nevio, Livia, my parents, and Marca. Mom is playing nice with Dad, though she seats Marca between them. I'd prefer to sit with Gia or Grace and avoid the awkwardness at my designated table, but as the host, Z needs to sit with the guests of honor, and he insisted I sit with him when we were arranging seat placards this morning.

I adore his proud ownership of our relationship, but it's come without explanation. I'm not the type to go along with things blindly. It takes all my patience and all the newly developed trust I have in Zeno to set aside my anxiety.

Christiano doesn't show for dinner, nor does he arrive in time for dessert. After we raise our glasses in toast to the happy couple, Ari approaches our table and whispers to Z. He takes out his phone and places a call that doesn't appear to be answered. Then another.

Goose bumps rise along my arms, despite the summer temperatures. The concern on their faces tells me all I need to know. Something's wrong.

Zeno excuses himself to talk to the man he'd first introduced to me before dinner. Savio joins them, and the three men exchange a few words before excusing themselves. I instinctively stand and walk to the group along with Ari.

"Z, what's going on?" I pull him aside and try to look casual so as not to alert the other guests.

"We can't get ahold of Christiano or his men. We're going to his place to make sure there's not a problem."

"Is Ari going?"

"Yes, it's her father."

"Then I'm going too." The words are out before I've thought them through. A week of uncertainty has worn through my patience. I have to know what's going on.

Z frowns at the conviction in my eyes and glances at Ari. "Okay. Let me tell Mom what's going on, and we'll go."

We receive a few curious glances from the guests, but we try to look unbothered as we make our exit. Ari and I squeeze in the back seat of Z's Range Rover with Savio while their associate sits in front with Zeno. When we pull up at the De Bellis mansion, all is quiet. The men step out, pulling guns from thin air and instructing Ari and me to stay in the car.

I've never seen Ari look so anxious. She's always so composed that a bouncing knee and white knuckles speak volumes.

"It's going to be okay," I assure her, clasping my hand over hers.

"When he didn't show up, I called, but he didn't answer. I tried his bodyguards, but they didn't answer either. That's never happened before."

"Could they have gone somewhere without phone service?"

She chews on the inside of her cheek as her wide blue eyes connect with mine. "I don't know," she whispers like a lost child.

Minutes later, Zeno marches toward the car. Ari scrambles to open the door, and I slip out of the car behind her.

"What's happened?" she asks.

His piercing gaze touches me before he places both hands on Ari's arms. "There's been an attack," he says calmly. His voice is surprisingly soothing. "I'm so sorry, Ari, but your father didn't make it. We've called an ambulance, but he's already gone."

Her chest expands with the news, rocking her body backward like the ricochet of a gun.

Christiano was a monster, but he was also her father. Her only parent. I can't imagine what she's feeling.

I push forward and envelop her in a hug. "Oh, God. Ari, I'm so sorry."

Her body trembles beneath me, her hands slowly rising to cling to me. "I need to see him," she whispers.

I pull back and look at her, then at Z. "I'm not sure that's a good idea."

"Ari, you don't want to do that," Z chimes in.

Ari sidesteps me toward Zeno with surprising ferocity, jabbing his chest with a manicured finger. "I'm going to see him." Her voice is absolute. She will not tolerate being challenged.

Z raises his hands in defeat.

Ari starts toward the house, and I follow in her wake.

"Where the hell do you think you're going?" Z barks, rushing to catch up with me.

"With her. I'm not letting her go in there alone."

He spews a litany of curses but doesn't fight me. It's a good thing, too, because I've shifted into mother-bear mode. Ari needs a woman's strength with her, and I'm not going to abandon her. If she needs to see her father, then I'm going with her.

Her footsteps slow as we enter the house, but she doesn't stray from her mission. We pass an enormous man lying in a pool of blood. I remember seeing him outside the elevator at Christiano's city apartment. He may have been huge, but a bullet to the chest ended his life as quickly as it would any other man.

Savio and the fifth member of our party stand in the kitchen, both on their phones. A second body lies at their feet. Ari and I slowly make our way over. Our heels clack against the marble floors, echoing throughout the cavernous room. The house is eerily silent. I've never seen a tornado or experienced its aftermath, but this strange helplessness can't be far off the feeling. The quiet insignificance of stumbling across a disaster after the fact.

Christiano is on his stomach. It's a small mercy. We can't see his face, but his finely suited form is unmistakable. Like the other man, blood pools beneath him in a viscous puddle.

Ari and I come to a stop some twenty feet away from him. I'm locked in a trance until I hear her stilted breaths beside me. Tears stream down her cheeks, and her face is as white as the marble floors at our feet.

"Come here, honey." I pull her into my arms and move her away from the sight of her father.

Savio ends his call and walks to Zeno. "The others are coming from your place."

"Cops will love that," Z murmurs. "A whole crew of people fucking up their crime scene."

"What are we going to tell them?" the other man asks.

"What we know," Z answers. "He was meeting with someone before joining us at the party. When he didn't show, we came looking for him."

I start to process what the men are saying and am struck by how unusual it is that the police were called. The Mafia likes to handle its matters privately. But this was the boss. Maybe that makes a difference.

The whole thing is so unusual. What are the odds that Christiano is murdered when Zeno was in the process of defying the man? It's awfully coincidental. Had he hired a hitman or maybe enabled an enemy to do his dirty work for him? Both options would create loose ends that worried me. And what about Ari? Would he have sent someone when she possibly could have been hurt as well?

I'm not sure what to think. Z said he'd handle Christiano, and it makes sense that killing him might have been the only way, but I had intentionally ignored that possibility. It's such a dangerous proposition. Killing Aldo was one thing, but killing the boss of the Giordano family is far riskier.

Within minutes, several familiar faces from our dinner party appear at the house. Each looks more merciless than the last. How could these men be one and the same as the smiling revelers at Hardwick? Their personalities had flipped like two sides of a coin.

"Jesus Christ," one spits. "Looks like a hit. Who the fuck would do this?"

"You check the cameras yet?" another asks.

"Turned off," Savio confirms. "Whoever was behind it knew what they were doing."

"So, we got no witnesses and no film. We can't even go for retribution if we don't have any fuckin' clue who's behind it."

Tension swells in the room around us.

"That's not our only problem," the first man says. "He hadn't even named a new underboss. Now the whole organization will be fucking chaos."

The others grunt their agreement.

"Actually," Savio replies. "Christiano spoke to me this morning. He was ready to announce that Zeno would be his next in command."

All eyes, including mine, swivel to Z.

"It's true," Ari chimes in, her voice empty. "He was telling me before I went to the party tonight that he planned to announce Zeno's promotion at dinner."

Christiano had chosen Zeno as underboss? But how? Why would he have changed his mind? And if Savio knew, had he not told Z? Was that why they'd spoken in Zeno's office before dinner? If so, why hadn't he told me when I asked what was going on?

I'm so lost, but there's no time for confusion. Sirens quickly fill the air around us.

"We can discuss this later," Zeno orders. "If any of you prefer not to give a statement, I suggest you head out the back. The rest of us should step out front."

Everyone follows his instructions without question. We're there giving statements for almost two hours. When the authorities finally release us, we take Ari back to Hardwick with us and get her set up in a guest room. Her father's house is now a crime scene, and she's too exhausted to drive back to the city. Fortunately, they allow her to collect the overnight bag she'd brought with her and a few items from the house.

Once we've updated Elena and seen to Ari, Z and I retreat to his bedroom. We sit on the bed and address a barrage of missed texts and calls until Z tosses both our phones onto the dresser and wordlessly leads me to the bathroom. He turns on the shower, then helps me from my dress. I step into the steaming water while he undresses, then wrap my arms around his middle when he joins me.

We stand silently in the spray of water for long minutes, absorbing strength from one another.

"Z, do you think we could be in danger?" The question has been haunting me all evening. If Zeno wasn't responsible for Christiano's death, then someone else was. Would that person want the new underboss dead as well?

He lathers soap in his hands and massages my shoulders, drawing a moan from deep in my throat.

"Danger? That's inherent in my line of work, but no, we're not in any imminent danger." The smooth and relaxed baritone tenor of his voice is reassuring and confident.

I lift my gaze and study his face, searching for answers. "Were you responsible for Christiano's death?"

"What makes you ask that?" His voice grows husky, and his hands trail down to graze around the outside of my breasts. When his thumbs pluck at my nipples, a bolt of lightning zings straight to my core.

I gasp and arch, pressing my chest into his capable hands. "I don't know. It just seems awfully convenient."

"Maybe from our perspective, but we weren't the only ones who had a problem with Christiano."

That's true.

Z rinses us and lifts me into his arms, leaning my back against the shower wall. I gasp at the shock of cold. His lips slant over mine, stealing my remaining breath. When he pulls away, I open my mouth to ask another question, but he silences me with a single thrust, driving deep inside me.

"No more questions." The command is ragged and absolute.

I don't argue. I can't. Not while his cock is melting my insides.

Zeno's hunger for me is palpable, my thirst for him insatiable. We grope and thrust and devour one another as though these will be our last seconds together, but instead, this is only the beginning.

"Now nothing can come between us," Z pants between thrusts. His thoughts must have taken him to the same place as mine.

I squeeze my legs tightly around his hips, trying to guide myself toward that precipice I sense clamoring in the distance. Zeno fucks me with savage intensity. It is all I can do to hang on like a palm bending with the winds of a hurricane. I don't normally come from penetration alone, but his punishing thrusts slap his body against my clit in a way that stokes a fire in my veins. My orgasm barrels into me. I claw at his back, unable to stop myself. Zeno doesn't seem to mind. His release comes seconds after mine, a roaring animalistic fury. He pants and clings to me, his movement slowing as our bodies normalize.

When my feet lower to the ground, Z has to keep me upright while my legs recover.

"I've got you."

And he does. Mind, body, and soul.

CHAPTER 17

I'M ALONE IN ZENO'S BED WHEN I WAKE THE NEXT MORNING. IT'S still early, but he's already gone. After the events of last night, I imagine his days will be busy for some time.

I decided to search for him, hoping he didn't have to leave for the city. I slip on one of his undershirts and a pair of pajama pants I brought over a few days earlier. After giving my teeth a good scrubbing, I head downstairs. As I reach the last couple of steps, Zeno's voice resonates from the sitting area around the corner. My initial reaction is relief that he's still here, but then his words register.

"I never thought I'd tell you this." His voice is gentle but grave. Is he talking to Elena or someone on the phone? Whatever he's about to say is serious. Anyone with any decency would retrace their steps and allow him a private conversation. I am apparently not that person. Instead, I creep closer to the wall separating us and shamelessly eavesdrop.

"I know about your relationship with Antonio Banetti. I've known for a long time." He's talking to his mother, listening to my suggestion and telling her the truth.

I'm so incredibly proud of him and touched that he took my advice to heart.

Silence follows his admission. Elena must murmur something. I don't hear her, but Z continues as though responding to her.

"It is. I was so angry at first, but over the years, I've realized that relationships are complex. Rarely are things one-sided and as simple as black and white. I know who you are, so I trust that you had your reasons for what happened."

"I never wanted you to think poorly of your father. You adored everything about him."

"Maybe more than I should have," Z admits. "No one is perfect, and we'd all be better off accepting that."

"I'd like to explain a little if you're willing to listen."

Z is quiet, but he must nod or give some assent for her to continue.

"When I agreed to marry your father, I was young. We didn't know each other well, but I thought I knew enough that we'd be happy together. I didn't learn until a few years later that he'd been in a relationship with someone else for many years."

My suspicions were right. Not only did Silvano have another woman but Elena also knew about the relationship. I can't imagine how painful that would be.

"I never told him that I knew. It was an accident that I even learned of his life in the city and the woman he loved. At least, I assume that was the case. They were together for a long time. Something happened about the time you were ten. He stopped spending so much time in the city, and I stopped things with Antonio. Silvano and I made a real effort at a relationship. That was when I had the miscarriage. I'd been so hopeful the baby was going to be a new beginning for us, but when I lost the pregnancy and became depressed, things slipped back to how they were. It was Antonio who helped bring me happiness again." Elena's voice is filled with love—the kind of love I always wanted for my father. He *is* a good man and deserves all the joy in the world.

"Another relationship?" His words are laced with pain.

"I'm sorry, I would prefer you not to think poorly of him, but if you're going to know the truth, you should know all of it."

"I agree. I'm just so stunned. He preached loyalty and honor every chance he had—having a mistress isn't *loyal*."

"That depends on your priorities. He was loyal to the family and what they expected of him. He tried to be loyal to his heart by not abandoning the woman he loved. And he was *always* loyal to you boys."

"Just not you." Z is quiet for several beats of my racing heart. "Well, I truly am happy to hear that Tony has been such a positive part of your life. I regret that I spent so many years hating him."

"That's the thing," Elena says warmly. "None of us are perfect. We're all doing the best we can in the circumstances given."

Z pauses. "Do you know if Dad had other children with this woman?"

"I, ah … I don't. I never pushed to learn about their life there." Her tone changes with a sort of wariness or … guilt?

Zeno must also sense the shift. "I know about Nevio, Mom. You've no need to worry."

"You do?" she asks incredulously.

"Yes. I secretly ran tests to confirm my suspicions back when I first moved to the city. It doesn't change anything, at least as far as I'm concerned. I suppose that's why I decided to tell you what I know. Nevio's paternity doesn't change that he's my brother, and who you choose to love doesn't change my love for you."

"Oh, Z," she whispers.

From the sound of it, the two hug, and I have to wipe at tears pooling on my lashes. I'm so grateful they've finally been open with one another.

"I didn't handle things back then as I would now, and I'm sorry for that," Zeno offers quietly.

"No need for apologies," she assures him. "You know I'm so incredibly proud of you, and it fills my heart with joy to see you so happy with Luisa."

"I won't do what Dad did, you know." His voice is barely above a murmur, and I have to strain to hear him. "I'll devote my life to making her happy."

"I know you will, sweet boy. I see how much you love Isa. You two are already in such a better place than your father and I ever were."

I'm not sure my heart can stand much more love without bursting at the seams. I wipe at my eyes again to make sure there's no evidence of my eavesdropping and pray any redness can be attributed to waking up. After taking a deep breath, I walk around the corner in my best just-came-down-the-stairs impression.

"Hey!" I grin. "Am I interrupting?"

"Not at all," Elena beams. "Come have a seat."

I walk toward Zeno with the intent of sitting beside him, but he yanks me onto his lap. I squeal with surprise and peer at Elena, hoping our display of affection doesn't make her uncomfortable. The grin on her face is the antithesis of discomfort. She truly is ecstatic for us.

"Zeno and I have been having a heart-to-heart, but I

suspect you already know everything we've discussed." Elena looks at Zeno questioningly.

I go stock-still, sure I've been busted for eavesdropping.

"Yes, I've already told Luisa everything," Z admits. "I hope it doesn't upset you that I shared something so personal."

Oh, thank God. They don't know I was listening.

My lips hitch in an awkward smile.

"No, not at all. You two shouldn't have secrets between you. I wouldn't want that for you." She looks at me and grins mischievously. "You gave me quite the scare when you first moved back in with your parents. I kept seeing you with Nevio and didn't know what to do about it—like the day you two were under the trees together."

"Under the trees together?" Zeno's voice takes on a predatory edge as his fingers dig playfully into my ribs.

I squirm with a giggle. "You mean the day the housekeeper broke the window?" It's the only time I can recall being under the trees with Nevio where Elena could have seen us.

"Yes!" She laughs. "Only because I was freaking out and told her to break it. I had to stop you two from doing something you'd regret. Then you moved up your date, and I didn't realize it. When I found out, I worried to death. I talked to your father, and he assured me nothing happened and that he'd take care of it." She pauses, growing serious. "I hope it doesn't upset you to hear me talk about him."

"Not at all. I'm glad he has you, actually. I don't know how I didn't see it before, but he cares deeply for you."

A radiant blush warms her cheeks, and her gentle smile speaks to her own love for him.

I squeeze Zeno's hand and continue. "Did he tell you he's divorcing Mom?"

Z shifts to catch my gaze. "He is? You didn't say anything."

"It's been a crazy couple of weeks." I shrug and turn back to Elena.

"He told me he was filing," she confirms.

"I heard them argue the other day when he first told Mom. She knew about you guys. She even knew about Nevio."

All the color drains from Elena's face. "I had no idea."

"It's not a huge deal. I suppose Dad told you that Mom was with someone else, too."

She nods. "Yes, I knew the girls weren't his. I'm just surprised she wasn't bothered by my relationship with him."

"Honestly, you had something to offer her. She never cared enough about Dad to justify confronting you and possibly losing her place at Hardwick. I think she figured she could keep the information in her back pocket as leverage, but she didn't know about Dad's vasectomy. In a way, I guess their secrets canceled each other out."

"Well, at least we're all moving forward." Elena breathes a deep sigh, her shoulders sagging with relief.

I peer at Zeno and gnaw on my lip. "Yeah, no more secrets. Soooo, it's okay that I told Gia, right?"

Z's eyes widen ever so slightly in rebuke.

"I had to talk it through with *someone*. And Gia wouldn't tell a soul. However, that means Nevio and my younger sister are the only people in our families who don't know the truth. I can't help but wonder if Nevio should be told. I would never say anything myself, but it's bound to come out eventually, and personally, I think he deserves to know." I glance between mother and son with an apologetic expression. I want to speak my mind, but it's a sensitive subject, and I don't want to upset them.

Z looks to his mother and shrugs. "I suppose it's up to you."

Worry creases her forehead. "I don't want him to hate me, but maybe you're right. I'll have to think about it."

I give her a reassuring smile.

"Well, then," Z says, patting my leg. "I've got an appointment with my lawyer in a few hours. I need to get cleaned up and head to the city."

It's Sunday, which is an unusual day for meetings with lawyers, but his boss was murdered last night. I imagine that qualifies as an emergency.

Elena jumps up. "I'll cook some eggs. Sausage or bacon?"

"Bacon," Zeno and I say in unison.

I giggle and poke Z in the ribs—payback for his earlier tickles. He grunts and slaps my backside as I scurry after Elena.

One Month Later

"Hey, you two! What's with all the boxes?" Ari walks up to where Zeno and I are waiting for the lobby elevator at his city apartment. *Our* apartment. I've been staying with him for a couple of weeks, but we're only now officially moving all my stuff. It's strange to think of his place being mine too.

"It's moving day. Classes are starting soon, so I needed to get settled in the city." I haven't seen much of Ari in the last month. We've both been busy adjusting to major life changes. Now that Christiano is gone, Ari's life is her own, and freedom looks good on her. She was already beautiful, but now her hard edges have softened. She seems content in a way she didn't before. "What are you up to?"

"I've decided to sell Dad's apartment and am meeting with a real estate agent to start the process. I thought about

429

renovating and keeping the place—it has phenomenal views, as you know—but I'd rather move on."

"That's understandable."

Ari's gaze lingers on Zeno. "How've you been, Z? Adjusting to your new position?"

His lips quirk upward fondly when he looks at her, and I get the sense that something passes between them.

"No complaints here." He glances at the elevator doors, which have opened and closed with other passengers while we've been chatting. "If you're looking to sell, though, I might be in the market."

I peer back at him, brows raised.

He shrugs. "The security's better on the top floor. More space. We could live in my place while we renovate the other—make it somewhere we're both at home."

I'm stunned, but what he says makes sense. And if memories of the prior owner won't bother him, then they won't bother me. I'd only been to the place once. "Okay." I look back at Ari with what must be a cartoonish smile.

She throws her head back and laughs from deep in her belly. "Okay, then. You give me a call, Z. We'll figure something out."

We take the elevator together, Z and I exiting on our floor while Ari continues upward.

"She seems like she's doing well," I say as we walk my stuff back to the guest bedroom, where we decided to stash things until I have time to go through them. "I'd say she's much happier without her father around."

Ari had been subjected to endless rounds of questioning about her father in the weeks after his shooting. From what Zeno tells me, no one has been able to pinpoint who took out the Giordano boss. The investigation isn't closed yet, but he doesn't think anything will come of it. If the family itself can't identify who instigated the attack, how could the cops have any hope of getting answers?

I've thought about that night a thousand times over and tried to reconstruct my memory. Like waking up from a dream and knowing the details will fade if I don't concentrate on preserving them. I feel an inexplicable need to remember.

"Did I ever mention that I had a long chat with the Guardian of the Gate about a week after Christiano was killed?" I follow Zeno into the living room, my eyes glued to his muscular back.

"Who?"

"You know, that new kid who works at the entry gate. I think his name is Adam, but after that first day when he wouldn't let me in, I dubbed him the Guardian of the Gate."

"I don't believe you mentioned that." He checks the stack of mail on the entry table, probably wondering where on earth I'm going with my story.

"He's not such a bad kid. Grew up in a small town in Jersey and did a couple of years in the Army."

Z cuts his eyes at me, brows raised impatiently.

I plop onto the sofa and open my phone. "It was funny. He made a joke about people always being in a hurry. Said he saw you flying past the front gates the night of the engagement dinner. I explained that it couldn't have been you because you were at the house with us, but he swore up and down that he'd seen you. Said he's learned the vehicles of all the residents." My eyes drift over and collide with his.

I hadn't mentioned the conversation I'd had for good reason. A sound part of me wondered if it might be true. Zeno had a substantial amount to gain from Christiano's death. And while I'd seen him pacing in his office, I haven't been able to shake the feeling that all of the events of that day were incredibly ... convenient.

Z prowls around the couch toward me. "I was at the house with you all evening. You saw me."

"I saw a man in your suit pacing in your office."

He lifts his chin and rubs his neck. "I suppose Savio and I could have changed suits. He could have pretended to be me, waiting in my office while I raced over to kill Christiano, but that would mean we were in on the plot together."

"Indeed, and I've struggled with finding ample motivation for him. Christiano was his uncle, after all. Why would Savio want him dead? Now, Ari, on the other hand. I've thought about Ari over and over. Thought about how demure she was around Christiano and how violent he was toward me—about those security cameras that were miraculously disabled. But what I've thought about the most is how upset she was when she saw her father dead and how grief could look strikingly similar to relief."

"That is an impressive scheme you've envisioned."

"It is rather imaginative, isn't it? No evidence left behind for the authorities, a slew of witnesses could attest to the fact that you never left the estate, and who would think to question Ari's loyalty to her father? It only works if all three of you were in on it together, but if that was the case, it would nearly be the perfect crime."

"Except for you," he says quietly. "You questioned."

"Only because I had insights no one else would have."

Z leans in to prop himself over me using the back of the couch. Our faces inches apart, he drowns me in his turbulent gaze.

My heart skitters at his nearness, and my mind races with curiosity over what he'll say.

A minute passes before he lowers his mouth to my ear. "White wine or red?" he breathes seductively, effectively burying our conversation six feet under.

My own breath hitches before I can answer. "Red."

He slowly pulls away and strolls into the kitchen, and that's how I know we are meant for one another. Because Zeno De Rossi has killed for me, not once but twice, and it doesn't bother me in the slightest. He did what was necessary to keep me safe. I would do the same for him.

A love like ours is worth preserving at all costs, which is why this conversation will never happen again.

"What's for dinner?" I ask brightly, lifting from the sofa to join him in the kitchen.

He meets my gaze appreciatively. "Steak."

"Celebrating, are we?" I arch an eyebrow. It's our first official night living together, and it's sweet he's memorializing the occasion.

"Absolutely. You get the wine poured, and I'll start the food."

TWO HOURS LATER, we take our wineglasses onto the balcony with full tummies and tired feet after a full day on the go. Z sits on the lounge chair with his legs on either side to make room for me in the middle. I lie back against his chest and hum approvingly when his arms wrap around me.

"It's a beautiful night," he murmurs.

"It is, and dinner was excellent. Thank you." I sip from my wine before he takes the glass and sets it on the table beside us to hold my hands in his. The wind blows steadily up between the buildings, giving us a perfect breeze as we admire the city below. I take in the splashes of neon color but am easily distracted by the sight of Zeno's hands touching mine. Holding and caressing.

"I never imagined I could be this happy," he says softly.

His warm breath drifts past my ear. "Or that one person could change my life so completely."

"For some people, change is a dirty word."

"Well, in this case, change was a *very* good thing. You brought light to my world, Isa, and I want you with me always." His right hand lifts from beside us and produces a sparkling diamond ring between his fingers.

My lungs cease functioning. I can't breathe or think through the rush of emotion. All I can do is watch in bewildered awe as Zeno takes my now trembling left hand and slowly slides the ring onto my finger.

"Luisa Banetti, you are the most authentic, loyal, and passionate woman I've ever known. You live life on your terms, and I admire every single thing about you. I want nothing more in this world than for you to be my wife." He closes my fingers around his and brings my hand to his lips for a kiss. "Will you marry me, Isa?"

My watery gaze drifts from our hands back to his face as I twist in the chair toward him. Placing my ring-clad fingers on his cheek, I bring my lips to his. "Yes, Zeno. Forever and always, *yes*."

5 Months Later

"Two girls—identical, no less. They're going to have their hands full." I lean against Zeno's side as we watch Livia open her next shower gift. We decided to throw one giant shower at Hardwick rather than coordinate several smaller gatherings among different groups of friends and family. After weeks of planning, the event is finally here and unfolding seamlessly.

Liv is seven months along and enormous. They learned at their first doctor visit that the couple was expecting twins. Identical girls, as they were told at a later ultrasound. It's a good thing they have money to hire help because I can't imagine Liv taking care of one baby, let alone two. She's fussed endlessly about how the girls are messing up her body, but I know she adores the attention she receives from a twin pregnancy.

"We'll need to keep a close eye on Nevio. The stress won't be easy on him," Z murmurs close to my ear.

"Yeah. At least he's done well leading up to this."

The couple's wedding was small, but Liv made sure to indulge in opulent selections at every opportunity—insisting on peonies because simple roses are too basic and rush ordering a dress from the most exclusive bridal boutique in the city. I don't want to know what the event cost. I don't even care. All that mattered was that Nevio played his part graciously, and Livia was deliriously happy.

I try not to think of how much they remind me of my parents.

Elena did decide to tell Nevio about his parentage and the affair. We were all worried about how he'd take the news, but it went surprisingly well. In fact, I think it gave him the justification he needed to reconcile who he is and why he has always been so different from the other men in his family. It also eased the sting of my rejection and gave us another avenue for connection. Between that news and a strict schedule with his therapist, Nevio seems to be finding contentment in life. He and Zeno have even started to spend time together in small intervals.

Liv and Nevio may remind me of my parents, but their story is unwritten and open to a world of possibilities.

Ripping through tissue paper, Livia pulls out a matching set of leopard-print bows from a shiny gift sack and swoons. "Oh ... my ... *God*! These are the cutest!"

Nevio raises his brows and shakes his head, making me laugh.

"Isa"—Gia snags my attention from behind—"would you

mind terribly if I went on home? I'm not doing so well." Her face is positively green.

"Of course not. Go home and get some rest!" I squeeze her hand and smile at Carter, who hovers behind her with worry on his face.

The two are rarely apart, especially after they announced their own pregnancy a month earlier. Ever since, Gia has struggled with horrible morning sickness. It hasn't allowed much of a honeymoon period after their wedding. They exchanged vows in the most lovely, touching backyard ceremony I've ever been to. Boston stood by his father as best man, and Emily was a bridesmaid. Both children were utterly smitten with their new stepmom. And now, the family is over the moon with anticipation of its newest member.

Carter's sister, Cora, has kept her distance, much to everyone's delight. She showed up for the wedding but went back to the city first thing the next morning.

It's been an eventful six months since I first returned home for what was supposed to be a short visit. While the early days were turbulent, the seas have been calm and skies clear ever since Christiano's death. The investigation into his death has been closed without any further leads. With the backing of Savio and a majority of the other capos, Zeno took the helm as boss of the Giordano family. And as they'd planned when they were younger, Savio is now Z's consigliere. The two are inseparable. Savio even purchased Zeno's old apartment, but the renovations of our new place are still underway, so we aren't moving until they are complete. He still has no desire to live at Tuxedo Park, but that hasn't been an issue since we spend most of our time in the city.

I'm almost done with school and have even managed to write half of my book when I wasn't studying or planning weddings and showers. Besides Livia and Gia, I've had a wedding of my own to plan, though Zeno and I decided on a private destination ceremony for ourselves. We leave for Aruba the day after Christmas, a mere two weeks away. No one is going with us. They wanted to, and several people argued heartily that they shouldn't be denied access to our big day, but we weren't interested in pleasing others. Our wedding will be a day only for us. Heartfelt vows spoken to one another on the shores of paradise with no stress or expectations. Just Zeno and I together.

When we return, we'll host a world-class reception at a luxury hotel in the city where we can celebrate with all our friends and family. The arrangements have been made. My gown is ready, and my heart is full.

"Earth to Luisa." The hum of Zeno's masculine voice draws me from my thoughts.

"What?"

"The presents are about done. What comes next?"

"Oh, we'll thank everyone for coming and let them know they can stay as long as they like."

"That shouldn't be too long. Forecasters have upped the chances of snow for this evening."

I peer outside to the overcast skies. "That would be amazing. I'd love to see a little snow before we head to the beach."

Z wraps his arm around my back. "Amazing for you, but Ari and Grace and several others will need to get back to the city before the roads get bad."

My eyes drift to my childhood friend who stands along the wall with her girlfriend, the two gently leaning into one another. After adjusting to the reality of her father's death, Ari began to flourish in her new life. She took over the management of one of her father's restaurants, and she and Grace became an official couple. Without Christiano around, the Mafia couldn't care less about her sexual preferences. As for the Larsons, though, they have struggled with understanding their daughter's relationship. They love her enormously, but they still refer to Ari as Grace's friend rather than partner or girlfriend. Hopefully, they'll come around with time.

I'm delighted for them. Grace is happier than ever and is working full-time for a theater company. She's kept her apartment, but the two spend almost all their time at Ari's place. I wouldn't be surprised if that arrangement becomes more permanent when Grace's lease is up.

The situation with my parents has been a little touch and go. Elena offered to help find Mom a new job at another house in the area, but I knew that wouldn't go over well. Mom has been convinced she won the son-in-law lottery and never has to work again. I've been reluctant to enable such entitlement, yet I can't seem to justify turning her away when we *do* have so much wealth. She is my mother, after all.

Zeno and I came to an agreement with Gia and Carter to jointly provide a fixed monthly stipend for Mom under the strict stipulation that no other allotments will be made. If she gets herself in trouble with her spending or gambling, that will be her problem. We are providing her more than she probably deserves.

She moved into an apartment a few weeks ago and has given Dad minimal recoil over the divorce. He's stayed at the cottage and can often be found at Hardwick, but he and Elena haven't openly proclaimed a relationship. Maybe they never will. I can't say what will happen, but both are happier than they've been in a long time, and that's enough for me.

With Livia and Mom out of the cottage, Dad gave Marca the choice of taking over Gia's job at Hardwick or going to school for her associate's degree. Much to my delight, she chose school and has become surprisingly engrossed in her studies.

"I suppose I'll start cleaning up," I tell Z.

Livia is on her feet, giving a tearful thanks to her guests. A double dose of hormones has wreaked havoc on her already volatile emotions. Fortunately, Nevio's laid-back personality has kept him seemingly unfazed. He hands her a tissue, and the two begin saying goodbye to their parting guests.

An hour later, all that remains in the house are those of us here for the night. Nevio helps Liv waddle upstairs to rest, and Elena disappears along with my father. The two house-keepers scurry about, collecting dishes and discarded wrapping paper. Wanting to help, I gather several punch glasses near our seats to take to the kitchen. I set them on the counter and pause before leaving when I spot an extra stack of printed "Oh Baby" napkins left out on the table. I pick one up and run my fingers over the custom floral design around the edges. They matched perfectly with the floral arrangements and other décor. I was extremely happy with how well it all turned out.

"Sorry about that," Zeno says as he joins me at the table. He'd had to take a call while we were sending off the last of the guests.

"No problem." I smile at him and peer back down at the napkin.

"Something wrong?"

"No, I was just debating whether to throw these away or keep them." My heart begins a frantic dance in my chest.

"Keep them?" he asks, confused.

"I've debated all day how to tell you—" I peer into those aqua eyes I adore so deeply as tears burn in my own. "I wasn't sure until this morning, but it looks like we'll be needing a shower of our own come summer."

Zeno is momentarily motionless, his lips slightly parted. "You're pregnant?" he breathes.

I nod, desperately hoping his casual attitude about children wasn't simply a show because I hadn't meant for this to happen so quickly. We'd discussed me getting off birth control, but who would have thought I'd be pregnant the very first month? Not me.

Banishing my fears, Zeno displays a triumphant grin as he yanks me into his arms and spins me around. I squeal and laugh, clutching him tightly. When he slows our dizzying circles, my feet touch back down, and our gazes lock in a silent communication of ardent love.

"I didn't think you could make me any happier than I already was. But as you are so good at doing, you've proven me wrong. I love you *so fucking much*." His lips melt into mine, a sensual glide imparting every ounce of his passion and devotion.

Our journey to this place in time may have been arduous, but now that we're here, I can unequivocally say the struggle was worth the reward. I love Zeno De Rossi with all my soul and will continue to do so until the end of time.

Thank you so much for reading *The Savage Pride Duet*! The *Pride and Prejudice* cast of characters is long beloved to so many of us, and I truly hope I did each of them justice.

Bonus Chapters

As much as I love the intrigue created by a single point of view, I know many of you are desperate for a glimpse of the story from Zeno's perspective. Now that everyone's secrets are exposed, you can read the four chapters I've written detailing key scenes of Luisa and Zeno's story from the vantage point of our enigmatic hero. Nine thousand words of behind-the-scenes action and explosive desire you won't want to miss!

Scan the QR code below or head to my website at www.jillramsower.com/pages/bonus-content to read the *Savage Pride Silent Prejudice Bonus Chapters*!

Where to go next!
You have two main options:

First, *The Savage Pride Duet* is set in my *Five Families* world. The original series begins with *Forever Lies*, in which Alessia gets stuck in an elevator with a mystery man who turns her life upside down. Start there to see where this mafia world began.

In the alternative, *The Byrne Brothers* series branches off to focus on the bad boys of the Irish Mafia. There is some character overlap since the books are set in the same world, and you'll even learn a little more about the mysterious Renzo Donati…

In *Silent Vows*, the first book in *The Byrne Brothers* spin-off series, Noemi Mancini has been promised to a ruthless Irishman. He represents everything she hates in the world yet summons her darkest cravings. She wants nothing to do with him, but if she tries to refuse him, her father will kill her. There is no escape, and the worse part is, a part of her doesn't want to.

***

Keep in touch!

Make sure to join my newsletter and keep in touch!

ACKNOWLEDGMENTS

Femenist, realist, romantic—Jane Austen was many things, but above all, she was an inspiration. As a female author myself, I am humbled by her trailblazing ambitions and insightful commentary of the world around her. When I decided to write a modern retelling of her classic tale, *Pride and Prejudice*, I worked hard to maintain the themes she so eloquently wove into her writing and endeavored to craft modern-day versions of her beloved characters. I'm incredibly proud of how this duet came together, especially because it was so important to me to honor the original work.

I hope you enjoyed reading the first part of Zeno and Luisa's as much as I enjoyed writing it. Things get crazy in the next installment, so buckle up!

When I began the journey of transporting Darcy and Elizabeth into a modern-day world of danger and deceit, I knew there was only one place for their story to begin. I was young when I first viewed the magnificent estates at Tuxedo Park, yet I can still remember their impact with such clarity. The gated entry sat beneath a canopy of ancient trees, leading to a winding drive around the lake where homes steeped in history dotted the hillsides. I felt as though I'd passed through a gateway in time rather than a security checkpoint.

I'd like to thank a dear family friend, Peter Regna, for providing me the opportunity for such creative inspiration. Everything about Tuxedo Park was perfect. The exterior Spanish accents of his estate were used to craft my vision of Christiano's mansion, while memories of the interior became the historic halls of Hardwick. Peter couldn't have possibly known a simple visit would make such an impact, but it did. And I think it's a beautiful reminder of how we are all capable of making a positive mark on others' lives with the simplest of gestures.

ABOUT THE AUTHOR

Jill Ramsower is a life-long Texan—born in Houston, raised in Austin, and currently residing in West Texas. She attended Baylor University and subsequently Baylor Law School to obtain her BA and JD degrees. She spent the next fourteen years practicing law and raising her three children until one fateful day, she strayed from the well-trod path she had been walking and sat down to write a book. An addict with a pen, she set to writing like a woman possessed and discovered that telling stories is her passion in life.

Release Day Alerts, Sneak Peak, and Newsletter
To be the first to know about upcoming releases, please join
Jill's Newsletter. (No spam or frequent pointless emails.)

Official Website: www.jillramsower.com
Jill's Facebook Page: www.facebook.com/jillramsowerauthor
Reader Group: Jill's Ravenous Readers
Follow Jill on Instagram: @jillramsowerauthor
Follow Jill on TikTok: @JillRamsowerauthor